THE
DOMINIONS

STARS & SHADOWS

ISBN: PB: 979-8-9921837-2-6; eBook: 979-8-9921837-3-3

Book Cover by Cameron L. Jimenez

First Edition 2026

For Maddie,

Thank you for being my person.

Thank you for showing me the kind of friendship that knows no bounds.

No matter where & No matter what.

THE COUNCIL

PROVINCE	SATRAP	VICE	
BRIENZA	KING BALTHASAR	(THE SHIFTER)	
SVEABORG	ASTAROTH	COATL BARDICK (THE SNAKE)	
ELYSIA	EGIN	ALOYSIUS ROOK (THE SKULL)	
VALHOL	ARITON	SOREN THANE (THE SPEAR)	
LORCA	ORIENS	TARUS LUTHER (THE STAR)	
TAKAMA	PAIMON	FALLON MALVINA (THE SPARROW)	
THE MIDLANDS	MAYMON	TRISTAN SHAW (THE SCYTHE)	

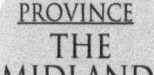

BOOK
TWO

STARS & SHADOWS

PROLOGUE
The Council of the Gods

The Dominions were gathered around a large, round table.

Clouds floated beneath the feet of seven grandiose thrones, each spaced evenly around the marbled counter.

Fragments of sunlight peeked through the cracks in the puffy vapors, illuminating the cosmos, and a faint haze fell over the scene, as if the compounding power of the Dominions had to be dimmed in order for the gods to assemble.

The entire setting looked as if Ianoda himself had suspended the Authorities in the boundless air.

No words were exchanged amongst the deities as they waited, staring intently at the lucent everflame glowing in the center of the veiny, marbled tabletop.

Acananas strummed his elegant fingers on the marble, a restless air radiating from his immortal body. He dragged his divine eyes around the room, surveying the Dominions presently seated.

Sophrosyne and Mehar sat patiently to his left, kindred

twin spirits always perfectly aligned in their repose. Castitas, perched in the throne directly opposite Acananas's, hummed softly as she waited. Beside her sat Dayala, the liveliest of the bunch, renowned for her gifts of service and aid.

Acananas's gentle gaze landed at last upon Sabri, the undeclared mediator of the group, and they exchanged pleasant smiles. The two divinities had always been fond of one another.

A final, seventh chair remained empty at his right hand, and he studied it intently.

The throne was hewn of alabaster stone and adorned with embellishments of sparkling gold. The long, towering back stretched towards the heavens, and an assortment of large, glittering diamonds covered the head. On the side of the white stone rested two golden catches, mirroring the clasps affixed on each of the other six thrones. The fasteners had been specially constructed to hold the Swords of the Dominions.

Lastly, Acananas dragged his eyes to the sculpted emblem resting in the center of the throne. Plated in polished gold, the carving of a seven-pointed star rested.

A rousing breeze whipped across the open skies, stirring the clouds beneath his feet. Acananas blinked, and when he reopened his eyes, the seventh throne was occupied.

"My apologies for the delay," Ithran uttered, readjusting himself on his chair.

The Dominions all murmured expressions of understanding.

"Is it done?" Acananas asked, a sense of tension entering his voice.

Ithran nodded and pulled out a small, weathered key, covered in brushed gold.

The Dominions stared at the metal.

"It has been a long time," Sabri murmured.

Acananas nodded and reached across the table to take the key from Ithran. "Not long enough," he sighed.

A stillness fell over the group as he ran his hand across the jagged surface.

"The last was Mikkal, was it not?" Castitas asked, a soft kindness filling her voice.

Acananas nodded once more. "The last Warrior of Prae-nuntius."

Sophrosyne sighed and added, "I had always hoped we would never need another."

Mehar and the other gods murmured their concord, all except Acananas, who remained silent.

The agreeing mumbles promptly fell quiet, and he could feel the blazing eyes of the Dominions boring into him.

He slowly peered up from the key, and looking into each of their awaiting gazes, he declared, "The worlds will always need a Warrior."

PART
ONE

THURISAZ

"And on the wings of abominations shall come one who makes desolate, until the decreed end is poured out on the desolator."
— Prophesy 77 of the Recorded Visions of the First Oracle
(Unsanctioned Edition)

CHAPTER ONE

Iskander Blaidd had been bred for war.

Born for destruction. Crafted and honed over time into a fatal weapon.

Forged like a sword against flame, his skills were sharp, superior—utterly lethal. And he swore the death-kissed darkness rolling through his veins had been gifted to him by Anubis himself.

Iskander stared deep into the monarchical eyes peering up at him through the smoke-filled haze. His own gaze was half-glazed over as he tried to shake off the dizziness swarming his mind. He struggled to focus on the blank, dark eyes burning into him. His stare drifted to the corner, landing on the blood red diamond. The bleeding crimson resembled a deep, smoldering flame.

The monarch's eyes lured his attention back to her, as if her condemning gaze was able to forcefully burrow into his mind, tugging harshly at his past.

The playing card's queen, tyrannical in her demand for his memories, leered at Iskander from the playing table. Perched atop the dark, distressed wood, she sat patiently waiting for the opportunity to consume his unleashed memories from the presence of her throne.

He picked the card up from the oak table, and glimpses of the past flashed through his mind. He tried to fight against its pull, knowing the battle was lost against his clouded mind, and he tumbled into the dark recollections of long ago.

Iskander's small legs dejectedly dragged him through the near-empty streets of Valhol.

Holes were worn through the sides of his boots, and a small, too-light jacket hung over his shoulders as snow began to fall from the sky.

His teeth chattered, and his ungloved fingers, tucked snugly beneath his arms, went numb from too many hours in the cold. As he wandered through the city, searching for a place to stay, the setting sun dissolved, and the cold cover of night took its place.

The blood on his lip had dried—frozen over from the winter air—and his right eye was swollen shut.

He waded through the quieting streets, the faintly lit luminos lining the alleys the only light to guide his way.

Iskander was not sure how much longer he could traverse between the buildings before he would need to find shelter.

He did not think he would survive a night out in the brutal cold, much less an entire Valhollian winter, but he also knew he had an equally slim of a chance of surviving the group Home he had just left; a place so similar to the many he had lived in before—with daily beatings and too few portions of food.

But being bastard born to a mother who had not sur-vived his birth, Iskander never had any other option. He had jumped between Homes for years, riding out the cruelty until the beatings became too much to bear, and then he would pack his few belongings and move on to find the next.

He took in a breath of the icy air, and a sharp pain splin-tered up his side. At ten years old, Iskander did not know much about broken bones, but he was fairly certain some-thing was cracked on his side.

When he accidentally tracked snow inside the Home with his boots, his mistake had been met with several fists to the face and a wooden rod to his side; evidently, to ensure he would not ruin the wooden floors again.

Once Iskander had been able to peel himself off the floor, blood still trailing down his lip, he crawled to the room he and the other children shared, packed a bag, and never looked back.

He walked for hours through the cobblestone streets, knocking on the different doors of places he had heard were rumored to take in kids off the streets. He wasn't above beg-ging; he had done it plenty of times before, and his boyish-ly handsome looks and charming nature had always helped him wiggle his way into a Home and a warm bed.

But with the purple shiner and bloodied face, Iskander's best asset had been rendered unusable, and every Home he tried to stay in claimed to be full.

As he hobbled down the street, clutching his side as he breathed in sharp, frostbit air, a door creaked open behind him and a soft voice called out, "Over here."

He spun around to find a small girl, maybe two or three years younger than him, peeking out from a cracked door and waving her hand frantically as she motioned him over.

Iskander looked both ways down the alley, unsure if he

should trust the young girl, but when a whipping blast of frigid wind blew past and ripped straight through his too-thin jacket, Iskander threw caution aside and slipped inside the cracked door, into the darkness behind.

The warmth of the space crashed into him like a wall of fire. His fingers felt like tingling splinters as they thawed, and his cheeks and ears burned.

The girl placed a delicate finger to her lips, and Iskander nodded, understanding the request to stay silent. She turned and soundlessly strode down the hall, past a set of stairs on the left that climbed to a higher level. He trailed behind her, sure to avoid any squeaking floorboards as he walked. She stopped halfway down the corridor and twisted the knob on a short door tucked beneath the stairs. She gestured towards the cramped space, and as she moved, her light auburn hair fell in front of her face.

Iskander took a breath and ducked inside.

He quickly glanced around the tight closet. He found nothing but discarded stacks of papers and a loose deck of playing cards. The Queen of Diamonds sat atop the incomplete stack, and the monarch stared at Iskander intently, as if she was watching a salient moment unfold from her throne.

The girl went to close the door, but just before she shut it all the way, she leaned into the narrow space, her voice pulling Iskander's eyes from the card. "It's not much, but I'll figure out a way to get a blanket for you tomorrow. Maybe a pillow."

He nodded, grateful for the reprieve from the winter air. "Thank you."

She went to close the door, but he gently pressed a hand against it before it latched. "What's your name?"

She smiled, the expression so full of light. "You can call me El."

He nodded. "I'm Iskander."

Iskander tried to force himself from the memory, but his head was heavy and clouded.

It had been sixteen years since that night, and in that time, he had never once let himself feel any pity for the abandoned boy he had been. He had discovered that lesson early on in his life; he had learned that those who are not fed love on a silver spoon learn to take it from the tips of blades.

So that was what he had done. Instead of running from the darkness, he learned to embrace it. He'd shoved down the burning rage inside him for so long and watched as it grew and festered in the dark.

And he would continue to let that darkness deep within grow and grow, until the time came for him to finally unleash it.

It pushed him—the darkness—fueled him and molded him into a vicious warrior. Aided him in becoming the ruthless, cold, and dominating General of the Vanguard—the Amarok's fiercest legion of warriors.

It was what molded him into a warrior worthy to be part of the Septant.

So, when Iskander met El, in that sea of darkness raging inside him, a small flame of hope began to burn.

He stayed there, hidden in the shadows of the stairs, for two years until he bonded with his wolf, Conri, and left for the Citadel. But every summer, when the Citadel went on break, he would take time to return to Valhol and visit El.

Through the years, she became his friend, his sister—a reminder of the small shred of goodness left in the world. She was his family and his home, and even in the brokenness that surrounded them, they had built a friendship that could withstand the dark.

But fate was cruel, and it had set him at a table and allowed him to pick up a spoon and taste what he would never have, because Iskander's little house of cards fell apart even quicker than it was built. Founded on beatings and broken promises, he supposed deep down he had never really believed it would last. But he never thought it would have collapsed in the way that it did—in brutal, unrelenting devastation.

He had never seen any glimmer of light, or hope, in any of the people he had met during his time in Valhol, except El—the small, shining beacon in his sea of darkness. So, Iskander had known early on that the safe space he had come to cherish would eventually be choked out. But he never, even in his worst nightmares, thought the crumbling home he had built in his mind would be because the burning flame—the flame from the unexpected sister he had come to love—had been extinguished.

Iskander finally pulled himself from the memories wreaking havoc in his mind. He tried to ground himself as his head began to spin. Too much ale.

Iskander stood up to leave The Wet Dog, a seedy tavern nestled deep in the Slums of Lorca. The room spun.

Shit.

He took one step towards the exit, and the world tilted. He had a strange sense of falling, slowly, before his body hit the liquor-soaked floors. And then there was nothing but darkness.

CHAPTER TWO

Dawn broke over the cloudy horizon as Asha secured the last strap on Uriel's harness. He huffed out a breath of warm air into her hand that smelled of sulfur.

A scuff of boots rattled off the walkway behind her.

She turned around and froze. Anselem was walking down from the Aviary shelter with Kapheria, her saddle already fixed against her midnight feathers.

"What did you do?!" Asha gasped.

Anselem's eyes went wide.

"You cut your hair!"

He ran a hand through the waves that now only fell to his shoulders.

It looked good. *Really* good.

He shrugged. "It was time for a change. A new start."

She simply gaped at him. He laughed, that newfound brightness gleaming in his emerald eyes. "I would have thought twice about it if I had known you'd be so upset, Seven."

She frowned. "Your hair was so pretty."

Anselem raised a brow. "Yes, because *pretty* is certainly what every warrior wants to be called."

"Some of us warriors don't mind being called pretty, *Eros*." She rolled her eyes and added, "And you know what I meant."

He let out a light laugh. "Are you upset I don't tell you how pretty of a warrior you are, Ash?" His tone was teasing, but Asha's cheeks still burned, nonetheless.

He took a step closer, looking down into her eyes. "Although we might be here a rather long while if I start to tell you how beautiful you are." He smirked, and Asha's heart did that stupid little flip that she hated. "And we *do* have a rather rigid schedule to stick to."

She forced her face to stay neutral. "Are you done with your satirical commentary?"

The mischievous twinkle that made her heart flutter flickered in his eyes as he replied, "Not even close."

She stepped away and walked back to her firebird, pretending to fix something on Uriel's saddle so she could avoid those burning emerald eyes. As she twisted the leather strap, her eyes caught on the singed skin poking out from beneath the cuff of her sleeve. She stared down at the E branded on her inner wrist and brushed her fingers across the scarred skin.

The Brand had been there, seared into her flesh, since the day she bonded with Uriel and her power manifested fourteen years ago. A permanent Mark to remind her, and every other magic-wielding soldier in the kingdom, of the Leadership that owned them and the wicked king they answered to.

"Don't worry," Anselem said, eyes following hers towards the E. "You're not expected in Valhol for another week. We have time."

Asha nodded, knowing there was little she could do if Soren Thane, the Vice of Valhol, commanded her to report to the base early.

She had only been commanded by the Brand once before, shortly after she found out her brother had been killed, when she refused to leave her barracks room at the Valhollian Fort. The only people she'd let into her room in the days following the news had been Nina and Dolion, her two closest friends in Kappi training.

After a second straight week of missed lessons, Vice Thane had commanded her to return to training, invoking the compulsory magic woven into the Brand.

Asha could still remember the searing pain that shot up her arm as she lay in her bed. It had burned, like a white-hot flame twisting tightly around her wrist before jetting swiftly up her arm. An invisible trail of singeing flames licked along her skin as the fire climbed towards her temples, coiling vehemently around her skull until they settled in her mind.

A single, fire-wrapped echo rang through her mind, forcing her upright from her tear-soaked pillow: REPORT TO VICE THANE.

The mandate echoed over and over, blocking out every other thought wading in her mind, every other morsel of reason and purpose. Until all that remained was the singular standing belief that she needed to go. That she wanted to go. To obey.

The burning in her mind did not subside until she followed the command and made her way across the fort. With each step, the unseen fire slowly dwindled, and the screaming echo to obey faded softly. Then, as she twisted the knob and stepped through the threshold into the Vice's office, the fire in her mind sputtered out with sudden finality, as if the flames had never been there in the first place.

She remembered watching as the haunting echoes of her forcefully fabricated beliefs drifted away and settled quietly atop a pile of cooled embers.

Asha was not sure she would be able to defy such a command again if Vice Thane were to invoke the compulsory Brand. She was unsure if she would be able to fight it, now that her magic had been unlocked and her iron bands removed.

She did not think she could.

"He won't," Anselem said quietly, as if reading the thoughts swimming in her head.

Asha glanced over at him.

"I sent a few requests up the chain of command," he added. "It will take at least a week for them to make a decision and sort through arrangements."

Asha raised her brows, but Anselem did not elaborate. "What about after?" she asked, fidgeting with another of Uriel's straps. "How am I supposed to go to the Forgotten City with you if I am caged up in Valhol? You know Vice Thane hardly ever permits soldiers or warriors to leave the Iron City."

Asha knew Anselem had been itching to go to Verloren ever since Raziel, the Secret-Seeker and Lord of the Boeotian Manor, had revealed where the Empress of the Forgotten City resided and how to access the undiscoverable city resting in the heart of the Kunlun Mountains. But Anselem had put off going for weeks. For Asha.

He had promised after their enlightening evening at the Boeotian Manor, as the pair stood beside one of the thermal springs at Sveaborg Base, that once Asha graduated from Soturi training, he would travel with her to the Midnight Castle and burn the entire city of Montu to the ground. For her brother, and his bright life that was cut too short.

"Why else do you think I put in a request to have you reassigned to Elysia?" Anselem asked, a wide smile spread across his handsome face. He brushed a hand down Kapheria's dark feathers.

Asha's eyes went wide. "You did what?" she asked, gaping at the Septant warrior.

Anselem's smile vanished. "I just figured it would be easier for me to request you for classified assignments if we were at the same fort," he explained, shifting uncomfortably on his feet. "But," he added, turning away from Asha's gaze, "if you would prefer to stay in Valhol—"

"No!" she shouted, cutting him off. Heat rose in her cheeks as the eagerness in her tone boomed across the space.

The smile returned to Anselem's face. "Good," he replied.

"Good," Asha echoed, turning from his gleaming eyes. She stuffed several more articles of clothing, along with an additional dagger, into the side pockets of the saddle and fastened the buckles.

She heard Anselem strap a final item down to Kapheria before calling over to her, "Ready?"

Asha turned toward him, a wide grin stretching over her face. "I've been ready for this for years."

The fire in her eyes that was dim for so many weeks sparked, and the embers in her soul once again began to burn. A reignited flame, much different from the one she held before, but equally as devastating.

This time, the desire in Asha's heart was not simply for a Mark upon her arm or a title before her name. This time, the fire burning through her veins was for blood.

It was a blaze-filled promise to destroy every last person responsible for harming the ones she loved.

It was for Mathieson.

For her mother.

For Anselem.

For Nina.

Because one thing Asha had learned during her time in the Nameless Place was that those who are forced to lick their wounds soon find their own taste for blood.

She climbed atop Uriel and fixed an orb around her head. Anselem followed suit, and with a simple nod, the firebirds launched into the sky and set off for Aaru.

Three days.

That was how long it would take them to fly to Montu. Longer if the weather was poor and the firebirds' wings became too heavy with rain.

Anselem had instructed Asha to pack light. Uriel and Kapheria would be able to travel faster with less of a load to carry, and Anselem was certain they would not have to worry about the approaching winter until they made it to Lorca.

He initially wanted to avoid the frost-kissed city, instead opting to travel straight across the kingdom and fly directly over the Redwood Forest and into Brienza. But Anselem knew avoiding the Capital, and the lavish Gilded Castle set within its center, would be the best option for steering clear of any overly interested eyes.

The Capital only had a small presence of firebirds stationed at their small, seaside Fort, Cadeyrn's Shore, named after King Balthasar's great-grandfather, and two additional phoenixes would have drawn too much attention. Especially when Kapheria, the Commander's *Firebird of the Night*, was well known throughout the kingdom's army.

So, Anselem decided the best option would be to travel north and cut through the foothills of the Iron Mountains, stopping in Lorca for a day to rest before they made the final flight to Montu.

Admittedly, a small part of Anselem was happy the adjusted plan allowed them to avoid spending a night camped in the Redwoods. He had heard many tales in his days of fighting about the creatures who occupied the forest. There were never many details, and most of the stories conflicted, but the one consistency amidst the legends was that the Kindlings, the *People of the Woods*, were not a folk that took warmly to outsiders.

As they sailed across the Gulf of Ahti and entered the skies above the mainland, Anselem, at long last, allowed himself to think of the place where they were headed. Of the Midnight Castle, the prison buried deep beneath its grounds, and the warrior he had left behind.

His chest tightened as memories filtered into his mind. Memories of a dark cell, a betrayed brother, and a slaughtered friend.

He realized, as the Darkness started to creep into his heart, no one had ever told him that sometimes things are not truly over when they end. Like a book with the last chapter torn out, he had been left to wonder, for years, what was on the missing pages. The lack of closure was tough on the soul, writing out the final words to a book with ink that would never dry.

But as his mind raced, Anselem smiled, his cracked heart pushing away the shadows, and instead filling with a long-forgotten light.

Because now, he was finally making his way towards the fulfillment of a promise he had made long ago, in a cage underneath the Midnight Castle, to one day burn the entire kingdom to the ground.

"For the Harbinger shall not come to bring peace, but a sword. And when a crowned rider, saddled atop a horse of snow, emerges amidst the fray, the Warrior shall be revealed in fullness, for that which is hidden shall be brought to light."

— The Truth Foretold: A Chronometry of the Warrior of Praenuntius
(Transcribed from the Original Language)

CHAPTER THREE

Iskander had drunk himself into such oblivion, he swore he'd heard the voices of the gods last night.

Maybe he really had, for that split second between when he stood up and when his body smacked the floor.

He remembered that much, at least.

That's how almost every night had been for so many of the past months. And this was how so many of the mornings would be that followed.

He would wake with a splitting headache, oftentimes in a new stranger's bed, and he would crawl out from the blankets and force himself into some sort of functional state. And then, every evening, he would go back and do it all over again. Because the burning ale he shoved down his throat was a Hells of a lot easier to swallow than the fact that she was never coming back.

Iskander did not open his eyes. He took in his surroundings, the sounds, the smells; he gathered every bit of information he could before deciding to open his lids.

It smelled like stale ale mixed with cedar and snow. And the soft, crumpled sheets beneath him felt familiar. He cracked open an eye and was nearly blinded by the light pouring in through the window.

He was in his bedroom. Alone.

His room was simple, with tall oak ceilings and a large window that covered nearly the entire east-facing wall overlooking the peaks of the Iron Mountains. A large bed covered in a thick, cream blanket rested against the center wall, furthest from the door. Dark, ebony wood furniture furnished the remainder of the space, and a secondary oak door, opposite the windows, led into the bathing chamber.

Iskander had no clue how he had gotten back, but he thanked the stars for having made it home. Not the gods, he hadn't thanked them for anything in a long while.

He dragged himself out of his bed and into the bathing chamber. He leaned over, throwing ice-cold water from the wash bin onto his face. His head was *pounding*. He stayed bent over for a long moment, unsure if he was going to vomit or pass out again, until the wave of nausea subsided, and he was able to bring himself upright.

He stood in front of the long mirror hanging just above the wash bin and paused. He stared into his silver eyes, flecked with onyx. They were dimmer than they had been before, like the moon hanging in the night sky had burned out.

His midnight hair fell just past his brow, and the normally soft waves were twisted into a knotted mess. Even his face looked grim, his usually sun-kissed skin having gone pale.

He looked like Hells.

Felt like it too.

He heard his door creak open and instinctively reached to his waist, grabbing for a blade that was not there. He whipped his spiraling head around to see Imara leaning against the doorframe with her strong arms crossed. His shoulders untensed.

"You know it eventually stops being called grieving and eventually starts being called *having a problem*, right?"

Imara Fellowes—his fierce, unwavering Second of the Vanguard.

Her long, chocolate brown hair was pulled back neatly and wrapped around her head like a crown. She kept her fair skin covered under thick winter leathers and light gray fighting gloves. She had a single, long blade fastened at her side. Dark circles hung beneath her hazel eyes, but standing in the morning light, even Iskander could admit she was pretty.

And although Iskander had made some questionable— *very* questionable—choices in his life regarding whose bed he would fall into, *that* was a line even he would not cross. He did not mix business and pleasure. And he was quite certain Imara would have slit his throat before the words had finished falling from his lips if he'd ever been brazen enough to ask.

"Good morning to you too, Miss Sunshine," he mumbled.

Imara simply stared at her General and let out a long, unamused sigh before flicking the scroll in her hand onto the onyx desk in the corner.

He walked over to the table, his head still pounding, and untied the leather strap securing the paper.

"Did you find it?" His eyes scanned over the enclosed writing.

"Yes. And you're not going to like it." Her voice sounded tired, as if she hadn't slept.

Iskander dragged his eyes over to Imara, her face worn but unreadable. "Tell me."

Imara let out a long breath. "It's in Montu."

The ringing in Iskander's head stopped, and his body went rigid. He could feel the darkness running through his veins begin to stir.

Iskander avoided the memories of Montu. He avoided returning to the time when he and the rest of the Septant were held captive in the depths of the city's castle for months. He avoided remembering what *she* had done to him—made him do.

And he avoided the shadows he had descended into once the Septant had broken out, how he had still been wallowing in those shadows when El was killed.

He thought he had known Darkness before she died; he thought his time in Montu was the deepest place he could travel in the abyss.

But Iskander had learned throughout his life that just when he believed he had reached the bottom of the blackness, fate always found a way to pull him down further.

The world stopped turning the day El died. Iskander felt it. In his bones. In his heart. In every fiber of his being, he felt it. The sun stopped being warm. The night stopped being cool. The birds no longer sang. When she died, the world as he knew it did too. A part of him did too.

Grief was all he had left of her now, so he held on to it so tight his fingers bled.

"THE MOST SACRED OF SECRETS MAY NOT GLITTER, BUT THEY WILL BE HIDDEN
BENEATH, BURIED IN A VAULT OF GOLD."
— THE FORMATION OF PERSEIS: AN EXCLUSIVE ACCOUNT OF THE ESTABLISHMENT
OF THE GILDED KINGDOM

CHAPTER
FOUR

Asha and Anselem had flown for the entire day, stopping only twice to stretch their legs and give the firebirds time to rest.

The pair had made it to Eastbourne, the small trading town tucked between the southern foothills of the Iron Mountains and the eastern edge of the Redwoods, when Anselem decided it was time to take up camp for the night.

He gathered a bundle of sticks and branches to create a fire, and Asha, who continuously practiced controlling her magic, offered to ignite the kindling. It took a few attempts for her to shape the flames in her palm into a tempered size and direct them into the broken branches.

After her final benchmark at Soturi training, Asha learned she was able to summon the burning flames within, but still needed to work on regulating the amount of magic she pulled from the depths of her power.

As she focused on the sparks igniting in her hands, her mind drifted to the thrum of power stirring beneath the surface of her skin—the power she had been undeniably given by the Dominions—and she wondered why the gods had gifted her the Kratos of fire-wielding.

Nearly all magic wielders—and many creatures without unlocked magic—knew there were seven sects of elemental magic present in wielders. One faction graced by each of the Seven High Gods.

Water and earth were the two most common forms of the Dominions-blessed magic. Used primarily for harvest and growth, the wielders with Kratos bound to the earth and water elements often ended up in the Kingdom's flatlands once their fighting years had concluded. They spent their final days discovering new ways to reap bountiful harvests for the citizens of Perseis and garner the best produce.

The few who possessed scarcer—typically violent—forms of the earth and water gifts were often forced to remain within their combat units.

Fire and air were less common elements, but both were often found in nearly every large warrior group. These Kratos were the most pivotal for combat, and those who possessed fire and air magic were most often the fighters placed on the front lines for the devastating impact their power could wreak upon their enemies.

Light and darkness were infrequently granted gifts, and the way a wielder channeled his or her power could deem their Kratos as an even rarer ability.

Asha had only met a few light wielders in her life, and the majority of those had utilized their magic to either illuminate spaces in the night or to heal. The most common use of light wielders was found in the Rapha, who Asha knew all too well were brilliant at utilizing their healing light to bind a broken body back together.

CAMERON L. JIMENEZ

But Anselem—he was the only lightning wielder she had ever known.

Spirit magic was the final power granted by the Dominions. It was the rarest of all the gifts, with nearly every wielder displaying different variations of the power.

Only one in every several thousand warriors was chosen by the final High God of the Dominions, Acananas, and blessed with his favor.

Many wielders argued the gifts of Spirit Magic were intrinsically mixed with the enduring remnants of Mind Magic—a magic form that had belonged long ago to the Virtues before the breaking of the Authorities in the Annihilation. Others argued that the two were fundamentally separate, and the powers of the twenty-one Authorities had never intermingled.

Lastly, and even more seldom than Spirit Magic, a warrior would display a power so unique that it was undoubtedly granted by one of the fourteen Disavowed Gods.

The Council always claimed that powers from the Thrones and Virtues *occasionally slipped through the cracks,* and that the warriors gifted with Kratos from the hidden Authorities should feel blessed to have been so lucky to find the lost gods' favor.

But Asha knew the truth behind Leadership's counterfeit praises. Those who displayed powers from the Thrones or Virtues were often never seen again, as the Council took them away to test and research their magic. And if they were seen again, they had been forced to serve in one of Leadership's *personal* cadres. Asha had never learned what servitude in those units meant, and she was not sure she ever wanted to.

The final option for those gifted with magic from the Virtues and Thrones was the appointment of the Satrap's Vice—granted only to seven warriors in the Kingdom.

34

The warriors with the rarest magic were referred to as the Elska—*the Precious.*

Until Sveaborg, Asha had never met a soldier who wielded magic from the Thrones or the Virtues. Mathieson had once told her of a Fader he had met on an assignment after Soturi graduation who could disappear at will, and her mother had referred to the minimal time she spent working with a Time Bender long ago; Anselem had even mentioned the traitorous Septant warrior—Balam—had been a Shield.

But Asha had never met any of the wielders with those gifts until she encountered the Vices.

She did not know if the other Elska projected an otherness from their being, as though the very energy they radiated may be unlike the rest of the warriors. But she knew the Vices—the Elska with the strongest possession of power—certainly emanated an otherworldly essence.

As Asha's mind wandered, she allowed the rippling flames to course through her body, and after a few minutes, a small burning fire blazed before them.

Filled with exhaustion from the long day of flying, the pair sat in comfortable silence, enjoying the warmth of the flames as they handed a loaf of bread and cheese to one another.

"You said you don't know much about the Skia, right?" Asha asked.

"I don't know anything about the group," Anselem answered. "Why?"

Asha anxiously fiddled with the leather string around her neck, twisting it around in her fingers. "They must be important, whoever they are, if the Vices were talking about them. Answer to them."

Anselem nodded his agreement, remembering the hushed conversation he and Asha had overheard in the early hours of the morning as they tucked themselves into a shadowed corner of one of the Base's open colonnades.

"What about the Vices?" she pondered, glancing over to the Soturi Commander.

"What about them?"

"Do you know who they are? I just figured with your position you might..." Her words trailed off.

The corner of Anselem's lips tugged upward. "That I might have what? Worked with them before? Been in cahoots?"

Asha rolled her eyes. "No one uses the word *cahoots*, *lieutenant*."

He let out a breathy laugh. "No, Seven, we never worked with any of them, thankfully. But I have come across some of them over the years."

She tilted her head.

"You know of the Vice assigned to Sveaborg."

Asha winced as an image of the Snake slithered into her mind. Her cold hands turned icy as the face of Major Coatl Bardick swam before her eyes.

Anselem cleared his throat, as though it had gone thick at the mention of Sveaborg's Enforcer. "I only came across the Spear once, not counting the encounter in the colonnades at the Base a few weeks ago."

Asha's jaw clenched as the unveiling words of the Vice came crawling back to her.

Soren Thane. The Vice of Valhol—notorious enforcer of Satrap Egin.

Asha would remember his name until the day she crossed the blood red letters off her list.

The first time she had ever glimpsed the Vice, she was eight years old. His harsh face was the first one she saw when the burning magic finally stopped ripping through her small body after the Bonding.

He'd held a bone white key in his hand, and she looked down at her arms through tear-filled eyes. She'd blinked the blurriness from them and found two iron bands fixed above her elbows. When she'd glanced back up, she had seen past his familiar ash-blonde hair and the deep-brown Soturi leathers she had come to find comfort in over the years, and looked deep into his piercing glare and saw there was no kindness in Soren Thane's black eyes. She remembered thinking he looked too young to hold so much darkness in his gaze. No more than twenty-three.

But that was how every Enforcer was rumored to be.

Plucked up by the Council soon after their manifestation, the Vices were sent off to an undisclosed location somewhere in the kingdom. And when they returned from their unaccounted sabbatical nearly a year later, with their newfound title in hand, the light in their eyes was no longer present. Only Darkness remained.

The unfeeling executors of the Council's will.

"I never met the Sparrow, but from what Sacha and Einar have told me about their time in Takama, her magic deals with the influence of desire and emotions. And from what they say, she's damn good at it."

Asha recalled the names of the warriors from Anselem's recounting of Montu—Einar and Sacha, the two Pontos warriors belonging to the Septant.

But the name that more prominently rang through her mind was that of Fallon Malvina, the Sparrow. The only female in the widespread collective of Higher Leadership.

Asha would bet a great deal of gold that the Pontos warrior who answered to Satrap Paimon was every bit as beautiful as rumors claimed if her alluring voice in the halls of the Base gave any rightful indication.

"Blaidd has worked with Tarus Luther on a few occasions, but he said he never learned what magic the Star possessed. Tristan Shaw is the Enforcer over the Midlands. We have rarely ever gone on assignments there, but Kage mentioned he worked with the Scythe when he was on a mission south of the Straight." Anselem paused for a moment, collecting his thoughts. "Kage never spoke specifically about the Scythe's gifts. It seemed as though the Vice's power was too dark for even him to recount." Anselem took a deep breath. "It had something to do with Death."

Asha's eyes went wide.

"Not a Revenant," he clarified, "but something loosely related."

Asha nodded, knowing no one who had ever been gifted the power to speak with the dead had ever lived long enough to tell the tale.

"I don't know who the Shifter is," he admitted, his voice strained. "None of us do. He was assigned to King Balthasar a year ago when his old Vice—the Sickle—was killed in a battle near Erebus."

Anselem went quiet, and Asha counted the names and monikers the Commander had already listed. Six in total. One was left.

The Skull.

Anselem's jaw clenched tightly as he met her awaiting eyes.

"Aloysius Rook," he breathed. The name sounded sinister, as if it carried Darkness in its very syllables.

"He's an Illusionist. One of the best the realm has ever known. He burrows into your mind, your thoughts, your memories, and creates false perceptions. He can make you see or hear things that aren't there."

Asha's body was tense as the Commander continued.

"It's not permanent. Once he releases your mind, the

mirage wears off and the haze subsides, allowing you to return to reality." The tenseness in Anselem's voice did not abate as he added, "But whatever he made you do—whatever *your own mind* made you do—that's irreversible."

Asha was quiet for a long time after he finished, fidgeting with the leather string hanging from her neck. Her fingers trembled, and she tried to shove the fearful thoughts of the Vices from her mind, but the effort was futile.

"What's that?" Anselem asked, pulling her from the infiltrating thoughts. She looked over and saw he was staring at the thin rope twisted in her hand.

She pursed her lips as she moved her hand towards her throat and pulled out the leather rope tucked beneath her flying jacket. A thin metal key was tied to the end.

Anselem's eyes went wide, and he arched a brow. He stared at the long, gold-plated key in her hand. "What is that?" he repeated.

"I don't know," she replied. "I didn't think it was anything. But then you told me about the Divulgence Key, and I thought... I'm not sure what I thought. But I believed it might be something important, so I kept it."

She stretched out her arm, and he opened his hand. She placed the key in his calloused fingers. He turned it over several times in his hands.

"Where did you get this?" he asked, not taking his eyes off the key.

"The Adaro King gave it to me."

His gaze whipped up to meet hers. "What?"

She nodded. "When I was under the Lake."

He blinked.

"He said it was because I freed them from the Sea Serpent. I didn't correct him to tell him I was just saving myself..."

Anselem looked back down at the ancient key.

"Do you think it could be the Divulgence Key?" Asha asked.

He shook his head. Mathieson had described the key to the Septant before they went to Montu, so the warriors would know what to look for.

The Divulgence Key was made of marbled onyx, with the carving of a lion's open jaws fastened to the top and two blood red diamonds fixed in the beast's eyes.

"No, but I think it's *something*. It feels... old. Other. It's the same feeling I had when I sent my magic into the Lake to find you."

He handed it back to her. "Just keep it safe for now. We will figure out what its purpose is."

She nodded and pulled the leather rope back over her head, tucking the key beneath her jacket.

She was quiet for a long while, staring into the flames before her, her expression blank, and he knew she had disappeared into the Darkness inside her mind. Disappeared into haunted memories of the Vices and the ruthless one with a serpent's sneer.

"Where did you go?" he asked softly.

His voice pulled her from the memories she was drowning in, and she dragged her eyes over to him. The burning inside of them was dim. Nearly extinguished. But a faint spark still hung on. Still survived.

"I just feel... empty. Like a part of me is so fractured I'm not sure it will ever be able to be filled again."

Anselem nodded, his heart full of understanding.

He wanted to hold her. To pull her in close and remind her again that everything would be okay. He offered a closed smile instead.

She turned her eyes back to the fire and sighed. "I don't even understand why you put up with it—with me. With my chaos and shadows, and the Darkness that seems to follow me wherever I turn. It seems like a very unwise choice to surround yourself with endless gloom, *lieutenant*."

He could hear her trying to force the humored, insulting tone into her voice, could see the attempt at reviving the banter they had thrown each other's way for months—the banter that masked so many other feelings they refused to acknowledge between them.

He turned to face her, but her eyes were locked on the flames. His voice was low, but steady, and full of truth as he replied, "Because you're fire, Asha, and I've been cold my whole life."

He meant it. Not because of the flames that rolled through her veins, or the sparks that lit her wondrous eyes; no, Asha was the entire essence of fire—beautifully lethal, strong, fierce. And she was desperately loyal, for she would burn herself to ashes for the ones she loved. But, above all, she was the first thing Anselem Eros had ever found in his life that truly made his cold heart feel warm.

She was quiet while she stared into the embers. He did not think she believed him.

Anselem pulled his gaze from her and settled it on the crackling fire. "Maybe we feel empty because we leave pieces of ourselves in everything we used to love," he whispered.

He felt her sapphire eyes turn to him, but he did not move.

And with a quiet voice, full of a vulnerability he so rarely ever heard from her, she confessed, "I just hope that when I am gone, someday, somewhere, someone will pick my soul up off the pages of the story I leave behind and think *I would have loved her*. Despite my Darkness, despite the demons running through my mind and the horrors I have seen, they would read the pages of my book and still choose to love me."

As she spoke, she did not realize the warrior sitting be-

CAMERON L. JIMENEZ

side her had gone still.

Because she was not just part of his book, she was *the* book. And he knew in his heart, if they did not end up together, he would always leave one last page blank, just in case.

CHAPTER

FIVE

"So, what do you want to do, General?"

Iskander cut his eyes at Imara. He hated when she called him that, and she knew it. But he figured it was only fair she got a jab in after dragging his unconscious body out of The Wet Dog the evening before.

"Right now, I want to wash off the remnants of last night and give myself a moment to think."

She raised her brows and looked him over once. "Thank the gods, because I'm not sure I would have been able to sit at a table with you all morning. You reek."

He rolled his eyes but gave her a grin. "Always the charmer, Fellowes."

She flashed a smirk as she pushed off the doorframe. "I'll meet you in the Hati Keep in an hour."

The Hati Keep was the western tower of the Twin Keeps built within the Citadel. Its sister tower, the Skoll Keep, re-

CAMERON L. JIMENEZ

sided on the east side of the fort.

Iskander nodded and, without another word, Imara disappeared down the hall. A moment later, he heard the front door to his two-bedroom cottage on the east side of the Southgate District slam shut. He let out a breath.

He pulled the chair out from beneath the desk and crashed onto the seat. The wooden legs groaned under his weight, and he rested his elbows on the desk before him. He rubbed his temples as he looked over the papers once more, studying every detail.

Iskander scoffed as he read the last line for the second time. He figured the gods must enjoy tormenting him by this point in his life.

He shook his head and rolled the scroll back up, binding it with the cut piece of leather.

Perhaps he didn't need to go retrieve it. Or maybe he could send a handful of his best warriors from the Vanguard to go in his stead.

Iskander let out another irritated breath, already knowing he would never choose the secondary option. He was many things, most of them undesirable, but he had never let the word 'coward' crawl its way onto the list of words he chose to describe himself.

Darkness rolled inside him, and black shadows began to creep out from his body, swirling around him. He shoved them down, throwing a leash around his power.

His head was still pounding. He stood, nearly knocking the chair over as he forcefully rose, and strolled into the washroom.

He stripped off the sweat and liquor-stained clothes clinging to his body, revealing the well-honed muscles he had earned from over a decade and a half of training. His skin was covered in black ink that stretched over his arms and legs. The only place left unmarked by the splintered thorns of inked darkness was his back, covered with the star-dust wing of his Septant tattoo, and the outer part of his right forearm, which held his Amarok Mark.

Centered on a vertical line stretching the length of the lower part of his arm, the Amarok Mark held the seven stages of the lunar cycle, with stardust swirls scattered around each of the moon's phases.

His hands gripped the sides of the wash basin, and as he stared into the dim silver eyes reflecting back at him, all he could see was loss.

The hardest thing wasn't the pain he felt, though there were days when Iskander believed it would swallow him whole. No, the most painful part was the people around him who expected him to have already picked himself up from the fall, to be healed, while he was still lying on the ground, his blood not even finished pouring out.

And if Iskander was honest with himself, he was not sure he even knew how to heal. Like a shattered mirror that had been fastened back together, there were cracks in his heart he knew would always remain. And the only way he knew how to cope with the endless dark was to drift off into oblivion until all he felt was numbness.

He was tired. In his mind and soul, he was so, so tired. Like grief had swallowed every morsel of life inside his body. And Iskander wasn't sure there would ever be a day when he would not carry the heaviness of the grief he felt for the loss of his sister. He was certain he would miss her forever, like the stars miss the sun in the morning skies.

He pushed himself away from the hanging mirror and climbed into the icy water resting in the basin beside him. A sharp breath pulled through his teeth as his bare skin dunked beneath the surface, and in a swift motion, he thrust his head beneath the frigid water.

He stayed under the water for a long time. It was quiet—peaceful, as if the horrors of the world could not enter the silence he encountered within the depths.

Once his lungs began to burn and cry out for air, and the shadows inside of him started to creep out and create a muddy picture within the tub, he finally allowed himself to pull his head from under the water.

As his face broke through the surface, he gasped in a deep breath, gulping down air. His shadows drew back into his body, leaving the basin filled with clear, unclouded water.

He ran his hands through his hair and took in a final, steadying breath before he forced himself back together and donned the mask of the General, a façade he had crafted so well over the years.

And just like that, Iskander Blaidd shut his emotions off.

He quickly washed and dressed, pulling on his light gray, fleece-lined leathers, and threw a midweight jacket over his shirt.

Everything in his closet had been tailored to fit him perfectly. With his towering height and large, coiled muscles, Iskander had never been able to fit into the traditionally issued uniforms.

He ambled into the kitchen, which opened into a small sitting room with a tall, stone fireplace in the corner. The ceilings were vaulted in the main room as well, matching both his own bedroom and the secondary one down the hall.

The height of the ceilings was why he had chosen the cottage—along with its location on the outskirts of the city—because every part of the home, excluding the halls, held high, towering ceilings.

Aside from the added luxury of not having to duck in his own home, the desire for the open feeling came from the many memories Iskander held of being forced into cramped spaces as a child.

And now, with even the few happy memories of his time in the Home with El tainted, Iskander was even more thankful he had chosen a place with an open feeling, for he tried to avoid his mind wandering towards memories of his sister at all costs.

Imara had left fresh-baked bread on the table for him, along with a basket of eggs. He sighed. He truly did not deserve his Second.

Iskander sauntered across the room to the burning fireplace. That was one of the first skills of lesser magic he had learned when his powers manifested—a rune that ensured a lit fire never went out. He had spent too many nights in his childhood enduring the brutal cold, and Iskander ensured he would never experience that fate again.

He took one of the iron rods from the holder beside the fireplace and held it in the flames, waiting until the tip of the spear burned bright red. Once it had heated, he walked across the sitting room to the cooktop in the kitchen.

He lit a small piece of flint with the burning rod, and the coals beneath the iron bars began to heat. He placed a skillet on top of the bars before he walked the rod back over to the fireplace and placed it inside the holder.

Two cracked eggs were thrown into the pan, and a sizzling echo filled the room. He grabbed the kettle sitting on the counter beside the cooktop and poured water from the clean basin in the corner. Once it had been filled, he put it above a second flame. Opening one of the cabinets above him, Iskander pulled out the ground-up beans he brought back from one of his missions south of the Straight.

He opened the sealed top of the container and peered inside the steel can. There were only a few spoonfuls left of the deep brown grinds. His lips pursed, but he proceeded to scoop out a small amount of the grounds onto a thin piece of paper.

A crackling pop sounded from the skillet, followed by a loud whistle from the kettle. Iskander removed the eggs from the fire, plopping them onto a plate he had pulled from another cabinet, and he quickly took the container with boiled water off the cooktop.

After pulling a mug from one of the shelves, Iskander folded the small piece of paper into a conical shape, placing it inside the mug. The boiling water from the kettle was poured over the grinds, and Iskander let it steep until a deep, rich liquid filtered through the paper and filled the cup. The smell of the brew saturated the room, mixing in with the frying eggs beside it. It was rich and bold, with a balance of strong and sweet notes all blended into a warm, distinct fragrance.

He splashed water over the two open flames, watching as they swiftly simmered out among the coals.

He took the plate and his drink—*jahvah*, the natives of the Southern Continent had called it—and sat at his quaint, ebony wood dining table to eat his breakfast.

On the opposite side of the room from the fireplace, next to the dining table, stretched two large windows overlooking the Iron Mountains.

A blackbird with a snow-white underbelly soared past the window, heading south towards Orevein. Iskander took another sip of his *jahvah* as two more flittered past, following closely behind the first.

It was still early in the year for winter to begin, but over the last week, the temperature had begun to drop more rapidly than normal for the eleventh month. And with signs of the snowbirds already beginning their departure south, Iskander knew this year's winter would come early and quickly.

He made a mental note to tell Imara to ready the winter sleds for the Vanguard. The last thing he needed was for his warriors to be immobilized if a strong snowfall came and the Amarok were unprepared.

He shoveled down the last of his breakfast, savoring the remaining few sips of his deep, rich *jahvah*, and set the dishes in the secondary, small wash bin beside the cook top and headed for the door.

A brisk wind cut through his open jacket as soon as he exited the cottage. He bolted the door with a locking rune, buttoned his jacket tightly, and headed towards the city center.

Iskander lived in a remote corner of the Southgate District, far enough away that he could enjoy some quiet solitude from the bustle of Lorca's busier districts.

His boots crunched on the newly fallen snow as he made his way through the Canis district towards the Citadel.

Only a light dusting had fallen the night before, but he knew that the heavier storms would arrive soon.

Even with the snow covering rooftops and balconies, the Canis district had seen better days. Located just east of the Slums, many of the buildings had adopted the same rundown, derelict look of their neighboring district. The only difference between the two communities was that the Canis district seemed to have kept most of the crime and questionable citizens out of its homes. But even the purity of the newly fallen snow could not hide the look of the crumbling walls and broken roof shingles.

As he waded his way through the streets, soldiers and warriors on their way to and from the Citadel stopped their steps and addressed him with a salute. He nodded at each of the Fenri and Amarok, acknowledging the several greetings he received, and continued wading through the streets until he reached the south entrance to the Citadel.

Even from beyond the towering stone walls, colored with marbled blue-grey hues, Iskander could see the magnificent Keeps of the Citadel.

As he crossed through the arched entrance, the Twin Keeps came forth in all their glory. Two perfectly circular towers stretched high towards the clouds above, each climbing thirty stories into the sky. Golden spires were fixed around the top floors, with open arches surrounding the lookout points.

Iskander turned left towards the Hati Keep, passing by the remarkable golden statue fixed in the center courtyard. Surrounded by marbled benches and garden shrubs, rested the statue of Selene, Goddess of the Moon—*the all-seeing eyes of the night*.

The goddess, intricately carved from various reflective metals, was beautiful. She wore a golden crown with a silver crescent-shaped moon in the center and held the reins to a chariot drawn by three Amarok wolves. A pair of golden wings, encircled with silver stardust, splayed out from both sides of her back. Carved meticulously into the platformed stone at her feet read the Amarok dictum: *When the moonlight fades, may you outlast the stars.*

A small collection of Fenri and Amarok warriors was gathered by the statue, stopping on their way to class to pay their respects to the goddess and seek wisdom.

A bitter feeling washed over Iskander as he passed by the statue of Selene, and he swore her carved, golden eyes watched him as he made his way towards the Hati Keep.

He would always be grateful to the Goddess of the Moon for gifting him Conri, but he still held a fair amount of resentment towards *the all-seeing eyes of the night* for allowing El to be taken from him.

He did not know what kinds of deals and arrangements were made between the gods and goddesses, but he held no doubt in his mind that the Goddess of the Moon wielded a great deal of influence within the divine realm.

He continued his way down the stone path, and just before he pulled the handle to the marbled blue-grey door that would take him into the foyer of the Hati Keep, he glanced back one last time at the statue fixed across the courtyard, and he swore he saw the goddess's eyes narrow the slightest bit.

CHAPTER

SIX

Anselem debated all day about whether they should stop for the night at the base of the Iron Mountains, north of Orevein, or if it was better to fly across the city of Lorca and rest at the western shore.

He decided to head to Gull's Landing, the small port village outside of Lorca on the coast of the Hoarfrost Sea.

Orevein would have been the better option, giving the warriors an opportunity to find lodging inside the town and seek respite from the frigid winter air that arrived earlier than expected.

But the Commander knew the pair could not afford to draw attention to themselves by renting a couple of rooms for a single night, firebirds in tow.

And staying at the base of the Iron Mountains without a formal shelter seemed like one of the poorer choices Anselem would have made throughout his life. So, consequently, he decided they would tough out a few more hours of flying through the frozen air until they made it to the coast.

The shores of Gull's Landing were nothing like the comforting, glowing coastline of Elysia. In his hometown, the waters nearest the sand were lit at night with the high concentrations of bioluminescent algae gathered along the shore. The soft, steady waves of the Seidon Sea lapped up against the pure white sands, and the crests unceasingly glowed with bright blue and green lights that matched the city's dragon glass buildings that lined the streets during the day.

But the frigid shore of Gull's Landing was Elysia's counter opposite. The rich, black sand stretched on for miles, and a littering of ice chunks was scattered across the dark grains, having washed ashore from the glaciers floating in the Hoarfrost Sea. Sparkling against the moonlight, the ice blocks looked like glittering diamonds, polished by the harsh wind and water.

Anselem found a small stretch of sand that was uncovered by the icy boulders and set up camp under the midnight sky.

As the firebirds had soared further and further north, even the warmth of the sun above was unable to fight against the bitter chill that had seeped into Anselem's flying leathers. And as soon as the daylight faded, the biting cold had worked its way deep into his bones and refused to depart.

The pair gathered dried driftwood, and the whipping winds cut through Anselem's winter leathers. He assumed Asha was experiencing the same discomfort, but she never once voiced her complaints.

In fact, Asha had been quiet for the better part of the day.

After they gathered the wood, Asha sat beside the pile and stared intently at the planks. She summoned the flames more quickly than on the first night.

As he pulled some dried meat and bread from one of the sacks strapped to Kapheria, Anselem fixed an orb around the fire, shielding it from the harsh winds and protecting the warriors from any noxious fumes the burning driftwood could emanate. He reminded himself to thank his Pontos brothers the next time he saw them for sharing that helpful bit of information on one of their past missions.

Once the fire began to burn steadily, Anselem sat down beside it and wrapped one of the thick wool blankets he had packed around his shoulders. Asha sat across from him, curled up in the other.

The crackle of the fire and the soft howl of the wind were the only noises on the shore. He pulled his gaze from the flames and stared up at the snowcapped peaks of the moonlit mountains in the far distance.

Occasionally, a ripping gale would cut through the place where they made camp upon the sand, causing the fire, even beneath the orb, to tremble, threatening to extinguish the only source of heat.

Anselem pulled the blanket closer around his broad shoulders.

It would be a long night.

Asha sat across from him, a matching blanket curled around her. Her eyes were fixed on the distant peaks with narrowed focus, as though she could see straight through the Iron Mountains and to the river-strangled city that rested on the other side.

"I used to think we told each other everything," she whispered.

Anselem turned his head slightly, watching her from the corner of his eye.

"I thought after Mom and Dad were gone, we knew that we were all each other had left."

54

A long silence stretched between them, filled only by the wind threading through the stones.

Asha shrugged, her voice low. "I think I knew it the last time I saw him. He came to Valhol a few months before my Final Testing. He didn't say anything, but... I could see it in his eyes. There was something he wanted to tell me. He'd always been easy to read."

Anselem's brows raised, but he quickly buried the flicker of surprise that surged through him. Mathieson Raynor had been many things, but easy to read had never been one of them.

"I think he might have known it was the end," she went on, gaze still fixed on the snow-capped peaks. "That it would be the last time we saw one another." She paused, her gaze softening with memory. "We went to the Temple of Frejya. I think it was one of the few places we still felt safe after Mom died." The pain in her expression ebbed, replaced by a soft, sad smile. "We used to call it *a place that remembers time*."

Anselem's voice lowered with reverence. "The Temple of the goddess who blessed the Warrior of Praenuntius," Anselem murmured.

Asha gave him a grave look and nodded.

The Warrior of Praenuntius was a legend lost to time. A Harbinger of Reckoning. He was the Chosen One of the High Gods, the soldier called to usher in the end, sent not to conquer, but to cleanse.

The God of Light had watched as darkness festered across the world for millennia, as cruelty and corruption spread through every kingdom like rot. And so the High Gods of Ianoda's Authority chose the Warrior as an answer—a divine fire meant to wash the world clean. He became the Chosen One who lit the First War, igniting a clash between the divine forces that shattered the known world. Continents were split, the sky tore, and the very laws of reality were rewritten.

At the war's end, the Warrior vanished. But from his ashes rose the seven kingdoms, each carving its piece of the new world from what remained. In the early days, kings and queens claimed warped versions of his legacy, rewriting the Warrior's legacy to suit their own reign, reshaping truth into myth. The early kings venerated him, most vilified him, and those of recent centuries tried to erase his memory completely.

His name was outlawed in much of the Northern and Southern Continents—stripped from texts, burned from archives, cursed in courts. And yet, the story endured—passed from tongue to tongue in whispers and rhyme, stitched into tales and carved into hidden stone. The truth lived not in books, but in the stubborn breath of those who refused to forget.

And, like all great tales that begin in darkness, some still secretly believed he would return—rising as an echo to finish what the First Warrior could not. Reborn to eradicate Darkness from the world once again—this time, in fullness.

Anselem looked back at Asha. "Do you believe the old stories? That he'll return one day or that there will be another?"

Asha didn't answer right away. Her gaze stayed on the mountains, unmoving, as if she were listening for something only she could hear.

"I've seen what the Darkness does," she said. "How it spreads. How it devours." She exhaled, slow and cold. "I don't know if I believe anymore that this world can change. That it can heal and be better than it is. Not really." Then, softer, barely audible, like a confession slipping between her defenses, "But some part of me still hopes for it. Some part of me still holds on to the belief that Ianoda hasn't forgotten us. That the Authorities see what we endure at the hands of

King Balthasar and the Council. What the people of other kingdoms endure. And I hold on to that fragment of faith that there's another coming—someone who will finish what the First Warrior couldn't." She looked down at her hands, then back at the peaks. "Someone who will build something better from the ruins. Someone whose efforts will last. Someone who will forge a better world."

He nodded, the only comfort he could offer, and watched as she slowly slipped away into the dark corner of her mind she had made after the Tartarus.

His stomach clenched. "Truth for a truth?" he asked.

She raised her head to meet his gaze, the dark shadows clearing from her eyes, and a soft smile pulled at the corners of her mouth. She nodded.

He dragged his eyes back up to the Iron Mountains, and in a voice so low, he was unsure if it carried across the distance to where Asha sat, he asked, "Did you ever encounter the Snowskulls living so close to the Iron Mountains?"

Asha's composure faltered, and she tilted her head, puzzlement spreading over her face. Anselem knew the question had taken her by surprise, having intended to distract her from the Darkness attempting to creep in.

The Snowskulls were the Mountain Folk of the North. More legend and fable than fact and truth, but Anselem had always admired the half-human creatures rumored to live deep within the Iron Mountains, for the clan had always rejected the rules of the world, determined to live by the ways of their own laws and code.

With its ruthless nights and unforgiving winters, throughout hundreds of years, the North became the Hells' territory, and the Snowskulls were beholden to no gods.

They answered to no outsiders, kings included, electing instead to observe a leader of their choosing—the Snow Sultan.

57

Anselem had never heard of any name given to the Sultan; he wasn't sure there even was a leader in the savage lands of the North, but the lack of acclaim the ruler's personal name carried was offset by the realm-renowned reputation of the Snowskulls themselves.

Rumors of the Mountain Folk had been passed down through generations. The tales were always centered around the wild, undomesticated practices of the half-humans, never failing to highlight the vicious, merciless, and outright brutal customs they took part in. From child sacrifices to ritual burnings, the Snowskulls had earned a nefarious and appalling reputation.

Anselem had never known which parts of the stories were true. Like most fables, he realized that the legends had likely become dramatized over time. But he also knew there was a good possibility that the creatures who chose to stay hidden in the deepest, darkest corners of the realm might very well have been every bit as carnal and merciless as the tales of old described them to be. But, in fair-mindedness, he figured that any people who dared to settle as the base of Hells' doorstep were presumably well acquainted with the God of Death. And too many encounters with Anubis was enough to send any rational creature towards spiraling insanity.

"Once," Asha replied. Her eyes left the fire and turned to the snowcapped peaks beyond. A gust of chilled wind ripped through the air, rustling the fire. Asha pulled her blanket closer to her chest.

"I expected them to be different," she said simply. "I had heard so many of the tales growing up that in my mind I envisioned these grotesque, menacing frost monsters of the North." She let out a deep breath. "But they were beautiful. In their own unique and unconventional way, but beautiful nonetheless." She brought her hand up to her cheek, to the spot where the crescent-shaped scar was carved into her skin. The same one he saw so many months before when they sparred in the rings high above the training grounds at Sveaborg.

"There was only one. I came across her when I was searching for flint to make more arrowheads."

Asha proceeded to tell Anselem all about the Mountain Folk of the North.

She told him how the creature's skin was snow-white, blending in perfectly with the surrounding winter mountains, that she almost hadn't seen her. But what caught her gaze was the faintest gleam of the high sun as it glinted on the pale blue gemstone fixed into the center of the Snowskull's forehead. It matched her glowing blue eyes, and the band it was fixed on wrapped around her head in an intricate, interlaced pattern of shimmering white fabrics.

The rest of her body looked the same. A pale, snow-white color, covered in a thin, laced, shimmering white fabric, as if she were immune to the splitting cold temperatures of the North.

But the most incredible part of the ensemble the creature donned was the white, glittering antlers that protruded from her head, just above her deer-like ears. Asha had never seen a creature so stunning.

"She was caught in one of the traps the Hunters of Valhol had set." A flash of disgust flickered on Asha's face. "Even as a child, I used to hear the Hunters brag about the 'monstrous creatures of the mountains' they killed."

She was quiet for a moment before she continued, her voice lower than before.

"It was a game for them. Sport. Like they got some twisted pleasure from hunting down their neighbors simply because they were... different."

She let out a long breath. "I think I would have under-

59

stood it," she explained. "I would have understood their boasting and joy if they had been hunting true savages. If the Snowskulls were the monsters we were made to believe. But as I stood below the iron-laced net, staring into the glowing eyes of the creature, I could see there was depth and understanding and... Light."

Anselem knew Asha had seen too many midnight eyes void of light. Eyes that held only shadows and Darkness. And he also knew she understood the difference between the ones that had been drained of all goodness and the ones with life and hope still swimming beneath the surface. He just had not realized that this was not a new revelation for her, but one she had known for quite some time.

"So, I set her free."

Anselem blinked. Asha touched her cheek again.

"And after she fell onto the snow-covered ground below, she gracefully pulled herself to her feet, and I remembered the only thought that came to my mind was that she was so tall." A soft, breathy laugh escaped her mouth. "Perhaps it was just because I was so small at the time."

Anselem raised a brow. "At the time?" he teased.

She rolled her eyes, but the smile on her face remained. "We can't all be half-giants, *lieutenant*."

A grin tugged at the corner of his mouth. He never thought he would love the sound of his title until he heard it spoken from her lips.

"She said nothing to me once she rose to her feet," Asha continued. "I'm not sure if the Snowskulls even speak the common tongue, but no words were needed. I could see the gratitude in her eyes.

"I remember her head whipping up and her eyes looking past me, to something buried further back in the woods that my ears could not hear. And just before she turned to leave, disappearing into the surrounding whiteness, she pulled her hand to my face, and with her long, cobalt blue nails, she cut my cheek."

Anselem's eyes widened and dropped down to the crescent-shaped scar on her face.

"It didn't hurt. It barely even bled. Honestly, it wasn't even deep enough to scar yet—" She motioned to the small, faint silver curve on her face. She shrugged. "I don't mind it," she added, "it helps remind me that sometimes things are not always as you have been told. It reminds me that there might be other people—other beings—out there who also have hope of better days and a better world."

She stared back at the peaks of the Iron Mountains, as if she could look beyond the darkness of the skies and see through the trees to a long-lost creature who was grateful for an unjudging mind and a second chance.

"After she took her hand from my cheek, she disappeared into the forest. It was only minutes later when a group of hunters came by the trap. I hid in some nearby bushes so they wouldn't see me." She pulled her eyes from the mountain tops, centering them back on Anselem. "And to think, I spent so much of my life believing the Snowskulls were monsters simply because of the tales I had been told." She sighed. "But I suppose that is how it will be."

Anselem tilted his head to the side.

"Until the prey is permitted to speak, every story will glorify the hunter."

Anselem stared at her, enveloped by her mind, her words. Lost in the way she saw the world, so differently from others.

Like the moon, there was a side of her so dark, even the flaming stars could not glow within it; there was a side of her so cold, even the sun could not warm it. But within the darkness and the cold, there burned a fire so great, no shadows could douse the flames. A fire built of hope and faith, and the dream of a better world.

Another whipping wind sliced through their camp, and he watched Asha creep closer to the fire, her boots nearly inside the flames.

"Come here," he said, his voice casual and level.

He pulled open one of the sides of his blanket, and even in the dim light of the fire, he could see Asha's brows raise.

He rolled his eyes. "Oh, calm down. I'm just trying to make sure neither of us freezes to death. It would put quite a damper on the trip."

She smirked, and to his surprise, she picked herself up from her place and walked around to where he sat, plopping down onto the sand next to him. The scent of jasmine and vanilla wrapped around him. She looked up at him with those burning sapphire eyes that killed him.

"No jokes about body heat? Or having in mind ways to warm us up?"

Anselem laughed and replied, "I will refrain as long as you keep your snide comments about me being cold to yourself."

He could see the redness flush across her cheeks, and he knew she recalled the remark she made at the thermal pools back at Sveaborg.

He chuckled. "Just body heat for survival, Seven."

She nodded once. "Survival."

Her side was pressed against his, and he could already feel the heat generating between them. He leaned in closer, pulling her against him. They stayed like that for a long while, comfortably sitting in uninterrupted silence, enjoying the warmth shared between one another, until Asha's eyelids grew heavy, and each of her blinks became slower and longer.

"We should get some sleep. Early start tomorrow."

She nodded again, and the pair resituated themselves on

the half-frozen ground. He felt her body still shivering from the cold, and he wrapped his arms around her, pulling her against his chest.

The softest smile curled at the corner of his mouth, and he swore he felt the faintest of sparking embers ripple out from her hands when his arms encircled her.

As he closed his eyes, the warmth of her body pressed closely up against his, and he knew no better feeling.

Between seas, galaxies, and moons, he was thankful to have stepped on the same land and dreamed under the same stars as her.

And as he drifted off to sleep, he dreamed of better days and a better world. And he dreamed of the woman beside him—the warrior who would change it all.

CHAPTER

SEVEN

Iskander's head was hammering against the sides of his skull by the time he made it up the winding staircase and into the top floor of the Keep.

When he walked into the meeting room, Imara was already seated at the white oak table, with dozens of papers spread in front of her.

As he entered, she said nothing, but the devious flicker in her eyes told Iskander she had purposefully chosen the top story meeting room to torment him and the shattering hangover he was nursing. He narrowed his eyes at his Second but did not comment.

He circled the table and looked over her shoulder, studying the scrolls stretched across the wood.

Seven separate manuscripts were splayed out, each containing detailed notes and descriptions of a unique and distinctive staff.

For the past two years, Iskander had been searching for the lost scepters. He had learned of their existence long ago, on one of the many sleepless nights he spent locked under the Midnight Castle.

Iskander turned onto his side, the rickety bed creaking beneath his weight. Bed was a kind word to describe his sleeping arrangements—a battered cot was a more accurate description of his makeshift bunk crumpled in the corner of the damp cell.

"Are you awake?" a scratchy voice whispered through the dark.

Iskander silently sat up and looked across to the cell opposite his own. The guards had stopped supplying magic to the hung luminos hours earlier, and Iskander's eyes were partially adjusted to the endless dark filling the room.

A shadowed silhouette of Mathieson sat upright in his cell. No other warriors in the room stirred.

"Yes," Iskander replied, his voice equally as hoarse.

It had been two months since the Septant was captured, and Iskander had hardly spoken in the time that had passed.

A long, silence-filled moment elapsed after he replied, and Iskander leaned his back against the wall, unsure if Mathieson had asked simply to know he had a friend with whom he could share the dark.

But, as Iskander began to once again close his eyes, Mathieson's broken voice crept back through the air. "Can you do something for me?"

Iskander's eyes broke open, and he stared across the lightless space. His brow bunched, confused as to what he could help his brother with while locked inside a cage. "I can try."

"When you get out of here, I need you to do something for me."

The General did not reply as the weighted words drifted into his cell. Mathieson's singular use of 'you,' rather than 'we,' was not lost on him. He did not reply.

"I need you to give me your Word," Mathieson added.

Iskander's eyes narrowed in the direction of his brother's voice. Mathieson had never asked any of his brothers for a favor; much less enacted their Word in the process. "Tell me what it is, and I will consider it," Iskander asserted, his hushed voice calm and contemplative.

A long pause of silence filled the space between the warriors.

"Your Word, Iskander," Mathieson finally responded, earnestness coating his words.

Iskander sat in the quiet dark for a long while, determined to hold to his long-standing covenant to never make bargains without first knowing the details of the deal. Even if the deal was with his brother.

But perhaps it was the mind-numbing monotony of sitting in endless dark, or perhaps it was his need for something other than the haunting memories of Kalevala's bedchamber to fill his thoughts, or perhaps it was the small inkling of curiosity that had been sparked within him at Mathieson's solemnity, but after decades of holding true, Iskander Blaidd broke his longest standing self-covenant with five simple words.

"I give you my Word."

Mathieson let out a long exhale, as if he had been holding his breath while he waited for his brother's answer.

Then, in hushed whispers, as the four other warriors slept soundly beside them, Mathieson proceeded to tell Iskander everything he knew about the Crowns of the Six Princes of Shadows.

The Princes were not of this world but were born of another; molded from Darkness itself, formed within the deep-

est level of the Seven Hells.

Mathieson told him of the tales of old, and of the First War, how the Lords of Light and Darkness fought one another, and their battle ripped through space and time. He explained how the Princes of Shadows, the Lord of Darkness's henchmen, served the Dark King with unwavering loyalty, equally satisfied to rip apart worlds and wreak havoc upon the souls that resided there.

He then explained what the Princes—the Wraiths of War and Ruin—had left behind when they were cast out from this realm and left to wander in the empty spaces between worlds, forever seeking to find a way back from the Hells.

The Princes of Shadows each enclosed a small fragment of their Dark Power inside six carefully hewn staffs, leaving the majority of their Darkness buried inside their soulless forms to utilize for governance over their appointed Province of the Hells.

The staffs were specially hewn relics, made for harnessing the overwhelming Dark Magic of the Princes without breaking. And, most importantly, they were made to serve as a gateway for the Princes to reenter the realm when the staffs were wielded.

"How do they reenter?" Iskander asked, his voice full of dread.

"The staff needs only to be touched, and the gateway will be opened."

The blood drained from Iskander's pale face. "Bloody moonlight," he swore, his head reeling with the information. "But why would anyone want to open a gateway for a Prince of the Hells?" he asked, disbelief winding around every word.

Mathieson was quiet for a moment before answering. "Because the Dark Power placed inside the scepter can be claimed by the soul of the one who wields it."

*Iskander's mouth went dry. "And these staffs are just…
floating around Darnella carelessly?"*

"All but one."

Iskander remained silent.

*"Before we came here," Mathieson explained, "I was
able to track one down. I stole it from King Nemuri."*

*"That wastrel of a king from Taidana? The one who sat
lazily in his castle while his kingdom rotted around him?
Who lets every vagrant, thief, and assassin flood his streets
while he does nothing but lounge on his throne?"*

"That's the one."

*Iskander ran a hand through his hair and rubbed his
eyes. "Where did you put it?"*

*One of the warriors at the other end of the room shifted
in his bed, turning on his side. Mathieson was quiet for a
long while until the soft, rhythmical snoring returned.*

*A clattering skipped across the floor, and a small ob-
ject landed at Iskander's feet. He reached down and picked
up the hard, metal item. He ran his fingers across the cool,
smooth surface. He felt the two forked teeth jutting out at the
end and a circular outline, with etchings Iskander's hands
could not make out in the dark, rested at the top. A leather
strap was tied to one end.*

*"The Alpha Key. It will allow you to enter the Ossuary.
It's where I stored the first staff. It is in the western side of the
Iron Mountains, not far outside of Lorca."*

*Iskander ran his hands over the key again, and, even
with the iron shackles locked around his wrists, he felt the
faintest hum of power extending from the key, as if the magic
resting inside of it was reaching out to his own.*

*"I don't know where the other staffs are at, but that is
what I need you to do when you get out of here."*

*"Why can't you do it?" Iskander whispered, unsure if he
wanted to hear Mathieson's response.*

Mathieson ignored the General's question and continued, "There is a box inside my room in Valhol, in the corner closet, tucked in the back. It has a journal with notes and the scrolls you will need to begin looking."

Millions of questions flew through Iskander's mind, but he did not voice them. He began making a list of all the things he would need to do once the Septant broke out of the castle, and, for the first time in decades, Iskander prayed to the gods of old that the box Mathieson had left behind in Valhol would still be sitting in the corner closet where he stored it.

"And Iskander?"

"Yeah, Raynor?"

A long pause followed, and through the darkness stretching before him, Iskander could feel the shift of Mathieson's stare, as if his gaze had turned away from the General and landed on the four sleeping warriors to his right.

Mathieson's voice broke through the stillness. "Don't tell the others."

And with those four sealing words, like an iron branding flesh, Iskander felt the Binding Mark of his bargain etched onto his skin.

Imara pushed two of the documents to the far side of the table, pulling Iskander from his memory. He glanced at the separated scrolls, markedly set apart from the other five papers lying on the table. The removed manuscripts held sketches of the two staffs that had already been procured.

A staff made from a pale blue rock and hooked in a sharp, curved shape was etched onto the first paper. A second, crafted from a deep-burned copper, with a whittled pig carved into the top in plated bronze, sat beside the first. Both procured staffs had the engraved, seven-pointed Crown etched into the top of their hilts.

The two pictures depicted perfectly detailed imitations

of the real staffs locked inside the Ossuary.

Mathieson had secured the first staff long before he asked Iskander to find the remaining six Crowns, but Iskander was wholly responsible for obtaining the second.

When he returned from Montu, he quickly found the box Mathieson had left for him. It did not take Iskander long before he solicited the help of Imara to decipher the cryptic messages hidden within the scrolls and pages.

Iskander's Second was able to uncover the hidden meanings buried within Mathieson's journal, as well as decode the text scrawled onto the scroll containing the image of the staff of deep-burned copper.

With clandestine research and a handful of favors, the duo called in to several trusted mentors, Iskander and Imara discovered the staff belonged to King Gulliver, the appointed monarch to the Crystalline Thone.

Iskander wasted no time before heading south of the Straight, and although he had no idea what to expect when his ship landed on the shores of Delphagia, a voracious king with an insatiable hunger for fine wines and sumptuous foods was not what he anticipated.

It took Iskander less than a week to find the copper staff and steal it.

The Delphagian King, excessively consumed by the endless parties he hosted at his amber-hued castle, maintained a constant state of drunkenness and overindulgence that unfailingly lulled him into a state of unconsciousness even the most persistent of servants could not rouse.

Night after night, cloaked in Septant black, Iskander watched from the shadowed windows of a nearby rooftop, witnessing the never-ending rotation of food and drinks that poured into the central ballroom. Tables were stuffed full of rich delicacies from across the Continents, and an endless river of luxurious wine unceasingly flowed down the monarch's throat.

Platter after platter, all filled with rare cuisines and opulent sweets, was set in front of the delighted king, and each plate whisked away by serving hands had been licked clean. The entire scene made Iskander's stomach roll.

But the most unbelievable act Iskander witnessed in the opulent dining hall of the Amber Castle was the sight of the drunken king ceremoniously crashing onto the polished floor each night.

Every evening, before the castle clock tower struck midnight, King Gulliver's mindfulness left his esurient body and remained eternally lost until the ravenous revelries of the previous evening had the chance to wane.

The unlucky servants closest to the king's side when his lifeless body hit the floor were forced to haul the portly monarch up to his bedchambers and lob his insentient body onto the massive bed—a ruler too far gone to hear the whimpered cries of the starving citizens filling the streets below.

On the third evening, after King Gulliver was dragged to his room, Iskander slipped inside the castle, veiled in a cloak of shadows, and snuck his way into the monarch's chambers.

He silently made his way over to the copper staff sloppily resting against the corner wall and carefully wrapped the rod in an iron-laced blanket. Without a single stir in the king's gluttonous slumber, he made for the window, staff in hand, but before Iskander slithered into the night, he ensured the King of Delphagia's snores had thundered for the last time. The courtiers unremorsefully found the king lifelessly sprawled out on his floor the next morning. No one ever questioned the misplaced staff.

After procuring the second scepter, Iskander sailed to Perseis. He did not rest until he made the entire journey back to the Iron Mountains.

Once he arrived in Lorca, Iskander followed the de-

CAMERON L. JIMENEZ

tailed instructions outlined in Mathieson's journal to find the
Ossuary and lock the Crown inside.

He curled his way through the iron tunnels until he
reached the secret chamber located far below the frigid exterior of the frozen mountainside. The burned-copper staff,
carefully wrapped up in his hands, felt heavier than the stone
steps of the Citadel Keeps as he wound his way deeper into
the Continent's core.

He rounded the final turn, and a towering, two-story
door peered down at him, glaring at Iskander with a primordial, foreboding glower.

The door looked old—ancient—as if it had been crafted in a time before the First War. It was molded into a perfect circle, with weathered, gold plating, and the image of
an enormous dragon with seven heads, ten horns, and seven
crowns intricately carved into the metal. A sentence from the
ancient language—a language lost from the people of Perseis for many millennia—was etched above the door. From
Iskander's studies at the Citadel, he knew the six ancient
words etched into the top of the stone: *The Wraiths of War
and Ruin*. Another phrase the General could not read lay beneath the door.

Resting in the middle of the primordial door was a single onyx keyhole.

Iskander pulled the Alpha Key from the leather cord
hung around his neck. A humming tingle of magic radiated
through his body; the same sensation he experienced the first
time he ran his hands over the cool surface under the Midnight Castle.

The key was made of translucent, obsidian dragon glass,
the rarest of its kind. And fixed at the top of the key's hilt
was a carved engraving of the three most powerful marks of
creation and new beginnings.

The picture of a new moon dwelt in the background,

72

a symbol of veiled potential, marking the inception of the lunar cycle and signifying the unseen forces that shape one's life.

Lying inside the circled moon phase rested a flickering flame of fire. Fire to embody purification, and the ability to both destroy and illuminate.

Beside the flame sat a droplet of water, an enduring symbol of renewal and a reminder of life's fluidity—the essential nature of change.

With a steady hand, Iskander gently placed the key into the latch and unfastened the bolt. The ancient hinges slowly creaked open, and he stepped inside the Ossuary.

The walls of the sanctuary curved to create a round room with vaulted ceilings stretching two stories high. The ceiling was plated with overlapping gold and onyx shingles. On the ground, a vivid, finely crafted mural lay untouched, preserved without blemish or scuffs.

Resting in the center of the far wall sat a caged archway, with a rectangular onyx stone centered behind gold bars.

Three ungated archways lined each side of the center cage, and on the far-left side of the room, placed inside the first opening, sat a pale blue staff, erected on top of an onyx platform.

The platform was decorated with intricate gold patterns, and gilded letters from the ancient language—the *Language of the Founders*—stretched across the base of the stand. A large, circular gap, seemingly the home of a missing object, rested beneath the letters. Three overlapping triangles with the outline of an eye were carved into the center of the void space.

The five other openings, absent a staff, matched the first.

Iskander ambled over to the first archway and studied the staff closely, careful to heed Mathieson's warning and avoid touching the rod for fear of unlocking the Prince's gateway.

The staff was hewn from pale blue rock, and it bent downward in a sharp, hooked shape. The carving of a large snail was whittled into the hilt, and just below the handle rested a seven-pointed Crown. The Crown chillingly and persistently emitted wisps of inky Darkness.

Stepping away from the eerie coils emanating from the Crown, Iskander retreated to the middle of the room and stopped in front of the barred opening fixed in the center.

The golden bars covered the entirety of the opening, and between the gaps in the metal dowels, Iskander could see the seventh platform resting inside the archway.

It similarly matched the surrounding six podiums, but unlike the others, no triangular-etched gap dwelt below the ancient inscription. Instead, six orbital locks were embedded into the wall, one beneath each of the bars. And seated on top of the platform, in place of where the others had left blank spaces with empty posts to store the staffs, a small, obsidian chest sat atop the stand. There were six tiny keyholes fixed against the front of the gleaming black box.

Iskander found no way to open the gilded bars, and, with the covered staff still weighing heavily in his hands, he quickly made his way over to the second arched opening and attempted to place the copper rod inside the post atop the onyx platform.

But before he was able to place the rod onto the stand, the magic inside the sanctuary shifted, and a soft glow radiated from the archway on the far side of the room. The gilded letters below began to glimmer.

Hesitantly, Iskander pulled the staff back and walked to the far side of the Ossuary. As he approached the glowing archway, the stirring magic in the room began to settle, and Iskander gently placed the staff into the post of the sixth podium, opposite the one made of pale blue rock.

Careful to avoid touching the staff, Iskander unwrapped the covering, exposing the second Crown of Shadows. More inky Darkness coiled from the metal emblem.

After placing the copper staff into its stand, Iskander quickly exited the vault and had not opened the doors to the Ossuary since.

Iskander's eyes trailed over to the scroll marked with dark ink directly in front of Imara. A chill ran down his spine, and his stirring shadows coiled to the surface of his skin.

The image of an onyx staff, with deep cracks that looked as if they were filled with red burning magma, was painted across the parchment. The clamping jaws of a lion were sculpted into the handle, and mirroring others, an ominous seven-pointed Crown rested just below the hilt.

But the eerie staff painted on the scroll was not what caused the shadows within Iskander's veins to shift. It was the five midnight-black letters Imara had written beneath the picture. The simple name of a haunted city where she had finally tracked down the next staff's location. The same circled name Iskander had read in his cottage an hour earlier.

Montu.

"TO BURN FOR THEIR BONDED SOLDIER IS THE ULTIMATE SACRIFICE. TO FEARLESSLY
GIVE THEMSELVES TO THE RISING. A SHATTERING BURST OF FLAMES AND FIRE AND
LIGHT. AN EXPLOSION OF HEART AND MIND AND SOUL. IT IS THE TRUEST FORM OF
LOVE WHEN A FIREBIRD FREELY GIVES ITS LIFE FOR ITS WARRIOR, UNTIL THERE IS
NOTHING LEFT OF THEM BUT ASHES UPON THE WIND."
—VOYAGE: A DETAILED HISTORY OF THE ODYSSEY (EDITION II)

CHAPTER

EIGHT

Asha was not sure what to expect when the warriors landed
outside Aaru's capital the following evening—but laughter
and children running through the streets were not on the list
of things she had imagined.

The city responsible for inflicting such heinous acts
against the people she loved seemed like it would harbor a
cloud of Darkness over the entire space. Instead, far below
the high hillside where the pair was perched, the vibrant,
luminos-lit streets of Montu were bustling with smiling citizens. Joy-filled merchants beckoned to those passing by,
hoping to make a sale to interested customers, and various
aromatic scents of spiced meats and other decadent foods
filled the streets, wafting their way up to where Asha and
Anselem waited.

The city looked pleasant, and Asha's jaw clenched.

Anselem, fully cloaked in Septant black, shifted his

weight beside her, his only sign of unease.

She brushed the back of his gloved hand with hers as she brought it up to her face, securing the mask beneath her hood in place.

Tonight, they would both be Assassins of the Night.

The sun had dipped behind the snowcapped mountains hours earlier, and the warriors landed in an open field high within the mountain's trees half an hour before the last of the daylight dissipated.

They waited several hours after sunset before venturing out of the forest to ensure their arrival would be covered by the surrounding sky's darkness.

Anselem and Kapheria, the *Firebird of the Night*, flew just under the belly of Uriel, shading his snow-white feathers from any looming eyes below with her midnight shadow.

After they landed, the warriors wound their way through the dark forest until they made it to an icy rock ledge. The uncovered edge provided a perfect view for the Soturi to take in the city's layout below, as they were determined to find the best route to reach the Midnight Castle undetected.

The Midnight Castle rested atop a small hill on the far side of the city. Its towering, onyx walls were not far from the lively, buzzing city center of Montu.

Asha wondered if the Aarun citizens, hustling across the cobblestones and running from shop to shop, knew of the horrors lurking behind the obsidian walls. Or if the people knew of the appalling acts their queen was responsible for executing.

"If we can stick to the shadows of the tree line, I think we will be able to make it to the edge of the city and scale one of the buildings, then we can take the rooftops across," Anselem explained, his voice low and calculating. She followed his hand, pointing to the most accessible building on the outer border of the city.

Asha nodded her agreement, scanning the buildings that zigzagged through Montu, fairly certain the two of them would be able to make quick work of climbing the brick wall and bounding between the closely set structures.

Her gaze trailed over a dozen different paths they could follow across the stunted city skyline. As she took in the short buildings, they reminded her of the restricted heights back home in Valhol—only a handful stretched higher than three stories.

"When we get to the castle, we can slip around to the south side of the wall. Unless something has changed, it should be unguarded at this time of night."

Asha took a deep breath and nodded.

I am a master of my fear. I have power beyond measure. I am unbreakable.

"Ready?" Anselem's hooded head turned towards her, but between the shadow cast over his eyes from the cloak and the mask pulled above his mouth, Asha could not see his face.

"For years," she answered, a devious, imperceptible smile on her face. She resecured the bow fastened to her back, along with the full quiver, and turned to look one last time at the vibrant city below.

Just as they had planned, the pair followed along the shadowed line of the trees until they made it to the city's edge. Anselem quickly scaled the side of an exterior building, and Asha was tucked in close behind him. He knew it shouldn't have surprised him that climbing walls and bounding between rooftops was yet another skill she profoundly excelled at, but he was still impressed. And he made every attempt to keep his mind focused on the mission at hand, refusing to let his eyes wander to the Septant black outfit she donned. It suited her.

After they made their way across the city, careful to avoid the luminos-lit terraces, Anselem and Asha worked their way around to the south wall of the Midnight Castle. He threw a prayer of thanks up to Ianoda and Tyche, the Goddess of Luck, that his presumptions had been correct, and the exterior south wall remained unmanned by guards at night.

Anselem looked over the smooth, onyx stone, attempting to find a place where the warriors could climb.

His eyes devoured the wall, but he found that the cutouts the Septant had used on their previous mission had been filled in, and the footholds they had used to scale the wall no longer remained.

He swore.

Asha stepped up beside him, her golden bow unlatched from her back. She pulled her hood back, and Anselem's brow crinkled. Then he watched as she pulled a clawed arrow from her quiver. He pulled his own hood down.

She leaned in close to him, keeping her voice as low as possible. "I'm not sure it will work, but I brought it just in case."

She handed him the makeshift arrowhead, and he studied it. Asha had crafted the head from Elysian steel, sturdy and strong enough to hold a warrior's weight. He had no clue how she had carved the head into a shape intended to grasp and catch onto the side of a rimmed edge, but there was no time to ask.

It would work.

As long as the interior side of the southern wall matched the one he climbed years ago on the north, Anselem knew the steel claw would catch.

He nodded, stifling a rising laugh. He couldn't believe

the woman before him was still able to surprise him, but he supposed that was how it would always be with someone like Asha. Forever full of wonder and awe.

She nodded in reply and quickly began fastening a rope on the end of the claw. Once she had finished, he took the makeshift arrow from her and twisted into it a final locking knot, one he had learned from Einar in Septant training.

She raised one brow and gave him a look that said *You are definitely going to teach me that.*

He winked, handing the claw back to her. *After we are done wrecking Kingdoms, Seven.*

She smiled, threw her hood back over her head, and nocked the arrow into her golden bow, the rope still tied to the end. Anselem followed suit with his own.

Even from under the hood, he knew that her eyes were filled with concentration. Her fingers grazed her mask-covered cheek, and he could see the way she shifted her arms, accounting for the change in the arrow's weight, the difference in its flight path. She closed her eyes, feeling the faint breeze passing by, and just as she opened her blazing sapphire eyes, she let the clawed arrow soar up the wall.

Anselem held his breath as steel clicked against stone, the claw gripping onto the inside rim. His heart thudded, and neither he nor Asha moved for a moment after the impact.

A minute passed. Then another.

And once Anselem determined no guards were yelling, nor any sentinels rushing through the south gate, he let out a whooshing breath.

He held out his hand, and Asha placed the rope in his palm. He looked up, the onyx wall towering nearly three stories high, and gave a strong pull. The claw, gripping the interior edge, did not budge.

He glanced down at Asha, and as she looked up at him, her hood shifted back the slightest bit, and he could see the faintest spark inside her eyes. He smiled beneath his mask.

Asha looked up the wall towards the awaiting carnage, but Anselem continued staring at the side of her face. He continued staring down at the woman who had healed his broken soul and whispered, "Until we are ash and embers."

She broke her gaze from the onyx stone above and nodded, embers sparking in her eyes. "Until we are ash and embers," she promised.

Then Anselem grabbed the rope in both of his hands and began his climb towards their awaiting death.

As Asha crested the top of the wall, she tried to slow her jagged breaths. Her forearms burned, and she knew without checking that bloodied blisters had formed beneath her gloves.

She crouched beside Anselem among the battlements, both making themselves as small as possible, and took in the suffocating sight of the Midnight Castle.

The castle had been crafted millennia before, and the passing centuries and harsh Aarun winters seemed to have deeply impacted the deep obsidian structure. Once celebrated as the bright heart in the lively city of Montu, the stone castle had hosted endless parties overflowing with sweet melodies of orchestras and the rumble of excited citizens who had gathered by the thousands in the glittering halls to celebrate glorious times and maritime conquests. Even amidst the endless winters in the Kingdom of Aaru, the smell of flowers had forever flowed through the castle's hall, giving the illusion of a never-ending spring within the snowy walls.

But joyous parties and bellows of royal laughter had not permeated the halls of the midnight fortress for decades.

Even the obsidian stones themselves looked darker than centuries past—more gruesome, less alive. Like the excitement and merriment that had been so prevalent amongst the visiting citizens was sucked from the castle, removing the sparkling brightness that had rested within the onyx walls.

Now, as she stood atop the battlements on the south side of the Midnight Castle, Asha could see the sadness resting within the fortress.

Dozens of thin spires and towers loomed over the snow-coated bailey. Flying buttresses and pointed arches stretched up towards the night sky, their black stone melting in with the obsidian sky. Towering, dramatic windows extended up the interior walls, allowing the overhead moonlight to pour inside the fortress's vaulted halls. And if it were not for the sinister feel emanating from the heart of the fortress, the palace would have been bewitchingly beautiful in its darkness.

Asha's gaze dropped from the obsidian walls to the grounds below. Dozens of guards fitted in silver armor were scattered across the snow-covered grass. Some of the sentinels were stationed at fixed posts; others were scurrying in and out of gated doors marked by lightly lit luminos.

Asha was surprised to find the castle so busy at such a late hour. She gazed down the interior wall, trying to determine if there were any footholds carved into the interior stone for the warriors to climb down. She was unable to make out any openings in the dim moonlight.

Asha and Anselem had only briefly discussed what they planned to do once they broke into the Midnight Castle. All the options began with lighting the wooden portions of the ancient castle ablaze. They would figure out what to do with the stone structures after they were inside.

Glaring down at the guarded grounds stretching out from the castle, Asha knew she would be able to take out a dozen of the half-asleep sentinels from the safety of the wall before the Aarun soldiers even knew there was a breach.

She studied the fixed posts, making a note of where each of the guards stood as she determined the best order to engage the men without her arrows giving notice to the others.

The number of guards rushing in and out of the obsidian doors began to dwindle.

Anselem shifted his weight beside her, and she knew that when the presence of the guards was low, it would be the best time to attack.

Asha reached behind her back, aiming to unlatch the bow from her back.

Her fingers brushed against the smooth golden arch of her bow when one of the luminos hanging about an exterior door flickered, and the midnight hinges flung open.

Asha dropped her hand.

The world stopped spinning.

The air ripped from her lungs, and a ringing sounded in her ears.

She froze. Her entire body went numb.

The next thing she knew was the distant feeling of falling, and before she could register what was happening, Anselem's hands were beneath her arms, catching her before her knees cracked against the wall's obsidian stone, and she tumbled over. Then his hand slipped over her mouth, smothering a shredding sob that had escaped her lips.

Everything felt so far away. Moving in slow motion.

The last thing Asha saw before the darkness around her swallowed her whole was her brother, walking across the courtyard, bound by iron chains.

She watched in roaring silence as he was escorted by a faction of guards into a shadowed door of the Midnight Castle, and an obsidian lock closed behind him.

Mathieson.

> "THE GREATEST WARRIORS WILL ALWAYS FIND A WAY—OR ELSE THEY WILL MAKE ONE."
> — THE GREAT STRATEGIES OF WAR

CHAPTER NINE

Anselem's head spun, and his sure-footed feet trembled.

No.

No.

No.

His hands, one clutched around Asha's waist, the other covering a shredding scream attempting to escape from her throat, were shaking.

He had died.

Mathieson had died.

Anselem had watched it. Lived it.

The memory was burned so violently into his mind, he still woke with a raw throat on nights he relived it in his dreams.

His scarred heart began to tighten, and his throat felt like it was closing. He couldn't suck in enough air.

Math was *alive*.

And Anselem had left him here, a tortured prisoner, for months—years. The guilt within began to swallow him, thrusting him down and into the Darkness.

He shoved back. Climbing to the surface. Lightning ripped to the surface of his skin, buzzing just within reach, readying itself for the attack.

Now was not the time.

They needed to get out, to leave. They had to form an entirely new plan, a *real* strategy.

It was no longer a colossal massacre, but a rescue.

Only seconds had passed, but it felt like a lifetime.

Another muffled sob sounded against his hand. Asha sucked in a breath.

He gently pulled his palm away, moving it to the side of her head as he spun her around, placing his thrumming hands on either side of her face.

"Seven, focus." Tears rolled down her face, and for a moment, the image of her before him blurred. He felt the cool, wet streaks that trailed down his cheeks.

He blinked twice, pushing the tears from his emerald eyes and regaining his focus.

His voice was low but stern. "You have to pull it together, Asha."

Tears continued to flow from her sapphire eyes, but they slowed.

"We can't stay here."

She broke his gaze, turning her eyes down at the onyx door the guards had forced Mathieson through. He waited for her to contest him, for the fighting words he expected to roll from her lips.

But they did not come.

Her mind swirled as she worked through the implications and the new choices they would have to make.

Anselem watched as Asha's tears slowed, dwindling until they came to a complete stop, leaving behind wet streaks on her cheeks that matched his own.

A punishing calmness crept over her shoulders, settling into her bones with enough rage to fuel entire armies.

Her magic stirred beneath his hands, and Anselem could feel the burning warmth begin to pour from her body.

She finally turned her sapphire eyes back to meet his, and Anselem once again saw the burning flames sparking within. The same embers that had been dimmed for so many weeks. And the fire he beheld blazed brighter than any he had ever known.

Asha dropped her voice low, and as she spoke, a lethal coldness wafted over her words. The iciness held such conviction and promise, Anselem carried no doubt the warrior standing before him meant every single word.

"May Ianoda have mercy on my enemies, because I will surely not."

CHAPTER TEN

Asha and Anselem landed on the black sand shores of Gull's Landing.

She had not uttered a word since they abseiled the side of the Midnight Castle's outer wall. Anselem had also remained silent as they made their way back across Montu and climbed the frosted hillside overlooking the city, where they had left Uriel and Kapheria.

On the flight back to Perseis, even the firebirds seemed to sense the need for quiet, for Asha had not felt the familiar tug down the Bond from Uriel.

She was sure her phoenix somehow knew.

Without words or explanation, as the bonded pair often interacted with one another, Uriel knew Math was alive.

Asha was sure of it.

After she dismounted, her boots deeply digging into the dark sand, Uriel nuzzled his head into her side, a quiet, comforting gesture. And for the first time since seeing the wave of ash-blonde hair disappear through the onyx door, Asha smiled.

Her brother was alive.

She ruffled the snowy feathers of Uriel's head and turned to Anselem.

His face was carved of stone, still riddled with shock, but underneath the composed face of the Commander, Asha could see the flicker of hope, the burning joy that had replaced a Darkness that had always been present in his emerald eyes since she first met him.

They stared at one another for a long moment, silence filling the space between them, until Anselem took a step towards her, a sigh of relief rushing from his lungs.

A tear of joy—a joy she thought would be lost from her heart forever—slipped from her eye, and she flung her arms around Anselem's neck. The unexpectedness of the embrace nearly knocked him back, but he quickly regained his footing, scooping her up and wrapping his arms around her waist.

Relieved tears of joy and laughter poured out from the warriors.

"He's alive," he breathed into her hair.

A sob of joy was Asha's only response, and for the first time in years, she thanked the gods for answered prayers.

Anselem placed her gently back on the sand, and as she looked up into his emerald eyes, now brighter than they had been before, she smiled and thanked the Dominions for sending her someone who understood the depths of the joy she felt. Someone who also understood the depths of the Darkness she had endured along the way.

Because she knew those with shattered souls were always the ones who loved harder than most. Once they had dwelt in the Dark, the broken understood how to cherish the things that shine.

"Let's go," he stated simply, turning away from the waves and looking towards the City of Wolves neatly nestled at the base of the iron mountainside.

Asha's brow crinkled. "We're going into Lorca?"

Anselem had only taken a few steps away from the shore, towards the frost-coated ridgeline in the distance, when he turned back, a wide grin spread over his face, and answered, "I think it's time you meet the rest of the Septant."

Nearly a year and a half had passed since Anselem visited Lorca, but the City of Wolves was mostly left unchanged. He guided Asha through the evergreen trees, trailing a worn path that stretched from the city to the sea, and as the warriors emerged from the dense, surrounding forest, the Commander looked back at the Hoarfrost shores and realized how much ground the pair had covered.

As the duo approached the South Gate, Anselem whispered, "Pull up your mask."

Asha obeyed and pulled her hood down further as well to fully obscure her face.

Lorca was surrounded by tall, pale-blue walls. The only entry and exit points to the city existed at the two monstrous iron gates located on the north and south sides. As he approached the gate, guarded by two Fenri soldiers, Anselem reached into the breast pocket of his obsidian jacket and took out a gold pin.

He fastened it to his collar and walked forward with the unwavering confidence of the Commander.

One of the gate guards, dressed in the customary light grey uniform of the Fenri, stepped forward as Anselem and Asha approached. He opened his mouth, as if to stop the pair, before his eyes caught the detailed, golden wing pinned on Anselem's jacket. The Fenri soldier's eyes flared wide, and he quickly stepped aside, saluting the Septant warrior.

Anselem nodded to the soldier in acknowledgement and motioned for Asha to enter first.

"After you, brother."

Asha said nothing in response as she sauntered in, donning the swaggering walk she had honed long ago.

Anselem smirked beneath his hood, thankful for her haughtiness and natural ability to wield such unwavering confidence even trained soldiers did not question the too large leathers and the too short stature for her to be one of the Septant warriors.

Neither of them spoke for several blocks once they made it through the gate and coiled through the streets of the Southgate District.

The city was alive, Lorcan citizens running every which way. Some were heading to the north side of the city towards the Merchant's Guild, trying to find deals of goods the traders had received from the evening ships that had come to port at the Docks, or to indulge in dinner with friends at the various restaurants lining the main row. Other citizens were headed west, to the Artist's District, planning to enjoy an evening of music or live theater. Uniformed Amarok and Fenri warriors were also scattered throughout the streets, mostly headed towards the center of the city, to the Citadel.

Occasional frostbitten winds cut through the air. Anselem removed the pin from his collar as they continued their way through the city and entered the Canis District.

"Where are we heading?" Asha asked, her voice low and quiet.

Anselem could see the towering, blue-marbled walls of the Citadel from where they stood. Luminos lined the top of the bastions, and an outline of shadowed figures monitored from the top. He looked over to the moon hanging in the sky.

It was late in the evening, well past dinner time, but the Citadel was strictly guarded at all hours. He knew he would never be able to sneak Asha in without another Septant pin.

He only had one other option—a plan he and his brothers had formed years before, when there was a dire need to get messages to one another without detection.

"To the Merchant's Guild. There is a shop I need to visit."

Asha did not ask anything further, and a smile came over Anselem's face.

Lorca was… different. Not in a bad way, just so unlike her mountain hometown of Valhol. It was busier, or perhaps it just seemed that way when everything took place above ground. And unlike the stunted skyline of Valhol, many of the homes and buildings of Lorca stood several stories high. But, contrary to the pristine streets and well-kept constructions of Valhol, many of the buildings in Lorca reminded her of the Temple of Freyja—crumbling and half broken down.

As they turned down street after street, she wondered if the entire city was the same—disheveled and squalid. That was until they turned onto a wide, main pathway, and she could see, only a few streets over, the lively, spirited people dancing to the music drifting through the city streets. She paused for a moment, watching the joy-filled faces, and her heart swelled. It was like looking through a glass mirror and seeing, even for a fraction of a moment, the world she hoped one day all Perseisians—all Darnellans—would experience.

She smiled, stepping forward to follow after Anselem, but when she turned her head, she saw he had not continued his walk, but he too was watching the scene before them, like outsiders looking through a glass wall at a life they one day hoped to enjoy. A glimpse of the promise of a better life ahead, a better world.

She walked forward, stepping beside him. She brushed the back of her gloved hand against his, pulling him from his trance. He glanced down at her but said nothing. He didn't need to. There was an unspoken understanding between them.

They continued north, walking past a towering wall crafted from blue and grey marbled hues. From everything Kaira had told her, Asha knew it was the Citadel—the heart of Lorca.

Another half hour of Anselem guiding them through questionable streets and past a curving bay holding a collection of boats lined around the edges, the warriors finally made it to the Merchant's Guild.

Asha's stomach rumbled as decadent spices and unfamiliar scents wafted through the air. She could make out the scent of freshly baked bread and the traditional dishes of Perseis, but as they passed an uncountable number of restaurants and shops, the variety of aromas filling the air mixed to form a mouthwatering smell.

They turned off the main row of shops, down a narrow street lined with unlit alleys on each side. After a few blocks, they came to a maroon-painted door. An iron knocker hung in the center, and Anselem picked it up in his hand and swung it against the door three times, followed by a pause and an additional four knocks.

The street was quiet, with no figures looming outside the painted doors. A latch unlocked from inside, drawing Asha's attention back to the door. The hinges creaked open an inch, and Asha could faintly make out wrinkled features with beady black eyes and a white beard.

She was not sure when Anselem had placed the golden pin back on his collar, but she saw the unblinking eyes of the man behind the door glance down at the wing. He then dragged his harsh gaze to Asha and back to Anselem.

The man said nothing, only shaking his head once, a silent refusal to let Asha in.

Anselem began to protest before Asha cut in, "I'll be fine out here."

Anselem tore his eyes from the doorman, looking both ways down the street before bringing his gaze to meet Asha. She could see the hint of worry behind them, but she also saw the confidence and trust he had in her ability.

She pulled her hood back slightly, giving him a reassuring smile. "Unless you think someone else out here is up to your level of sparring, I'm pretty sure I will be fine, *lieutenant*."

She winked before shoving her hood back down.

His jaw clenched as he replied, "I'll be quick."

She nodded, stepping away from the door, and watched as Anselem dipped inside and disappeared behind the maroon door.

She heard the latch lock after the hinges closed.

Like the rest of Lorca, Al's was unchanged since the last time Anselem had been there. There was hardly any furniture in the small room, and the navy-painted walls were still chipped along the baseboards. It smelled of firewood, and a small haze filled the room. Only two dimly lit luminos filled the space. One hung from the center of the ceiling; the other was set on the desk in the far corner.

The ancient man, too, was much the same. A few of the lines around his eyes sat deeper than before, and his all-white hair had shed the few remaining speckles of black. His deeply tanned skin was paler than Anselem remembered, and, in his old years, he figured the man had finally begun to spend fewer hours out in the water under the harsh sun.

But the ambiance of the space and the visual look of the man had never been the basis for why the warriors used Al's services.

First was his inalterable vow of silence—for Al's tongue had been cut out many years back when his fishing boat was overrun by Smaragdus pirates. Second was Al's rare magic.

Al graduated as a Pontos warrior decades before, but when his iron bands were finally unlocked and his powers did not manifest for more than a year, Leadership declared him unusable, casting him out from the military. It was not until several years later, when he had found a decent-paying job on a fishing charter working for Sacha's grandfather, that Al discovered his gift.

Holding a colossal swordfish in his hands, struggling with the beast's weight as it flailed back and forth on the deck, Al willed the fish into the steel tub on board the ship, and as his hands touched the flapping fins, the fish flickered into the storage bin beside him. Sacha's grandfather was the only crew member on the deck with the young Pontos. It took him years to master his craft, but, over time, Al learned to flicker objects to far-off places. He kept the manifestation of his magic quiet, for he did not wish to return to the rule of a Leadership that had cast him aside; so, Sacha's grandfather told no one, until the day he lay on his deathbed, when his grandson came to visit him once more.

Knowing Sacha was bound by his Septant Oath of loyalty, he made his grandson promise to honor the man's wishes and remain unknown. When Sacha agreed, giving his Word to his grandfather, he shared Al's gift with the warrior.

Al was shocked the first time Sacha showed up on his doorstep, but, over the years, Sacha created a relationship with the Deliverer, and Al agreed to use his gift to help the

94

Septant warriors whenever it was needed.

Anselem placed a silver coin on the table. The Deliverer handed him six cream letters with matching envelopes, a burning candle, and a stick of obsidian wax.

Anselem held the papers in his hands, staring down at them for a long moment before handing two back.

He looked down to see Al's beady eyes filled with heaviness. He cleared his throat and nodded, taking the two unneeded letters.

Anselem sat down at the small, oak desk. The only items covering the desk were a small luminos, a quill, and a glass jar of black ink.

Anselem sighed deeply and wrote down the same sentence onto all four letters:

MEET AT THE MOUNT AT SUNSET ON THE NIGHT OF THE HALF-MOON.

As they walked through the city, Anselem had studied the glowing light in the night sky, determining only three nights remained until the half-moon.

It would be a quick response for everyone to meet in Elysia. The firebirds could cover the distance from Lorca in that amount of time easily, and Kage was likely still at Sveaborg. He would make it.

The other three warriors were questionable, depending on where the Vanguard was currently stationed and which ocean Einar and Sacha were roaming.

He folded the papers, placing each note neatly inside its respective envelope. Then he took the stick of wax and held it over each letter, melting it down with the candle flame until it dripped onto the paper. Once a small, liquid pool of wax formed on the envelope, he took the pin from his jacket and pressed it into the onyx wax until it hardened.

The sacred Seal of the Septant.

❖ ❖ ❖

Asha stood in the center of the quiet street, alone for the first time since seeing Mathieson.

Her mind began to race, emotions flooding her heart.

Relief, shock, guilt.

So many foreign feelings, so little time to properly sort through them. But the one feeling that continued to push its way to the forefront was one she had not known for years—joy.

Lost in her thoughts, Asha did not sense the cloaked figure approaching until it was too late.

A hidden form emerged silently from the shadows. Strong hands grabbed her, pulling her back against a tall, sturdy body, and dragged her into one of the unlit alleys lining the narrow street.

"I've prayed I would be the one to send you to your grave," a rough, deep voice growled beside Asha's ear. She caught a glint of steel in the moonlight as he moved his arm upward.

Asha thrust her hand between the slashing knife and her throat, catching the sharp blade before it pierced through her skin. He pressed the steel harder towards her neck, ripping into her leather gloves. A stifled cry escaped her lips as the blade sliced into her palm. Her heart thudded in her chest as she pushed with all her strength against the blade, the knife digging deeper into the skin.

From the corner of her eye, Asha saw the shadows in the alleyway shift. An adumbral figure approached from the left as lightning cracked across the sky.

"I would choose your next move very carefully," Anselem growled.

Asha could see the dagger he had pressed up to her captor's temple.

Deafening silence was the only response that came from the man with his knife pressed to her throat. He did not slacken his hold on the blade.

Anselem's voice dropped low, his tone darker than death. "Hello, Iskander."

"THERE IS A TENDERNESS IN THEIR HOWL, AND LOYALTY IN THEIR BLOOD. THEY
BEND FOR ONLY THEIR CHOSEN ONE."
— THE AMAROK: A DETAILED UNDERSTANDING OF THE CANINE BOND

CHAPTER

ELEVEN

Iskander dropped his hand and shoved Asha away. She laughed as she turned around to face him.

"Apparently, whatever gods you prayed to didn't bother to listen, little pup," she mocked, flashing him a wicked smile, the same one she knew always grated Anselem's nerves.

"Well, at least she's pretty, Eros, if you have to deal with that vicious mouth on her."

Asha flashed him another taunting smile as she tore the bottom of her shirt and wrapped it around the cut on her hand. He looked her up and down, taking in the Septant black leathers she wore.

"I'm going to like this one," she said, turning towards Anselem.

Anselem laughed. "Why, because he tells you you're pretty?"

"No, although it is good to know the man has fabulous taste," she drawled, another grin dancing across her face. "I like that the pup barks back a little. I've become bored with all your niceness, *lieutenant*." She winked at Anselem, and he only chuckled.

"Call me that one more time. Please. I dare you," Iskander seethed, his hands balling into fists.

Asha flashed her eyes back to the General, and burning frost danced across her fingertips before she transformed it into scorching flames, then dripping water. She flicked a drop at Iskander, and the droplet splashed into his face. The swaggering smile she loved to don flickered on her mouth. "Still dare me?" Asha taunted.

Iskander's eyes went wide as her raw power flashed in her hands. "You're a Thurisaz."

"A what?"

Anselem and Iskander exchanged a look.

"Anyone want to let me in on what that means?" Asha asked, an edge to her voice.

Anselem ignored Asha's questions and instead followed up with one of his own. "How did you know we were here, Blaidd?"

Iskander cut his eyes at Anselem, giving him an impatient look. "You should know well enough that I have ears in all parts of my city, Commander."

Anselem nodded in approval, as if he would have set his operations up in a similar manner to the General's. "And why are you trying to kill Asha?"

"Yeah," Asha chimed, "why *are* you trying to kill me? Doesn't the Blood Oath prevent you from doing that?"

Iskander's eyes narrowed and locked on Asha. "Who says I don't believe spilling your blood might be worth my untimely death?"

"You and your massive ego would probably present a

strong argument for remaining alive," Anselem replied.

Iskander cut his eyes at the Commander. "Well, the Blood Oath says nothing about bringing her an inch from Death," he replied sharply. He turned his sneer back to Asha. "I'm sure Anubis would *love* to tangle with your charming personality."

"He's tried," Asha answered, rolling her eyes dismissively. "On more than one occasion. Unfortunately for you, our *charming personalities* didn't mix too well. You know, that whole *desire to stay alive thing* thrumming through my veins and whatnot." A smirk curled on her lips. "But I *have* heard Death rather enjoys the company of cocky assholes, so you might be in luck." She threw him a derisive wink.

"Again," Anselem said, attempting to break up the back-and-forth insults, "why exactly are you trying to kill Asha?"

Iskander did not turn towards Anselem. He held Asha's stare for a long while before he answered, "She killed my sister."

Asha's brow furrowed. "Who is your sister?"

The onyx flecks in his silver eyes expanded until they grew so dark they matched the night sky. "My sister was Elanina Aerol."

Asha's ears rang, and then the world went quiet.

Nina.

Anselem's voice broke through the stillness, but it was muffled. "El was for Elanina?"

Iskander managed to tear his eyes away from Asha and pin them on Anselem. "Yeah, why?" he replied curtly. He cut his eyes back to Asha. "What the Hells is wrong with her?"

Asha forced herself to crawl back from the Dark, but her voice was quiet as she said, "Nina. I knew her as Nina."

Iskander just stared at her blankly, not understanding what his sister's name had to do with anything.

She glanced at Anselem, and he nodded. She sucked in

a deep breath, and Asha told Iskander Blaidd exactly what happened on the day she killed his sister.

When she finished telling the story of what transpired at the Final Testing of Algae and who was truly responsible for the events that unfolded, Iskander simply stood there, his face blank. But she could see the graveness in his eyes, and she knew that he had descended back down into the same kind of Darkness she knew very well.

"And that isn't everything," Anselem added.

Iskander slowly dragged his eyes over to the Commander.

"Math is alive."

Iskander blinked. Once. Twice.

"She still has him in Montu. And we are going to break him out," Anselem concluded.

Iskander stood there, unmoving, for a long time. "I need a drink."

"I need several," Asha replied.

He looked over at Anselem, shaking his head. "You're going to need Neith."

The Commander sighed but nodded in agreement.

"Who's Neith?" Asha asked.

Iskander shot a look at Anselem but replied, "I've never met her; I've just heard a lot about her. But she's... an old friend of Eros's."

Asha's brows raised as she looked over at Anselem.

"Thanks for that," he said bitterly to Iskander. He looked at Asha. "Not a friend, just someone who helps me with information from time to time."

Information—she had heard him use that word before. Her cheeks went hot.

Anselem glared at Iskander, and Asha caught his eyes flip back and forth between the two of them.

"So, are you in?" Anselem asked.

"Is that really even a question?" Iskander snipped.

"Good. Now let's go get those drinks and sort out the details."

"There's a place down in…"

Anselem cut him off. "There's no way in the Seven Hells I'm going to The Wet Dog, Iskander."

The General flashed a mischievous grin. "What? Last time we were all there, we had a grand time."

Anselem didn't budge.

Blaidd rolled his eyes. "Fine. Then it's either The Den or Duke's."

"What about The Fox Hole down the street?"

"Can't."

"The Broken Bow over in the Heights?" Anselem tried.

Iskander shook his head.

"What about—"

"Let me save you the trouble before you list off every bloody tavern in this city," Iskander snapped. "It's either The Den or Duke's."

Asha wasn't sure she wanted to know what this man had done to get himself kicked out of nearly every bar in Lorca. And she also wasn't entirely sure she wanted to find out the kind of bar he *hadn't* been kicked out of.

Anselem looked over to Asha. "Duke's it is."

"I'm going to find some food first, I'm starving. I'll meet up with you two afterward."

"Same here. I'll be right behind you," Anselem replied.

Asha nodded, leaving Anselem and Iskander alone in the alley as she headed back towards the main row lined with restaurants and shops.

"He's really still alive," Iskander breathed. It was more

of a statement than a question, as if Iskander was still trying to convince himself.

Anselem nodded.

"He's going to kill you, you know."

Anselem's brow furrowed. "What?"

A wolfish grin appeared on Iskander's lips. "I saw it the second you looked at her."

"I don't know what you're talking about." Heat flashed through Anselem's body.

Iskander rolled his eyes, "Seriously, Ans?"

Anselem didn't respond.

"Fine, deny it all you want," Iskander said. "But if even *I* can see the way you light up when she's around, her brother sure as Hells will."

Anselem ran his fingers through his hair and sighed. "That's not what she needs. *I'm* not what she needs. So, Math can see whatever he wants, and you can too, for that matter, but it doesn't make a difference. What I want doesn't make a difference."

Iskander stepped towards his brother—not by blood, or law, or Oath, but his brother by choice—and put a hand on Anselem's shoulder. His voice grew softer, a tone he rarely used. "What you want matters, Ans. And maybe you can't see it, but you aren't the only one who looks at the other like the whole world could crumble around you and you wouldn't blink."

Anselem turned his gaze towards Iskander, and he tried to smother the hope rising in his chest.

"She looks at you the same way. You're both just too damn stubborn to acknowledge it."

"We are friends."

"Friends don't look at each other like that, Ans."

He sighed.

Iskander looked past Anselem, down the narrow street,

as if he could still see Asha swaggering past the buildings. And when he turned his eyes back to Anselem, his voice was low as he said, "Just know there's a fire burning deep inside that girl's eyes. And before this is all over, she will make kingdoms fall and monsters wish they had never been born."

Anselem released another deep breath as he looked down the alley after her obscured shadow. "Let's just all survive Montu, and I'll figure it out later."

His voice sounded indifferent, but Anselem could feel the spark of hope that had already caught fire inside his chest, and flames were beginning to burn.

"UNTIL YOU ARE NOTHING BUT STARDUST AND SHADOWS, MAY THE LIGHT GUIDE YOUR WAY."
— ARTICLE I, SECTION I OF THE VANGUARD CODEX

CHAPTER TWELVE

Duke's was on the south side of the city, deep within the Canis District. Anselem figured it was a better option than The Den, which bordered the high-crime area of the Slums. He took a deep breath before opening the tavern door, but even the last breath of fresh air did not save him from the assault of sweat and stale ale that smacked into him as he entered the bar. The entire place smelled of lost hopes and dead dreams.

Several patrons, already well into drunkenness, glanced his way as he crossed the threshold. Their eyes quickly turned away after sizing him up, assuredly recognizing it would be a fight they would not walk away from. Iskander followed in behind him, and a few friendly calls rang out as he entered.

Anselem shook his head.

He didn't judge his brother, gods knew Anselem himself had made many questionable choices in how he chose to deal with the Darkness that haunted him, but he was admittedly concerned.

Iskander made his way over to a corner booth.

Asha walked in last, her hood pulled back to expose her long, ash-blonde braid and striking eyes, and Anselem's fists curled at his side as the attention of every seedy man in the bar fixed on her.

He slowly made his way over to where Iskander sat, and a barkeep was already fetching the table a round of drinks. He sat opposite the General, and Asha slid in beside him. He glanced around the room, marking the exits and the lingering eyes.

"I assume the others already know since you were at Al's," Iskander noted.

Anselem nodded, turning his eyes to him. "I'm sure your letter will be waiting for you at home."

Iskander pulled a cream paper from his jacket pocket, an unbroken, obsidian seal pressed on the front of the envelope. "It seems our friend's magic has advanced in his old age."

Anselem stared at the letter in Iskander's hand, the same one he had written only half an hour before. His eyes widened. "Impressive."

Iskander tucked the letter back into his pocket. "So, what's the plan?"

"You're not going to read it?" Asha broke in, brows raised.

Iskander's intense eyes turned to the Soturi. "I'm sure Anselem can just as easily tell me when we are meeting."

Asha did not respond.

"Evening of the half-moon." Anselem felt both the warriors' eyes turn to him.

"Bloody moonlight, Ans, that's only three days," Iskander grunted in annoyance, downing several gulps of his ale.

106

"Where are we meeting?" Asha asked, unaware of where the Septant held their meetings.

Anselem looked around before addressing her question. "In Elysia. I'll give you specifics when we are... elsewhere."

Asha nodded.

"Will you be able to make it?" he asked Iskander.

The warrior took another large drink from his glass. Anselem and Asha had not touched their mugs.

He wiped the foam from his lips with the back of his thorn-inked hand. He nodded, arrogance in his tone, "Of course. What kind of question is that?"

Anselem rolled his eyes, and he caught the slight widening in Asha's eyes.

Apparently, Iskander caught it too as he turned his attention to her. "Just because I can't fly doesn't mean my wolf doesn't soar like the winds above, *Kappi*."

There was a bitterness in his tone, a harshness he still held. He thought Asha would let it roll off her back, to ignore the disdain and the barking tone. What he did not expect was for her to lean forward, a lethal calm seeping into her voice as her power hummed within her, radiating from her body. Anselem could feel the surge of power beside him. He knew Iskander could too, for his shadows, masked by the dimness in the tavern, began to coil around his fingers.

"If you want to go outside, *General*," she hissed, "and settle whatever issue you're still holding against me, let's go. But I will not let you sit here and throw insults towards a title your sister gave her life for."

Iskander's shadows recoiled, and his face dropped. Anselem had never seen the warrior silenced. He always had a snipping reply. And before his brother could find words, Anselem's mouth dropped, and he watched coils of shadowfire ripple out from Asha's fingertips, matching the ones that had disappeared from Iskander's.

They lasted only a moment, but both the warriors saw it, and Iskander's silver eyes went wide.

"I loved her," Asha continued, "she was my family too. And I get it. I get why you hate me. I hate myself too for what I did. But I love her enough to keep moving forward. To try... To try and let it go. And I'm not sure I ever will. But I will try—for Nina."

Anselem was not sure if it was the sincerity in her tone or fear from the destruction that would surely ensue from having to fight against Asha's raw power with his own, but Iskander leaned forward, his voice full of the death-filled darkness that rolled through his veins, and said, "Give me your Word."

Anselem's head snapped over to his brother, and the gravity of the statement he had used.

Asha did not balk. Anselem was not sure she understood the implication of the words he had used or if she was simply fearless. From the endless hours she put into researching the Septant, Anselem was certain she realized the meaning of Iskander's question.

She replied with evenness in her tone, "I give you my Word."

Iskander studied her for a long moment, recognition flickering through his silver eyes, then he leaned back from the table and grabbed the mug before him and lifted it to her, nodding once, and finished his glass.

Silence filled the table, and Iskander dragged his eyes to Anselem. "What?"

"What the Hells is wrong with you?" Anselem growled.

Iskander smirked. "Mad I claimed a Binding with Asha before you, Ans?"

Rage boiled inside the warrior, but he kept his face schooled in the unexpressive mask he had learned to wear long ago. He leaned forward, unleashing the faintest ripple of his own devastating power. The luminos in the room flickered, and an electric buzz filled the space between the men.

Anselem's voice was dark as he smirked and replied, "If you think any man can lay claim to Asha Raynor, you're going to be in for a rude awakening, Blaidd."

He meant it. If fables were real, then Asha was the kind of queen no prince or king would ever be able to control. She was not made for pretty gowns and delicate parties. She had not been created to stand in the shadow of a man. No, Asha had been born for battles and the wrecking of kingdoms.

Iskander chuckled. "Calm down, Eros. It wasn't Binding."

He rolled up his sleeves, revealing a myriad of splintered thorns of darkness. But among the ink covering his arms, Anselem did not see any fresh tattoos from the Binding.

The Binding was another of the many powers the Septant Mark granted the warriors.

Entrusted to always be true to their Word without fault, the powers bestowed upon them by the gods ensured all magic remained in balance. And because the warriors could never falter from their given Word, they had also been granted the power of the Binding, which allowed a Septant warrior the ability to ask another to pledge their word, with the consequences of the agreement to be a permanent Mark inked on both of their arms.

The result of breaking an Oath made with the Binding was death; the only caveat was that the Septant warrior had to have intent on Binding the individual to himself when he asked the question, a matter none of the warriors took lightly.

"Now that I've passed your little test, can we move on to bigger issues?" Asha's voice broke through the tense air.

Silver eyes, flecked with darkness, continued to stare into Anselem's deep green from across the table. He wanted to rip the stupid little grin off Iskander's face.

Asha huffed and stood up. "I'm going to get something else to drink other than... whatever this is." She motioned to the lukewarm ale in front of her.

Iskander reached across the table, sliding her mug across the gnarled wood, and shrugged. "Suit yourself." He downed half the drink in one breath.

Asha shook her head and sauntered off to the bar.

Anselem stared at Blaidd through narrowed eyes.

Iskander chuckled. "Oh, calm down, Ans, I'm only having fun."

He glanced over to Asha and then back to his brother. "I wouldn't push her buttons too much if I were you."

Iskander took another gulp, the liquid in the glass sloshing around as he placed it back on the table. "I'm pretty sure I can handle little Miss Raynor."

Anselem did not roll his eyes or shake his head. Instead, he looked at his brother with such seriousness in his eyes, Blaidd straightened in his seat.

"She has been through the Hells. So, believe me when I say, you *should* fear her. She is the type of warrior who looks into a fire and instead of shying from the flames, she smiles."

That was when it clicked. Anselem saw it in his face. Iskander knew that he was not simply talking about the raw power pulsing through her veins, or the loss of loved ones, though both were enough to fuel the rage of any warrior. No, Iskander understood there was a Darkness inside of her that he knew very well. A Darkness that could swallow the world whole.

He dropped his voice. "So, you see it too," he stated. It was not a question.

Anselem nodded.

"It's her," Iskander whispered. "He was looking into it for her."

Anselem nodded again.

Iskander tore his eyes from the Commander, glancing over to the ash-blonde Soturi across the tavern. He blew out a breath. "Does she know?"

"Not yet. I wanted to be sure before I told her. I figured if anyone would recognize it, it would be you."

Iskander brought his silver eyes back to Anselem. There was no offense held within the silver pools of moondust. Iskander Blaidd had always known who he was, what lived inside his veins.

"Tonight," Anselem promised. "I'll tell her tonight at your place."

Iskander picked up his mug once more and winked. "Have fun with the one bedroom."

Anselem rolled his eyes, picking up his glass for the first time. "You're unbearable."

Iskander laughed, and Anselem smiled. He had missed his friend.

But the laughter did not last long before they heard a glass shatter on the ground across the bar, their heads whipping towards the noise. Both warriors instinctively palmed hidden daggers.

Across the tavern, Asha had a sleazy, half-drunk man's face pressed down against the wooden bar top. His arm was unnaturally twisted behind him.

Her voice carried across the space. "It's such a shame your mother never taught you how to keep your hands to yourself."

A cracking snap of bone echoed through the air. A pitiful cry sounded from the grimy man's mouth.

Asha released the man's deformed arm. It hung limply by his side. She turned to face the other ogling men. "Anyone else need a lesson in manners, or have we learned from our friend here not to put our hands where they don't belong?"

Silence filled the room, broken only by whispered grumbles and coughs. She grabbed her glass from the barkeep and headed back to the booth in the corner.

Anselem caught the look on Iskander's face before she returned; a mixture of impression and amusement had flashed over it.

"So, what did I miss?" she asked, plopping down next to Anselem.

"We are going to stay at Iskander's tonight, then head to Elysia in the morning. We will come up with a more concrete plan with everyone once we are down there."

She nodded.

"Where are Kapheria and..." Iskander turned to Asha.

"Uriel," she finished. "They are down at Gull's Landing."

"I need to head down that way in the morning to take care of some things for the Vanguard before I head out. I'll let them know to meet you at the cottage."

"And that will still give you enough time to get there?" Anselem asked.

Iskander scoffed. "Seriously, Ans?"

He laughed. "I just wasn't sure if Conri had enough run time lately with all your late-night escapades."

"I'll let her know you think she is out of practice."

Anselem chuckled. "You're just mad she hates everyone but me."

"Sounds like another bonded beast I know," Asha commented.

Iskander laughed. "Kapheria hates you, too?"

Asha nodded. "Undoubtedly. Though I think she might be warming up to Uriel a little."

Anselem rolled his eyes. "She doesn't hate you."

Asha raised a brow.

"...Much," he added.

Iskander laughed, and Asha joined.

They talked casually until Asha and Anselem finished their drinks. Iskander ordered another.

"I think I am going to head out since we have an early start." Anselem looked over to Iskander. "Are you going home later, or will you find somewhere else to sleep?"

Iskander raised his newly filled glass. "The night is young; the options are endless."

The night was very much *not* young. It hadn't been for hours.

Asha stood up to leave with him. "I think I will head back with you if that's alright. Not sure I want to rely on this one to show me the way to his cottage." She gave Iskander a wink.

"You two are no fun."

Anselem shook his head and laughed, scooting out of the booth to stand beside Asha.

She turned to leave but paused, twisting back around to Iskander. Her voice was soft, quiet, and based on the expression that crossed the General's face, her question had taken him by surprise. "Where did you bury her?"

Iskander's throat bobbed, but he composed himself before he answered, "She is in Crescent Gardens."

Asha nodded and turned to leave, not wanting to press the warrior for anything more. She could see the flash of pain in his eyes.

Anselem waited a moment to follow her, looking down at his brother. He said nothing as Iskander placed his full mug on the table and stared at it for a long time. Then, he pushed himself out from his seat and called after Asha, "I'll tell you where it is on the walk home."

CHAPTER THIRTEEN

Asha ran her fingers over the smooth glass orb tucked in her pocket as she stood in the threshold of Iskander's second bedroom. The glass was cold, so contrary to the warm air filling the cottage.

As the trio walked back, Iskander guiding them through the disheveled streets of Canis and telling Asha all about El, they passed by an open store. The glass orb was set on display in the front window, and, without explanation, Asha jetted inside the store, leaving the two Septant warriors out on the frigid street.

The shop owner said he would part with the orb for a single silver coin. Asha fished inside her coat pocket, not caring to haggle with the man, flicked a silver piece to him, and slipped the orb into her pocket. The men asked no questions when she slid back onto the street, and the trio continued south to Iskander's cottage.

Asha nervously twirled the ball in her hand, over and

over.

There was only one bed.

It felt like a scene from one of those romance books Kaira loved to read. The same ones she forced Asha to try, swearing to the gods she would love them. Asha never admitted to her friend that she was right. After she read the first one, she was hooked.

Reading about it was one thing, but being in the middle of the scene herself? That was something else entirely.

"I'll take the couch," a husky, accented voice muttered behind her. She jumped at how close it sounded. She turned around and looked up into his jade eyes, darker in the dim light of the hallway. She nodded, unsure what to say.

He turned and sauntered down the hall towards a wide, open room at the end. "We have some things we need to discuss first."

Asha pulled off her jacket and laid it on the forest-green blanket covering the bed. She walked silently down the hall, and the warmth filling the cottage air burned hotter. She pushed the long sleeves of her top up to her elbows and took a seat in one of the matching black fabric-covered chairs flanking either side of the large, cognac couch. As she folded into the seat, she took in the open space, the high ceilings, and the roaring fire beside her that seemed to never dim. Her focus settled on the two warriors seated before her.

Iskander was sunk into the second black chair directly across from her, and Anselem was to her right, resting in the middle of the leather couch. She saw Iskander's eyes flash to the bare skin on her forearm, covered in misty tendrils of ink.

"Don't start looking at me like I'm fragile," she bit. Her voice was cold.

His silver eyes flicked up to hers and narrowed. "You don't get out of my insults that easily, *Kappi*."

A smile tugged at the corner of her mouth. It was nice to have another warrior see her Marks for what they were — signs of survival. They were something that had happened to her, yes, but they were not who she was.

"Good, little pup. I'd be disappointed if you lost your bark so quickly."

He rolled his eyes but grinned before looking over to Anselem.

Asha dragged her gaze to the Commander. He took a deep breath. "Tell me," she stated, her voice full of strength, braced for whatever news he was about to unleash.

He cleared his throat. "I think you're a Thurisaz."

His voice was unwavering, but he kept it low, as if he did not wish to speak the words into existence.

She said nothing, only looked back and forth between the two warriors.

Anselem glanced at Iskander, and the General nodded. Anselem continued, "Do you know what that means?"

She shook her head, but deep within her she could feel her power begin to roll, as if in answer to a calling, a likeness.

"You feel it, don't you?" Iskander asked, and her sapphire eyes burned as they met the cold fire within his moondust silver.

She nodded. "How?"

Anselem released a loud breath. "He's half-Thurisaz."

Shadows began to coil around Iskander, filling the space beside and above him. She felt a pull towards the magic pouring from the General.

"Your magic recognizes mine as the same," Iskander explained. "There is a familiarity it feels drawn to."

She did feel it, like the power within her was beckoning to be unleashed, as if it wanted to reach out towards the swirling shadows. The smoky tendrils surrounding Iskander recoiled, and the reaching feeling of her power declined.

"We will always feel it when we are near one another, but it is much more manageable when the other has their power restrained. When you're grounded with your mental walls in place."

He glanced at Anselem, as if to verify he had used a similar explanation for her when he first taught her how to ground and control her magic. Anselem nodded once in silent confirmation.

As she tried to digest everything the General told her, Asha's head whipped to Anselem, and the overwhelming feeling she had experienced in the bar washed over her again. A crackle of light flashed between his fingers. It was different from what she felt when Iskander's shadows snuck out from his veins.

With Iskander, it felt like her power wanted to join with his, to form together, and dance with one another. With Anselem, it was as if she could feel the overwhelming magic running through his veins, and her own power needed to consume and devour it as its own.

"You feel mine too, don't you?"

She nodded, grabbing the arms of the chair to ground herself. She could feel Iskander's eyes burning into her, but she did not move her gaze from Anselem.

The crackling stopped, and her breathing slowed.

"What the Hells was that?" Iskander asked, his voice uneasy.

Asha and Anselem kept their eyes locked with one another as Anselem answered the Amarok, "She can feel my power too."

Asha turned to Iskander and, with genuine curiosity, asked, "You can't?"

He shook his head. "No. I'm only half-Thurisaz, which means that I have the power within me, and I can recognize others—it's how I recognized your power—but that's it. I don't feel... whatever you just felt."

"So, what am I? What does it mean?"

A long silence filled the room. The warriors looked back and forth between one another.

Anselem was the first to speak. "It means you hold the power of pure Chaos."

How in the Seven Hells was this girl alive? Iskander thought. His own power—the raging darkness inside him, gifted to him by Anubis—was the only reason he was still alive. The Chaos running through his veins was enough to nearly kill him the first time it manifested. The only way he was able to keep it under lock was from the equally powerful darkness that had made a home inside of him long before. The Chaos was what made his shadows so strong, so lethal. But even Iskander, with years of practice, had never been able to find a way to wholly harness the burning flames that ripped through him whenever he unlocked the Chaos.

His mentor, Seraiah, a Grand Master at the Citadel, helped him for years before they discovered how to separate the Darkness in his veins and the Chaos in his blood. Through many trials, Iskander found the most specific balance of allowing a fractional amount of Chaos through the channels of his mind to help fuel and aid in making his shadows stronger, but in that balance, Iskander had locked the majority of the Chaos within, to keep from burning himself alive from the inside out. And the Chaos inside of him was not pure; if he was honest, he likely wasn't even half Thurisaz, but he had no true way of measuring it. He just knew that his Chaos accompanied his shadows, manifesting years after the darkness had crept out for the first time in smoky coils from his body. Not the other way around. The Chaos complemented his power, allowing it to draw the needed strength, but it was not his given power.

He had no clue how Asha was walking around with pure, unfiltered Chaos running through her veins and was still alive.

"What do you mean she can feel your power, too?" Iskander turned to Anselem, a brother he had fought beside too many times to count, and he had never once felt the electric power rolling through Anselem's veins.

To Iskander's surprise, Asha replied, "It's like my power wants to join with yours," she said softly, looking at him.

She turned her eyes over to the Commander. "And with you, it's like I can feel the power running through your veins and my own needs to consume and devour it. Like it wants to take it for its own."

Anselem nodded, his mind sprinting a million miles an hour. Iskander's brow crinkled, shock washing over him at his brother's response. Anselem looked like he was simply working through an uncomplicated battle plan, not sitting beside an all-powerful warrior whose magic quite literally wanted to swallow his own. But Anselem sat there unfazed, as if he trusted the Soturi with his life.

"So, what does this mean?"

"I'm not sure. All we know is that you two," Anselem motioned to Iskander and Asha, "are the only ones Chaos has chosen."

Iskander interjected, "He means we are the only two Chaos has chosen that haven't combusted into a ball of raging fire as soon as it manifested."

Anselem shot him a glare, and Asha's eyes went wide.

"What?" she breathed, her voice low and muted.

Anselem nodded. "Every other Thurisaz we know of hasn't made it past manifestation."

"Honestly, I have no clue how you're standing here right now, Kappi."

"How do you know all of this?" Asha asked.

The Septant warriors looked at one another before Anselem turned back to Asha. "Mathieson was researching it before everything happened in Montu."

Asha took a deep breath. "So, you're telling me that everything, including possibly my life, so I don't... combust, rides on us breaking Math out of the Midnight Castle?"

"Yep. Pretty much," Iskander replied, picking at his nails.

She nodded. "No pressure." She was quiet for a long moment before she turned to Anselem, a Darkness filling her sapphire eyes. "Do you think he knew?"

Iskander had no idea who *he* was, but from the way Anselem's body went rigid, he figured the referred man was likely the one responsible for at least some of the misty tendrils of ink scattered across her arms.

Anselem shook his head. "I'm not sure, but I don't think it's likely. Your power hadn't manifested yet."

She nodded, lost in dark thoughts. Anselem's face looked grave, as if he wished he could pull her from whatever sinister place she had visited in her mind.

"I'm heading to bed," Iskander interrupted, pulling the warriors back into the presence of the cottage. "You sure you're good on the couch, Ans? I'm sure I can find somewhere else to sleep if you need." He winked and flashed a grin.

Both Soturi laughed, and Anselem replied, "I'll be fine out here."

He pulled himself up from the armchair, crossing the room towards the hallway. "You sure? I know of a room with a pretty blonde occupying it, not too far away. I'm sure I would be welcome."

Asha let out a soft laugh and snipped back, "As long as you're okay with sleeping on the floor with one eye open, Iskander, then absolutely."

Iskander feigned hurt. "And after all my generous hospitality."

Asha rolled her eyes but smiled at his teasing tone. "Just because my power wants to be near you, doesn't mean I do."

Iskander waved his hand in dismissal. "Fine, fine. Best to not come between you two love birds anyway."

And with those parting words, he sauntered to his room, catching a death glare from Anselem and the flushed cheeks covering Asha's face before he disappeared down the hall.

❖ ❖ ❖

Asha rose from her chair. "I guess I should go get ready for bed, too. Early day tomorrow." She could still feel the warmth on her face from Iskander's parting words.

Anselem nodded, rising from the couch. "Do you need anything?"

She shook her head, stepping around the square mahogany table set between the seats.

She said nothing as she walked towards the hall, but his deep, husky voice stopped her before she left the room. "Are you okay?"

She turned back to look at him from across the room. His shoulder-length hair was half pulled back from his face, but a few strands had come loose throughout the evening, falling in his eyes.

His beard was thicker than he normally kept it, not having time to shave during their travel. But even under the gruff exterior and worn leathers, she could still see the kindness in his eyes, still see the beauty of his face as the light from the endless fire danced across it.

She realized she had been silent for too long when he asked again, "Truth for a truth?"

She smiled, "Sure."

He walked around the couch and came to where she stood next to the cutout in the hallway. "Are you okay?"

"No," she replied simply, before expanding on her answer, "but I'm not afraid." His brow crinkled, and the look on his face made her smile. She loved that she could still surprise him at times.

"I'm not afraid of going to Montu, of facing the queen and her army. I'm not even afraid of everything I learned tonight. My power... I'm not sure how to explain it, but it feels like it is part of who I am, and I learned long ago to stop being afraid of myself."

Anselem said nothing, but looked at her with such intensity, it compelled her to finish her thoughts.

"My only fear is letting him down again. Of failing and not being able to get him out."

Anselem nodded, and she could see in his eyes that he understood. That deep within his soul, there lingered guilt and Darkness from leaving Math behind.

She reached out and touched his arm, whispering, "It wasn't your fault."

His emerald eyes met hers, and she held his gaze, willing him to believe the sincerity within her words. "Your turn, Seven."

She dropped her hand back to her side as she contemplated what to ask. As the seconds passed, a grin tugged at her mouth, but she pushed the question aside, searching for another.

"What was that?" he asked, his interest piqued.

She laughed softly. "Careful there, *lieutenant*, it might not be one you would enjoy answering."

His brows raised before his expression was replaced

with a sly smirk. "Try me."

A swaggering smile curled on her lips as she looked up at him and asked, "Are you truly alright with sleeping on the couch?"

A flicker danced in his eyes, but he kept his face composed. "Yes."

Asha's cheeks burned. That was *not* the response she had hoped for, nor expected. "Then I will leave you to it," she replied unemotionally, turning on her heels and heading down the hall.

She grabbed the knob on her door and twisted it open, but just before she entered the room, his tall, broad silhouette appeared at the end of the hall and called down to her, "Next time you ask a question, make sure you're more specific with your words, Seven."

She was not sure if he could see the confusion on her face in the dim light, but he finished his explanation whether he could see her expression or not. "If you had asked if I *wanted* to sleep on the couch, you would have found yourself with a much different answer."

Before she could respond, his backlit figure disappeared around the corner, and a wide smile spread over Asha's face as she entered the room.

She changed into the silk nightclothes she had packed, hopeful they would have spent more than only one night in covered lodging with a fire and bed. Exhaustion hit her like a wall as soon as her head hit the feathered pillow.

She huffed a near-silent laugh. Iskander Blaidd was many things, but Asha had to admit the man had wonderful taste in bedding. She rolled her eyes as she stretched out her legs, *probably because the bedroom is the only place the majority of his guests get to see.*

But as Asha lay in bed, curled up in the thick blankets, her mind ventured away from Blaidd and settled on the other Septant warrior down the hall. She wondered how his hands would feel tracing her curves. How his lips would feel pressed to her collarbone. She wondered if he would turn his back to her to sleep or if he would hold her and keep her warm. Would he dream of her if she were right by his side?

And for once, as she drifted off to sleep, her mind was filled with happy thoughts instead of the rippling Darkness of the Nameless Place.

Anselem had been asleep for only a couple of hours when throat-tearing screams rang out from down the hall. He was up on his feet in a flash, heading down the hall towards Asha's room. He nearly collided with Iskander as he barreled out of his room.

Anselem stopped for a moment, looking at Blaidd who, like him, was only wearing short, black bed-shorts. He had an unsheathed dagger palmed in his hand.

"I got it."

Iskander looked him up and down, noticing there was no blade in his hand.

"It happens every night," he called over his shoulder to him, continuing down the hall to Asha's room. Before he opened the door, he looked back at his brother, still standing in the threshold of his room, and Iskander nodded. Understanding filled his eyes before he disappeared back into his bedroom.

Another scream ripped through the air, and Anselem opened the wooden door and ducked inside.

He crossed over to the side of her bed and saw that she had thrown the covers off in the midst of her nightmare. He sucked in a breath and forced himself to focus past the midnight silk nightgown she was wearing, the same one that had burned into his memory from months before when he stood in her doorway at Sveaborg. He pushed his desires away and kneeled beside the bed, placing a soft hand on her shoulder. He gently shook her.

She sprang awake, sitting upright and gasping for air. Sweat clung to her back, and a few pieces of hair were matted to her face. She gripped his arms, and he held still as she focused on calming her shallow gasps. A few minutes passed before her breathing returned to normal, and once it had, he pulled himself slightly back to look down into her eyes. "You okay?"

She nodded, knowing the memories of being trapped back inside the Nameless Place had passed, and she was no longer there.

Realizing she was safe, Anselem pulled himself backward, suddenly all too aware of the lack of clothing between them.

She held his arms and looked up at him, her eyes lined with silver. Her voice was nearly gone from the screaming as she rasped, "Stay. Please."

He nodded, and she slid to the side, creating a space in the bed for him. He knew she would never want him in the same way he wanted her, but he promised himself that no matter what she was able to give him, he would take it. He promised that even at his darkest, he would always find a way to be her light.

Because before he had ever met Asha, Anselem only thought there were two kinds of love. The kind of love someone would kill for, and the kind of love they would die for.

But Asha—she was the kind of love he would live for.

As he slid under the sheets, he wrapped his arms around her and pulled her close against his chest. Moments later, exhaustion swept her under, and she drifted into a peace-filled sleep.

CAMERON L. JIMENEZ

And for the first time in months, Asha slept through the night without another nightmarish scream shredding through her lips.

"To bear the gift of Light, one must first survive the burning. From the faintest spark, a flame is born—and from that flame, the fiercest are forged. They are like everflames, the undimming fires that darkness cannot touch. They are the strongest of us, not because they burn, but because they refuse to fade."
— Inheritance: A Guide to Understanding the Gifts Bestowed by the High Gods
(First Edition)

CHAPTER FOURTEEN

When Asha and Anselem woke early the next morning, Iskander had already left, and the cottage was quiet.

They dressed in their flying leathers, and Anselem threw together a quick breakfast of the last few eggs left on top of the kitchen counter. A light knock sounded at the door, and Asha looked over from the cognac couch where she was sitting, tearing her eyes from the snow-brushed mountains outside the window.

She rose from her seat and walked down the short hall-way, pulling the heavy, wooden front door open.

A beautiful woman with long, chocolate brown hair and a light gray uniform stood beyond the threshold. Asha's brows crinkled.

The woman looked her up and down once before remarking uninterestedly, "Odd. Blondes aren't usually his type."

Before Asha could throw a jab that would likely cut the woman at the knees, Anselem slipped into the space behind her and interjected, "Imara, it's good to see you. This is Asha." He glanced at the Soturi beside him and back to Imara, adding, "Asha Raynor."

Asha noticed a titillating light fill in the warrior's eyes when she saw Anselem, but the blood quickly drained from her face as she realized she had just insulted a Septant's sister.

Imara opened her mouth to apologize, but Asha cut her off. "It's fine. I've met Iskander, I would probably have thought the same."

She nodded, and Anselem added, "Imara is Iskander's Second."

"And to think I was told all the Saints had been killed in the First War. You must be blessed with the patience of the Dominions to put up with Blaidd's mischief."

Anselem laughed, and Asha caught the twinkle in Imara's eye when she looked at him again. That same tinge of jealousy she had felt at The Golden Sail reared its head.

"He's not here," Anselem told Imara, "he left early this morning. I thought he would have told you."

"He did." She looked over to Asha. "He just failed to mention he had multiple guests."

Multiple.

Had he mentioned Anselem was here, and *that* was why she came? Asha forced herself to keep an even, unmoved expression.

"Did you need something?" Anselem asked.

She certainly wanted something, Asha thought.

"I just needed to pick up some papers," Imara answered without hesitation. Maybe it was the truth, or maybe Iskander's Second simply happened to think quickly on her feet.

Anselem pushed the door open wider, giving the Amarok room to enter.

"Thank you, Commander."

Imara lingered a second too long next to Anselem before heading down the hall and into Iskander's bedroom.

Anselem closed the front door, and Asha raised her brows.

"What?"

She smirked. "Oh, nothing, *Commander*." She kept her voice low, but a joking tone filled the space.

Anselem teasingly narrowed his eyes. "Don't start with me, Seven. It's far too early." He sauntered down the hallway, back towards the kitchen.

Following closely behind, she replied, "I'm not starting anything. It's not my fault if some people," she motioned to Iskander's closed bedroom door as they walked past, "seem to be overly excited for the morning time."

He shook his head, and Asha almost laughed. Either the man was clueless about the effect he had on women, or he simply did not care.

"Eat your breakfast so we can leave."

She gave him a swaggering smile. "Is that an order, *Commander*?" She winked at him.

He snagged one of the pieces of fresh bread he had placed on her plate.

"Hey!"

He took a bite, and a wide smile curled on his lips. "You're going to be left with no food if you keep pushing my buttons, Seven."

She snatched one of the biscuits off his plate. "Thief."

He laughed, but Asha joked with him about Imara no more as she shoveled down her lukewarm breakfast.

As Asha finished her food and scooped up the plates in front of her and Anselem to wash in the basin, Imara ambled back into the room. The guardian lingered near the hall, her face set in a neutral expression.

"I'm heading out," she called over, her voice carrying

strongly across the room. "Thanks again." She lifted a rolled scroll in her hand.

Anselem nodded. "Of course. It was nice to see you, Imara."

The warrior smiled. "You as well." She turned to Asha. "It was nice to meet you."

"Likewise."

The Amarok turned and disappeared down the hall. Asha began scrubbing the dirty plates beneath the water. She heard the front door latch shut but said nothing as she continued to brush the dishes clean.

A warm tingle ran down her back when Anselem's voice snuck up behind her, whispering in her ear, "Did that lie taste bitter coming off your tongue, Seven?"

She whipped around, splashing water and accidentally clanking the plate in her hands against the side of the basin.

His face was mere inches from hers, but he did not back away.

"What lie?"

He smirked. "*Likewise*?"

She narrowed her eyes. "I'm sure she is very sweet."

"Is that right?"

She nodded, heat threatening to rise in her cheeks.

"Jealous, Asha?"

So, he *did* know the effect he had on women; he just saved them from the humiliation of rejection by feigning naivety.

But his question reminded her so much of a reversed situation months ago that she could not miss the opportunity to toss his own words back at him.

"If you want a distraction, Anselem, that's your choice. I don't care who you sleep with."

Her tone was not harsh but instead held a hint of question within it—as if there was a hope swimming within her words that he would tell her he had no interest in the striking Second of the Vanguard.

He leaned in close, placing his hands on either side of her, gripping the basin behind her. She braced herself for the scent of amber and citrus that would wrap around the air, for the buzzing wave of his power that she could always feel rippling out from him when he stood close.

He stared down into her eyes, and for a moment, she felt happy to be lost in the seas of green.

"Liar," he breathed. His eyes broke from hers and trailed down to her lips. He stood so close she could feel his heart racing inside his chest. Her own thudding beat matched the speed of his, as if there was a storm raging in her heart.

She knew she shouldn't feel it. She knew she should shove it down, that he didn't feel the same. It was just the game of distraction they had always played, and now, with everything that had happened in the last two days, she was certain he wanted a distraction. And she had not forgotten his words to Iskander the night before, that she was *unclaimable*. Asha knew he didn't mean it as an insult, that he truly believed in her and her ability to thrive beyond the shadow of a man, but the smallest part of her questioned whether he also believed it because he had no desire to ever try to pursue her himself.

But knowing all those things did not stop her heart from fluttering when he looked at her with such intensity.

Because in those rare moments when he stared at her like that, those moments when, for a fraction of a second, she allowed herself to hope, she felt the beautiful depth that existed between them. And she knew he had awakened a part of her soul that she had tried to keep buried for a long time. But as she looked into his emerald eyes, she was aware that for as long as she knew him, there was a part of her that would never return to sleep.

His eyes sparked as he broke the silence. "Ash." Her name sounded like honey on his lips, and the word was filled with such longing it came out almost like a plea. Warmth spread over her as she tilted her head up, but as he leaned down, she turned her head to the side.

"I can't," she whispered.

Because Asha did not want distractions, nor mediocre love. She wanted someone she could drown in.

He stood up straight, pulling himself a step back. Even with the space between them, she could still feel the twirling dance that played in the air between them. The electric charge of their powers as they intermingled, as if they recognized the other.

"I'm sorry. I just thought…"

It was so strange to see him fumbling for his words.

"I'm sorry. I didn't mean to make you feel uncomfortable."

He took another step, back and Asha could see the guilt washing over his body.

She shook her head, taking a small, half-step towards him. "You didn't make me uncomfortable, Ans." The tension in his shoulders eased the slightest bit. "I just… I can't do a distraction. It doesn't work for me." She left the rest unsaid, as she too often did. She did not mention that if she let herself cross that line with him, there would be no going back. She would give him every piece of her fractured heart. He would be her undoing, and she could not allow herself to give him the deepest part of herself for something that was only a distraction for him.

"Asha, you're not a distraction—"

Before he could finish his thought, before Asha could allow her heart to swell with hope, high-pitched screeches rang through the air from outside.

The warriors' eyes flared wide, and they grabbed their

jackets, hanging on the back of the dining chairs, and ran out the front door.

Midnight black feathers rolled across the snow, tumbling with icy snow-white plumes. Snow was flung into the air from the ground beneath the beasts.

But as Asha and Anselem rushed across the grass, they heard no snarls or clamping of beaks. Another small screech sounded from Kapheria.

Anselem halted, and Asha came up behind him, stopping by his side. A loud, bellowing laugh exploded from him.

"What in the Seven Hells..."

"They're playing. Like damn children in a snow fight."

Asha's brow crinkled, and a small, muffled laugh crept out.

Anselem whistled, and Kapheria immediately ceased, quickly crawling to her feet and standing upright.

Uriel rolled off his back, shaking the snow from his feathers. As the warriors walked over to the firebirds, Uriel kicked one last ball of snow up, hitting Kapheria in the chest. She snapped at him, and Asha swore there was a twinkle in his eyes.

"Get your phoenix under control, Seven," Anselem called over, a smirk on his face.

She shrugged as she neared Uriel, brushing the feathers on his head as he leaned down. "It's not my fault that all the males in this warrior group are shameless flirts."

"Only with you, Ash." He winked, and her cheeks went warm.

It's just a joke, he didn't mean it, she thought.

"He most certainly did."

She flashed a narrowed glance at the Commander. "Stop doing that!"

"Doing what?" he asked innocently, pulling himself onto Kapheria's back and settling into the saddle.

Asha followed suit, climbing atop Uriel, and called over, "Reading me. It's annoying."

He grinned and shrugged. "I rather like it. Although it would be much easier if you didn't try to always hide what you're thinking from me."

She rolled her eyes. "That's the point, *Commander*."

Anselem frowned and scrunched his nose. "I don't like that one as much."

Asha's brow furrowed.

"Commander. I don't like it."

"You don't like *Lieutenant* much either, if I recall from many months ago," she countered.

Uriel spread his wings out beneath her, restlessly ready to take flight.

"I don't mind it now. It grew on me."

Asha wondered if it was for the same reason Seven had become so endearing to her—that she was the only one who called him by the title. Everyone else either called him Eros or Commander.

He smirked, and Asha knew he had somehow read the thoughts racing through her mind once again.

"That's exactly why, Seven."

And before she could scold him, Kapheria launched into the air, her midnight feathers swallowing the dawning sun as she soared overhead.

Asha locked an orb of air around her head, gave Uriel a swift kick, and followed the pair into the sky.

The warriors flew to the open, snow-covered foothills at the base of the mountains.

They dismounted, leaving their firebirds in an open field below, and climbed up the snowy hillside until they reached a latched gate with three moon phases cut out inside the center of the wood.

Asha took a deep breath and looked over at Anselem. There was nothing but understanding and kindness in his warm, emerald eyes. He reached out, gently taking her hand in his.

"I can go with you, or I can wait here. Whatever you need."

She loved that about him. She loved that he always gave her the choice. Even when she could see in the depths of his eyes that he wished to be by her side in case she needed him, he would always let her choose. And he would always trust that she was strong enough to do it on her own.

She squeezed his hand. "This is something I need to do by myself."

He nodded, squeezing her hand once before letting it go. "I'll be here whenever you are done."

She nodded, her throat feeling too tight to reply, and turned to face the waist-high gate. She took a deep breath, the cold air stinging her lungs, lifted the latch, and entered the sacred grounds of Crescent Gardens.

She wound her way through the snow, trying to stick to places that looked like a stone path covered lightly in powder. She ventured off the walkway a couple of times before she made it to the final line of gravestones. Iskander had given Asha very specific directions, and as she neared the end of the line, her heart sank into her boots. Perfectly carved into the headstone rested seven words:

ELANINA AEROL
LOVING SISTER, WARRIOR, AND FRIEND

After Nina died, the world kept turning, and Asha never forgave it for that.

For a long time, in the midst of her silence, Asha thought she could cry her back to life. Or, perhaps, she'd hoped the tears that fell from her eyes would have been loud enough for Nina to hear them and come back home.

She kneeled beside the stone. Her throat felt tight.

"Hi, Nina." She let out a long breath as tears began to swell. "I miss you."

The first drop fell from the corner of her eye.

"I wish time had been kind to you," she began. "There is so much I wanted to tell you. So much I wish I had been able to share." More tears slid down her cheeks and wet the snow-coated grass beneath her. "But now I will whisper them to the stars, hoping that you're there."

She was quiet for a long time, and new snow began to slowly trickle from the sky.

Asha had always heard that what didn't kill her would make her stronger. But it hadn't.

She survived, but she was not stronger for it. It was a tragedy that would simply and forever be scorched upon her heart.

"I'm so sorry I couldn't save you." Her voice cracked as the words came out. "But thank you for saving me."

Asha pulled out the glass orb tucked away in her cloak; the same one she had bought the previous evening when she spotted it in the storefront window. She set it on top of the headstone.

Through blurred eyes, she raised her hand above the translucent globe and, with grave focus, watched her magic seep out and light an eternal flame inside the glass sphere.

She smiled down at the flickering flame, pressing two fingers to her brow.

"Until we meet again, may you live on and burn well."

And with tear-streaked cheeks and a heavy heart, Asha pulled her cloak tighter to her chest and walked back down the stone path.

CHAPTER

FIFTEEN

The warriors flew nonstop until they reached Elysia. They traveled all day and through the night, stopping only once for Kapheria and Uriel to rest before heading back into the skies towards the City of Glass.

As they neared the sleeping city, dawn broke through the clouds, and rays of morning sunlight illuminated the buildings below. It had been a long time since Anselem had visited his hometown, but from the skies overhead, the city looked much the same as when he left it years before.

Even from high above, the view always managed to steal his breath.

The city had been crafted thousands of years ago, before the time of the First War, when dragons still roamed the earth and humans still held bonds with the magical beasts.

The early settlers of Elysia crafted the city from the remnants of dragon glass, a material that not only withstood the destruction of battle over the centuries but also gave the city a preternatural feel.

As the rays peaked into the sky, the sun glinted against

the glass buildings, sparkling and reflecting a prism of oceanic colors. Blues and greens and hints of deep purple radiated off the glass walls, painting the city in a haze of watercolors. Narrow canals, filled by the glowing saltwater of the Seidon Sea, wound their way through the city, and paddle boats holding early risen citizens were scattered amidst the pale blue water.

Anselem had traveled to many places in his life, across Perseis and throughout the kingdoms south of the Straight, but he had never found one he loved as much as the one he called home. He pulled his gaze from the beauty beneath him and looked over to the warrior gliding through the air beside him. A full, genuine smile filled his face as he saw the awe and wonder burning within her sapphire eyes. Her long, blonde braid flowed behind her, and his heart was filled with boundless bliss, thankful he was able to share another piece of himself with the warrior.

He whistled, pulling Asha's locked gaze from the city below, and nodded his head towards the coast. She glanced to the side, looking at the docks along the sea, and gave him an understanding nod.

Anselem pulled once on Kapheria's reins, and the firebird tucked in her midnight wings and barreled towards the seaside ports below. Moments later, both firebirds and their riders landed gracefully on the sandy white shores, just outside the glass walls of the Elysian Fort.

"You never told me it was so beautiful here," Asha called over to him, her faint green orb disappearing from around her head.

He released his own orb and took in a deep breath, smelling the salty citrus air. He pulled a single slinged leather bag from one of the compartments strapped to Kapheria's saddle. He looped it over his shoulder and pulled it around to his front. He strapped his dual swords to his back, the same place he always kept them whenever he wasn't riding.

He smiled as Asha walked over, catching the multitude of daggers sheathed along her waistband, and the warriors left Uriel and Kapheria to find a place to rest after their taxing journey.

"I'll have some of the Kappi cadets tend to them and bring some food."

Asha nodded. "Could you have one of them send a message out as well?"

"What kind of message?"

Asha tilted her head back, staring up at the tall, glimmering sea green walls of the fort. "Kaira should be stationed here. I think we need her at this meeting."

Anselem watched her eyes as they took in the refracting light as it crossed the dragon glass.

"I'll see that it is done."

She nodded, pulling her gaze back down to meet his. "I've never seen it before—dragon glass."

Anselem smiled. "Sure you have."

Asha raised a brow. The towering doors to the glass wall opened, and a soldier ran out, heading over to meet them.

Anselem pulled one of the swords from his back, the same one he had given to her for her final benchmark. As it caught in the sunlight, it glinted, sparkling and reflecting off various shades of blue and green. *Soulmaker.*

Asha gasped and looked up at him.

He shrugged. "I can't tell you all my secrets, Seven." He winked and sheathed the blade on his back just as the Kappi cadet reached their side.

The soldier looked young, no older than fifteen. He was likely on gate-duty and spotted the two firebirds when they landed on the shore and was ordered to come greet the riders.

"Good morning, Sir." He nodded to Anselem. "Ma'am." He gave a second nod to Asha.

"Good morning," Anselem replied, greeting the soldier in Elysian. Before he allowed the soldier another word, Anselem asked in the common tongue, "I need to meet with Cathan."

The kid's amber eyes went wide, and he glanced between Asha and Anselem several times before he hesitantly nodded.

The soldier turned to head back, but before he took off in a run towards the glass gate, Anselem called out, "Tell him an old friend from Enyalius would like to chat."

The soldier looked back, nodding once more, and took off in a run, his loosely braided deep-brown hair flowing behind him.

Asha crinkled her brow, and Anselem laughed. "More secrets you can't tell?"

He chuckled. "We're not supposed to let anyone know the name of Septant Training, Seven."

Asha's eyes flared.

No more than five minutes passed, and the glass gates opened wide. An older warrior, with deep-honey brown skin and white hair, stepped out from behind the glass doors and began a slow, methodical walk towards Asha and Anselem.

Without a word, Anselem stepped forward, and Asha quickly followed, heading to meet the man halfway between the sandy shores and the white stone walkway at the entrance.

"Anselem," the man greeted, in a rough, gravelly voice. He stuck out his worn hand, scarred and marked from years of battle.

"Overseer," he replied, grasping the warrior's hand. His grey eyes shifted to Asha. "Sir, this is—"

"Asha Raynor," the Overseer interrupted, finishing the Commander's statement.

She stuck out her marked hand and he took it, his grey eyes staying locked on hers.

"I have wondered how long it would be until we met."

She said nothing as he released her hand. He held her gaze for a long time before dragging it back to Anselem. "I will ensure the cadets see to both Uriel and Kapheria."

Anselem nodded, and Asha remained silent, studying the Overseer.

She had learned many things about the title during her research on the Septant. The Overseer was the warrior in charge of training the seven warriors, always a former member himself before age or injury claimed his active role in the unit. But the one common theme Asha discovered throughout the entirety of her research was that none of the Overseers were ever named. Not even the Septant warriors themselves were informed. She assumed 'Cathan' was a name the warriors used to inform the gate guards that they held positions high enough to garner the Overseer's time.

It was as if acceptance of the position erased the Overseer's name from history, forever lost in a sea of namelessness.

"Where is she?"

The Overseer studied him for a long moment. Asha could only assume Anselem was asking of Neith.

"The Spinner is at home."

The Spinner?

"We will all be at the Mount at sunset."

The Overseer nodded, but instead of answering Anselem, he turned to Asha and stated, "I will ensure Miss Samson gets your message."

Asha's eyes narrowed, but she held her tongue. The old man smiled, but before he turned back towards the glass gates, he looked back and forth between the warriors, and his grey eyes landed on Anselem. "Iskander is right, you know. He is undoubtedly going to kill you."

Anselem's face went red, and Asha's brows pulled together.

The Overseer ambled down the white stones, disappearing behind the glass gates and into the fort.

After the white-haired warrior vanished behind the blue-green glass, Asha turned to Anselem and said, "Another secret you can't share?"

As Anselem hurried down the slowly lightening streets, he filled Asha in on everything, all while trying to point out the different buildings and the city districts they passed as they made their way to Neith's.

He explained the Overseer's gifts and how, upon accepting the position, the leader was blessed with a small fragment of each of the Septant warrior's powers. Anselem did not know how or in what way the Overseer gained the powers; he only knew that it happened as soon as the position was accepted, and that he added more gifts to his collection each time a new Septant warrior was appointed.

He told Asha about Kage's magic, how the Examiner was a Transferent—a mind reader—capable of determining the thoughts and questions wading within one's mind. And Kage's ability was one of the greatest Leadership had ever seen—able to not only determine conscious thought, but also subconscious thought, as his gift sifted through the ideas and mental pictures swimming within another's mind. That was how the Overseer had been able to know what was going on in her head, for he possessed a small snippet of the powerful gift Kage harnessed.

Lastly, he explained who Neith was and the dark powers the Spinner wielded. Her gift of wisdom over war and her ability to weave the outcome of battles had not been granted to her by the gods, but rather had been given to her long ago by a dark force she refused to mention after she found a way to break free from the chains used to imprison her. Since gaining her freedom from the dark forces, she wiggled her way onto the Septant's payroll, and for the last few centuries, she provided insight and knowledge into the predictive outcomes of battles and gave guidance on the best strategies for the warriors to utilize.

Asha's eyes went wide as they turned another corner. "Kage has Mind Magic?"

Anselem nodded.

Asha was quiet for a moment, the clamoring of boots against the white-stone walkways the only noise filling the street. "If he is gifted by the Virtues, why did the Council not appoint him as a Vice?" she questioned.

Anselem's jaw feathered, as though the concerning thought had crossed his mind before.

"The positions were all filled when he came into his power. And Kage... he has done a very good job at keeping his Kratos hidden."

Asha believed the Transferent must have done an *incredible* job at hiding his power, for the Satraps had the authority to replace their Vice whenever the desire struck them.

A wave of horror washed over her as another possibility entered her mind—perhaps the Satraps *were* aware of Kage's power, but the Vices already in their ownership wielded gifts even more valuable than a mind reader...

Anselem abruptly stopped in the middle of the street. The shuffling of citizens grew louder as the sun rose in the sky.

He looked down at Asha and suddenly, with strained

words, he uttered, "This was not how I wanted to show you Elysia."

She looked up at him with kind eyes, as if she understood the special place his home held in his heart, and then glanced over at the rising sun. "I would love nothing more than to come back when we have time and for you to show me every corner of this city." She brought her gaze back to his tired face. "But until then, show me what you can and promise me that we will return so I can see it all."

The graveness on his face disappeared, and a smile replaced the disappointment. The fact that Asha wanted to know about the place that had played such an intricate role in shaping who he was, for good and bad, brought so much joy to his heart; all he could do was smile. "I promise."

She smiled, looping her arm through his, and they continued down the street, now filled with Elysians hurrying in all directions, and Anselem noticed the slightly slower pace she walked, as if she wanted to savor the beauty of the city surrounding them for as long as possible.

As they continued towards Neith's, Anselem found his own pace had slowed to match hers. And each new street and every monumental building they passed, he told her all about his home, and his heart was lighter than it had been in a long time.

Asha had never seen a place so stunning. As they wound their way down the alabaster-stone streets, crossing bridges that arched over clear, ice-blue channels snaking through the city, Asha couldn't help but gape at the oceanic rainbow of light covering the city like a blanket. She had never known the reason behind the city's name, but after seeing how the sunlight reflected off the walls of dragon glass and danced

CAMERON L. JIMENEZ

across the stone streets and white buildings, painting them a rainbow of blues and greens, she understood how the City of Glass had earned its name.

Anselem had already guided them through two quarters, the Market Square, filled with endless merchant stands setting up for the day, and Luminsend.

Anselem told her the true name of the Luminsend Quarter was the Luminiferous Quarter of Awakening, but the people who lived in the district simply called it Luminsend because it was located on Luminos Street and there was a large cul-de-sac at the end.

He noted with a smile that the citizens had quickly transitioned to the name when they realized the original title was more than a mouthful to state every day.

The entire quarter was lined with strings of glass orbs hung between the buildings, and Anselem told her that Luminsend was even more beautiful at night, when the dragon-glass orbs, lit internally with lesser magic, reflected the light from within and the blue and green colors refracted off the orbs in every direction.

"Do you still have that key with you?" Anselem asked quietly, his eyes fixed on an inconspicuous-looking door ahead. Asha instinctively placed her hand against her neck, feeling for the metal hidden beneath.

She nodded as they neared a matte black door.

Anselem looked around and leaned towards her. He kept his voice so low it was inaudible to any prying ears as he explained, "That door just ahead leads to the Undercroft. It is the hidden vault for the Septant."

Asha did not react, keeping her gaze locked straight ahead as she took in the information.

"It is enchanted with an ancient spell, and Iskander also secured it with several locking Runes. It is impossible to enter without the Septant Mark."

Asha slowed her pace as they approached the black-oak door.

"If you want, I think it would be a good idea to lock the key from the Adaro King in there until we figure out what it is for."

Asha nodded and carefully pulled the key from beneath her shirt and discreetly handed it to Anselem.

He looked over her shoulder and down each side of the street. "I will be right back."

Asha nodded her head, understanding she would not be able to enter the impenetrable space.

As Anselem turned to enter the door, she grabbed his hand. He looked down at her with bunched brows.

She silently dug inside her jacket pocket and pulled out a gold-plated pendant with emeralds encircling the edges.

Three overlapping triangles were etched into the metal with a singular, engraved eye in the center.

The amulet from the Hound.

"Put this in there as well," she whispered, running her thumb across the carved symbol.

Anselem stared at the golden piece with narrowed eyes. He nodded, gently taking it in his hands, and disappeared into the Undercroft.

The Commander was only gone for a short time before he reappeared on the busy street. The warriors exchanged no words as Elysian citizens hurried past, and they quickly fell into step amongst the crowd, continuing their trek north-ward through the city.

As they exited Luminsend, turning another corner, Asha stopped in the middle of the street. A small gasp escaped her mouth as she beheld an open square, and set within the center was a large, cylindrical tower, crafted from alabaster stone at the base. But what took the breath from Asha's lungs was the rainbow-stained glass the soaring tower was constructed from.

Every other wall in the city had been crafted from traditional blue-green dragon glass. But this structure, in the heart of Elysia, was made from dragon glass of every color. Hues of reds and yellows, blues and greens, and every shade of orange wrapped their way up the curved walls. A rainbow of light danced across the grounds of the square.

"The Illuminary Pillar of Knowledge," Anselem whispered. Asha did not pull her eyes from the tower, but as the low tone of his voice reached her ears, she noticed the deafening quiet that surrounded the square. It was so different than the bustling and lively sounds filling the rest of the city.

He kept his voice low as they continued across the square. "We call it the Lightpost."

She tore her gaze from the tower and looked to the Commander, her brows crinkling.

He smiled. "I'll bring you back here at night, on the full moon, and you will see why."

There was a twinkle in his eyes, and she smiled, glad to see such excitement filling his face. She took a final look at the Pillar before the warriors continued through the square, slowly making the rest of the way to the Spinner's home.

As dawn vanished and day broke brightly into the sky, Anselem at last reached the Spinner's luxurious townhome on the north side of the Diamond District.

The street was quiet, with only a handful of citizens walking along the pristine sidewalks. Dozens of homes lined the street on either side. Each of the row houses was built from expensive neutral-colored stones, and lush green lawns, filled with hundreds of white rose bushes, lined the front side of the homes.

Anselem rolled his eyes, unsurprised that the Spinner chose a home located in the most affluent area of the city. She had always maintained a preference for opulence.

Her rowhome stretched three stories high, crafted from glittering onyx rocks and tall, arched windows. An alabaster door was perched at the top of three large steps, and the outline of a woven web stretched across the right side of the white wood.

The warriors stood on the street, outside a small, knee-high iron gate surrounding the Spinner's perfectly manicured front yard. To the citizens passing by, the townhouse looked no different than the other luxurious properties lining the street, but as Anselem approached the gate, he could feel the dark magic woven into the encompassing iron, preventing any uninvited guests from entering the grounds.

From the tenseness in Asha's shoulders, he was sure she also felt the wall of magic stretching before them.

Her voice broke through the quietness around them. "Truth for a truth?"

He looked at her and nodded, but she kept her gaze locked on the webbed door.

Her voice was quiet as she asked, "Is there history between you two?"

Anselem knew the type of history she was alluding to, and he let out a long breath. *That* was certainly not the question he expected her to ask.

"Yes," he replied honestly. "Once. Years ago, when I was young and drunk and more than a little stupid."

He could not read the expression on Asha's face. She said nothing.

"Does it bother you?"

She was quiet for an extended moment, as if trying to sort through her feelings. She turned her burning eyes to him. "No," she replied softly, then added, "and yes."

He tilted his head to the side. He was thankful she'd been honest, but he was still unsure what to make of her answer.

She sighed. "She is very beautiful." Asha said the words as if they were an explanation, as if she could understand his choices simply because of Neith's looks.

He had never seen the warrior seem so unsure of herself. And although he had no way to explain what it was that existed between them, he knew what they shared was something real, and the only thing he wanted was for Asha to know his past meant nothing to him. All he cared about was what lay ahead. *Who* lay ahead.

He stepped towards her and put his fingers gently beneath her chin, raising her eyes to meet his and said with equal strength and vulnerability, "I'm not beautifully broken, Ash. I was ripped to shreds from the inside out. And for a long time, I was lost, searching for a place to land. And I have a past filled with a lot of regrets and many choices I wish I had not made. But if all those choices had to happen to lead me to you, I would make them all again. I would endure them all again. Because the one thing I know for certain is that every set of eyes before yours made me feel empty, and when I look into yours, I feel seen. For the first time in my life, I feel understood."

Anselem had formed a handful of great friendships in his life. He had brothers with whom he had forged a lifelong bond.

But with Asha, it was different.

With her, it was a friendship where she saw every dark and shattered part of his soul, as if her own had been crafted from the same star long ago, and when she looked inside his heart, she never once thought to shy away from his brokenness.

She did not break his gaze, but looked deep into his

eyes, a fire flickering within the sapphire, and nodded. And for the first time, whether she was aware of it or not, she did not try to hide the thoughts swimming in her mind as she silently said to him, *Tell me all the horrible things you have done, and let me love you just the same.*

Anselem's heart raced in his chest, and as she responded, he realized she had not intended to utter the silent words she had spoken to him.

"I see you, Ans."

His mind could not focus. He barely heard the hinges of the front door squeal open, and the only thing that brought him back to reality was the sultry voice that called from the door, "If it's not my favorite Septant warrior."

Anselem dropped his hand from Asha's face, stifling the irritation pulsing through his veins as he turned to face the Spinner. He schooled his face back into the unemotional mask that he always donned and called over to Neith, "I'm only your favorite because you've never met the others."

Anselem felt the wall of magic drop and walked towards the front door. Asha was by his side, donning the swaggering persona she had carefully mastered.

"Even if I had, I'm quite certain you'd still be my top choice, Anselem." She turned her foxlike eyes to the ash-blonde warrior beside him, looking her up and down. "Hello, Fireborne."

Asha's fire-filled eyes narrowed, and an arrogant smile curved on her lips as she replied, "Hello, Spinner."

Neith smirked, as if she too could see the dark Chaos living inside the Soturi's veins.

She looked back at Anselem. "Would you like to come in, Commander?"

He nodded, and the two warriors stepped into the home of the Spinner.

Neith was dressed in a nude-colored gown, fitted at the top like a suffocating corset, with long flowing layers of tule that reached the ground. She wore matching, see-through sleeves that connected to the top of the corset and left her shoulders uncovered. Her long, dark hair was swept to one side and flowed down to her waist in silky waves. Her neck, ears, and fingers were covered with diamonds and gems wrapped in gold, each piece of jewelry looking more costly than the last.

As the Spinner turned from the entryway, the train of the dress trailed behind her, swinging back and forth with the sultry sway of her hips. She guided them through the entryway, her uncovered back bared to them, exposing creamy, unblemished skin, save for two marks set in the center of her shoulders. Scars, Asha noted from their jagged curve, as if someone had taken a blade to her skin in a frenzied attempt to extract something.

The Spinner entered the sitting room off the foyer, her layers of tule blooming out beside her. Asha wondered if she always dressed in such extravagant gowns, or if the wonderous woman had somehow been notified of their impending arrival.

The interior of the house seemed an extension of the outside, with luxurious onyx floors, pristine cream-colored walls, and gold accents that wrapped around the staircase banister and the ornate chandelier hanging inside the doorway.

The home looked as though it were not lived in, without a speck of dust or dirt to be found on the caramel leather couch or the perfectly placed pillows. There wasn't even an indentation on either of the crisp, pure-white chairs that faced the couch, and yet the untouched room felt welcoming. Asha attributed the cozy feel to the soft burning blaze on the far wall. The fireplace stretched all the way to the high ceiling.

She took a seat in the armchair closest to the fire, expecting to feel warmth radiating from the flames, but as she settled into the seat, she noticed there was no heat spreading out from the embers. Asha looked closer at the flickering blazes, encased by translucent glass, and she realized the fire was an illusion, a phantom image produced by magic and enchantments.

"I don't do flames," the Spinner interjected, turning Asha's gaze away from the glamour. Standing beside the couch, Neith's eyes were locked on the fabricated fire as she added, "But I have always enjoyed their beauty."

There was a longing in her voice, a sense of desire. She forcefully pulled herself back into the townhome, shaking off the many wonders sifting through her mind. "To what do I owe the pleasure of a house call, Commander?" Neith's honeyed voice returned, as if she had replaced a mask she had crafted centuries ago. The Spinner took a seat on the couch, the nearly transparent, nude-toned layers bunching around her. She crossed her long legs and stretched a delicate, thin arm over the back of the couch.

Anselem, who had unhooked the dual blades from his back and leaned them against the chair beside Asha, cleared his throat. "We have a meeting at the Mount at sunset."

Neith thrummed her red-tipped fingernails, painted the same crimson color as her lips, against the leather. She gave him a wicked smile. "You're not even going to say 'please?'"

Anselem's jaw feathered, and the Spinner laughed.

"So tense, Ans. You used to be so much fun."

Asha shifted her weight but stayed silent. Neith's fox-like eyes dragged over to the Soturi. "And why are you here? I usually don't deal with Kappi."

"Soturi," Asha corrected, her voice unfazed.

Neith raised a brow. "Congratulations."

She smirked and turned to Anselem. "You have always had eyes for strong-willed women."

Asha forced herself to keep her body loose, but from the twinkle in Neith's eye, she knew the Spinner was enjoying toying with her.

Anselem's head turned towards her, and she glanced over to him, meeting his emerald eyes for only a fraction of a second.

But that was all it took.

One look into the emerald oceans, and somehow, in some way, without a spoken word from his lips, Anselem said to her, *There is only one strong-willed woman I have ever had eyes for, Ash, and I'm looking at her.*

He pulled his gaze away, turning back to the Spinner, and it took everything within Asha to keep her jaw from hitting the floor.

Did he just speak to me? she wondered, confusion and amazement fighting one another within her mind.

"Name your price," Anselem replied, ignoring Neith's previous comment.

A sly grin pulled on her lips. "Anything?"

Anselem stiffened, and rage thrashed through Asha's veins. Not jealousy, not envy. Pure, ice-filled rage for the implied payment the Spinner alluded to. As if the warrior seated before her—as if the godsflaming Commander of the Septant—was nothing more than a pretty face and a well-honed body made to service her desires.

Asha leaned forward, and Neith's foxlike eyes cut over to the Soturi. She smiled, a grin crafted of venom and fire, and with a voice colder than ice, Asha warned, "I suggest you choose your price very carefully, Spinner. Or else you may become well acquainted with the flames you very clearly like to avoid." Asha released a drop of her power, letting the embers within her sapphire eyes burn like wildfire.

Neith stiffened and dropped her hand from atop the couch, placing it in her lap. Asha swore she saw the red nails grow longer, sharper, as if the Spinner was readying her claws for a fight. Neith's dark eyes narrowed. "Be careful with whom you choose to tangle, girl."

Asha did not balk, even as the Spinner released the bindings around her dark magic, and it barreled towards her. But just as her power nearly collided with Asha, it halted, and the Soturi stared deeply back into Neith's wide eyes. "Perhaps it is *you* who should be careful, Spinner."

Neith released a whoosh of breath and muttered something in Elysian. She looked to Anselem, but he did not move, did not reply, as if he was letting Asha be the one to guide the conversation.

"I will be there."

Anselem nodded and stood, grabbing *Soulmaker* and his secondary, unnamed blade that leaned against the armchair. He fastened them against his back and dug into his pocket, pulling out an indigo-colored velvet pouch. From the rattling of metal inside, Asha assumed it was filled with pieces of gold—*many* pieces of gold.

The Spinner shook her head, still visibly astounded. "I do not need gold."

Anselem flung the sack onto the couch, and it softly bounced off the leather before resting atop the cognac cushion. "A Septant always pays his debts." He turned for the door, pausing in the opening between the sitting room and the foyer to wait for Asha.

She gracefully rose from her chair, Neith's foxlike eyes trailing her every move, and just before she joined Anselem at his side, readied to exit the townhouse, she looked deep into the stormy seas of the Spinner's gaze and saw the flicker of ancient Darkness prowling within her beautiful frame. But in that fleeting moment, within the Darkness she peered into, Asha also saw an intricately woven web of iridescent silk. A web crafted and spun to hold back that same raging Darkness living inside her mind.

"I see you, Spinner," Asha whispered, and Neith's eyes slightly widened. "I see your Darkness. But I also see how you desire to fight for the Light."

And with those final words, Asha walked out of the townhouse, leaving the Spinner behind, still seated upon the couch.

And for the first time in centuries, a smile of hope curled on Neith's mouth, and a single tear slid from her eye.

"THEY MOVED AS ONE—SILENT, BLINDING, ETERNAL. WHERE THEY PASSED, SHADOW WITHERED, AND THE EARTH REMEMBERED THE LIGHT. BORN NOT OF FLESH, BUT OF HEART AND WILL, THE LEGION WAS AWAKENED IN PURE LIGHT TO STAND AGAINST THE DARKNESS THAT DEVOURS ALL THINGS. DEATH COULD NOT TOUCH THEM, FOR THEY CARRIED THE FLAME OF VIRTUE THAT BURNS BEYOND THE VEIL. AND IN THEIR EYES, THE END OF DAYS WAS NOT FEARED, BUT FULFILLED."
— FRAGMENT IV OF THE RECOVERED PASSAGES FROM THE LOST TOMES OF THE LEGION

CHAPTER SIXTEEN

Asha and Anselem slipped out of the webbed door and onto the white rose-petalled front lawn of the Spinner's house.

They had not made it more than a quarter of the way down the stone path, leading towards the main street in the Diamond District, when the hinges creaked open behind them.

The warriors turned around, and the Spinner glided across the alabaster walkway, her layers of nude tule splayed behind her.

As she approached, Neith looked singularly at Anselem and said, "I found the answer you were seeking."

She glanced over to Asha, as if she were requesting permission to divulge the information in front of her. When her foxlike eyes turned to the Thurisaz, Asha could see the faintest smudge at the corner of the perfectly placed charcoal lining her eyes.

Anselem gave an assertive nod, but Asha could see the tenseness in his shoulders.

"It was not easy," Neith confessed. "Your predecessors used another name long before they ever claimed the Septant."

Anselem's gaze sharpened, but he stayed silent.

"It is hidden in the Throat of the World," she went on. "A cavern carved into the bones of a mountain that never knows daylight. A place where statues of forgotten gods kneel in endless shadow. Where the air tastes of salt, and the roar of the sea shudders through the stone as though the Deep itself keeps vigil over the place." She paused, holding the Commander's gaze. "The Obviator will know the way."

Anselem's jaw tensed, and he gave the Spinner another curt nod. "We will see you tonight," he replied.

He turned on his heels and continued down the path, exiting the grounds of the Spinner's home.

Asha followed closely as they ambled through the opulent streets of the Diamond District.

He glanced over to her, and just as he was about to open his mouth to explain, Asha interjected, "You can tell me later."

Anselem arched a brow. But that was when he saw it on her face—the utter exhaustion.

He nodded, knowing the warrior had far too many other revelations from the last several days swimming in her head for him to stack any more onto the pile.

"After we get through all of this," he agreed. And she smiled softly as the Commander guided her towards the center of the City of Glass.

Anselem and Asha walked several blocks before they found an inn with a vacancy and requested a room.

The Commander wouldn't chance visiting the loft he

had purchased years ago in Luminsend, for he knew there was a good chance the Council had lurking eyes in all parts of the city.

The innkeeper was a scraggly old woman with deep-set wrinkles in her tanned face, and dark brown hair streaked with grey. She gave Anselem an odd look when he requested a room at such an early hour, but she accepted his coin and handed over a key with a short wooden rod connected to it. The room number was etched within the oak.

The quarters were simple, but clean. A decent-sized bathing chamber connected to the bedroom, and a large bed sat in the center, cloaked in crisp white sheets and a navy blanket.

Anselem waited patiently in the bedroom while Asha bathed and washed off the grime and dirt from several days of travel. When she returned, her unbound hair was still damp from washing, and she smelled of vanilla and lavender mixed with the soft scent of sandalwood soap and the faintest hint of citrus that seemed to always linger in the air of his hometown. She had changed into one of the black, short-sleeved shirts he had packed in the leather sling bag.

His shirt.

Falling just above her knees, the shirt was entirely too large for her, but the sight of her in his clothes knocked the breath from his lungs.

She gave him a soft smile as she walked past, and it took every ounce of self-control he possessed to keep from reaching out and pulling her into him. He let out a long sigh and went into the bathing chamber, feeling a strong need to clean off the dirt and sweat sticking to his body from the days of flying.

When he came back into the bedroom, his wavy, shoulder-length hair was clean and untangled, and he had it pulled back into a loose bun. Asha had already collapsed onto the bed and fallen asleep, and Anselem, also exhausted from too many days without rest, smiled, thankful she felt safe enough to fall into a deep slumber. He pulled the deep blue curtains over the window, blocking out the daylight, and crawled under the cozy, white sheets.

He was asleep before his head hit the pillow.

Asha felt like she was floating, wrapped up in the soft embrace of the clouds. She cracked open her eyes. The room was dark, except for a small sliver of light creeping in through a narrow opening on the far side of the room.

Asha shot up, her heart racing.

"We're fine. We have time."

She didn't know when his deep, accented voice had become one of her favorite sounds, or when she had begun wishing that he would never cease speaking, simply so that she could continue to hear it; she just knew that she could listen to the calmness of him for the rest of her life.

She rubbed her eyes, glancing at the broad figure sitting in the corner. Suddenly, the space beside her in the bed felt cold. Empty. As her eyes focused, she realized the light pouring in through the window was not supplied by the moon, but rather by the remnants of the dimming sun.

"How long have you been up?" she asked, her voice hoarse from sleep.

"Not long."

Her head ached. She needed more sleep. The shadowed outline of his figure rose, and the wooden chair beneath him moaned against the shifting of his weight. He walked to the window and raised his arms. A moment later, deep orange light poured into the room. Asha squinted as the sunlight illuminated the space.

He was already dressed in his leathers; all traces of grit and mud having vanished from the black material. His long hair was pulled back in a bun, with two shorter pieces had escaped from the leather tie, falling loosely in front of his face. His beard was dark and thick, much different from the close-cut trim she had always seen him wear. She realized, again, that she must have been silently staring at him for far too long when a smirk appeared on his lips and a matching twinkle flickered in his eyes.

She pulled the covers off, the cool air in the room swarming over her, and swung her legs over the edge before placing her bare feet onto the wooden floor. Her unbound hair fell to her waist, and as she stood beside the bed, still wearing Anselem's oversized shirt she had stolen from his bag, she watched the Commander's emerald eyes slowly trail down her body.

When he raised the emerald seas back up to hers, there was a hunger, a wildness lurking inside them, and he pressed his hands against his sides, as if it was the only thing keeping him from abandoning all reason.

She could see the ragged rise and fall of his chest, and a warmth pooled inside her.

Asha took a step towards him, her voice low, "I hope it's okay that I borrowed it." She glanced down at the black shirt draped over her body.

He nodded slowly. The voice that escaped from his mouth was unlike any she had ever heard from him before, filled with unrestrained desire and need. "More than okay."

She took another step, crossing the last of the space between them, and gazed up at him. A piece of hair fell in front of her face, and he gently raised his hand, tucking it behind her ear. His hand did not return to his side, but instead slid softly behind her neck, his thumb brushing the side of her face, and she was certain he could hear the thundering beat inside her chest.

He gazed deeply into her eyes and said, *You are not a distraction, Seven. You are a storm raging inside my heart. You were the waves that crashed against my broken soul and threw me out into the tempest. And at first, I was lost, for there was no shore in the savage place of my soul, but as I waded through the waters, I knew I would not have it any other way. You helped bring me back to life, you helped me once again find my footing. You helped me heal. You are by far the most beautiful place I will ever get lost in.*

Asha could not breathe. She felt every word, every declaration deep within her bones—within her soul—as if a part of him, and a part of her, had been crafted by the gods from the very same star.

A chime rang in the distance, and Anselem broke his gaze to glance out the window.

When he looked back, she knew he could see the silver lining her eyes. He smiled and pressed a kiss to the top of her head.

"We have to go," he mumbled into her hair, and just before he pulled away, she wrapped her arms around him.

They stood like that for a long while, until the final chimes of the clock tower bell ceased and the echoing rings went silent.

And as they stood there, arms wrapped around one another, Asha realized that in the moments when she thought she would never be anything but broken, Anselem was the one who always gave her hope. And when he wrapped his arms around her, she was reminded that she was still worth loving, brokenness and all.

Anselem wound his way through the nearly deserted

streets as the sun sank in the sky and the heavens painted swirling hues of pinks and oranges across the city.

Asha, now dressed in clean, black leathers, stayed glued to his side as they quickly made their way down the alleys and towards the Mount.

The Mount was the Septant's long-held meeting room. Tucked in a secluded back room of The Glass Lantern—a popular, upscale tavern in the heart of the city. The Mount had served the warriors well for decades, providing a central place that did not draw attention to the patrons who visited.

But the location, as well as the inconspicuous nature of The Glass Lantern, was not the only reason the Septant chose to continue utilizing the meeting room in the back. The true benefit of the Mount resided within the walls themselves.

Twenty years earlier, a Septant warrior found a way to erect a spell upon the walls of the Mount, barring anyone beyond the room from hearing what was discussed inside. The enchantment also projected a shield around the space, prohibiting any outside wielders from utilize magic to see who had gathered inside.

"Are you going to tell me how you do it?" Asha asked, breaking through Anselem's focused mind.

He continued down the street, turning another corner, but glanced over at her with a crinkled brow.

"How do you speak to me without saying anything?"

Anselem smiled, slowing his rushed pace, and looked at Asha once again. *I have no clue what you're talking about.* He winked, and she lightly slapped him on the shoulder. He laughed softly. "Truthfully, I don't know."

Asha scrunched her nose in response. Anselem turned and continued down the alley.

"I don't," he continued. "I've never heard of anything like it before, besides Kage's gift. And even with him, it's not like he *speaks* to us. It's more so that he just sees whatever is floating through our minds. Like pictures."

"How come I can't speak to you, but you can speak to me?"

Anselem's eyes slid over to her again, his footsteps never ceasing in their steady pace. "You can."

Her eyes flared wide, and she tilted her head.

He shrugged, "I think it's probably just easier for me because I've had years of experience opening and closing my mental channels to access my power. I'm guessing the more practice you have, the easier it will be."

He turned down another street and saw the blue luminos of The Glass Lantern shining in the distance.

"Interesting," she replied.

Anselem nodded. "Very."

"What's interesting?" a soft, kind voice rang through the air from behind them.

The two warriors spun around, and bright gold eyes greeted them.

Asha flung her arms around the Amarok so fiercely, the two women nearly toppled over. Laughter sang through the air.

"Thank the gods," Asha exclaimed, her voice carrying down the street. A few passing citizens glanced over at the commotion as they walked by, surprise flashing across their faces.

"Lieutenant Eros," Kaira acknowledged, nodding to Anselem.

He gave her a soft smile. "Eros is perfectly fine, Kaira."

"Or you can call him Commander. He loves that," Asha interjected.

Anselem rolled his eyes, and Kaira's golden stare widened. Asha glanced up at the sky, taking in the last remnants of the setting sun. Dusk had finally found them.

The moon, dimly visible through the pink and orange

clouds, began to fill, only half of its contents having been poured out. She glanced over to Anselem, a questioning look upon her face.

He nodded. "You have five minutes before we need to head inside."

Asha turned to her friend and said, "Then I'd better catch you up quickly." For the next several minutes, Asha told Kaira everything that had happened in Montu. She told her about the Septant and each of the warriors, about Neith and the minimal amount of information she had learned about the Spinner, and she told her how she needed her friend's help to come up with a plan to free her brother from the Midnight Castle.

Kaira's eyes were wide as the Soturi spoke, but Anselem could see the brilliant mind working through the hundreds of ideas floating within the golden pools.

Asha finished her spiel of information with a single offer to her friend: she could walk away, with absolutely no animosity or malice held for her choice within her friend's heart, or she could agree to help, and tie herself to a decision that could very possibly lead to death.

Kaira smiled, the sentiment warm and filled with love as she replied, "I told you long before, you are the Warrior. And I promise to follow you, to stand beside you as we walk through the Hells. Until we make it out the other side."

A full grin broke across Asha's face as she took her friend's hands in hers. She pulled Kaira in, giving her another long embrace filled with gratitude and love.

Kaira's words settled in Anselem's mind, and he smiled. Asha Raynor—the Warrior. The one who holds the hope of a better world.

"How precious," a sultry, spine-grating voice sang from the corner of the intersecting street.

Anselem twisted around, his jaw tightly clenched.

Asha released the Amarok from her arms; a small flame flashed through her sapphire blue eyes. The warriors said nothing as Neith crawled out from the shadows forming from the rising night.

"What? Not going to introduce me to your little friend, Ans?"

Kaira's always kind eyes narrowed, and a darkness he had never seen her display danced within the gold.

Anselem shook his head and turned to the cobalt-colored door, lit by a pair of neon blue luminos anchored to the wall beside it. He pulled on the latch, and the door creaked open as he tugged it towards him. As the sun finally set within the sky, the Commander stepped into The Glass Lantern and the three powerful women followed in behind.

The tavern was Elysia's most high-end alehouse. With swanky, onyx leather booths curving into private half-circles, gold-plated ceilings with intricate designs, and luxurious crystalline chandeliers hanging in a single row through the center, the tavern remained the most favored establishment for the wealthy. The affluent spent many evenings gathered around the gold-rimmed marble tables dispersed throughout the main room, smoking opium and drinking the finest wines.

The large, arched windows allowed in heaps of natural light, and the last of the setting sunlight drifted in through the glass openings, illuminating the bar and reflecting off the hundreds of bottles lining the shelves behind the barkeep.

"Oh, how *divine*," Neith purred.

Both Asha and Kaira followed the Spinner's gaze as she tracked a man walking across the room, heading towards the back—Iskander.

Asha caught a flash of intrigue flicker in Kaira's eyes.

"No one told me the Wolf was so... delicious," Neith drawled.

Asha rolled her eyes and scoffed. "He has a name."

"And I'd like to scream it," she replied, the words coated with lust-filled wishes.

Anselem smirked. "Now *that* is a pairing I would love to see who'd make it out alive."

Kaira said nothing as Asha elbowed Anselem in the side and the four of them followed Iskander, disappearing through a solid mahogany door into a private room in the back of the tavern.

"NOT ALL SHADOWS BELONG TO BEASTS. SOME MOVE ON TWO LEGS, CLOAKED IN QUIET SMILES AND SHARPENED BLADES. THE NIGHTSHADE ASSASSINS ARE FEAR MADE FLESH. THEY STRIKE WITH VENOM SWIFTER THAN ANY SHADOWED SERPENT AND VANISH BEFORE THE ECHO OF THEIR DEEDS CAN BE HEARD. MERCY DOES NOT KNOW THEM; LIGHT DOES NOT FIND THEM. AND THOSE WHO CROSS THEIR PATH SELDOM LIVE TO SPEAK THEIR NAMES."
—BLADES BENEATH THE LIGHT: AN OVERVIEW OF THE FORBIDDEN TRADES AND THE MASTERS WHO RULE THEM

CHAPTER

SEVENTEEN

Iskander's head rolled.

He leaned against the back wall, his arms crossed in front of his chest.

Anselem, Asha, and two other women trailing behind the Thurisaz filed into the room, and he forced his spinning mind to settle.

He was drunk.

He'd arrived earlier than expected at The Glass Lantern, and although the tavern was *extremely* different than the typical establishments he frequented, Iskander had always been able to flourish among the wealthy, especially when he found himself surrounded by dozens of women with endless gold and unfulfilled desires for a charming male gaze. He drank, and drank, whispering sweet nothings and empty compliments into the lonely ears of the women as they continued placing glass after glass of ale in front of him, each hopeful the beautiful warrior seated at the bar would choose them as the one he wanted to escort home.

Anselem nodded as he walked through the door, and Iskander inclined his head in acknowledgement of his Commander.

Asha's burning sapphire eyes landed on him next as Anselem stepped to the side, but if she was surprised he'd been able to make it to Elysia in such a short time, her face showed no indication.

But the burning eyes and the familiar impact of power that filled the room when the Thurisaz entered were not what cleared Iskander's drunken stare. What sobered him, what ripped him so violently from the hazed filter of his mind, was the golden eyes of the Amarok warrior that filed into the room directly after.

Her eyes looked as if all the gold that had birthed the Gilded Castle was poured into them; a gold so rich and brilliant it was as if she held the sun in her soul and her eyes were the window through which it shone.

She was the most beautiful woman he had ever seen.

Her long, dark hair was twisted into dozens of braids, all wrapped together atop her head and cascading down from the leather strap tying the strands together. Iskander's gaze, pulled from the lure of her eyes, landed on her lips, beautifully set on her deep, rich skin. Light grey Amarok leathers hugged her curves, and a stitched insignia—the Skull of the Elysian Vice—was sewn onto her shoulder.

A quiet, but powerful voice broke through Iskander's enchantment. "Commander."

Anselem nodded towards the men lining the wall beside the General.

Kage and Sacha had been waiting inside the Mount when Iskander rolled into the room. His brothers hadn't changed much since the last time he had seen them.

Kage's eyes looked a little more tired, and his dark hair was slightly longer. Sacha's deeply tanned skin looked a little darker from the countless hours he spent in the open water, and his usually clean-shaven face sported a light shadow of stubble, but his hair remained the same as the last time Iskander had seen the Pontos—cut short, all the way to the skin.

The three warriors exchanged quick pleasantries, attempting to brush off the tenseness among them after many months apart. It was the first time the group had gathered since Montu. Since Math.

The Mount had not changed much either in the last few years. Deep oak bookshelves still lined the back wall, filled with bound journals, and forest green paper covered the three remaining sides. Even the ornate, opulent chandelier hanging above the center table looked untouched, its burnished gold metal still perfectly polished. The runes carved into the baseboards were undisturbed, and Iskander wondered if there had not been a single soul who had entered the space since they last gathered.

Sacha, standing on the opposite side of the large oak table, was the next to speak. His soft voice was practical and serious as he relayed, "Einar is on an assignment near Peitho."

Peitho was one of the kingdoms south of the Straight, in the southernmost hemisphere of Darnella. It would have taken the Pontos at least two weeks to make the journey to Elysia.

Anselem nodded in understanding and sucked in a deep breath. Kage went still beside him, and he knew the Soturi had read his Commander's mind. The two warriors exchanged a glance, and Iskander could see Anselem was aware that the Examiner now knew Mathieson was still alive.

"Is it true?" he breathed, his voice unsteady and weak, uncharacteristically different from the unemotional exterior he always displayed.

"Yes," Anselem replied and turned to Sacha. The Commander caught the warriors up to speed, detailing all the events that had unfolded over the last several days.

Kage and Sacha remained silent, their faces unreadable. As he finished explaining what had occurred, Sacha's ocean-blue eyes drifted over to Asha. His stone-cold expression softened, and a soft smile appeared on his angular face.

"It's nice to finally meet you."

Asha's sapphire eyes, the same ones that matched Mathieson's, brightened, and a soft smile curled on her lips.

"This is the first pleasant introduction I have had with a Septant warrior. It's nice to know some of you brutes are capable of propriety."

Sacha raised his brows, and his eyes darted between Anselem, Iskander, and Kage.

Kage held up his hands innocently. "Don't include me in that bunch. Asha and I have had nothing but amiable interactions."

Asha laughed softly. "I suppose that is true." Asha's smile did not meet her eyes, and the brightness burning within them darkened the slightest bit. Iskander saw the flicker of sorrow that passed over Kage's face as he glanced down at the smoky ribbons etched into her skin. He still had no idea what had happened to the girl, or where the dozens of scars and tattoos wrapping around her arms had come from, but he was certain Kage knew something about the person who had delivered them.

"Do I even want to know what the two of you did?" Sacha interjected, looking between the Commander and Iskander.

Anselem smirked, glancing at Asha. "You'll learn quickly that she can sometimes be a stubborn pain in the ass."

Asha glared at him with narrowed eyes. "And I'm sure you already know, he is *always* a pain in the ass."

Kage suppressed a grin, and Sacha's eyes went wide, shocked by the audacious reply of the Soturi. He turned his surprised gaze over to the General. "And why was your introduction so unpleasant?"

Iskander smirked, and from the corner of his eye, he saw Kage's face go pale.

"You tried to kill her?!"

Iskander shrugged and flashed a grin. "Water under the bridge, right, Ash?"

When he glanced over to the Soturi, Asha rolled her eyes at him, and beside her, the golden-eyed woman had her fists clenched at her side.

"What is wrong with you, Blaidd?" Kage asked, clearly seeing the memories of the scene within his mind.

"I'm not sure we have enough time to start down that long list," Asha answered.

The Amarok beside her smirked.

"You adore me," Iskander countered, flashing a swaggering smile that rivaled Asha's.

"I'm fairly certain you say that to every woman," Asha replied, "and I highly doubt every woman in the realm adores you, *General*."

She said his title like it was an insult. But under the flowing annoyance and the stinging bite in her voice, he could hear the faintest hint of a teasing tone.

He laughed. "I don't need every woman in the realm to adore me, Kappi. Just the ones I want." He winked at the Thurisaz.

She rolled her eyes, but he could see the faintest bit of light reenter the burning sapphire.

"Are you two done?" a sultry voice interrupted, dragging Iskander's gaze over to the dark-haired woman.

He had learned very little of the Spinner over the years, but from the Commander's rarely shared insights, Iskander had gathered enough information to know he did not trust her.

Neith had found Anselem several years back in an amoral place south of the Straight. He had never asked what questionable mission the Commander had been on to garner a visit to a land wicked enough to house the dark magic billowing inside of her, a Darkness vastly different from his own, and Iskander was not sure he ever wished to discover why the warrior had been sent.

What he did know was that Neith possessed a magic capable of spinning and shaping the threads of battle, offering insightful wisdom and sagacious strategies for the Septant to utilize for gaining an advantage over their enemies.

But just the same as all dark-hearted creatures, the Spinner always required a price for her knowledge, and Iskander could only imagine the hefty fee she had demanded for this meeting.

He supposed that was the greatest difference in the darkness which ruled his mind and the shadows that filled the Spinner's soul—even in the raging dark that permeated his veins, Iskander had always held on to a small inkling of Light. A shining droplet of humanity that survived in the wrathful sea of his darkness. But the Spinner—her soul harbored nothing but blackness.

He never discovered the motivation behind the Spinner's choice to help the warriors, but he was certain her intentions were singularly self-serving, even if he had never been able to find any evidence to support his beliefs.

She wasn't an Oracle. Anselem had quelled those inquiries the first time he brought the Septant wisdom from one of his meetings with Neith, explaining the Spinner had never once claimed to possess prophetic insights into the future. She merely told the Commander her magic allowed her to give advice on war, and she was able to spin the threads of battle in particular directions. But unfortunately, she had no way of knowing what the outcome would be.

Iskander remembered seeing the disappointed faces of his brothers, hopeful for the ultimate advantage in war—the visions of a prophet. But he also remembered rolling his eyes at the sanguine looks that disappeared from the warriors' faces when they realized the advantage they had desired most would not be met by the minimally insightful words of the Spinner.

Mathieson had called him a cynic, claiming he never held on to any hope for a better future. Iskander had simply scoffed, knowing that the magic of an Oracle had not been granted to a single inhabitant of Darnella since the time of the First Kings, many millennia ago.

He wasn't a cynic. He was a realist.

Anselem sighed, huffing out an irritated breath, and introduced the Spinner, as if the dark magic stirring within her wasn't enough of a cautionary indication.

"And this is Kaira," he revealed, motioning to the breathtaking Amarok. She nodded to the group, and one of her twisted braids fell in front of her shoulder. She brushed it behind her back with delicate fingers.

Kaira.

Something shifting inside the General. The faintest slip of the veil around his cold, dark heart.

The Commander claimed the attention of the room as he looked to each of the gathered warriors, his eyes landing last on Asha. He smiled down at the Thurisaz, a light filling his eyes that Iskander had not seen in his brother for a long time, and declared, "We are going to break Mathieson out of the Midnight Castle."

Silence filled the room. Deafening silence.

Anselem broke his gaze from the Soturi, meeting the warning looks from Kage and Sacha. The Commander's body stiffened.

"What is it?"

Sacha remained quiet—the undeclared arbitrator of the group. Iskander also stayed silent, his position and support already having been voiced to Anselem in Lorca.

Everyone's eyes turned to Kage, who bared the weight of the warriors' stares with resolute poise.

"How are we supposed to break him out when we are not fully operational? Last time we had all seven of us and—"

"This is not last time," Anselem said, cutting him off. His voice was stern and strong, the unwavering voice of the Commander.

Kage nodded, assuredly reading whatever thoughts were crossing through Anselem's mind.

The uninvited voice of the Spinner filled the room again. "I would not have thought Zindel would be the uncooperative one. He seems so... submissive."

There were very few times anyone used Kage's first name. It was an unspoken understanding in the unit that the Soturi loathed his first name, and Anselem had always made a point to respect his wishes.

Kage's jaw flexed. Shadows coiled around Iskander's hands. Neith's eyes drifted down to the smoky darkness encircling his arms. She smirked and rolled her eyes in dismissal, as if the roaring darkness in his veins could not touch her. Anselem flexed his hands, and Iskander knew the Spinner was testing the very last bit of patience the Commander possessed.

"Are you two willing to join us?" Anselem asked, motioning to Asha and the Amarok beside him. Kage and Sacha glanced at Iskander, and he nodded, confirming he was already on board.

Sacha was the first to speak. "Of course I will join."

Anselem turned his attention to Kage. The Examiner

studied him for a long time, as if an unspoken conversation was taking place between the two warriors.

Kage's face looked strained, as though he was fighting an internal war.

"You know I would do anything to get him back," he stated simply. "But someone will need to stay to cover for your absence. Leadership has already started asking questions about Raynor," he continued, glancing over to Asha. "And soon enough, they will begin asking questions about you as well, Ans. The last thing we need is for them to command her back to the fort."

Iskander glanced down at the Brand burned into Asha's wrist. The *E* had been seared with powerfully woven magic that was capable of forcing every warrior and soldier to remain loyal to the Council—as well as its commanded summons.

"If one of the Vices—or Dominions forbid, one of the Satraps themselves—summon her," Kage continued, "there's nothing I can do. But if I can run interference, possibly listen in to some of lower Leadership's conversations..."

His words trailed off, but the group knew the Transferent was speaking of committing high treason—not only by listening in on the confidential conversations and thoughts of lower Leadership, but also by using his Kratos to do so.

It was one of the most important rules established by the Council and subsequently reinforced by decree of the Perseisian King when he reordered the military. No soldier or warrior was permitted to utilize their powers against any members of Leadership, with specific emphasis placed upon the Council and the Crown. Breaking the established edict was punishable by Death.

Iskander had always wondered if the iron bands fixed onto the power-wielding children were simply another way for the Council to gain control over the devastating magic running through their veins until Leadership had enough years of influence and indoctrination to convince the bonded soldiers to never utilize their gifts on the ones who had enslaved them.

Anselem nodded, his mind beginning to race through viable options.

"If I stay, I can buy the two of you a few days. Maybe three or four. It should be enough time for you to get to Montu before they notice you're missing."

The rest of his implications went unsaid, but the group could read between the lines. Kage would do whatever he needed in order to buy them enough time to rescue Math before the warriors were reported missing, likely notifying the ones in Leadership closely intertwined with the Council.

He would play whatever part he needed for Mathieson—to save the brother he thought was forever lost.

"Two firebirds won't be enough," Sacha said. "And four days isn't enough time for me and Tasi to swim to Montu."

Anselem pursed his lips. If they were only able to take two firebirds, then Iskander was the only other warrior who would be able to go. They would need a space on one of the phoenixes to bring back Math.

"Can it be done with three of us?" Anselem asked, turning to Neith.

The Spinner went still, her foxlike eyes going dark. Even the whites had been filled with black. A ripple of magic filled the room. It felt odious and other, as if the Dark magic inside her veins was never intended to exist in their realm. The whites of her eyes returned, and the glossy haze that coated her vision receded. She shook her head.

"No matter how I spin the threads, I cannot find a way for you to recover him with only three warriors inside the castle."

The Commander and the Spinner discussed options and

various approaches, swapping back and forth between the common tongue and Elysian. Each plan Anselem threw her way, the Spinner would shake her head and confirm her initial evaluation—there was no way to save Mathieson with only three warriors. No matter how powerful the trio might be.

"Four?" he asked. His voice was steady, but Iskander caught the trace of desperation that swept over the word.

Neith's eyes glazed over once more, but she quickly returned from whatever dark place she visited after a very short assessment.

She nodded. "It will not be easy, but it is possible."

Anselem nodded, and Asha's burning eyes flicked over to him. When he did not meet her stare, Iskander knew there were ideas wrapped in atonement running through his brother's mind. Iskander's stomach crawled into his throat.

Spinning on her heels, Neith turned towards the exit. "I have another obligation I need to tend to," she announced. "You know where to find me if you need me."

Before heading to the door, Neith muttered something in Elysian to the Commander, her tone convicting and persuasive. Iskander only understood a few of the words, catching the tail end of her hushed whispers: "If you only have three, and you stay in his place, you will be able to get him out."

Ice-cold darkness ripped through Iskander's body. Shadows filled the space around him. "I don't even speak your language, and I know that sounds like bullshit," Iskander barked, breaking his long-lasting silence.

From the corner of his gaze, he saw a soft smile appear on the warrior with the piercing gold eyes.

The Spinner whipped her head towards him and looked him up and down, her eyes devouring him like he would be her next meal. Her stare lingered on his moonlit irises, a flicker of recognition surfacing, as if she had seen the silver pools once before and was trying to place the familiarity. Her dark eyes brightened with an unknown awareness, realization fluttering through the onyx, and a wicked smile unfurled across her lips. "And your name, wolfling?" Her voice was honeyed, wrapped with a sweet venom that threatened death.

He stared back into her foxlike eyes, his face set in its typical, harsh expression. "Iskander." His voice was low and husky. He slowly trailed his eyes down her curves, taking in every inch of her body, letting her watch.

She only blinked in response, her face showing no emotion, no intrigue. She turned on her heels once more and dismissively sauntered towards the door.

As she walked, he watched the sensual sway of her hips. His eyes darkened as she neared the exit, and the corner of his mouth twitched upward as he called over to her baldly, "And I'll make sure it's loud when you're screaming it."

Neith stopped dead in her tracks. Asha, Anselem, and the others went utterly still, their gazes shifting between the two masters of darkness.

A fraction of a moment passed before Neith glanced back, locking eyes with him. His face was schooled into a predatory smirk—the Wolf incarnate.

A wicked grin grew on Neith's face as the words she had used earlier in the evening settled in her mind. Then she drawled, "Just be warned, wolfling—I scratch and bite." She flashed her teeth at him in a taunting smile before turning back towards the door.

Iskander's growl carried through the room. "You'll moan and beg too," he promised.

Her eyes flashed once more, a libidinous twinkle sparking through them, before she crossed the threshold and disappeared into the tavern.

Iskander had no intentions of tangling with the Spinner,

but she didn't need to know that. He could play her games—flirt, taunt—until he had her wrapped around his finger. Until she truly did fall on her knees and beg him to take her to his bed. He was sincere in that promise; it had happened plenty of times before when he had played this sort of game—the begging.

And, if he was honest with himself, Iskander had ended up taking a lot of them to bed. But not her—not Neith. He would most definitely *not* be sharing his bed with the Spinner.

But he would continue to play the game until she gave him the information he needed about Montu.

The General's silver eyes were filled with flecks of onyx, as if the moon had passed through them and left behind a trail of stardust. She had never seen a man so beautiful, so alluring. His notorious reputation with women made a lot more sense now that she had seen the warrior.

He was tall, maybe half an inch taller than Eros, and his jet-black hair fell just above his eyes. It was ruffled, as if he had run his hands through it too many times throughout the day, and the locks looked like the choppy waves of a stormy, midnight sea. She could see the myriad of tattoos covering the exposed part of his arms, wrapping their way up the right side of his neck, stopping just beneath his ear, covered in metal rings. They looked like splintered thorns of darkness, as if night was quite literally running through his veins and had seeped through onto the surface of his skin.

His face looked tired, but beneath the stubble and dark circles, she could see his angular features and strong jawline.

But what Kaira most notably discerned was that, as beautiful as Iskander Blaidd may be, he was every bit as much of an asshole as Asha had described.

Kaira rolled her eyes. Sure, he was handsome, but she would rather pull out her own teeth than sit in a room any longer with such arrogance.

Egotistical prick, she thought.

After Neith slipped from the room, the remaining warriors began to discuss thoughts and strategies from the meeting. Asha pulled Anselem off to the side.

"Do you think you could teach me some Elysian? It would be super helpful in situations like this." There had been too many times when Asha was half lost with Neith's comments, the Spinner swapping back and forth from her native language to the common tongue.

Anselem smiled. "Of course. I would love to."

"Maybe just a handful of useful phrases," Asha added, unsure how much time they would have for practicing.

A crooked smile tugged at the corners of his mouth, and Anselem answered her, purring something in Elysian.

Her brows raised. "What does that mean?"

He leaned in close.

"Get on your knees." He winked. "I know how often you like to think about the sight of me kneeling before you."

Asha's face went red, and a wide smirk broke across her face. The phrase brought her back to the brazen comment she made in The Golden Sail months before.

She leaned in, her lips grazing his ear. "That one will be *extremely* useful."

As she pulled away, she could see the titillating twinkle in Anselem's eyes, and her entire body went warm. His expression mirrored the wide smile resting on her face as he added, "Only for you, Seven. You're the only one who could ever bring me to my knees."

Asha stared at him for a long moment, losing herself in the emerald seas. She could read every unspoken thought that waded in the deep green, and that was the moment she knew. Anselem Eros, legendary Commander of the Septant, would kneel for no one. No ruler. No crown. No converging enemy forces. But as she gazed deeper into his electric eyes, she knew he would kneel for her.

Kaira appeared by Asha's side, bringing Asha and Anselem back to the present. The Amarok gave her a look of sincere apology as she murmured, "Sorry to interrupt, but can I borrow Ash for a minute?"

Anselem smiled. "Of course. I need to go discuss some strategies with Blaidd." He gave Asha a wink and ambled over to the other side of the room towards the General.

Kaira raised her brows. "You are absolutely going to catch me up on everything that has happened with *that* in the last week."

Asha rolled her eyes and laughed. "So, what is your brilliant plan, Kai?"

Kaira opened her mouth to dismiss the compliment, but one stern look from Asha had her swallowing the denial. "What if we brought in more warriors?"

Asha gave her a contemplative look. "Who?"

"Jeremiah is stationed here, isn't he?"

Asha's eyes brightened, and she nodded. "Varrick and Ronin went to Takama and Lorca, but Jer said he was going to be stationed here."

"I think we need him since Kage can't go."

Asha nodded her head in agreement and turned to the rest of the warriors. "We need another Soturi."

She looked at Anselem, and without fully understanding how he had done it in Neith's home, she looked deep within his eyes and attempted to say *Jeremiah*.

Anselem's face remained unmoved, carved into the stone mask of the Commander. But just before she turned her eyes away, she saw the smallest nod of his head, and his emerald-green eyes brightened.

"The Septant does not elicit help from outsiders," Iskander growled.

Kaira scoffed. "Clearly, that isn't true if we are here." She waved her hand between herself and Asha.

Iskander's moondust eyes narrowed, and a darkness began to fill the silver.

Asha took a step towards the door, and Kaira mirrored her movement as the Soturi called over her shoulder, "We will be back shortly!"

A snarl erupted from Iskander's mouth as he barked back, "We. Don't. Need. Any. Help."

Kaira laughed, continuing towards the exit. "They say women are considered fragile, but I've never seen anything as easily wounded as a man's ego."

Asha looped her arm through Kaira's. "Gods, I adore you."

Asha flashed Iskander that swaggering smile that grated down his spine. Both women were laughing as they left the Mount.

Anselem chuckled. "And I had wondered who would make it out alive between you and Neith. Maybe I should have put my gold on Kaira."

Iskander was still standing in the middle of the room, dumbfounded. No woman had ever spoken to him like that before, besides maybe Asha. Certainly, never an Amarok warrior.

He managed to collect himself long enough to flash a

glare at Anselem.

The Commander shook his head. "I'm going to get us all a round of drinks. Gods know we need one."

Kage and Sacha nodded in agreement, offering to help Anselem bring back the glasses.

The three warriors made for the door, and Kage and Sacha quickly slipped into the tavern.

Before Anselem crossed the threshold, he looked back at his brother. "Don't even think about it, Blaidd."

"Think about what?" he snarled.

Anselem gave him a warning glare. "I'm serious, Iskander. Don't." Annoyance raked down Iskander's spine. Sometimes, he hated how well his brother could read his intentions.

He flashed a grin to mask the irritation. "What? Scared I'm going to make Asha's little friend fall in love and she's going to get hurt?"

Anselem looked at his brother for a long moment before he answered, "No. I'm afraid you will."

And with those parting words, Anselem disappeared into the chaos of the noisy tavern.

Iskander sat down at the table in the corner of the Mount, laughing—howling—at the idea.

Him? Fall in love? The concept was hilarious.

"POWER IN THE SOUTHERN KINGDOMS IS NOT BOUND BY A LAW OR LINEAGE. IT IS SHAPED BY
CHAOS AND CUSTOM. SOME THRONES CHOOSE TO FOLLOW THE RIGHTS OF OLD BLOODLINES,
BUT MOST ARE WON BY BLADE, STOLEN THROUGH BETRAYAL, OR GRANTED BY THE FICKLE
WILL OF THE MASSES. EACH KINGDOM CLINGS TO ITS OWN TRADITIONS. SOME CROWN THE
STRONGEST, OTHERS THE MOST BELOVED, AND A RARE FEW THE RIGHTFUL HEIR. BUT WHAT
UNITES THEM IS NOT ORDER; IT IS THE INSTABILITY OF THEIR RULE. AND IN THE SOUTHERN
LANDS, MADNESS REIGNS MORE FAITHFULLY THAN ANY CROWN."
– PAGE 72 OF THE COMPLETE GEOGRAPHICAL ARCHIVES OF DARNELLA: VOLUME II

CHAPTER

EIGHTEEN

Asha and Kaira ran—sprinted—back to the Elysian Fort.
Breathless, they reached the glass gates Asha had stood before mere hours earlier. She knocked, and a different Kappi
cadet opened the towering doors. When she asked him to retrieve Corporal Greystone, the cadet gave his apologies but
explained that it was not protocol for him to honor requests
without proper identification papers.

Kaira's face went blank, clearly understanding Asha
would not be able to give her identity to the guards to keep
on record.

"They won't let me into the Soturi quarters," she whispered to Asha under her breath, low enough to ensure the
Kappi could not hear.

Asha sighed, racking her brain for an idea. It wouldn't
help for Kaira to go in if she were unable to access the Soturi
quarters to find Jeremiah.

"Fine," she replied to the gate guard. "Then give my
message to Cathan and tell him the one whom he wished to

meet for so long is here."

The Kappi's dark eyes flared wide, and he swiftly nodded, closing the gate and disappearing beyond the glass.

They waited for a few minutes in silence. Kaira's eyes burned into Asha. She gave her friend a glance that silently said it was not the place for an explanation. Kaira nodded, and the two warriors waited with eager expectancy.

Moments later, the glass gates cracked open, and the old man with white hair and honey-brown skin stepped out.

He walked over to Asha, glancing briefly at Kaira, and settled his grey eyes on the Soturi. His ancient, gravelly voice was low, but it carried a powerful strength within it as he remarked, "You have no place summoning me."

"And yet here you are," she replied, her voice even.

The Overseer studied her, and she did not waver as she held his intense gaze.

"Bring him home."

Asha nodded, her heart full of promise. The Overseer raised his wrinkled hand to the side of his head, curling his fingers towards his palm once, as if giving a directive for action. As soon as the Overseer moved, the gates opened, and out walked a tall, lean warrior with golden-brown hair and tawny eyes.

A wide smile broke over Asha's face as he strolled down the stone path.

She broke her gaze from Jeremiah long enough to look back at the Overseer. "Thank you."

He nodded once and turned, heading back inside the glass fort.

As Jeremiah reached the two warriors, Asha threw her arms around him, and he wrapped his own around her. He gave a swift hug to Kaira once they broke from their embrace, and then he looked at the two warriors and asked, "So, are you going to tell me what's going on?"

❖ ❖ ❖

The three warriors ran back to the Mount, with Asha and Kaira attempting to fill Jeremiah in between ragged breaths. By the time they reached the tavern, he understood the most important parts—that Mathieson was still alive, they were going to break him out of the Midnight Castle, and she needed him and Khalfani to make it happen.

Without hesitation, Jeremiah agreed to go with them to Montu, and before they entered the tavern, he grabbed Asha once more, squeezing her so tightly she knew how happy he was that Mathieson was alive.

When he let her go, she looked up at him—the brother she had found and loved by choice—and smiled. "Thank you."

Jeremiah returned her smile, his tawny eyes bright with excitement, and replied, "Always, Ash."

Iskander's voice, full of irritation, welcomed the trio as they walked back into the Mount. "I'm not sure why we need to wait for the princesses to make a final decision on what we are going to do."

Asha entered the room first and replied to the General with an equal amount of bite in her tone, "Because you know damn well you need me to pull this plan off."

Kaira sauntered in close behind and added, "And I meant it when I said more Soturi warriors couldn't hurt."

Jeremiah strolled into the room last, nodding at Anselem and Kage, who both returned his greeting.

Iskander's eyes went wide. "Why the *Hells* is Eirikr Balthasar with you?"

Everyone in the room went still, and their gazes whipped back and forth between Jeremiah and Iskander. The excitement stirring in Asha's stomach went sour.

"What?" Jeremiah asked, bewilderment filling his voice.

"You're Eirikr Balthasar, Crown Prince of Perseis."

Jeremiah's face was blank, and he blinked. "Who in the Seven Hells is this guy, and what is he talking about?" Jeremiah asked, turning to Asha.

Asha, for once, was at a loss for words, confusion written all over her face. She stared at Jeremiah until a slow Darkness began to creep into her sapphire eyes.

"Ash, don't."

Fire began to roar inside of her.

Had he lied? This whole time, had he lied to her? Betrayal sliced through her like ice.

"Seven, hear him out." Anselem put a calming hand on her shoulder, but Darkness began to seep inside his own emerald seas.

"Asha, it's me. I have no clue what he is talking about, but I am me. I'm not a crown prince. I'm not the king's son. I'm just me."

Iskander cut in, "You may not be a crown prince, but you are certainly King Balthasar's son."

Asha's burning eyes flashed to the General. "Explain."

"Explain what?" Iskander bit back.

"Why do you keep calling him Eirikr Balthasar?"

"Because he is."

"No. I'm. Not." Jeremiah snarled.

"Ah, look, the puppy has some bite," Iskander mocked.

"If you're going to get a jab at him, at least be creative enough to come up with your own insults, Iskander," Asha fired off. "Plus, he's a Soturi," she added, rolling her eyes, "not an Amarok. So, the dig makes no sense."

"Would you prefer I call him a featherhead?" he sneered.

Asha scoffed, and Iskander simply waved a hand, dismissing her.

Anselem turned to the General, his brotherly tone nowhere to be found as he donned the authoritative voice of the Commander, "Blaidd, stop being an ass and explain yourself."

Iskander huffed a breath and pointed to Jeremiah. "I'm telling you, he looks exactly like the crown prince."

"And when would you have met the prince?" Kaira questioned, breaking her silence on the matter.

A cocky smile spread over his face. "I've been to the Gilded Castle a few times."

She raised a brow, not entirely believing his claim. "And why would *you* have been invited to the castle?"

Iskander leaned forward in his chair, that arrogant smile plastered on his face as he looked Kaira in the eyes. "The queen invited me."

Kaira's face was stone.

Asha glanced over to Anselem, and she let him read every word in her eyes. *He did not.*

He nodded, a humored grin pulling at the corner of his mouth that she could tell he was attempting to keep hidden. *He most certainly did.*

Asha whipped her head back to Iskander. "You had an affair with the queen?!"

Iskander's moondust eyes were still locked on Kaira's as Asha's words filled the room. He slowly pulled them away.

He shrugged. "It was a couple years back."

Asha laughed. "I knew I was going to like you."

"For something other than my dashing good looks?"

Asha rolled her eyes. "Not even in your wildest dreams, Blaidd."

"That's too bad, Ash, because my dreams of you and me are absolutely feral." He smirked once more and winked.

Anselem's body stiffened beside her, and she could see the look of death he shot towards Iskander. She silently brushed the back of his hand with hers, and he turned his eyes away.

Calm down, he's trying to rile up Kaira, not you, Asha said to him silently, in the way only the two of them understood.

I'm not riled up. You'll know when I'm riled up.

Oh, will I? She winked at him and brushed the back of his hand once more with hers as she redirected her attention to Iskander. She could see the blush of red on Anselem's face as she turned.

"Okay, fine. So, you have clearly been to the castle. What does that have to do with the crown prince and Jeremiah? Since I'm assuming the only part of the castle you saw was the inside of Her Majesty's chambers."

"Whoever said we always stayed in her chambers? There are so many places for late-night fun inside a castle."

From the corner of her eye, Asha saw the heat rise in Kaira's cheeks. She rolled her eyes at the General, and he threw her a playful wink.

"Just get to the damn point, Iskander," Anselem scolded. "I'm getting tired of your reminiscing."

"So testy tonight, Ans." Iskander huffed, turning towards the Commander. "I saw the crown prince several times in passing when I was at the castle. And Eirikr Balthasar looked exactly like *him*." He pointed to Jeremiah.

Jeremiah was still, but his face was fixed in an expression of pure confusion.

"Are you sure?" Asha asked, the Darkness starting to creep back in. She saw Kage palm a dagger from the corner of her eye, but he left it sheathed at his waist.

"On my Word."

Asha turned to Jeremiah. "And what do you have to say?"

"He's lying."

Asha could feel a new crack starting to form in her heart, and tears threatened to pool in her eyes.

Not Jer.

"He gave his Word." Her voice was low, cold, broken.

Jeremiah's eyes flashed as he realized the implication. "Well, on *my* Word, I'm telling the truth. I'm not the crown prince."

"That's not how that works, kid," Iskander snipped.

Tears began to swell in Asha's eyes. "How could you?" Her voice cracked on the question.

"Ash, look at me. Look in my eyes. I'm not lying to you." Jeremiah's eyes had filled with tears of their own as he watched his friend's—his family's—fragile heart begin to crack once again.

"Wait." It was Kaira's soft, low voice that broke through the Darkness swarming Asha's mind. Everyone turned to face the Amarok.

"You said you were from Brienza, right?" Kaira asked Jeremiah.

Asha barely remembered all the details of her Tribe; it was a miracle Kaira was able to recall the tidbit of information she had learned only once, months ago, during the first time she met with Valorous. She loved her friend's brilliant mind.

Jeremiah nodded.

Kaira shifted her gaze to Asha. "What if they're both telling the truth?"

Asha wrinkled her brow, and her friend stared intently into her sapphire eyes as she worked through it. Asha's eyes flared, and she had never loved Kaira's mind of steel more. "Holy Hells."

Kaira nodded in response.

Iskander was the first to speak. "Would either of you like to bring the rest of the group up to speed?"

Asha tore her eyes from Kaira's and settled her blazing stare on Jeremiah. "What if you're King Balthasar's stolen heir? The firstborn twin of the crown prince?"

"IT IS WITH UTMOST SADNESS THAT THE KINGDOM OF PERSEIS DECLARES THE CROWN PRINCE TO BE PRESUMED DEAD AND FORMALLY PASSES THE FUTURE INHERITANCE OF THE KINGDOM TO PRINCE EIRIKR BALTHASAR, THE NEWLY APPOINTED HEIR OF THE GOLDEN THRONE." — THE DOCUMENTED ROYAL STATEMENT OF KING VISERYS BALTHASAR OF PERSEIS, IN THE SECOND YEAR OF HIS REIGN

CHAPTER NINETEEN

Everyone in the room stared at Jeremiah.

"That's impossible," he whispered. "The heir was presumed dead decades ago."

"They never found a body," Anselem countered, his eyes locked on the Soturi.

Jeremiah shook his head. "Someone would have noticed. I lived in the same city for Dominions' sakes!"

"When did you bond?" Kaira asked, her voice soft and kind.

"When I was eight."

"So, you lived in Elysia for most of your years then."

Jeremiah nodded, his mind racing behind his tawny eyes.

Asha looked at Anselem.

"It's possible," he said unemotionally.

Jeremiah whipped his head up. "It is *not* possible."

"I'm with the kid," Iskander interjected. "Certainly *someone* would have noticed a boy walking around who looked identical to the crown prince."

Everyone was quiet for a moment.

Kaira was the one to reply. "Not all of us are privy to frequenting the castle, General. How would we know what the crown prince looks like?"

Iskander flashed her a swaggering grin that rivaled Asha's. "Jealous of my time with Her Majesty, Kaira?"

"I'd rather eat glass."

"Can you two shut up for five minutes?" Anselem broke in. He began pacing, his face distressed. He ran his hand through his hair before he headed towards the door.

"Where are you—"

"Just give me a minute," Anselem barked, cutting off Iskander's words.

He threw open the wooden door and stormed into The Glass Lantern, bursting out the front door of the bar and into the night air beyond.

Everyone's eyes landed on Asha. She said nothing, simply turned toward the exit without a word, and followed Anselem out of the tavern.

He had not walked far down the cobblestone street when she silently caught up to him, confused about his abrupt change in temperament. The streets were quiet, with nothing but the distant scuffing of boots against the road several blocks away. He paced back and forth in the narrow alley, his fists curled by his side. His charming face looked distorted in the dim light, as if deep impressions of angst and worry had been acutely carved onto the surface.

Asha leaned against a nearby wall, standing in silence with crossed arms as she waited. Several minutes passed, and his breathing began to slow.

"Are you going to tell me what that was all about?" Asha asked, glancing back at the cobalt door Anselem had stormed out of.

He stopped a few paces away and turned his gaze towards hers. He took a deep breath. "There is obviously a lot more going on here than we originally thought, Seven."

She did not say anything, prompting him to explain his thoughts.

He huffed out a breath. "This goes well beyond Montu and Kalevala if the King of Perseis and his lost heir," he motioned to Jeremiah sitting inside the door, "are involved."

Her brow crinkled, but her voice was kind as she asked, "And? When has danger ever stopped you?"

"Since now!" he cried, his voice filling with something that resembled panic. His exclamation echoed down the street, reverberating off the walls of the surrounding buildings.

She took a step forward, closing the gap between them. "What's different now?"

He looked deep into her eyes, and his strong, domineering voice emerged no louder than a whisper as he replied, "You."

She blinked. "If it's because of the Blood Oath, Ans..."

He exasperatedly threw his head back. "Gods, Asha. You're so damn brilliant, but sometimes you're so blind. Don't you get it? It has nothing to do with the Blood Oath. It never has."

He looked down at her, deep into the fire burning in her sapphire eyes, and gently placed his hands on either side of her face. She said nothing; she only stared back, waiting for him to finish speaking.

"Not since I saw you at the first Division War," he continued, the words flowing from his mouth like the rapid rush of water from a newly freed dam. "Not since I stood there and watched you take a bow—a godsflaming *bow*—towards Moros while your arrow was still soaring through the skies. That was the first time I felt it. And I told myself for so long that it was just because of the damn Blood Oath. I told myself over and over that it was the only reason I cared. But it wasn't. Because deep down, I always knew I would have picked you. Regardless of any promise I had made before. Regardless of everything that had happened. Regardless of everything that might still happen. I will always choose you. It will always be you. You're not just my seventh reason, you're *the* reason. You are the end of my road. After a lifetime of missed chances and wrong turns, you feel like I'm finally home."

Asha couldn't breathe.

In that moment, every wall she had built up for so many years came crashing down around her, and everything became clear. She recognized that not only had Anselem seen the wars raging within her and still chose to stay, but he chose to stand by her side and fight them with her. She knew he was the one when he walked into her Chaos and never left. And like an all-consuming tidal wave, that was the moment Asha Raynor knew she had found the kind of love that would wreck kingdoms.

The wooden door behind them cracked open, but neither tore their eyes from the other.

"We have a problem," Iskander called over, breaking the silence between them.

For a moment, they did not move. And in that fleeting second of ecstasy, Asha knew of no better feeling. As they looked into one another's eyes, his soul danced with hers to a melody made purely of energy. Their chemistry created a magic unlike any other.

CHAPTER TWENTY

As Eros and Asha reentered the room, there was an apparent shift in the air. A palpable tether suspended between the two, as if something preeminent had occurred in the brief moment the warriors were outside that had perceptibly and earnestly tied them to one another.

Kaira's gold-filled eyes gauged the warriors who stayed behind in the Mount, quietly assessing if they noticed the same shift in the bond between their friends. The lack of respondent change among those gathered indicated no one besides Kaira had noticed the tangible connection emanating from the pair as they reentered the room.

"What's the issue?" Eros growled, his piercing eyes settling on the General. He was livid.

Iskander narrowed his moondust eyes, as much defiance as the loyal warrior would show. Kaira did not know much about the relationships of the Septant, but in the few hours she had spent gathered among them, she had learned the reasoning behind their titles.

Anselem Eros—the Commander. The head and leader

of the renowned warrior group.

Iskander Blaidd's title of General was generated from his highly held position commanding the Amarok's Vanguard, but it also translated to his position as Eros's Second within the Septant.

Zindel Kage, whom Kaira had quickly perceived from the tension that filled the air loathed his first name, earned his name of the Examiner from the unique magic pulsing through his body. No one had stated it out loud, but from the silent conversations that occurred between him and the other warriors, Kaira believed he likely possessed the powerful gifts of a Transferent.

No one had mentioned an accompanying title of the last Septant warrior present, Kaz Sacha, though Kaira knew from her months of research that each of the warriors was given a title upon initiation.

"Tell the princess that she's not going," Iskander seethed, pointing to Kaira. Her eyes shot over to him, but she said nothing, her face schooled into a cutting glare. Eros looked between the two of them.

"And why not?" a challenging voice asked.

Kaira turned to look at Asha. A formidable grimace was planted on the warrior's face.

The words that slipped from Iskander's lips were laced with venom as he replied, "In case you forgot, *Kappi*, you don't make the calls here. He outranks you."

The General nodded towards Eros, whose jaw was flexed at the tone Iskander had used towards Asha.

Asha took a step forward, shadowed flames filling her eyes. "You're right, I'm not in charge. But I do get to make the call of who rides with me, *General*."

Kaira had never known someone so capable of cutting a man so violently. Someone able to wield words themselves as vicious weapons; someone able to take a title, one of honor and respect, and twist it to sound as if it were a foul insult thrown from her lips. A smile tugged at the corner of her mouth. Iskander's perfect jawline tensed.

"You brought me back in here because you couldn't decide who was going with the three of us?" The Commander motioned to the two other Soturi warriors in the room before he turned to Sacha and raised his brows.

The Pontos rolled his eyes and nodded towards Iskander, as if to say, *You know how he can be*.

Watching the exchange, Kaira wondered if Sacha's title was perhaps the Mediator.

Anselem ran his hand through his hair and let out a long exhale.

"We have three firebirds. One will need to have an open place for Math for the return. So, only two can come with us..." the Commander was mumbling to himself as he sorted through the logistics, as if he had to speak out loud because his mind was too clouded with other thoughts. The Commander was quiet for a long moment before looking between Kaira, Iskander, and Sacha.

"Iskander is going."

Asha, still standing beside Eros, did not object, as if she too understood the need for the General's powers and skills.

Anselem shifted his body, turning to face Kaira and Sacha. "Let's hear your arguments."

Kaira's brow furrowed. She had always liked the lieutenant. He was poised and humble, with a lethal edge of confidence that had always intimidated her. But as he stood before the group, in full command of how the events would unfold, she could not help the tidal wave of surprise flittering through her. She had never known a leader who took the opinions of the warriors in his command into consideration. She knew it was likely the trait that had made him into one of the greatest warriors the realm had ever seen.

He nodded to Sacha.

"You know my strengths and my weaknesses without me needing to stand here and list them off, Commander. I am well acquainted with the Midnight Castle. I know how we operate successfully within this unit, and you know better than anyone that I will do whatever is needed to get our brother back."

Eros said nothing, not even a nod of acknowledgement for the warrior's words, before he turned his piercing eyes to Kaira. She did not shrink back from his domineering presence, holding her head high and strong.

Her voice was kind and gentle as she reached into her jacket pocket and pulled out a small, folded paper and replied, "I know why Kalevala kept Mathieson."

Deafening silence filled the Mount.

Asha couldn't help the smile that curled on her lips. Anselem gazed down at her.

You knew?

No, but I can't say I'm surprised.

The smile she expected to cover his face did not appear. He stared at her for a long moment before peeling his eyes back to Kaira.

His voice was strained with vexation, as if he was grappling with the impatience coursing through him, and it was beginning to win the fight. "And you didn't think that would be an essential piece of information to share while Neith was here?"

The smile on Kaira's face was wiped clean off, and her deep tan skin paled as the growling words of the Commander filled the room. Even Iskander refrained from making a snarky comment.

"I didn't trust Neith. I still don't trust her," Kaira declared; her voice filled with an apologetic tone. Every pair of eyes in the room shifted to the Amarok, but she kept her own locked on Anselem.

"That is not your call to make," Iskander growled.

As much as Asha wanted to shove her fist through the General's face a majority of the time, she was glad to know Anselem's Second would profusely and firmly stand against anyone who questioned his Commander—even Kaira.

Fury lingered within his emerald eyes, and she could see he was struggling with maintaining his limitless patience.

"You're right. It wasn't. It's not," Kaira replied, swallowing the pride in her chest that wrongly told her to stand her ground.

Anselem glanced down at Asha.

Hear her out, Ans.

His jaw flexed, but he did not respond. She brushed the back of his hand. The darkness wading in his emerald eyes subsided the slightest bit as he turned back to Kaira.

"You'd better have a Hells of an explanation if you want me to consider taking you with us." His words were sharp, but Kaira did not balk.

She took a deep breath and unfolded the letter. Her golden eyes flashed to Asha in request. She glanced down at the note held in Kaira's hands. She would recognize that paper anywhere; she had stared at pages identical to it for years, memorizing every detail etched onto the parchment. From across the room, Asha could not make out the frantic scribbles and smudged ink lining the page, but she nodded, knowing the warriors in the room could be trusted.

Kaira's eyes shifted back to Anselem. "This is the last page from Mathieson's journals. The very last entry he wrote before you left for Montu."

Iskander went rigid, and shadows swirled at his hands.

"Why do you have that?" he snarled.

Anselem raised a hand towards the General, the only motion necessary to indicate he was aware Kaira possessed the journals. Iskander's shadows recoiled, but his hands remained clenched at his side.

"It took me months to figure it out. His entries were not exactly easy to decipher," Kaira explained. "But when I was summoned earlier at the Fort, I figured there was only one reason why I would be called." She glanced over to Asha. "So, I grabbed this before I left." She lifted the paper in her hand.

She let out a long breath. "I'm sorry I did not say it earlier with the Spinner in the room, but the information I discovered wasn't something I believed you would want others to know."

Kaira's eyes shifted around the room until the golden pools landed on Asha.

Asha took in a deep breath, preparing herself for whatever catastrophic knowledge Kaira was about to reveal.

The Amarok took in a deep breath. "I think Mathieson is an Oracle."

Another wave of unadulterated silence filled the room. The air inside Asha's lungs felt as if it had been ripped from her chest. She felt Anselem's burning gaze burrow into the side of her face, but she did not move her eyes from Kaira's.

"How long have you known?" Anselem questioned. His voice sounded far.

Mocking laughter filled the space in response to the Commander's query, and Iskander's captious voice replied, "You're not seriously considering this, are you?"

Asha continued to stare at Kaira. Anselem shifted his weight beside her.

"It's true," Asha declared, her voice sounding distant.

She had suspected it. For months.

But hearing it voiced—hearing it spoken in a place other than the confines of her mind was strange.

She looked up to meet Anselem's eyes.

How long have you known? he repeated.

Sometimes she truly hated how easily he read her, as if she were an open book with every word in her mind written before him, like detailed notes.

A few months.

Pain filled his eyes.

Why didn't you tell me how you felt?

His question was heavy, loaded with more meaning than solely her feelings surrounding Math. Asha swallowed the lump in her throat. Her heart skipped, and her chest tightened.

I'm sorry. It was never something I planned on keeping from you. I was never certain just from going through his journals, and I figured since he was gone, it didn't really matter...

Even in her own mind, she could hear the rambling of her voice.

"Everyone out," Anselem ordered. A moment passed before anyone moved, then a shuffling of feet made their way to the door.

He glanced over to the departing warriors. "Don't go far," he instructed. Asha did not turn to see them leave, but she heard the creak of the door as the hinges swung open, followed by quiet boots on the floor and a latch locking as the door shut.

"I'm sorry," she whispered.

A smile pulled at the corner of his mouth. "Those are two words you never have to say to me."

Her brow furrowed. "You're not angry?"

Anselem took a step towards her. "Don't you get it, Seven? You could break my heart into tiny pieces, and I would still pick them up and put them back into your hands."

She sucked in a sharp breath.

"But no, I'm not upset."

Her heart beat so loudly against her chest she could hear it ringing in her ears. He took another step towards her, their bodies mere inches from one another. He brushed a loose strand of hair from her face and tucked it behind her ear.

Her voice was low, labored, as she glanced over to the closed door and asked, "Why did you make them leave?" Her mind raced, but blankness filled her thoughts. She struggled to find words when he stood so close. She couldn't find her breath when his presence filled the same space.

"Are you okay?" He asked, his voice gentle, so contrary to the commanding tone he wielded throughout the meeting.

She nodded. "Do you think we're wrong?" she asked. He studied her face, his eyes lingering on her mouth for a long moment.

He shook his head. "It was a possibility I had always considered. Even before Montu."

Asha's eyes widened and her brows raised.

He let out a long sigh. "But after everything happened, I abandoned the belief entirely. It never made sense to me that he would have known how things were going to unfold and still have chosen to go."

Asha nodded in understanding.

"Tell me what you want to do," he murmured.

As the words hit her ears, she realized why he had ordered the others to leave. She realized he would relinquish his control—his command—and do whatever it was that she wished. Choose whoever it was that she asked him to take.

She shook her head. "I trust you, Ans. I trust you to choose who you think is best."

His eyes fell to her lips, and she could feel his heart as it pounded against his chest.

"Thank you," he murmured. Asha said nothing as she looked up at him. She forced herself to breathe. He was beautiful, and she swore his eyes were spellbound, for she always found herself lost within them.

He traced his thumb over her bottom lip, and a soft gasp involuntarily escaped from her throat. Her sapphire eyes glowed, and the burning flames within them settled on his mouth.

She leaned into his touch.

"Not here," he whispered, his body tense with restraint. His voice was wild, as if he were fighting to constrain the desire pulsing inside of him. "Because there are many things I wish to tell you. Many things I want to say before I ever take that step. And here is not the place. Because I make no promises that once my lips meet yours, once your skin is underneath my fingertips, I won't lose myself in the need to make every inch of you mine, Seven." He traced his fingers over the line of her jaw, and her heart thudded loudly in her chest. Tingles washed down her back.

She had wanted his mouth on hers for months. She had told herself for so long that he did not care, that it was simply a mutual attraction between them, harmless banter, but as she looked into his eyes, inches from hers, she knew he meant every word. She knew he wanted to savor the moment.

A knock thumped against the door. Anselem huffed out a laugh and shook his head. "Impatient children," he muttered as he untangled himself from Asha and walked over to the door.

Asha attempted to compose herself as he opened the door, and the warriors piled back in.

The group waited for the Commander to speak.

"What else do you know from his journals?" he asked, looking over to Kaira.

Asha was quiet, her heartbeat still returning to its normal rhythm.

"I think he was moved to a different place in the castle."

"What do you mean?"

Kaira walked over to Anselem, the crinkled paper still clenched in her hands. The Amarok held it out so that both Anselem and Asha could see as she explained, "I will have to go back to the fort to retrieve the rest of the notes, but this line here," she pointed to the scribblings in the center of the page, which read: *Six cages will hold the loyal. Their Word will be all they have to keep them warm.*

"I believe he is referencing the cells the six of you were originally taken to within the Midnight Castle." From the corner of her eye, Asha saw Iskander and Sacha stiffen. "But here," she pointed to the bottom corner of the page. "He talks about a different place—a place he calls Nameless."

Asha ripped the paper from Kaira's hand. In her brother's scribbled writing, printed at the bottom in dark black ink, read: *You will find the answer you need when you reach the crossroads of Where It All Began and the Place Without Name.*

Asha's stomach rolled and her knees buckled. Anselem's steady hands were beneath her arms before she hit the floor.

"He knew," she mumbled, her voice cracking. Jeremiah and Kaira were right by her side as her body began to shake. The three Septant warriors in the room stayed silent.

"He knew that's what I would call it. He knew we would need to know how to get him out." Her voice was so low it was barely audible. She glanced up at Anselem. "He knew you would come for me."

Iskander had no clue what had happened. He had no idea what Nameless meant, or how it related to Asha. He had no clue why the warrior spiraled into a Darkness so gruesome that he was unsure he ever wished to know its origin.

All he knew was that as soon as the words left the lips of the Amarok beside him, his Commander was barking orders.

"Iskander and Kaira are coming with us," Anselem declared, his voice filled with an authoritative tone.

Sacha opened his mouth to protest, but a cutting look from Anselem silenced him. "Unless you can decode the rest of Math's journals in a single day, I suggest you keep your mouth shut."

Sacha nodded, aware that the Amarok before them might have significantly less training and skills, but her mind was a weapon the group could not afford to travel without.

"Kaira, go retrieve the remaining journals you will need. Asha, Jeremiah, and I will get the firebirds and meet you at the Grounds."

Kaira nodded. She grabbed Asha's hand and squeezed it once before exiting the Mount.

The Commander looked to Kage. Not a word was exchanged between the warriors, but from the corner of his eye, Iskander saw the Examiner nod his head and swiftly make his way to the exit, following behind Kaira.

"Iskander," Anselem thundered, calling the General's attention away from the warrior exiting the room. "Go to Cathan, ask him for two travel orbs. Ensure he makes the proper arrangements for Conri and Tala, then meet us at the Grounds. We leave in an hour."

Iskander nodded, but before he exited the secured walls of the Mount, he looked to his brother and asked, "Is anyone going to tell me what in the Seven Hells is going on?"

Anselem looked down at Asha, who had composed herself enough to stand, her shaking hands tucked tightly at her side, then pulled his gaze back to Iskander. "I know how to get Math out."

"Number 7 – Oracle (Divinus): Possesses the precognitive power of prophetic visions and insight."
– The Known Powers and Kratos of Magic Wielders (Abridged Version)
By Instructor C. Bardick

CHAPTER TWENTY-ONE

The Grounds of Sephone sat atop a high hill on the north side of the city, just outside the center of Elysia.

Even under the faint light of the half-moon, Asha could see the radiating beauty of the gardens on the hill. Dozens of silhouetted blue rain wisteria trees surrounded the space, their burgeoning violet petals sprinkling down towards the lush grass beneath the woody branches. Giant veins sprawled across the earth, covered by hundreds of bundled hydrangea bushes shaped into pinwheels of exploding color. A sweet, blossoming scent floated through the warm air, and Asha took in a deep breath, filling her nose with the sprouting aroma of greenery and blooming life.

The Elysians crafted the gardens hundreds of years before to pay homage to Sephone, the Goddess of Spring and Harvest. But, over time, the Grounds—similarly to the Temple of Freyja—had long been abandoned. Cast aside in favor of new gods and goddesses, the citizens believed would help bring restorative hope to a desperate kingdom.

Uriel shifted beside her, his snow-white feathers sparkling in the moonlight. She ran a soothing hand down the side of his neck. Anselem stood several paces away, securing the straps on Kapheria. Her onyx feathers were nearly invisible in the night.

"Where is Jeremiah?" he asked.

Asha glanced over to Khalfani as she stretched out her golden wings. "He said he was stopping to say goodbye to Tahira and then he would come straight here."

Anselem did not reply, his mind too preoccupied with planning. He retightened the same strap again, and Asha figured it was to give his hands something to do while they waited.

"What did you send Iskander to get?" Asha inquired, attempting to find a topic to distract his busy mind.

His head shifted to look at her. "What?"

"What is Iskander picking up?"

Anselem's brow crinkled. "Travel orbs."

"What's that?"

Anselem's hands stopped fidgeting with the straps, and he raised his brows. "Are you trying to distract me, Seven? Or do you truly not know what a travel orb is?"

Asha chewed her bottom lip and shrugged. "Both?"

He smiled, the tenseness in his shoulders abating. "Travel orbs were created for the Amarok and Pontos warriors when they fly. The warriors aren't taught how to create areal orbs with their lesser magic... I suppose most of the warriors never need to know. But for the Septant, some of our missions require us to adapt and conform to the strengths of the others. Cathan keeps the orbs in a vault. We have similar ones for the Soturi warriors to use when we go on sea-faring missions and need to go underwater."

Asha blinked. "Wouldn't it be easier to just learn how to make an aquatic orb?"

Anselem smiled. "Not all of us are gifted with powers of air, land, and sea, Seven."

She was quiet for a long time, searching her mind for another lost question to occupy Anselem's thoughts. "How come Kage couldn't read Balam's thoughts during the mission in Montu?"

Anselem's eyes spread wide with surprise. Whatever he had expected her to say, *that* question was certainly not on the list of possibilities.

His shock turned into a smirk as he replied, "Why don't you ask him yourself?" Anselem nodded to a place behind her, and as she turned her head, heat stung her cheeks.

Kage strolled out from the shadows of the wood line. His face was fixed like stone, unmoving. Asha opened her mouth to apologize, but Kage's words cut her off. "No need. It's a valid question."

She realized now that there were two warriors present who could read her mind, and the idea of her inner thoughts being put on display made her feel bare and exposed.

An uncommon grin curled on Kage's lips. "I'm not going to touch whatever *that* is," he remarked, glancing between Asha and Anselem, clearly referring to the abnormal connection between their minds. His eyes landed back on her. "As for me, put up your shields and stop screaming things in my direction, and I'll do my best not to listen."

She heard a chuckle from Anselem, and her face went hot again. She tried to build up the walls in her mind, but suddenly they seemed extremely feeble, as if the masonry was made of crumbling bricks and decaying mortar.

"To answer your question, Raynor, it takes a lot of focus for me to utilize my power when someone's shields are up."

She felt a scraping in her mind, as if sharp nails were dragging down the side of the bricks. She watched motionlessly as a block fell from the wall, creating a small hole in the barrier.

"All I need is a small space. A tiny crack to slip inside." As she listened, Asha focused on rebuilding the broken part of her mental fort, watching as a tiny tendril of golden light slipped in and out of the broken crack.

"And I try my best not to infiltrate the minds of my brothers." The Examiner took a deep breath. Anselem was silent across the field. "Balam was different, though. His gift of shielding also extended to his mind, and no matter how hard I tried, I was never able to break past his mental walls." Kage was quiet for a long moment. "That's how I couldn't read his thoughts. I had never been able to. And he knew that."

Asha realized that each of the Septant warriors held onto their own pieces of guilt and regret from that day.

Kage's quiet voice filled the air once more as he added, "Iskander is extremely good at blocking out Mind Magic. You should ask him to teach you." A small smile curled on his lips, "But even he still has a difficult time keeping me out if I truly want to find a way in."

"You wish," a cocky voice scolded from the shadows. Iskander stepped into the moonlit grass, and dark coils of smoky night trailed behind him like a tenebrous cloak.

Kage let out a soft chuckle.

"What are those?" Iskander queried, pointing down at the two scrolls rolled up in Kage's hand. The Examiner's smile faded, and he did not reply as he ambled across the grass and handed the curled papers to the Commander.

"Thank you," Anselem said softly.

Kage nodded.

Asha took a step towards Anselem, equally as interested in the papers as Iskander. He slowly unrolled the two scrolls, and Asha conjured a glowing ball of moonfire in her palm, illuminating the etchings on the paper beneath the midnight sky. The moonfire resting in her palm looked less like flames and more like a glimmering orb of light, similar to the strings of glass hung in Luminsend. A knot twisted in her stomach as she studied the pages, taking in the dark markings.

Impatience filled the General's voice as he directed another question towards Anselem, "Don't you think it would be helpful for your Second to be informed of what is going on?"

Kage went still, and Anselem remained quiet as he looked down at Asha. She took a deep breath before meeting his eyes.

It is not my story to tell, Seven. And I will never make you share it if you are not ready.

She looked back down at the scrolls. The first document was filled with a detailed map of the Midnight Castle. With outlines of hallways and stairwells, dozens of rooms, and hidden passageways. She was not sure what bargain Kage had called in to obtain the papers, but she knew the Examiner likely had some unconventional ways of retrieving the information he needed.

The second scroll was the one that scraped against Asha's raw nerves. Her trembling, sweat-slicked fingers gripped the curved paper so tightly, her knuckles went white. Her breath caught in her throat, and as she looked down at the black ink on the page, the last vestiges of color drained from her face. A detailed sketch of the Nameless Place rested in the center of the paper.

She had always wondered how Anselem and Kage found her. How they'd known where she was, and how to reach her. She'd always been too afraid to ask. She did not think she would ever want to know how the Examiner procured the map in the first place.

Asha took a deep breath and looked over to Iskander. A warm, caressing breeze brushed her face, cooling the sweat that had beaded on her brow.

Her voice felt thick as she held out the scroll, handing it to Iskander, and replied, "This is where he took me."

Iskander glanced at the paper, his eyes scouring over the map and the detailed lines of the drawing. His eyes settled on the dark dungeon in the center, far below, in the belly of the earth. He pulled his moondust eyes up from the scroll, and they landed on the scars and marks covering her forearms. He said nothing, but she could see the understanding, the sorrow that filled his eyes. And Asha shared with him her story. Her tale of Darkness and survival, and the friend that saved her in the midst of the endless gloom.

Silver rimmed Iskander's eyes as she spoke of Nina, of the sister he had lost and the friend he was glad she had known.

As she told her story, Jeremiah and Kaira silently returned, but Iskander's gaze never once left the sapphire eyes of the Soturi before him. When she finished her tale, the one filled with broken pieces and ugly truths, Asha realized that she was thankful to know a soul who understood the Darkness raging inside her heart as if it were his own. Another whose power stemmed from a shadowed place she had come to know intimately, a place of chaos and turmoil.

Iskander took her hand in his, a gesture so gentle and kind, Asha almost did not believe him capable of owning it. Power stirred inside her veins, a buzzing hum of recognition as familiar power called to its own.

His bright, silver eyes looked down into her flame-filled blue, and he whispered, "Do not let it harden you. Hold on to the parts of you that make you human. The parts that make you kind." He said the words as if he had great experience in dark places with brutal consequences and knew how they could alter the mind. How they could stifle the light and the joy in life.

kander.

She'd never taken the time to think about what it would
be like to have people in her life who understood the Darkness inside of her. It never seemed important. She never believed she would be around long enough for it to matter.

It was only after she gazed into a pair of emerald-green
eyes and realized she had found home. Only after she stared
into a pair of melted gold eyes and recognized she had found
friendship. Only after she looked into a pair of tawny-brown
eyes and understood she had found family. Only after she
looked into a pair of moondust silver eyes and knew she had
found another with whom to share the dark.

She never thought about what it would be like to be
known by people who understood her Darkness, because she
never believed anyone would be willing to stick around long
enough to help mend her broken soul.

Until now.

She looked to each of the warriors gathered, her gaze
passing from face to face.

The patient eyes of her friends. Her Tribe. Her family.

The warm air stirred as a breeze from the Seidon Sea
brushed past the Grounds.

Her eyes settled back on Iskander's, and she replied,
"Let's start a wildfire."

He grinned, the smile free from the wolfish sneer that
usually sat behind it, and the Darkness floating within his
silver eyes vanished. A brightness she believed he had not

214

known for a long while filled the moondust gaze staring down at her, and she responded with a joy-filled smile of her own.

Iskander took a step back, and Anselem gracefully filled the space before her. He tucked a loose strand of hair behind her ear. A soft smile was perched on his beautiful face, the kind that reached his sea green eyes. The kind he saved for only her.

Then he looked into her burning sapphire and said, *There's no one else with whom I'd want to wreck kingdoms, Wildfire.*

Her heart felt warm. Full. He was the unexpected blessing she had found in the Darkness that had ruled her life. She never expected him or the effect he would have on her heart, her mind, her soul. He was the calming light in the midst of the shadows, the soft patter of raindrops on a quiet morning. The ever-present peace in the middle of her brutal, destructive hurricane.

Kage cleared his throat, and Anselem's smile turned into a teasing smirk. Asha's cheeks burned as she threw her mental shields back up.

Turning to the Examiner, she mumbled, "Sorry."

Kage only shook his head, as if he were a tired parent dealing with a pair of love-drunk teens.

Iskander's snarky voice returned, filling the silent space as he remarked, "Is anyone going to explain what in the Hells that is, or are we all just going to continue pretending it's not happening?"

Asha rolled her eyes. "Good to know your sentimental feelings only last for two minutes." She pulled herself away from Anselem, and he kneeled beside her on the white stones set in the center of the Grounds. He began laying the scrolls out flat on the smooth rocks.

The group squeezed together, circling the papers. Kaira, standing beside Asha, leaned in, her voice low as she sneered, "Hopefully for her Majesty's sake, he realizes that timeframe was *not* a compliment."

Asha forced herself to stifle a laugh, her hand pulling up to her mouth. Iskander opened his mouth to reply, clearly having heard the insult, but before he was able to fire off whatever quick-witted reply he had primed, Anselem cut in, "Don't."

Iskander narrowed his eyes and glanced down at the Commander. He pressed his lips together and left Kaira's insult hanging in the air.

"And you," Anselem continued, glancing over to Kaira, "knock it off." His voice was harsh, authoritative, and Asha quickly realized the patience he held for her did not extend to anyone else.

He looked back down at the papers, a reticent dismissal of the bickering warriors. The unfolded scrolls were stacked on top of one another, the thin sheets overlayed to blend the separate drawings onto a single plane. Asha summoned the moonfire within her palm once again, and Anselem lifted the sprawled papers from the stones, giving her space beneath to place her hand.

Illuminated by the glowing light radiating from Asha's palm, the dark outlines of the Nameless Place rested in the very center of the map of the Midnight Castle.

Asha pressed her hands against her sides to keep still.

Jeremiah's voice broke through the silence as the group stared down at the marked pages. "Does that match up with where she kept you?"

Anselem shook his head and pointed to the south side of the castle's map. "We were here." His finger directed the group's gaze to a small, rectangular outline in the bottom corner. Ice rushed through Asha's veins. She dragged her eyes back up to the middle of the map, to the heart of the

Midnight Castle. The outline of the Nameless Place deeply encircled the central most room of the fortress.

Kaira kept her voice low, her eyes shifting to the bounded space, and asked, "Then what room is that?"

Adumbral shadows coiled beside Iskander. His moondust eyes went dark, and his gaze did not move from the outlined room. His voice was dimmer than night as he whispered, "The Chamber of Reflection."

CHAPTER
TWENTY-TWO

"If you don't loosen your grip, I'll shove you off myself," Anselem snapped. The lashing winds whipped past their faces, leaving rose-colored burn marks on the warriors' cheeks.

Iskander slackened his grasp.

Barely.

Kapheria let out a relieved exhale that was quickly swallowed up by the bitter gusts whisking past.

Iskander had always hated flying. Loathed it.

Perhaps that was the one gift the gods had granted him in his ill-fated life—that he had not bonded to a phoenix.

His arms and legs began to cramp shortly after the group took flight, courtesy of his unyielding, white-knuckled clench on Kapheria, and for the final stretch of the night's journey, his stomach sat inside his throat.

He kept his eyes locked straight ahead on the back of Anselem's head. He sipped in breaths, never entirely able to fill his lungs.

That was the other part of flying he hated—the air always seemed too thin. Even with the travel orbs.

Iskander's fear of flying existed as far back as he could remember. Every time the Septant conducted joint training in the air, he had to hide the shakiness of his hands and the limpness of his legs. It felt like the earth was shuddering beneath him, but he was the only one who felt the quakes.

The fear left a minimally confined space in his mind for any considerations besides one strong, persistent thought that rang through his head as he hung hundreds of feet in the air—one wrong move and he would surely end up in an early grave.

The lone benefit of the spiraling fear was that his entire focus stayed locked on the all-encompassing idea of tumbling through the skies and crashing into the snowy ground below. And that very thought saved him from revisiting the swelling Darkness accompanying the memories of the Chamber of Reflection. Iskander would never forget the time the Dark Queen brought him to the room.

The guards had blindfolded him, an obsidian cloth tied around his moondust eyes, but as they marched him through the castle, he counted every step, noted every turn.

The sentinels didn't even attempt to evade him, to turn down alternate hallways or bring him back towards the cell block deep within the underground—not that Iskander wouldn't have been able to tell, to gauge the circling paths and extra steps; but it was insulting they didn't at least try.

The guards had become sloppy in the months the warriors were held captive.

Or, perhaps, they were simply arrogant. Falsely reassured that the warriors would never find a way to break out.

They had come to retrieve him from his cell, as they did every night, and when they arrived, he figured that evening would be no different.

As always, they marched him up the winding staircase

and down a long, familiar hallway leading to the queen's bedchambers. His body went numb as he neared the onyx door. But before he heard the nauseating creak of the iron hinges swinging open, his weathered boots misstepped, and the sentinels shoved him down an adjacent, unfamiliar hall.

The hair on the back of his neck rose, and the chilled air wafting through the castle turned icy. The darkness in his veins began to stir, but was quickly winked out by the iron shackles fixed around his wrists.

He was guided down several winding halls, marking every step and turn his feet made. The scuffing boots ahead came to a halt, and he heard the rattle of a heavy key cling against steel, followed by a soft click as a metal bolt unlatched. The stirring shadows inside him ceased, as if they could feel the sinister Darkness ahead and recoiled.

A Darkness unlike his own.

His footsteps slowed as the sentinels ushered him towards the unlocked door. They forcefully shoved him inside, and the hinges creaked behind him. The metal door snapped shut.

He saw nothing but blackness.

"Hello, Iskander."

That voice.

Iskander could not wait for the day when his ripping shadows would tear the last breath from the strident lungs that gave the voice life.

The guards untied his blindfold.

Kalevala stood before him, wrapped in a layered, onyx robe made of sheer fabrics. Her deep red lips sat in a malicious smirk.

The air in the room was as cold as the witch's heart.

His silver eyes adjusted to the dimly lit luminos floating high above.

Three walls joined together in pointed corners to

construct the triangular shape of the room, and each side stretched roughly six stories high. The floor was made of dull, grey stone, with three overlapping triangles and a carved eye seated within the center of the lines.

But what made Iskander's darkness recoil was not the blood red hue of the lights suspended in the air, nor was it the bone-chilling air that frosted his skin. It was the hundreds of mirrors fixed against the towering walls. Not an inch of space was left uncovered as dozens of pieces of reflective glass twisted their way around the room, each echoing off one another.

Iskander attempted to swallow a lump in his throat, but his mouth had turned to ash. He left his face unmoved. He willed his body to return to the place of numbness he visited each night.

"Do you know what this room of mine is, Iskander?" Her voice was soft, but Iskander could hear the lingering wickedness in her tone. He could hear the yearning way his name always sounded on her tongue. It made his stomach roll.

He did not move. He did not speak.

Kalevala sauntered around the room, her picture reflecting off the hundreds of mirrors.

A spider's smile twisted on her face. "You know you won't be able to stay silent with me forever."

Five months. He had gone five months without uttering a word to the witch.

He spoke in hushed whispers to his brothers late in the night when they planned their escape, and many times, he talked to himself, just to remember he had a voice. To remember in the numbness, he was alive.

But not Kalevala. He never once spoke a word to the Dark Queen. Not since the first night she had the guards drag him to her bedchambers.

He'd fought. He took two of the sentinels out within a second, ripping out their throats with his bare hands. His shadowed darkness flared, cracking one of the iron shackles before the pain became too much to bear and his power withdrew. He rampaged, taking out guard after guard as they rushed in to help.

But the warrior's storm abruptly ceased when Einar was hauled into the room, a thick iron chain wrapped around his neck.

Kalevala gave him a choice—to join her in bed or watch his friend die.

When Iskander hesitated, the guards yanked the chain, cutting off Einar's air.

With tear-filled eyes, Iskander surrendered to the Dark Queen's wishes. She smiled, knowing she had discovered the warrior's greatest weakness, for Iskander Blaidd would destroy himself to save the ones he loved.

Iskander never fought the guards after that first night.

The vociferous voice broke through his numbed mind. "You won't even ask me why I've brought you here?" Her thin hand stretched out as she gestured to the mirrored room.

Iskander's heartbeat quickened.

He wasn't sure what kind of twisted fantasy the wicked queen had in mind, but he knew he would take no part in it.

He was barely able to disconnect himself enough to make it through each night, but having to watch? Having to have the picture, hundreds of times over, burned into his memory?

Iskander Blaidd was strong in many things, but he was not sure his broken soul was strong enough to endure that. And to spare his brothers, Iskander told himself he would find a way to end his own life before he allowed her to break his soul in a way he knew he would never recover.

Iskander did not move. He did not breathe.

Kalevala's white eyes narrowed. She raised her pale hand, with two fingers lifted, and pointed at Iskander. With a swift flick of her fingers, she motioned to the ground, and Iskander crashed to his knees, bone cracking on the stone floor. Another twist of her wrist, and his shirt tore in half, falling to the icy ground.

The dark, splitting thorns of ink spreading across his paled skin had multiplied, and the reflection of the Marks bounced off one of the cracked mirrors on the wall. His head turned, glancing to the side, and a different glass frame held a picture of his exposed back.

His Septant Mark stretched down the entire right side of his back. It looked so similar to the ones etched onto his brothers' skin, but the details of his Septant wing differed slightly. His tattoo looked as if it had been crafted by the moon, with intricately woven plumes of stardust, all arranged in various constellations ready to take flight through the night sky.

It looked exactly the same as Balam's.

Iskander forced his rising anger down as his shadows eddied within his buried fury. His skin burned as the shadows attempted to force their way from his skin.

A cackle sounded from the corner, and Iskander's eyes cut over to the witch.

"They want out, don't they?" she crooned.

Iskander could feel his twisting shadows withdraw, as if his darkness sensed the queen's piqued interest and wanted nothing more than to distance itself. As if his shadows knew the queen's Darkness did not match his own.

A spidery smile upturned on her crimson lips. "I was hoping we could have a different kind of fun tonight," she purred, stepping towards the warrior.

The pools of silver sitting in Iskander's eyes dimmed, as

if the last of the moonlight inside of his soul had been over-run by Darkness. She placed her chilled fingers under his chin and lifted his eyes to look at her.

"Before I came here, I was never told how enjoyable the men would be."

He jerked his face to the side, shaking off her cold touch.

She let out a harsh laugh and began to creep her way around the room of mirrors once more. "As much fun as an evening of pleasure in here would be, General, unfortunately, I have more paramount needs in mind."

Iskander's eyes focused on the circling queen, her lurking reflections prowling in the background. His face remained unmoved, carved of stone, but his mind awakened, and he shrugged off the numbness with which he had become well acquainted.

"Has your friend told you about this room of mine?"

Iskander's face was blank, but his brows threatened to bunch together.

"No?"

Iskander remained silent.

"None of you have wondered where I've brought Mathieson every day?"

Iskander's only response was a flickering of his eyes as they turned to the queen. The reaction elicited a fiendish grin from Kalevala.

"Or have you wondered, and he simply hasn't told you?"

Iskander did not move, but his mind raced.

He never asked his brother where he was taken during the day. Just as none of the warriors asked Iskander where he went every evening. He figured they understood, assumed they knew not to bring it up.

Iskander knew firsthand how he wished to never revisit his own haunted memories, and he presumed whatever horrors Mathieson endured each day were likely a topic he also did not want to relive each night, forcefully having to explain the dark memories to his brothers.

So, the warrior never asked, and Mathieson never offered.

"I bring him here, to the Chamber of Reflection."

As the name of the room fell from the lips of the Dark Queen, sinister chills rippled down Iskander's spine, as though the voiced title somehow brought the room and its mirrors to life. The stirring darkness inside his veins retreated, plunging far from the surface and deep inside his awaiting well of power, as if his magic knew the baleful nature of the room was an unsafe place for even Iskander's dark shadows to wander.

Kalevala's gaze dropped down to the iron shackles wrapped around Iskander's wrists.

"Do you want me to unlock them?"

The faintest glimmer of hope flashed through Iskander's eyes.

The queen motioned to the guards providing overwatch at the door. One of the men walked over to her side, the key to Iskander's shackles in hand.

A nefarious grin sat upon Kalevala's face as she added, "I only have one proposition for you before I take them off, Iskander."

His gaze drifted up to her red-flecked irises.

The queen twisted a separate key in her hand. It was markedly different from the iron one held by the sentinel. It looked made of marbled obsidian, with two glittering red diamonds resting at the head. The clamping jaws of a feline beast sat beneath the rubies.

Iskander lifted his gaze from the queen's key and up to her black-rimmed eyes.

"Join us," she offered, and her thin arms splayed wide, gesturing to the mirrors around the room. "And your power

can be limitless."

The dark magic of the witch burst from her body, filling the space. It reflected off the mirrors, and the enhancement of the queen's power packed the space around Iskander, until the air felt so thick with wrath-filled magic, he could hardly breathe.

Kalevala dropped her hands, and her magic receded into her body.

Iskander took a breath of untainted air.

"Imagine what we could offer you. What you could become," she purred, stepping towards the warrior.

The dark side of his magic, the portion that strengthened his shadows and enhanced his power, began to eddy, as if the shard of Chaos locked inside of him had been beckoned, as if it had been called home.

Iskander fought against the war raging inside of him, against the different prison he would be shackled in if he were to join the wicked queen and whatever dark forces she belonged to.

And for the first time in half a year, Iskander looked at the Dark Queen, opened his mouth, and growled, "I will let you kill me before I ever bow to a queen who dons a crown studded with the jewels of every innocent life she has ruined."

The white irises of the witch went dark, and black encompassed the wholeness of her eyes. "That can certainly be arranged."

A wolfish grin prowled onto Iskander's face as he replied, "Then I'll drag you back to the Hells with me."

Iskander returned from his memories as the midnight firebird landed gracefully on the snow-covered ground. Anselem slid off the back of the phoenix, and Iskander followed, rolling off the side and planting his feet firmly on the

ground.

His brother looked over at him, concern settling in his eyes. "Want to talk about it?"

Iskander shook his head, and Anselem didn't press him again about the Darkness creeping through his mind.

"In the days following the First War, the Mist was formed. Birthed from the foggy wisps curled at the forest's feet, it harbored the agonous storms stored within the heart of the earth—storms shaped from the loss and deaths of thousands of innocent lives. A vaporous tempest built from sorrow and rage."
— Legends of Darnella: An Extensive Collection of the Fables of Old

CHAPTER

TWENTY-THREE

Velsen was a simple village, with nothing distinguishable to attribute to the small parish, aside from the narrow river that rushed through the center, and the eldritch mist indelibly draped over the trees like a smoky cloak.

Small, modest homes lined each side of the river, with plain exteriors and bleak scenery.

The dullness of the township was one of the things Kaira hated most about it whenever she was forced to return to her haunted home village.

The other was the man who lived in the uninviting grey house down the street.

As they walked along the single path connecting the homes to the handful of shops serving the hamlet, Kaira noticed the river was no longer overflowing with rushing water as she once remembered; instead, the stream had dwindled to a soft trickle, with barely enough depth for the fish to swim upstream. She figured the early arriving winter and the piles of snow that would accompany the frigid winds would fill the river once again, and the rushing waters would return to Velsen soon enough.

A biting wind ripped through the air, and Kaira was unsure if the chill that ran down her back was from the cutting breeze or the sinister house they neared.

A comforting presence appeared at her side, and Asha grabbed her hand, wrapping it in her own.

Kaira's hands shook, and Asha held onto her tighter.

"I am a master of my fear. I am powerful beyond measure. I am unbreakable," Asha whispered.

Kaira nodded and repeated the line to her friend in hushed whispers.

Asha pulled Kaira close to her side as they approached her Uncle's home. She leaned in towards her friend, her voice low and filled with earnestness and love, as she murmured, "Every time you think you are broken, know this: you are never truly breaking. No one can break the sun, Kai. All you are doing is fracturing the glass barrier they tried to hold you in. Don't let anyone enclose you inside that glass; it was never meant to contain you. Instead, wreck it, splinter it into a million pieces, and become who you were always destined to be—the sun, boundless and eminent."

And she was not sure why, but Asha's words brought the smallest bit of comfort to her mind, and as Kaira walked past her broken childhood home, for the first time in her life, she held her head high, and her body did not tremor.

And her friend's hand stayed intertwined with her own, until they made it past the grey house and marched far down the rugged road.

The golden-eyed Amarok shook her head as she descended the crooked stairs, exiting the austere inn and making her way back down to the gathered group on the desolate street.

Iskander huffed out a breath. Another frigid gust of wind brushed down the street, sucking the breath from his lungs.

It was going to be a long night.

"They said they're full," the Amarok replied, pulling her light grey jacket tighter to her chest.

Beside Iskander, Anselem ran his hand through his hair, his face grim and tired.

"Aren't you from here, Kai? Is there no family of yours we can stay with?" the twin replica of the crown prince asked.

Iskander's gaze drifted over to the Amarok, but to his surprise, it was Asha who replied to the Soturi. "We will be fine outside, Jer."

There was a sharpness to her tone, one Iskander had never heard her use with her friend before, that very blatantly relayed to the Soturi that he should drop the question, promptly.

Iskander noticed the rigidity of the Amarok's body, and he swore he saw her hands begin to tremble before she shoved them into her jacket pockets.

Asha glanced at the Commander, and Iskander figured one of their inexplicable, unspoken conversations was taking place.

Iskander drew his moondust eyes back to Kaira, and for the fleeting moment she met his gaze, he saw Darkness wading within her golden pools.

"I might have enough supplies packed on Kapheria to make something work for the night," Anselem offered.

"And I stowed some extra blankets in the packs strapped to Uriel," Asha added.

Iskander said nothing, but he watched silently as the Amarok forced herself back from the Darkness, as if she was diving into the depths of her strength and forcing herself to choose the light. Her gold-filled eyes beamed. "I have a place we can go," she professed softly.

Iskander kept his eyes on the Amarok as Anselem, Asha, and Jeremiah turned their gazes to Kaira.

"You should still grab the blankets and supplies," she added, "but it will be a better option than sleeping in the open."

The warriors nodded, and the group made their way back toward the firebirds resting just outside the village.

After the warriors grabbed the thick blankets and the bread and dried meats Anselem had packed for the journey, Kaira led the group on a short walk further into the Redwoods, away from the sleeping village of Velsen.

As she entered the Mist, Kaira heard the faintest of screams echo in the hazy distance.

The half-filled moon hung brightly in the night sky, making it easy for Kaira to find the way through the trees. But she didn't need the light. This was a path she had walked so many times in her life, she would know the way if she were blind.

She turned north when she reached the tall pine with the bark singed off on its west side, smiling at the familiar sight that had brought her comfort for many years. She threaded her way through the trees for a few more paces until she came to the Olden Oak.

The ancient tree looked much the same as the hundreds of others filling the space, but as the group circled the massive, ruddy base, careful to avoid tripping over the monstrous roots bulging from the lush ground, a forest-green door with a worn, brushed-gold handle greeted the warriors.

Kaira ran her hand over the cool metal knob, and a smile

pulled up at the corners of her full lips. She twisted the knob and gently pulled open the curved door.

She looked down the spiraling stone stairs. The first three steps were illuminated by the hanging moon, but pitch-black darkness swallowed the remaining portion of the stones that plunged into the earth.

A small globe of light appeared beside her, and Kaira's gaze shifted to the warrior. A small ball of moonfire sat in Asha's hand. Kaira let out a relieved breath, unsure how she would have guided the group down the steep stairs without a fire-filled lantern.

She glanced back at the three men behind her. Their eyes were wide, but as another ripping gust of frozen air passed through the forest, not one of the warriors objected to the shelter—no matter how eerie the descending darkness appeared.

"This way," she murmured, her voice quieter than she wished it had been.

Kaira ducked inside the undersized doorway and began her descent into the darkness. The five warriors behind her followed inside the Oak in uninterrupted silence.

Iskander had spent enough years of his life wallowing in endless dark that his shadows unquestionably knew the difference between lightless dwellings that harbored threats and shadowed spaces that welcomed his darkness.

But as he descended the stone staircase, each step brought greater feelings of unease, because for the first time in Iskander Blaidd's life, he was unable to recognize the essence of the darkness surrounding him.

It was neither good nor bad. It was simply and entirely *other*.

As the group descended deeper into the Oak's center, the cold air from up above receded, as if someone or some-*thing* had cast it out. When he reached the bottom of the steps, his feet scuffed against the stone floor, and a mixed aroma of old, earthy smells washed over him.

He swore, for the faintest moment, that he noted the softest hint of lavender in the air, as if the flower had some-how seeped all the way down and into the roots of the Olden Oak.

"Ash, would you mind lighting the lanterns on the walls? There should be a handful with oil in them." Kaira asked softly.

The globe of moonfire resting inside the Thurisaz's hand flashed and shifted into controlled flames of fire.

Slowly and purposefully, Asha sent her magic out, sep-arating the flames from her palms, and lit the half dozen lan-terns hanging in the center of the short hallway.

The corridor led down to a large, open space at the end of the hall. The distant room was faintly lit by the last sus-pended lantern on the far side of the corridor, but the spacious space awaiting the warriors was not what drew the General's attention. It was the Ageless Library that composed the front entryway.

Thousands upon thousands of ancient books and man-uscripts filled the shelves, lining both sides of the narrow space.

Kaira marched ahead, the warriors standing behind her following silently, but Iskander lingered in the front space, his hands running over the spines of the archaic books. Many of the titles were written in the *Language of the Founders*, in characters and symbols he could not comprehend.

From the corner of his eye, Iskander saw a flash of flames appear in the room down the hall, followed by a con-tinuous glow that matched the light in the front space.

Before the General turned away from the shelves, aiming to join the others in the open room, his eyes caught on a leather journal shoved onto the center bookshelf. The spine was written in the ancient language in black hand-scripted letters, and it read: *The Wraiths of War and Ruin.*

Iskander pulled the book from the shelf, tucked it in his jacket, and ambled down the hall.

234

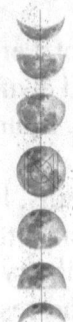

CHAPTER
TWENTY-FOUR

In all his years, Anselem had never witnessed a space filled
with such preternatural energy.

He did not trust the misty air that hung like a choking
cloud over the Redwoods, always skeptical of the tales that
accompanied the mist-filled haze—stories of lost travelers
consumed by hallucination-filled dreams, and disoriented
visitors swallowed up by the salt-scented smog, never to be
seen again.

He blamed the Kindlings and the unorthodox magic
practiced by the *People of the Woods* for the wicked fog that
hung over the Redwoods like a suffocating blanket.

According to the legends, the Mist appeared several
centuries ago, after the Kindlings had erected a new form
of magic—one rumored to be based in Seider Magic—when
the *People of the Woods* discovered their arboreous children
were no longer bonding to magic-releasing creatures.

And ever since the Mist resting over the Redwoods
appeared, the cloud of smog relentlessly haunted the folks
brave enough to venture into the forest's borders. And, over

the centuries, the number of Perseisians willing to voyage through the eerie terrain had dwindled to a scarce amount.

Anselem huffed out a troubled breath as he glanced around the spacious room.

A vast number of lanterns, lit from flames conjured in Asha's hands, covered the smooth stone walls.

Similar to the narrow library the group had just departed, a large array of bookshelves lined the curving granite walls. The shelves in the main room were not packed full like the ones lining the front foyer, and unlike the ancient texts scattered among the stands in the front room, the manuscripts in the main space seemed much newer, mostly all written in the modern language of Perseis.

Two curved openings rested on the side walls, one on each side, and opened to unlit, darkened halls.

Anselem wondered how far the underground space stretched, and who—or *what*—had created the Ageless Library. And more importantly, why did Kaira know of its existence?

Asha, Kaira, and Jeremiah stood in the center of the room, unfolding the blankets the group had brought with them underground. The air was much warmer within the covered earthly space, as if there was a cloak of magic wrapped around the area, warming it from within.

The trio spread the thick, wool coverings out on the stone floor, layering the blankets for added comfort. They needed a good night's rest before making their final flight to Montu the following day, for the group was not entirely sure how combative the conditions would be when they landed.

The two Septant warriors sauntered around the room, as if they were inspecting the space for looming threats.

"Kaira, do you know where these halls lead?" Anselem called from across the room, motioning to one of the unlit halls.

Kaira shook her head. "I never ventured past this room."

The Commander glanced at Iskander, and the General nodded once before making his way over to Anselem's side. The men pulled dual daggers from their waistbands.

"We will be back shortly. Just going to do a quick sweep of the halls to ensure we are alone down here. We can set up a watch rotation when we get back."

Asha nodded, and Anselem pulled one of the hanging lanterns from the wall before the warriors disappeared down the dark passage.

"Not sure I like that guy very much," Jeremiah remarked as he laid out the final set of bedding.

Kaira snickered. "Yeah, well, join the group."

Asha plopped down on one of the blankets, an audible sigh escaping her lips. "Iskander's not that bad once you get to know him."

Kaira's brows raised. "I thought he grated on your very last nerve."

Jeremiah collapsed onto another makeshift cot.

Asha shrugged. "It's complicated."

Kaira was right. From the moment she met Iskander, right after he removed the blade from her throat, his arrogance and the smug way he approached the world truly did grate on her very last nerve.

But when she glimpsed under the rough exterior and the harsh mask he wore for the world, and saw the brokenness—the Darkness—that shaped the warrior into the man before her, her heart softened at the reflection she saw staring back.

A matching image of herself, Darkness, and all. And not because of the Chaos that stirred within both of their veins, but rather for the deep wound from the loss of a gold-hearted woman that had been thrust inside their chests.

"Well, speaking of complicated things…" Kaira prodded, a mischievous smile on her face. "Tell us all about what's going on with you and Eros."

Jeremiah let out a soft chuckle and shook his head.

Asha rolled her eyes. "Later," she promised Kaira, and Jeremiah smiled, a silent thank you for sparing him from an uncomfortable conversation.

"You don't get let off that easily, Jer," Asha added, turning to the Soturi.

He feigned an exaggerated yawn and then laughed.

"How is Tahira?"

Jeremiah's eyes went bright, and a genuine smile stretched over his face. "She is wonderful. It's so nice to be able to see her again."

His words were filled with so much love and happiness that Asha was unable to hold back the smile that spread over her lips.

A twinkle sparkled in his tawny eyes, one Asha had never seen resting upon his face, not even when the warrior sat beside Tahira in The Golden Sail many months before.

"Tell me," she pleaded, excitement entering her voice.

Jeremiah rolled his eyes. "I always hate how you can do that."

Asha smiled widely.

"I got her a ring."

Asha tilted her head to the side and her brows bunched.

Jeremiah and Kaira both let out light chuckles.

"It's a tradition in Elysia," he explained, his smile full of eager excitement. "When a pair marries, the couple exchanges rings."

A rare squeal of excitement escaped from Asha's mouth, and she jumped to her feet and flung her arms around her chosen brother. "I'm going to have a sister!" she exclaimed, nearly knocking Jeremiah over.

A hearty laugh escaped his throat, and he responded, "Well, she has to say yes first, Ash."

Asha pulled herself back upright. "Of course she will, Jer. I'm so happy for you." Genuineness filled every word she spoke, and a warmth spread through her heart, filling some of the cracks with the faintest bit of light.

Kaira had a huge grin on her face as she softly said, "Congratulations."

Jeremiah turned his gaze to the Amarok and replied, "Thanks, Kaira."

"When are you going to ask her?" Asha inquired.

Jeremiah reached into his pocket and pulled out a dainty silver band. Set in the center of the metal was a topaz gemstone, sparkling in the flickering light of the lanterns.

"As soon as we get back," he answered, staring down at the ring in his hand. "I was going to ask her before I met you all at the Grounds, but I didn't want to rush off right after."

Asha nodded, staring down at the light blue gem. "She is going to love it, Jer."

The Soturi lifted his eyes and met the burning sapphire ones burrowing into him—eyes that had held Darkness for so long but were now filled with bits of light and love.

Boots scuffed from the opposing hall Anselem and Iskander had walked down, and the three warriors sitting in the center of the room were on their feet instantly, weapons in hand.

"All clear," the Commander called out as the two Septant warriors reentered the central room.

"The two halls connect and make a long loop," Iskander added.

"No big, scary monsters looming in the shadows?" Asha teased.

Anselem glanced down at the dagger held in her hand

as he sauntered over. A grin tugged on his lips. "Apparently not as many as in here."

Asha grinned and sheathed the blade. "One can never be too cautious, *lieutenant*."

As he approached her side, he leaned in close and whispered, "Don't worry, Seven. The last thing I intend to be with you is cautious. I have far too many untamed things in mind."

He pulled his lips away from her ear and saw a deep red blush on her cheeks, a bright, titillated glimmer in her eyes.

"Iskander," he called, addressing his Second.

The shadow wielder glanced over to the Commander, looking up from the corner where he had placed his bedding.

"Set up a rotation for the night watch. We will be back." Anselem threaded his hand through Asha's and headed towards the unlit, looping hallway.

"Where are we going?" Asha asked, her voice low in the stretching darkness. She held a ball of moonfire in her free hand, the glowing light leading the way.

"Not much further," Anselem replied, a tinge of playfulness in his tone.

As they walked, the light filling the hallway expanded, and Asha realized the moonlight igniting the space was not a result of the globe shining in her hand, but from beams pouring in from above.

Asha let the radiating ball in her hand dim until the narrow hall was only illuminated by the night sky overhead.

A small gasp escaped Asha's mouth.

The sight was breathtaking.

A wide gap rested in the ceiling, stretching several stories high, and opened into a broad break in the Redwood trees, revealing star-dusted skies.

Hues of purple and gold swirled between the collection of closely packed stars that were swept across the open sky. Hundreds of bright specks formed together to form a pinwheel in the midnight clouds, with bright washes of color strewn throughout the constellations.

It was beautiful and foreboding all at once, and unlike anything Asha had ever seen in her life.

"Stunning," she whispered, her voice barely leaving her.

"Completely," Anselem replied. But with her own sapphire eyes locked on the skies above, Asha did not see that the gaze of the warrior beside her was not set on the stars above. His eyes were wholly and entirely focused on the woman beside him.

As Asha took in the awe-inspiring heavens overhead, Anselem wandered to her side and turned his eyes upward.

"There are so many things we have left unspoken, so many feelings left to linger quietly in the silent words hung between us," he murmured, pulling Asha's attention to the man beside her.

Anselem broke his eyes away from the stars suspended high in the night sky, turning his full concentration onto Asha. "But I refuse to go into tomorrow, into the unknown peril that lies ahead, and leave what is held between us unvoiced."

Asha did not move; she did not breathe.

He smiled softly, and her heart skipped in her chest. When he spoke again, his accented voice was filled with genuineness and sincerity. "Sometimes I'm not sure you realize how terrifyingly beautiful you are."

He brushed a tender hand down the side of her head. "And I know most people do not see the vulnerable side of you that you keep hidden so well."

His hand caressed her face, his thumb brushing over her

cheek. It was warm and gentle, heating the place where the chilled breeze had nipped at her face. "But I saw it and I loved it quietly. I chose to love you in so many ways that I was unable to show you, so I showed you ever so softly in the silence between my words. You may think no one burns for you, or would die for you," he took in a steady breath, as if the words he spoke were ones he had never been more sure of uttering in his entire life, "know that I have burned quietly for you, and I die for you a little more each day."

Anselem looked into her burning sapphire, his emerald eyes bright in the moonlight, and as he stared into the flames sparking within hers, his gaze did not falter. He was unafraid of the power stirring within the cerulean blue. "Asha, I love you. I am *in* love with you. Today. Tomorrow. Forever. If I lived a thousand years, I would be yours for all of them. If I could love you for a thousand lives, it would still not be enough. The day I met you, I began to forget a life without you. You are not only the love of my life, you are the love of this entire lifetime, and every one I have lived before. Regardless of how many suns may rise and fall, I promise my soul will always find yours, time and time again. You are my home in every life, the love of all my lifetimes. And I am yours. Always. In this heart of mine, you will always hold the space. It will forever be yours, until there is nothing left of me but ash and embers. I will never find another that my heart will beat for. And when the time comes, and Death takes my hand, I will grab onto you with the other, because I intend for our souls to never part ways. And I promise to follow you, into every lifetime."

Tears streamed down her face.

Asha had never before felt so at peace, yet so on fire, all at once, knowing deep in her soul he was who she had waited for her entire life.

She leaned forward, closing the space between them, and

peered up into his emerald eyes. She lifted her lips to meet his, but paused, just inches from his mouth, and breathed, "I love you, Anselem Eros. I am yours, the way the sands belong to the sea, the way the stars belong to the sky. And I promise, as long as this heart of mine still beats, you will never be unloved. Your soul is forever entangled with mine, and I, too, will follow you—into every lifetime."

Silver rimmed his eyes as he looked down at the woman he loved. At the woman he had always loved, even before their souls ever met, even before their names were a whisper among the stars.

Then Anselem leaned in and pressed his lips to hers.

It was unlike any ordinary first kiss.

It was as if the world itself stopped spinning, a brief pause in time when it recognized the collision. It was as if two parts of a single soul had been searching for one another for a million lifetimes, across a million worlds, and after a million new beginnings, two halves of the same soul had finally found each other once again.

And then, they kissed.

CHAPTER TWENTY-FIVE

Anselem fell in love with her soul long before he ever touched her skin. And if that wasn't love, then he was not sure he knew what love was.

But the moment he tasted her lips, her skin, he realized he had never known how truly deprived he'd once been. Her kiss awakened his soul. He never knew a piece of his heart was missing until he found it hidden within her touch.

"Anselem," she breathed, pressing her body against his. His name came out like a plea on her lips, and he was certain he had never heard a more beautiful sound in his life.

That was, until she opened her mouth, inviting him in, and he traced her tongue with his. A soft moan escaped from her lips, and he knew it would be his undoing.

He had never before heard someone's voice and felt his knees sink in. Never heard a poetic string of words pulled together in a way that made his cold heart turn warm. Never tasted bliss on someone's tongue as they spoke. He did not attempt to make sense of it. He was not sure it was possible to even do so.

All he knew was that her moan brushed against the edge of his every weakness, and in that moment, he swore to both himself and the gods of old that if someone asked him what the song of love sounded like, he would have told them *her*.

His hands kissed hymns up her sides. He pulled his lips from hers for a brief moment, and his breath caught in his throat as he looked down at her.

A silent confession lingered in his eyes, an unspoken admission of how long he'd looked for a place to worship and, gods, how she put him on his knees.

Crackles of lightning flashed through the narrow hall. Anselem's hands trailed down Asha's sides, beneath her thighs, and he lifted her in one swift movement. Her legs wrapped naturally around his waist as he pushed her up against the cool, stone wall. He wrapped her hair in his hand and kissed her even deeper, as if he needed her body closer to his, as if he could melt into her touch and it would still not be near enough.

A crackle of simmering lightning snapped down the hall, and Iskander jumped to his feet, his mind not yet having found sleep. He left his makeshift cot crumpled on the ground behind him as he scrambled towards the opening.

"He will absolutely kill you if you interrupt them right now," Kaira called over, her golden gaze piercing Iskander in place.

The General said nothing, but his narrowed stare whipped towards her voice.

"If Ash doesn't do it first," she added, a curtness to her tone.

Jeremiah softly snored between the warriors.

Iskander scoffed. "She can try."

He continued his way towards the dark hall, a long blade held in his hand.

Kaira, sitting against a far wall underneath a dimly lit lantern, barked, "I mean it. They're fine. And Eros seriously will kill you if you interrupt whatever they're in the middle of."

Iskander's boots halted, and Kaira could see the warrior was quickly working through the situation down the hall.

Without a word, the General abruptly turned around and moseyed back to his bedding.

Kaira rolled her eyes and glanced back down at the leather-bound journal in her hands. She could feel the sharp glare of the General burrowing into her from across the room.

She peeked her eyes over the top of the papers.

"What?" she snipped.

Iskander's moondust eyes dropped to the book in her hands. He slowly pulled them back up to meet her golden leer.

"Is that Raynor's journal?" he asked, curiosity filling his tone.

Kaira stared at the warrior for a long time before answering. He had not yet lain back down on his bedding, as if he was waiting for her response before moving again.

She shook her head. "No."

His silver eyes narrowed. "What is it?"

She pulled her stare from the star-filled eyes of the General, and without reply, she returned to her reading.

Not a sentence into the page, the entire room went dark. Kaira felt a strong waft of air pass by her, like a hissing breeze. A moment later, the lights returned, and the swirling shadows that had engulfed the space vanished.

From across the room, Kaira caught a glimpse of the final fading coils of twisted shadows as they returned to Iskander's hands, and with the tendrils followed the book that had been resting in Kaira's lap.

Her stomach dropped.

"What in the Seven Hells!" she growled, crawling to her feet.

Jeremiah rustled on his blanket, but even the bickering barks of hostile warriors could not rouse the sleeping Soturi.

A smug grin pulled at Iskander's mouth as he glanced down at the journal in his shadowed hands.

Kaira wanted to smack the smirk clean off his perfectly hewn face.

She stormed across the room, heat pouring from her ears, and snatched the book from his hands.

"Didn't anyone ever teach you to respect your command?" he snarled.

"Didn't anyone ever teach you to earn it?" she seethed, turning back towards her spot across the room.

The General's scuffing boots were right behind hers as she crossed the open space.

He softly grabbed her wrist, spinning her back around.

Kaira flinched at the unanticipated touch, and her fist instinctively swung towards the General's face. Before she processed what she was doing, her hand brushed past Iskander's jaw.

Luckily, Iskander moved his head at the last moment, as if he had far too much experience with dodging smashing blows. Kaira's knuckles barely grazed his cheek.

She dropped her hand to her side, and Iskander's wide eyes slowly turned back to her.

Kaira knew Darkness was swimming through her veins. She knew Iskander saw it from the shocked look that crossed his face, replacing the initial fury. She shoved the surfacing feelings down, burying them deep inside.

"General..." Kaira began, intending to spew endless apologies, but Iskander's words cut her off before she could finish.

"Don't apologize. I shouldn't have touched you. That was my mistake." There was a knowing glimmer in his eyes—an understanding, as if to say he did not blame her for how she reacted to haunted memories. Did not judge her for how she survived. Did not require an apology for how she chose to repair what someone else had broken.

Surprise poured over Kaira like a devouring tidal wave.

"And it's Iskander," he stated.

Kaira's brows bunched together.

"Call me Iskander," he repeated. His voice was heavy, as if he did not like the title he had earned.

She nodded slowly, unsure how else to respond.

He bent down, picking up the journal she had dropped. "And this," he said, waving the book in his hand, "You can read the *Language of the Founders?*"

Kaira's wide gaze jerked up from the journal to meet his. A sharp inhale flowed through her nose.

It was the first time she had heard someone refer to the language in its proper form. The first time anyone had ever asked her about it.

She dropped her voice low as she replied, "You know the ancient language?"

Iskander shook his head, handing the bound pages back to her. "Unfortunately, I do not."

Kaira's brows crinkled together at the odd response, but she quickly smoothed them back out, forcing her expression into neutrality.

"But you do," he added, glancing down at the ancient characters etched onto the front page.

"Somewhat," she admitted, unsure of the warrior's unusual interest in the language.

Iskander studied Kaira, his eyes shredding through her external facade like a slicing blade. She forced herself not to balk from his daunting gaze.

After a too-long moment of silence, Iskander quietly replied, "Good to know," and turned back towards his cot.

"Good to know?" she challenged, stepping towards him, a revived sense of sureness having reentered her body. Her forceful voice carried through the open space.

Iskander slowly twisted to meet the Amarok.

"What's good to know?" a distant voice chimed through the tense air.

Kaira did not remove her gaze from the General's lustrous eyes. His moondust glare burned into Kaira as he looked down at her with an unnerving sense of disapproval.

"What's good to know?" Asha repeated, coming up beside the Amarok warriors. Eros followed closely behind her.

Iskander pulled his eyes from Kaira and mockingly replied, "She was just enlightening me as to why I shouldn't barrel down the halls when bolts of lightning began cracking through the room."

Red flushed across Kaira's cheeks at the brazenness of his words, but as she looked towards her friend, Kaira was stunned to find no matching flush painted across Asha's face.

Eros wore a proud grin, as if he could not be more honored to stand beside the woman at his side. Asha stepped towards Iskander and glared up at the General.

"I'd be careful with that mocking tone, Iskander; you wouldn't want someone to call you out on the longing haze that fills your eyes every time you look at a certain warrior in the room." Asha cut her eyes over to her friend.

Kaira wished she could evaporate into the discomfited air surrounding her. Or perhaps she would choose to ascend the oak staircase through the next room and let the Mist swallow her whole. Whichever option would more quickly pull her from the awkward nightmare she found herself unwillingly thrust into.

Iskander, ever composed, scoffed, and the dismissive sound somehow stung Kaira's pride even more than the embarrassing flutters that had ripped through her chest moments before. She struggled to keep her face composed.

"Not even in her wildest dreams," he replied, throwing Asha's words from the Mount into the open air like thoughtless waste.

Heat poured through Kaira's body, but the warmth was not founded in embarrassment or shame; it grew from a swelling pool of rage ripping through her.

"Nightmare," she sneered.

The three warriors turned towards her; Iskander's head cocked to the side.

"The only way you'd find me sharing a bed with you would be in a haunting nightmare."

Iskander clenched his jaw, as if Kaira's words hurt more than any others she could have thrown his way. As if he knew too well about disturbing dreams in unwanted beds.

Without another word, he dismissed himself, heading back towards his place on the far side of the room. The two Soturi warriors found cots close beside one another near the opposing wall.

Kaira slumped down into her bedding, tugging the thick, wool blanket up around her legs to block out the bite of the frigid winter air. She pulled the book back out, intent on returning to her reading, but the ancient letters scrawled onto the leather drew Kaira's gaze back towards the mysterious Amarok brooding in the corner.

When her gaze finally landed on the warrior, from across the room, his moondust glare burrowed into her golden oceans. His constellation-filled irises dipped towards the book in her hands, and her grip tightened around the worn leather. He pulled his gaze back up to meet Kaira's face, and the Amarok swore she saw the slightest flicker in his eyes, and then he softly shook his head.

Kaira was not sure what came over her when Iskander shook his head, but she knew, deep down, there was a part of her that was intrigued enough with the General's unusual questions to remain quiet; and so, Kaira tucked the knowledge away—a morsel of information stored in her mind of steel to share with Asha when the time was right.

"LONG AGO, THE DESERT ISLES WERE A VIBRANT AND PROSPEROUS KINGDOM. BUT, AS TIME PASSED, AND A LONG SEQUENCE OF PRIDEFUL KINGS DISMISSED THE GODS AND FOCUSED ON THEIR OWN RISE TO POWER, THE KINGDOM WAS THRUST INTO DISARRAY AND PANDEMONIUM. WARS WERE WAGED AND THE GODS OF STORMS AND SEA WREAKED HAVOC OVER THE ISLANDS, UNTIL THE CITIZENS WERE EITHER DECIMATED BY THE DEITIES OR VEHEMENTLY FORCED FROM THE LANDS, AND THE ISLES HAVE NOT BEEN INHABITED SINCE."
– PAGE 245 OF THE COMPLETE GEOGRAPHICAL ARCHIVES OF DARNELLA: VOLUME II

CHAPTER TWENTY-SIX

*J*eremiah *slowly drifted down an open colonnade, with high, carved arches encompassing the pathway on both sides. The passage looked too unadorned to be the inside of a distinguished castle, but the towering sand-sculpted walls and strong desert marble made him believe he was likely wandering through the halls of an ancient fortress.*

Through the gaps in the sandstone, Jeremiah's hazed vision swept across the surrounding landscape. The entire scene seemed subdued, like his senses had been dimmed to an insipid version of themselves.

The passing scenery was nothing he recognized. For hundreds of miles, an unending stretch of uninhabited desert poured across the land. Dried plants, clinging to their last breath of life, were erratically scattered across the rolling sand dunes, and thin, stacked rock forms, crafted from deep red dust, arose aimlessly throughout the sand-covered hills.

Every step he took felt more fabricated than the last, as if the entire view was illusory and false—like it belonged to another.

Jeremiah reached the end of the hall and rounded the corner. As he stepped out from under the cover of the concealed path, a monstrous figure abruptly halted his steps.

He swiftly tucked himself into a shadowed corner, hidden from the devastating glare of the beast's piercing eyes.

A golden blur of wingbeats flashed through the open air, and the familiar smell of sulfur filled the space. A long, lash-like tail, prodded with whetted spurs, spiraled behind the winged creature. Its head and neck were horned, and each prong gleamed like polished gold. Its ethereal eyes matched its golden underbelly, and midnight onyx scales covered the remaining spaces of the beast's body.

From the opposite side of the fortress, a raven-haired woman emerged from the fort, her sun-kissed hands assertively wrapping a leather cord around her neck. She tucked the thread into her shirt and glided across the field towards the dragon.

As she drifted across the sandy floor, Jeremiah could see two dark tendrils of smoke trailing behind her like stalking Reapers. He tried to focus through the murky haze pressed before him, but the image would not sharpen. As she neared the dragon, the tendrils hugged her so closely, it seemed as though the Shadow of Death himself were perched on her back, a perfect place for Anubis to watch from over her slender shoulder.

A low grumble rose from the creature's throat, and Jeremiah braced himself for the impending stench of roasted flesh.

As she approached the beast, she raised her hand and mumbled an inaudible command. The dragon settled and lowered its head in acknowledgement.

An otherworldly, immortal presence emanated from the woman, as though she had lived far more years than her youthful appearance depicted.

253

She spun to the side, stroking the side of the dragon's face with a gentle touch that did not match the dark aura surrounding her.

The mysterious woman embodied the entire essence of refined retribution, as if she were a goddess crafted from pure vengeance.

Her virulent nature rivaled the force of her devastating beauty, and Jeremiah was unsure if he had ever seen a human so beautiful. Two long scars stretched across her left eye, sweeping down past her cheekbone. A scattering of freckles danced across her nose, and in the setting sunlight, Jeremiah could see the dim rays reflecting off her eyes.

Her irises were painted in the purest shade of violet, with shattered galaxies sparkling through the center. The dark flecks of obsidian scattered throughout the vibrant purple held the memories of a thousand haunted years inside of them, as if the rancorous woman had witnessed too many tragedies to be counted.

"Jer!" a familiar, far-off voice cried. The world around him began to abrasively shift, as if his body was being violently shaken.

He looked back at the mysterious woman once more, the world fiercely shuddering behind her, and he watched as she climbed atop the gold-plated dragon, her long black hair stirring behind her. The last of the sunlight glinted off a glass object hung around her neck.

She glanced once in his direction, her narrowed eyes burning into the space where he stood. Jeremiah was motionless as her gaze lingered in the shadowed corner, as though she could feel his presence and realized it did not belong in the surreal place.

She uttered another inaudible command, and the beast let out a long, fire-filled screech. A moment after, the dragon launched itself into the air, and the pair took flight into the twilight sky.

Jeremiah swiftly turned around and headed in the direction of the anxious screams, back towards the opposing end of the fortress hall, where his trancelike walk began.

Jeremiah awoke to four warriors staring down at him. Asha wore a concerned expression, one he did not often see grace her charming face, and Eros's posture looked equally as perturbed.

"What?" he questioned, distress filling his tone.

Asha's panicked gaze shifted from Jeremiah to Eros, then over to Kaira. "You were sleeping..." Asha started, her voice struggling to find the words.

Jeremiah's brows bunched together, but he remained silent.

The Amarok General—the arrogant warrior Jeremiah had decided he was *not* a fan of—let out a loud exhale and rolled his eyes.

"Crazy over here," Blaidd stated, motioning towards Asha, "was violently trying to wake you, and you wouldn't budge. She started shaking you and screaming your name, and eventually you came to."

Jeremiah pulled his gaze from the General and settled it on Asha. A flicker of worry still sparked in her sapphire eyes, but the overwhelming pool of concern he had seen when he first awoke had mostly abated.

Looking at Asha, Jeremiah replied, "You'd think a man with such an extensive list of entanglements with women would have learned long ago how distasteful it is to call a woman crazy."

A smirk twisted on Asha's lips, and Jeremiah's shoulders untensed as the last of the worry lifted from her eyes. Laughing, Asha looked over to Blaidd and snipped, "I'd be careful if I were you, Iskander. It seems this *puppy* has some bite." She glanced at Jeremiah and winked.

Blaidd rolled his eyes and shuffled towards the exit, ducking beneath the archway and disappearing into the Ageless Library.

The faint light of dawn crept into the open space from high above. Jeremiah hurriedly collected his belongings and made his way towards the ascending staircase in the adjacent room, following closely behind his friends.

The mingled smell of freshly extinguished flames and woody parchment wrapped around him as he rushed past the packed bookcases. His hand lingered a moment longer than needed on the mahogany doorknob at the base of the stairs as he glanced backwards. His gaze brushed across the endless leather spines marked with the ancient letters of the Founders. The same enigmatic feeling that had swept over him during his elusive dream reemerged, and an eerie chill climbed up his spine.

Jeremiah tightened his grasp on the handle, and as he closed the ligneous door behind him, he prayed to the gods of old that it would be the last time he ever saw the Ageless Library lying beneath the Mist.

"Dragons were born of life's first Light and the untamed wild of flames—not beasts to be bridled, nor servants to be shackled. They were forged for law, for truth, their strength a vessel for wonder, not war. With breath that shaped cities and wings made to kiss the heavens, they soared not to conquer, but to create. Never were they meant for shadows, never for sorrow or chains or the merciless will of dark things. But the cruel truth of time carved them into creatures they were never meant to be."

— Page 27 of A Summarized History of Darnella's Native Creatures, Volume II

CHAPTER TWENTY-SEVEN

Standing in a shadowed tree line of the overlooking mountain peak, the Midnight Castle was exactly the same as Iskander remembered. With high obsidian walls crafted from smooth granite stone, and a bustling city with lively citizens resting at its heels, the entire picture looked unnervingly unchanged from the haunted memories burned into his mind.

Even the light dusting of snow settled on top of the buildings seemed untouched, as if the capital had been frozen in time—waiting for the warrior to return.

The group silently watched as the remaining light of the setting sun dipped behind the snowcapped mountains, and darkness filled the sky.

"It's almost time," the Commander announced from behind Iskander.

The General twisted around to face Anselem. He was clothed in traditional Septant black, matching the leathers worn by both Asha and himself. Jeremiah and Kaira wore their branch-issued uniforms.

Iskander shoved his hand into his jacket pocket and ran

his fingers over the rolled parchment.

"Everyone knows the plan?" Anselem asked, his voice unwavering.

The group had discussed the plan a hundred times over on the final leg of the journey, working through different responsibilities and various approaches. Anselem had devised an outwardly infallible plan, one that left the least number of outcomes up to chance. The group would not separate, and every warrior, no matter the circumstances, would stay unified until Mathieson was recovered and the phoenixes took flight back to Perseis.

But this was war—and Iskander knew better than most that nothing in war was guaranteed.

The General cleared his throat.

The entire unit shifted their stares to Iskander, along with the weight of a thousand judging eyes.

"I need to change the plan," he pronounced. His voice was steadfast, strong, but deep inside his chest, Iskander felt the rapidly unsteady beat of his heart.

Asha's fire-filled eyes burned into him, but Iskander did not move his gaze from his commander.

Confusion, anger, and something that resembled crushing pain flashed across Anselem's face, as if he believed his fierce, unwavering Second was about to shove a second unfaithful blade into his scarred heart.

He pulled the crinkled scroll from his jacket. He left it rolled, tied up with the thin leather strap, as he ran his hands across the ancient paper.

"Math is not the only reason I came back to Montu," he explained, his tone softer than the normally brash one he wielded.

From the corner of his eye, Iskander could see Asha's hands clench into tight fists by her side. He could feel the overpowering thrum of her power as it rose to the surface.

He looked up from the scroll, into the piercing eyes of the Commander. "But he is the reason I cannot follow your plan."

Anselem's expression softened, and his brows bunched together. The humming Chaos flowing through Asha's veins abated.

"I made him a promise. I gave my Word," he explained, leaving out the details of the bargain he had made with his brother long ago.

He pushed up the sleeve of his jacket, along with the thick shirt buried underneath, and showed Anselem the three distinct lines that made up his Mark from the Binding.

In dark-black ink, resting in the center of his forearm, surrounded by the Marks of splintered darkness etched across his skin, sat three equally lined bands that wrapped fully around his arm.

One line to represent each branch.

One line to represent the sentiments of blood, sweat, and sacrifice.

And one line to honor the three Oaths of the Septant: Law, Loyalty, and Life.

Law: an unfailing commitment to follow the Septant Codex without fault.

Loyalty: to the Brotherhood and, ostensibly, the Crown.

Life—the most sacred of the three: to willingly commit the entirety of one's life to the Septant, and, if required, follow the Oath even into assured Death.

"Tell me what it is," Anselem demanded, his eyes dropping to the scroll in Iskander's hands.

Iskander held his brother's glare and shook his head.

"I can't."

"What the Hells do you mean you can't?" Asha broke in, her voice filled with ice.

Anselem's eyes narrowed as he stared at his brother, his

gaze intently burning into the General's moondust eyes.

Iskander's gaze did not falter.

"Ehwaz," he commanded, his voice low and authoritative.

Truth.

The warriors of the Septant were all graced with exceptional skills and authority—the power of the Binding, the remarkable skill set of execution, and the unwavering loyalty of brotherhood.

But the Commander of the Septant was graced with authorities beyond the others.

Along with his ability to denounce a warrior from his position, stripping him of his title and sentencing him to a disgraceful death, the Commander was also granted the power of Veracity.

Anselem did not use the Veracity power often, as truth was a required attribute of the Septant warriors; but on rare occurrences, when a warrior chose not to be forthcoming—or in the even scarcer occasions when he *couldn't* be forthcoming—the Commander could wield his power of Veracity and force the warrior to share the truth. In the unlikely event the warrior was rightly unable to disclose the information, the Commander's proposition would permit him to claim amnesty through reprise.

Iskander let out a relieved sigh and repeated, "Ehwaz."

Anselem nodded, and Iskander returned the sentiment.

"I'm assuming you have something planned?" Anselem challenged, still undoubtedly aggravated.

"We're changing the plan *now*?" Asha questioned, her voice filled with venom.

Anselem glanced back once more at his brother, meeting his star-filled eyes, and nodded.

"All because *you* want to? Where was your brilliant plan the last two days when we were preparing?" Asha's words cut through the air like a slicing blade, ready to wreak havoc on Iskander's authority.

He slid his eyes to the Thurisaz. Her overwhelming power began to vibrate across the space. Iskander unleashed the restraints around his magic, matching hers with his own dark shadows.

"Not always fun to be left in the dark, is it, *Kappi*?"

Shadowfire swirled in Asha's hands, mirroring the tendrils coiling at his fingertips. "If you would like to know Darkness, Iskander, I can surely help arrange it."

Iskander let a devious smirk twist onto his lips as he replied in his naturally smug tone, "You seem to forget, I have known Darkness much longer than you, Asha, and my power does not shy away from yours."

For the first time since he met the Thurisaz, Iskander unlocked the barred doors in his mind, the ones holding back the consuming Chaos buried inside his soul, the same doors that he rarely opened more than a crack; the ones harboring the beautiful, glittering onyx inside his mind.

And for the first time in two years, Iskander unleashed his devastating Chaos, letting a generous amount of the burning obsidian rip through his veins.

His shadows swelled, kissing the tops of the trees towering forty feet above, and his darkness swallowed the entire open space, blotting out the last of the overhead sunlight.

His humming Chaos-filled darkness engulfed the air, and he felt Asha's power recede, as if the overwhelming presence of his shadows had scared her devastating magic into hiding. The Chaos burned, but he forced himself to remain unmoved, as if the additional amount of burning magic was not all-consuming.

"Iskander," Anselem barked.

And just as quickly as his shattering darkness had rushed out from his body, it withdrew, and the General slammed the

barred door in his mind closed, thankful for the instant reprieve he felt with the Chaos safely tucked back inside the
cage in his mind. He took a deep breath, his face still carved
of stone, and he prayed to the gods of old that he would not
have to open the door again when he made it inside the Midnight Castle.

Asha's eyes were splayed wide, along with the two warriors beside her.

"Seriously?" Anselem hissed.

Iskander broke his narrowed gaze from Asha's and
shrugged. "Someone has to put the princess in her place."

Anselem shook his head and sighed.

"We will have to split up," Iskander announced, continuing with the conversation as if nothing had happened.

"Explain," Anselem stated simply, the harshness having
left his tone.

Iskander flashed him an apologetic look, and the Commander huffed out a breath. "Fine. Tell me what you can,
and we will go from there."

Iskander nodded. "You, me, and Kappi will go retrieve
Math. The other two will go retrieve... this," he stated, holding up the rolled scroll.

The Binding lines on his forearm started to burn, as if
giving a warning that the General was treading on thin ice.

"I will tell them what they need to do separately."

Anselem nodded, his mind racing through various possibilities. "Neith said we can't do it with only three," the
Commander countered.

"We are not splitting up," Asha broke in, evidently having composed herself from the aftermath of Iskander's display.

Iskander ignored Asha and replied to Anselem, "The
Spinner said we could not do it with only three warriors inside the castle. I never said those two wouldn't be inside."

He motioned to Kaira and Jeremiah.

"Absolutely not," Asha barked.

"You don't make the decisions, *Kappi*," Iskander snarled.

"Mathieson would never agree to it. He would never agree to have two barely trained warriors go off on their own inside that castle."

"Well, your brother is the reason we are in this situation in the first place, so excuse me if I don't particularly care how he feels on the matter," Iskander growled.

The lined Mark on his arm began to burn once again, and the glare Asha shot his way was sharp enough to cut through Elysian steel.

Iskander didn't care.

When Anselem and the Thurisaz had shown up in Lorca mere days before, it was the first moment in two years he acknowledged the profuse amount of anger stirring deep inside of him.

Anger towards Mathieson for sacrificing himself.

Anger for forcing him to keep a binding secret from the last living souls he trusted.

Anger for his lies.

And when the golden-eyed Amarok avowed her theory concerning Mathieson's capacity to wield the power of an Oracle, *that* was the defining moment when the fury burning deep inside Iskander's bones finally burst through the surface.

Asha said nothing. Her blazing sapphire eyes held enough pain-inflicting promises in them that no commentary was needed.

Iskander broke her gaze and turned to the two warriors standing behind her. Their eyes were still wide, as if neither had fully regained their composure after his dramatic display of power moments before.

"You two come with me," he ordered, and swiftly marched into the shadows of the forest.

He did not wait to see if Jeremiah and Kaira would follow, but a crunching of boots on the lightly laid snow behind him told him the warriors had complied.

After walking deep enough into the forest to avoid the inquisitive ears of the Commander, Iskander twisted around to face the nervous-looking warriors.

It was in that moment, when he stared into the tense pairs of gold and tawny eyes, that he remembered how untested the warriors were. How, just as he did with his soldiers in the Vanguard, he would have to balance the roles of both commanding officer and teacher.

"The three of us," he motioned to the two warriors waiting beyond the trees, "are going to continue with the initial plan. We will sneak into the Chamber of Reflection, get Math, and get out. While we are finding him, I need the two of you to go and get this."

Iskander unrolled the ancient scroll, unveiling the detailed painting of an obsidian staff with cracks of molten red etched throughout.

Kaira took a step forward, closely studying the paper. Her brow crinkled.

"What?" Iskander asked, watching her gold eyes devour the ancient letters scribbled on the page.

"Where did you get this?" she whispered, not pulling her eyes from the scroll.

The Binding Mark on Iskander's arm flared once again and, ignoring her question, he asked, "Can you read it?"

Kaira shook her head. "Some letters. Maybe a word or so. But I would need to go back to Velsen. I made some notes in several of the journals in the Library that I think would help me decipher it."

Iskander nodded. "Well, until we can get back there, I

need you two to focus on getting *this* out safely." He gestured to the painted scepter before pulling out a second tightly rolled scroll.

The paper was much newer, with far fewer creases and wrinkles, and the parchment's color appeared brighter. He unrolled it quickly and laid the map of the Midnight Castle before the warriors.

Then Iskander explained his plan and told the warriors everything they needed to know about retrieving a Crown of Shadows.

CHAPTER

TWENTY-EIGHT

Darkness had fully engulfed the skies when Asha, Anselem,
and Iskander made their ascent.

When the three warriors had returned from the forest, they did not divulge anything about the secret mission
Iskander was sending Kaira and Jeremiah on.

So, left in the allegorical dark, Asha stuffed her annoyance for the General down so deep, it was already beginning
to fester.

Climbing the southernmost wall of the Midnight Castle,
the three warriors blended in so well with the onyx stone,
Asha herself struggled to see the two Septant warriors ascending the rope above her.

Kaira and Jeremiah went in a wholly different direction, heading towards the eastern wall. Asha did not know
how the warriors planned to enter the castle; she only hoped
Iskander had thought to give them thorough guidance on the
various entrances while in the forest.

Asha pulled herself over the crest of the wall, joining
the two Septant warriors crouched on top of the battlements.

Her shoulders burned from hoisting herself up the long, interwoven rope, and her breath was labored beneath the mask fastened across her face. She crouched down beside the men, resecuring the deep-black hood over her head.

The three warriors blended into the backdrop of the midnight sky.

Pure, unwavering Assassins of the Night.

Asha's eyes raked over the guards littered across the ground.

She pulled the bow from her back as she counted the final two soldiers moseying in through the gardens.

Eight in total. Three more than they had suspected.

Asha ran her hands over the arrows in her quiver. Once she took care of the guards below, she would have two to spare.

She silently knocked an arrow onto the bow and pulled down her mask. She let the wind lightly brush across her face. Felt the subtle pull from left to right in the air.

She raised the bow and aimed in her sights. From the corner of her eye, she saw Anselem hastily setting up the rope for the warriors to descend once the guards had been taken out.

"From the left," she whispered to Iskander.

His only acknowledgement was a swift nod, and inky tendrils of all-consuming shadows slowly coiled in his hands.

Asha took a final breath, relaxing the tenseness in her body, readying herself to execute the carefully formed plan the Commander had laid out for the warrior group.

A nearly undetectable shift echoed across the wind, and Asha adjusted her aim, accounting for the altered speed.

She took a final breath, and in the faint pause between heartbeats, she released the golden arrow and watched as it soared across the midnight sky, trailed by a wake of Iskander's swallowing shadows.

Asha had another arrow aimed in before the first one struck straight through the lowly guard's right eye, crimson blood splattering across the snow-covered ground. She did not pause to watch as the inky swells of Iskander's shadows consumed the entire scene, veiling the view from the surrounding guards to prevent alerting them of the invasion.

The duo picked off the remaining guards one by one, falling into a rhythmic cadence of destruction—the fatal dance of war.

Asha fired arrow after arrow into each of the remaining sentinels' skulls, and Iskander followed closely behind the gliding barbs with his pitch-black tendrils, ready to conceal the bloodied ground resting beneath the fallen men.

The warriors made quick work of the watchmen, taking out all eight sentinels on the south side of the castle before a single guard had a chance to call out a warning.

Asha's final arrow pierced through the last standing soldier as Anselem tied the finishing knot in the rope and threw it over the edge.

Asha secured her bow onto her back, and Iskander's shadows quickly returned from their places far below.

Bodies littered the ground, and the newly fallen snow, before pure and untouched, now sat blood-stained and death-marked.

A wicked smile curled on Asha's lips, and her burning eyes darkened as she looked upon the wreckage below.

She grabbed the rope in her gloved, calloused hands, and Asha finally began the descent towards her long-avowed revenge.

From atop the eastern wall, crouched tightly against the battlements, Kaira measuredly counted the number of doors lining the outside of the castle.

Third from the right.

Iskander had told them twice, ensuring the pair knew exactly which doorway to enter.

It was painted a deep crimson, and no less than a half dozen guards stood outside its entry.

Kaira swallowed a lump in her throat. Her fingers wrapped more tightly around the iron-laced blanket in her hand, and she forced herself to take a deep breath.

Jeremiah shifted beside her, grabbing his wrist. Kaira glanced down and saw deep red covering his fingers. "You're bleeding," she said, concern entering her hushed voice.

Jeremiah did not turn to meet her gaze as he wiped his stained hand on his leathers. "I'm fine, just scraped it on a jagged stone on the climb up," he whispered, his voice barely carrying the short distance between them.

She stared at him for a long moment.

"How long?" he asked, his attention fixed on the castle beneath them.

Kaira twisted her gaze, straining her eyes as she attempted to make out any adumbral figures perched atop the southern wall. The distance was too far, and all the Amarok met was darkness. "It shouldn't be much longer," she replied, knowing the three warriors on the south side of the castle had likely spent less time climbing the exterior wall.

That had been Iskander's plan—for Asha and the Septant warriors to take out the guards on the southern side of the castle and make their way inside. Jeremiah and Kaira were instructed to wait until the warning was sounded and the guards on the east side were pulled away from their posts.

Kaira scanned the grounds again, knowing her climb had likely taken much longer than the others based on the speed of Jeremiah. He had been kind, never venturing too far ahead on the rope, but Kaira knew she had slowed him down. Knew he could have scaled the wall in a fraction of the time if he had gone without her.

Her breathing was just beginning to return to normal when she saw a group of sentinels far below circle together, conversing in hushed whispers.

Her gaze flickered to the shadowed corners of the castle flanking either side of the crimson door. As she stared intently through the dimly lit sky, she saw a jolting movement stir within the shadows.

Three horrid creatures emerged from the darkness. Their skeletal limbs were stretched to an unnaturally long length, and oily, blanched skin wrapped around their bony structure.

Their depthless eyes matched the long, stygian nails protruding from their hands, and even from the distance atop the wall, Kaira could feel the Darkness radiating from their presence.

"What are those?" she breathed, her voice shaky and uneasy.

"Eligos," Jeremiah replied.

A shout sounded in the distance, and the gathered sentinels whipped their gazes towards the southern wall. The three beasts took off towards the cries, their movements erratic and inexplicably fast.

Kaira had been right; it would most certainly not be long.

With each step, Anselem's raging power was pulled further and further to the surface. Buzzing electricity crackled through his veins, and its accompanying thunder hummed just under his skin, itching to destroy and devour.

His footsteps were silent as he guided the warriors through the castle halls, unhesitatingly directing the trio through the passageways as if it were a path he walked every day of his life.

He had left no room for mistakes. No space for error.

Anselem curved down a dimmed hall, his feet quickly gliding past dozens of rooms. When he reached the end of the corridor, he veered right, heading down a high-ceilinged passageway.

His heart skipped, and his footsteps faltered as a large mahogany doorway at the end of the hall greeted him.

He would know that door until the day Anubis came to collect his soul—the image of it was permanently burned into his mind.

The door that harbored a haunted memory and a piece of his shattered heart.

The door that housed the room where he had killed his brother.

Anselem steadied his breath, forced his heart to slow, his mind to focus.

They only had a few minutes before the slaughtered guards would be found. Only a few moments left to find the Chamber of Reflection before the warning would be sounded, and the occupants of the castle would know the fortress had been infiltrated.

Only a few seconds until the Hells were unleashed on the Midnight Castle.

A deafening horn rang through the still air.

Once.

Twice.

Then, on the third and final blare, all Hells broke loose.

Sentinels far below erupted like a tempestuous storm, shouting orders and scrambling in all directions.

From atop the eastern wall, the scene underneath the warriors looked like unadulterated chaos.

Blades were drawn, and orders were howled over an endless string of curses running through the air. Men were falling over one another as they scrambled towards the direction of where their dead comrades lay.

Fear washed over the faces of the younger guards, as if the men had not believed a day would come when the castle would fall.

Another group of men, those seeming to lead the charge, looked vehement, with hands tightly wrapped around their swords. Their eyes were hungry, like they had been eager for battle for many years, soldiers thirsty for blood.

Kaira and Jeremiah crouched lower on the crest of the wall, hidden by the shadowed sky. Their eyes scoured the ground below, marking where each of the sentinels was repositioning.

And, amidst the pandemonium, the warriors saw that the deep red door was left unmanned.

Shrill screams and booming directives pierced through the silent air, tumbling violently down the slumbering halls.

The warriors' footsteps did not falter, did not cease in their pursuit, prowling closer to the castle's center. Closer to the sinister room lined with mirrors.

Anselem led them down another dimly lit hall, and the air turned icy. The luminos lining the walls were hazy, lit with a crimson hue that made the walls look as if they had been painted with blood.

The shadows rolling through Iskander's veins ceased, as if they had instinctively recoiled from the Darkness lurking at the end of the hall, just the same as the last time he stood outside the door, and he knew they had made it.

The General took a deep breath, his heart pounding against his chest as each step brought him nearer to the haunted room behind the door.

He could hear the mayhem that had arisen outside the walls as it continued to pour inside the castle. He knew it would only be moments before a brigade of sentinels came storming down the hall to greet them.

Anselem paused, stopping just outside the iron door.

He looked back at Asha, and the Thurisaz nodded, palming a dagger in her hand.

Then he pulled his eyes to meet his brother's. Iskander forced the rolling darkness back into his veins, opened the barred door to the Chaos swimming inside his mind, his soul. And he nodded, his moondust eyes having gone dark.

Anselem turned back to the entryway and took a single steadying breath. Then he reached out and opened the door to the Chamber of Reflection.

And as the Commander unlatched the iron handle, Iskander remembered the silent promise he had made himself the last time he had walked into the haunted room.

A promise to decimate every monster that had ever touched him. To destroy all the dark devils that twisted his brilliant stars into tormented shadows.

They had turned him into a nightmare, so he vowed to become theirs.

Jeremiah had no clue how he and Kaira had slipped inside the castle unnoticed, but he was thankful the General seemed to live up to his renowned reputation of excellent battle strategy.

As they flitted their way through the halls, he was thankful for Kaira's brilliant mind. Not once did she waver. Not once did she hesitate with which turn to take.

The Amarok guided them to the end of a towering hall, up to the base of an onyx door.

Jeremiah slung the iron-laced blanket over his shoulder and pulled out a second blade from his waistband.

Kaira glanced back at the Soturi, her golden eyes wide. Jeremiah nodded and took a deep breath. Kaira reached for the knob and swiftly pulled open the door.

Jeremiah poured into the room, twin blades at the ready. His eyes quickly scanned the open space, working his way across the room. Kaira filed in behind him, quietly shutting the obsidian door. It latched shut with a soft click.

Jeremiah's heartbeats slowed as he took in the room, not a guard in sight.

He slid his daggers into his belt and pulled the blanket off his shoulder.

The room was covered in bone-white and onyx decor, and a large, crimson blanket covered the bed resting against the opposing wall. The black walls were adorned with gold embellishments, and over the queen's bed rested a detailed carving of a bear with bones clenched in its jaws and blood dripping from its maw.

Jeremiah motioned for Kaira to remain put and quickly swept the adjoining two chambers of the queen's quarters. He found no guards positioned in either of the connecting rooms.

As he ambled back into the bedchamber, his eyes swept across the sinister room once more, catching on an object sitting on the far wall.

Lying in the corner, fixed atop an obsidian stand, rested a towering scepter made of onyx stone, with deep red fissures running up the shaft. The staff looked like it was formed of cracked magma, pulled from the depths of one of the Peithon volcanoes.

He slowly strode over to the wall, and as he approached the staff, he saw a faint swirling of smoky black shadows twisting around the hilt.

He took another deep breath and carefully wrapped the blanket around the Crown, cautious to heed Iskander's warning and refrain from touching the rod.

And just as Jeremiah lifted the iron-wrapped scepter from the stand, the hinges of the queen's bedroom door slowly creaked open.

Seven hundred and fifty-six.

That was how many days he had waited.

The number of nights that had passed since he had leapt from the obsidian wall.

The amount of time he had spent locked inside the castle, awaiting their return.

Two and a half long, boundless years.

There were many dark evenings spent alone inside his cell when he was not sure he could continue. Many sleepless nights when every part of him wanted to stop. For it to end. But he kept going. Because deep down, he felt he deserved to know what not giving up on himself felt like.

What not giving up on them felt like.

Not giving up on her.

The bell tower rang out overhead, shaking the mirrors curving around the room.

And as the final chime echoed through the space, Mathieson Raynor smiled, for he knew it was the night he would finally escape from the Midnight Castle.

"I BELIEVED IF IT WERE TO END IN FIRE, THEN AT LEAST WE WOULD ALL BURN TOGETHER."

– QUOTE FROM GENERAL ISKANDER BLAIDD OF ASSIGNMENT 878, ANNOTATED IN THE LORDS OF CARNAGE: REDACTED OUTLINES FROM THE MISSIONS OF THE SEPTANT

CHAPTER TWENTY-NINE

Thundering footsteps clamored down the hall behind them as the warriors slipped into the Chamber.

Asha crossed the threshold, and as she entered the mirrored room, the rising flames flickering beneath her skin winked out. A strong, scorching stench of iron-laced air singed her nostrils, and she was met with a thousand versions of herself staring back with wide eyes.

The warriors scoured the room, their gazes swiftly washing over the small space.

Asha went still. Her heart sank.

"Where the Hells is he?" growled Iskander, his voice filled with angst and agitation.

Anselem stood beside him, his mind blank.

He had done everything right. He had followed every clue, laid the perfect plan. Mathieson was supposed to be here. The Commander shook his head.

Asha's breath quickened, matching the speed of her racing heart.

Where in the Seven Hells was her brother?

276

Silence filled the Chamber, and Asha remained frozen in place as Iskander began pacing between the slanted walls.

She could hear the clamor of fists against the iron door they had entered, and the angry, barking commands of sentinels followed directly after.

Anselem's voice, barely louder than a whisper, cut through the room, "He's beneath us."

Asha turned to Anselem. Iskander's footsteps ceased.

The warriors looked at the Commander, and he only nodded, his eyes bright and full of promise.

Anselem opened his mouth to further clarify his claim, but his words were interrupted by an unnerving creaking from the door across the room.

The warriors all snapped their attention to the opposite side of the Chamber, to a secondary door wrapped in glittering onyx. The door's hinged lever slowly began to twist.

"Go," Asha whispered, praying Anselem would heed her command.

The General shifted to her side, and she felt the subdued tinge of his power stirring beside her.

"I will meet you at Gull's Landing," Anselem replied in a hushed tone. The Commander silently exited the room as the gleaming onyx door slowly opened.

Booming cracks of lightning snapped in the hallway behind them, but Asha and Iskander did not remove their gazes from the dark door.

Asha felt her presence before she saw her.

An overwhelming, wrath-filled essence poured into the room, amplified by the hundreds of mirrors. A raven-haired woman with white eyes, surrounded by endless black, sashayed into the room.

A devilish smile rested upon her crimson-painted lips, and her lean, pale body was wrapped in dozens of layers of sheer black fabric. An onyx crown, jeweled with blood red diamonds, rested atop her head.

The Queen to the Obsidian Throne.

"Hello, Iskander," she greeted. Her voice was falsely sweet, and she was unable to hide the traces of madness held within her speech. "It's nice to see you again." A smile that looked more like an unholy sneer crossed her perfectly painted lips.

Iskander went still at Asha's side, his hands tightly wound into closed fists.

The queen shifted her gaze to Asha, and as the wicked woman's eyes met the Thurisaz, a devious twinkle sparked in the endless Dark.

"The Promised One," she mocked, her voice cruel and forbidding. "Not what I expected." Her tone was harsh and incredulous, as if she were wholly unimpressed with the warrior standing before her.

Asha ran her eyes up and down the queen and smirked. Donning her swaggering tone, she countered, "Good to know I'm not the only one who feels as though the gods underdelivered."

Asha had been born a fighter. With grit and fire and steel in her blood. And perhaps it was not the life she would have chosen for herself, a life full of battles and war. Maybe she would have decided to lay down her arms, chosen to take the path of peace and amity. But Asha was not blessed with carefree days and quiet mornings. Asha was selected by the Dominions to be a fighter. A warrior. And it was a title she was determined to earn.

Kalevala's dark eyes narrowed, and she peered down her nose at Asha. She quickly replaced the hostile glare with a false smile, as if she remembered she had an underlying need to win the warriors' favor.

The queen clicked her tongue. She wasted no time with small talk, instead jumping directly into her proposition, as if she'd had many nights to compose the offer—as if she had known for years that the warriors would come.

"With the commoners," she started, motioning to the outside of the castle, towards the citizens she ruled beyond the walls, "your power is wasted. You don't yet know the depths of your greatness. You could become powerful— boundless. With us, you could become infinite."

The queen studied Asha with an intensity so vast, her white eyes burned through the air between the women. "But if it is not power you seek," Kalevala continued, her lips twisted into a dark smile as if she could see the thrumming power ripping through Asha's veins, "perhaps you will join us to save yourself."

Asha could feel her roaring fire as it swelled to the surface. She could feel the thrumming bite of the Chaos as it filled her bones.

The queen's gaze flicked to the door behind the Thurisaz, looking beyond the iron frame to the warrior who had disappeared down the hall. The queen's words turned icy as she added, "And if you will not save yourself, then perhaps you will join us to save *him*."

Asha's body went cold, and in the silence that followed, she admitted the witch was convincing.

Within the flickers of Darkness swimming in Kalevala's eyes, Asha saw that the queen's gift of persuasion had been learned long before, in a Dark place not of this realm, but another.

And she knew that the Dark Queen had quickly learned humans were desperately greedy creatures.

Slaves to power.

And Asha also understood that for those who possessed the greatest deal of power, others would line up at their feet, eager to fasten their own chains until every part of them was shackled and bound. And then, without pause or second thought, those desperate for the approval of the ones in power would place the keys to their freedom in the palm of their hand, subjected to a life of awaiting orders, and pleading for mercy and the liberty they willingly gave.

But Asha also knew she would much rather have dangerous freedom than peaceful slavery.

Neither of the chaos-wielding warriors replied.

"Join us. Both of you." Her eyes flashed back and forth before ultimately settling on Asha. "You don't belong with them," she hissed, her chin motioning towards the warriors outside the room. The warriors filled with Light in their bodies.

Her voice converted into an artificially sweetened tone as she turned to Iskander and added, "You know it, too. You have for a long while. The shadows in your veins could not have given you a clearer sign. Darkness is within you. It makes you." The queen paused as she glanced over to Asha, her final words spoken as a damning decree to both Chaos-wielding warriors, "Darkness *is* you."

Iskander spat on the stone ground, and a wolfish sneer rested on his face. The witch's eyes returned to face the General, and the corners of her deep-red lips turned up.

"And Iskander, if you would like your old room back, I'd be more than happy to make the arrangements."

That was all it took. A single, cutting comment to release the leash Iskander had fastened around his composure. To unlock the chain he held around his power. One perfectly placed remark to undo the years of training and experience the General had endured to sharpen himself into a perfect, unfeeling warrior.

A snarl ripped from Iskander's throat, and devastating shadows erupted from his body as he lunged for the queen, a hidden blade in hand.

He moved faster than any human should be able, like

roaring Darkness if the gates of the Hells were torn open, desperate to claw its way out of the burning fire.

He sprang forward like newly freed blackness, fleeing from the depths of the Underworld, as if wings had grown on the ends of its shadowed coils, dying for the chance to taste untainted air.

Swirling Darkness clashed into Iskander, and his own shadows were swallowed in its might.

A powerful, unseen force hurled him against the reflective wall. Several mirrors shattered upon impact, and fragments of glass littered the floor. A loud cry escaped from the General's mouth as his body collided with dozens of skin-slicing shards.

As Iskander's body crashed against the stone ground, Asha's power flared, white flames igniting in her hands.

The queen's eyes snapped wide. A wicked grin accompanied the shocked expression.

A trickle of blood dripped from Asha's nose as her power raged against the iron-laced air.

"If we can't have him, then surely you will be enough," Kalevala declared. Her words sounded like oil, slick and vile.

With an accent of blood and vowels that were the sound of metal clashing, Asha responded, "You have taken many things in this life that do not belong to you, but I will not be one of them. And I will gladly stand by and watch as you choke on the ashes of the dreams you have tried to burn."

Asha's head began to pound. She felt every ember of the obsidian light roaring through her veins, every rushing wave of burning magic as it swelled against the iron in the air.

Her heart started to thunder inside her chest. She couldn't hold on much longer to the summoned flames sparking in her hands.

The surrounding mirrors were created to enhance power, but as she stood in the center of the room, Asha felt the reflective glass seemed to only heighten the iron in the air.

The dark light rolling through her veins burned.

The queen waved her hand in the direction of the General, never taking her eyes off Asha.

Iskander thrashed on the floor, screams of agony escaping from his mouth. The broken shards of glass ripped into his limbs, shredding and slicing through his skin.

After an unending moment, he went silent and still. Blood began to pool beneath him.

Asha compelled her gaze to the General, and Kalevala cackled, the sound wicked and unsettling. "Join us, and I will heal him."

Swirling Darkness eddied around the Dark Queen as she thrust her wrathful power into the rest of the Chamber.

Asha forced her roaring fire to the surface, pulling deep from the endless depths of her Chaos, her mind straining to contain the formidable magic. Blood began running down her face, dripping onto the cold, stone tiles at her feet.

Flames piled around her, shielding her from the swarming Darkness encircling the queen.

Asha stepped forward; a path of fire lay before her. As she walked towards the General, her flames protected her from the Dark power filling the room, and she remained untouched.

And as she marched across the room, she walked on the flame-filled embers like she was stepping on the defeated souls of all of those who had ever doubted her.

She bent down and pressed two fingers to Iskander's paling neck. A faint thump of his heart continued to fight, battled to stay beating.

With lips made of glass and a voice cut from steel, Asha scowled at the queen and replied, "You think because I show kindness that I will bend? Have you forgotten who I am?

How foolish of you to forget what lurks beneath my skin. My bones burn with Hellsfire and Chaos, and I will burn this entire castle to ash with everyone in it if given the chance."

The queen stilled, a glower fixed upon her wrathful face.

The Warrior hauled Iskander to his feet, his limp form fighting to regain consciousness.

Asha began dragging the General from the Chamber, a ring of fire set around them.

She made it to the far door, and as she twisted the lever and pulled open the hinges, the queen's sinister voice carried across the room. "You will be ours," she declared.

Asha paused, and glancing back at the witch through the wall of fire, she answered, "I belong to no one."

Her soul danced to the beautiful rainstorms of dreams and freedom, and it would never move to a music made of possessive claims.

Asha did not wait for the queen's reply as she twisted around, Iskander still hanging from her side, and exited the Chamber of Reflection.

She waded her way through the sea of bodies littering the hall—the aftermath of Anselem's rage-filled storm. A trail of blood followed the warriors' footsteps, and Asha was not sure if the bloodstained ground was courtesy of her own ceaseless trickle or from the gushing wounds of the man beside her.

The flames around her slowly began to dwindle as her mind continued thrashing against her skull. She forced herself to focus, to keep her attention on each step forward.

She sent a frantic call down the Bond, praying Uriel would hear her plea.

The warriors made it to the end of an untraveled corridor, and Asha forcefully pushed the door open. The pair nearly toppled over as they exited the castle. Iskander's body had turned weak, and he lost his footing. Asha's flames winked out as she used all her strength to pull him back up-right, throwing his arm around her shoulder.

She had hauled his nearly unconscious form halfway across the grounds when she heard the exterior door crack open.

Asha whipped around, and her eyes stretched across the blood-splattered snow, locking on the exterior door. She attempted to summon her power to the surface, but no flames sparked into her hands.

Her breathing hitched, and her heart slammed inside her chest.

The queen exited the castle door, flanked by dozens of sentinels and three Eligos. The Shadowblades' long, skeletal limbs jerked erratically at their sides, and their lips curled back to reveal long, jagged fangs. Deep, throaty snarls ripped from the creatures' throats.

Kalevala floated across the snow-covered ground with ease, stopping a safe distance away.

Asha attempted to calm her labored breaths as she dove back into the pool of darkness in her mind—in her soul—searching for the smallest of embers within the ash.

The faintest of flames flickered into her hands, and the guards surrounding the queen shrank back.

The queen pursed her lips and called from across the grounds, "He will not make it. This is your last chance, Promised One."

With Iskander still hanging off her side, Asha looked the witch dead in her red-flecked eyes. An otherworldly Darkness twinkled in her gaze.

Asha dropped her voice low, iced over with her own personal edge of darkness, and she sneered, "A day will come when you think you are safe, and you have won. But I promise you, I will be back. And your joy will turn to ashes in your mouth. There will be no place you can turn without tasting me like blood on your lips. I will destroy you in the most beautiful way possible, and as I leave, you will finally understand why the gods pour the violence of storms into people."

The witch's eyes narrowed, but she did not move.

Asha held her red-flecked gaze for a long moment until she heard the familiar screech of her firebird close by. She turned and continued to drag Iskander across the grounds, blood unremittingly seeping from his leg.

The firebird landed forcefully, with flames pouring from his mouth, his talons digging into the muddy earth.

The Eligos charged forward, their spasmatic movements carrying them with otherworldly speed across the snow.

A low, rumbling growl built in Uriel's throat, but the firebird did not cower. He did not balk. He bent his feathered head low, stepped forward in front of Asha, and let out a loud, flame-filled screech as the Shadowblades crossed the remaining stretch of space. His white-hot flames cut through the creature's pale, bony skin. Dark, black blood stained the untouched snow, and tortured screams tore from the beasts' lungs as the firebird singed through the demons' skin. A burning reek filled the air. The warrior heaved Iskander onto Uriel's back, deep crimson staining his snow-white wings, and climbed atop the saddle.

She peered down at the queen, with features born from thunder and battle, and eyes flecked with ash. She sneered, a grin made for war.

Then Asha kicked Uriel, and the trio launched into the sky, powerfully striding towards the arms of Death.

From the ground far below, the Queen of the Obsidian Throne grimaced, knowing in the depths of her empty soul it would not be the last time she encountered the girl with the flame-filled eyes.

For Asha Raynor was not the type of warrior endless

armies would follow into mere battles; she was the warrior they would follow into a war.

CHAPTER
THIRTY

Uriel glided through the sky, the midnight horizon breaking into dawn as he headed for Gull's Landing.

Asha was closely monitoring Iskander, ensuring his unconscious form would not topple off the back of her firebird.

As soon as the pair launched into the clouds, Asha had dug into one of the side pockets of Uriel's saddle and pulled two small vials from the pouch. She shoved the first bottle into Iskander's pale hand, fearful he was losing too much blood. He hastily downed the pale green liquid, hands shaking furiously as he brought it to his lips.

The tonic worked quickly, slowly sealing the open gash on his leg and stopping the bleeding.

She handed him the second, light-yellow vial, and between labored breaths, he swallowed the draught.

Only a moment passed before he was lulled to sleep, his body desperate for rest and healing.

The warrior was still asleep when Uriel's feet touched down on the sandy shore.

Asha and Iskander were the last to arrive.

She glanced to her right and left. Kapheria's night-like feathers were no more than a hundred yards away. To her opposing side, a golden firebird lay resting just off the shore, and two warriors were running down to meet her.

Asha slid off the back of Uriel. Iskander's slumped body was still draped across the saddle.

Kaira and Jeremiah were by her side in an instant, helping drag the General off the back of the firebird.

The wind whipped across the shoreline, and a loud screech rang out from Kapheria. Asha's head snapped up, the whipping wind pulling a few pieces of her hair loose from the braid tied around her head.

Then she saw it—two towering warriors walking through the black sand.

Her eyes first met with Anselem's blazing emerald, and with a swift nod, he wordlessly assured her everything was fine, that they were unharmed.

Then, for the first time in two and a half years, Asha pulled her eyes over to meet a pair of sapphire irises matching her own.

A sob escaped from her lips.

"Go," Kaira whispered, assuring Asha they would take care of Iskander.

Without hesitation, without falter or second thought, Asha sprang to her feet and raced across the sand.

The rushing feet of the ash-blonde warrior down the shore matched her own, and at long last, after years of fighting through the Darkness, after months of drowning grief and broken hearts, Asha crashed into the warm embrace of her brother.

Tears poured from her eyes, and soft sobs escaped from both warriors' mouths.

It had taken Asha a long time to realize that not everything in life was meant to be a beautiful story. That sometimes, the Darkness wins. Sometimes, people must endure pain, and there is no light on the other side of it. Sometimes, they fight for what they love, and they do not triumph.

But this—holding her best friend close after years of loss and separation—*this* would forever be etched onto her heart as one of the most beautiful moments in her story.

✤ ✤ ✤

Mathieson had held it together for years.

Full, unremitting composure. Unwavering strength in a sea of endless Dark.

But when he held his sister in his arms, that was all it took for the steadfast Septant warrior to break. All it took for his walls to crumble and his shattered heart to open once again.

Tears flowed down his face, wetting his cheeks with long streaks.

Mathieson knew there was something incredibly beautiful about unconditional love. Something exceptionally poetic about having another with whom to share his past. A person who experienced the same memories of childhood; someone who knew every season of him, in every fashion of his life, and still chose to remain at his side. A person who loved the same family and mourned the same losses.

So much of what they had experienced in life had mirrored the other so closely, and as they grew up and travelled their own paths, he knew a large portion of who they each were now would always be made up of the pieces of who they had been together.

And that was who Asha would always be to him—his person.

"Hi, Fletch," he breathed against her matted hair.

She smiled, full and true, and answered, "Hi, Math."

❖ ❖ ❖

The warriors pulled themselves from their embrace.

Asha's eyes flared wide. Something dark was crusted on his face, and his shirt was torn to shreds, the fabric barely able to cling to his body.

"Is that blood?" she asked.

Mathieson chuckled. "Don't worry, it's not mine."

"That isn't reassuring."

He winked at her and replied, "Not all of us have the luxury of killing our enemies from hundreds of yards away, Fletch."

She smiled, thankful years in a dark cell had not dimmed all the sparks of Light inside of him.

He glanced over to the warriors across the shore. Anselem had joined Kaira and Jeremiah, and the trio was tending to the General, pulling blankets from the saddles to ensure he stayed warm.

"Let's take a walk," Mathieson murmured, turning towards the ice-blue water.

As he began heading towards the lapping waves, Asha caught the silver marks scattered across his skin as the dawning sun climbed further in the sky, illuminating the coast.

She dragged her gaze over the littering of Marks that scarred his body, the ink looking like an ancient tree pressed into the center of his shoulder, with dozens of limbs branching out from the trunk and stretching down his arm and back.

Staring at the ink, Asha's stomach twisted into a tight knot, and as she silently followed her brother down the sand, a haunting thought entered her mind.

She scoured the exposed portion of his arms, glimpsing at the woody branches and bare skin visible on his back from where his shirt had been ripped open. But Asha could not find any trace of the Marks she knew should be there. No hint of the jaggedly carved lines he had received from signing his name on an onyx-bound book with dripping, blood-red ink. No trace of the deal he had made with a devious devil in a Room of Secrets.

And when Asha did not see any signs of the binding deal, her heart sank, and she fearfully realized the branding ink was likely resting beneath the portion of his ripped shirt still clinging to his chest.

Directly over his heart.

Asha stood beside Mathieson, glancing back at the warriors huddled around the General.

"He will be okay," Mathieson promised.

Her burning gaze shifted to him, but he kept his eyes focused on the stretching ocean.

"Did you have a vision, or do you know that one from experience?" Her voice was inquisitive, but Mathieson could hear the faintest hint of tension in her tone.

A smile turned up on his lips. "I always knew you'd figure it out."

He shifted his gaze away from the crashing waves and onto his sister, whose own eyes were now fixed on a different Septant warrior, one with comforting green eyes and the governance of a Commander.

He let out a huffed laugh. "Now *that* was certainly not something I foresaw."

Asha turned her blazing stare onto him, and he could see her otherworldly power lurking within the flames.

"Does he know?"

Mathieson nodded. "I told him everything while we waited for you and Blaidd to land."

Asha nodded her head slowly. "How does it work?

Mathieson sighed. "It's like seeing fractions of what will ultimately unfold, but you have no clue when or where or even how it is going to happen. It's like sitting with the insight into something you never asked for, insight into situations and experiences that you know will eventually play out, but having no way to stop them. No way to help."

He took a deep breath. "Sometimes it's just quick flashes of an image or a word or phrase. Those are the ones I tried my best to record in my journals, hoping that later I would see something else that would help me fill in the blanks. But mostly," he paused, carefully contemplating his choice of words. "Mostly, it's just feeling alone and lost and perhaps a bit insane at times, like trying to fit the pieces of a puzzle together without ever seeing the original picture. And I just have to hope I'm putting them together in the right order. Have to trust that I'm getting it right, even when everything around me seems to be screaming that I got it wrong."

Asha was quiet for a long while, taking in all he had explained. Then her hushed voice broke through the extending silence. "Why?" she asked, the question coming out as a broken whisper.

He had expected it. It was the first question that had left Anselem's lips when they safely made it out of the Midnight Castle and onto the back of Kapheria.

"It was the only way," he claimed, attempting to make the assertion sound reasonable. He fumbled to find the right words, glancing back at the warriors on the beach. "At least, that's what I thought at the time. There were so many moving parts. I had to make sure you all believed I was gone. I couldn't tell you the truth. But I needed to make sure you had a reason to fight. To question. There are so many things that even I don't fully understand myself, but somehow, in my soul, I knew it was the only way for it to work out how it was intended to…"

He rambled, unsure how to justify a choice he had made to keep everyone he loved in the dark for so long. To validate a decision to lie and have the ones who loved him most mourn his death. His words trailed off as he lost the ability to find any defensible explanation without unveiling the secrets he needed to keep hidden—at least for a little longer.

"But Asha," he said, waiting for her eyes to meet his. "I never knew about the Nameless Place. I never knew what he would do in that dungeon. Not until many months after I leapt from the wall."

He remembered when the vision had come to him, late one night, when he was locked beneath the castle in his cell. He was sitting in the dark—alone, and cold, and hungry—and that was when everything clicked. Before, he had only known the notes written in his journals and the empty pictures he had been sent of a bare dungeon with merciless instruments of torment lining a nearby table. The images of blood-soaked floors and the rattling screams of a woman he could never see.

Everything was ambiguous and indistinct.

Until it wasn't.

Not until several months into his solitary imprisonment, when his power sent him visions of an ash-blonde warrior with sapphire eyes that matched his own, chained to the floor of the place for which he had never been able to find a name.

When the vision finished, fading into darkness that matched the suffocating space of the cell around him, Mathieson could no longer breathe. His body went hot, and his hands clammed. Vomit spewed across the stone floor, and he could sense the burning ink as it stretched up his arm and the Darkness entered his mind. He didn't even fight it.

Asha's body had gone rigid when Mathieson mentioned the Nameless Place. Her jaw clenched, and her hands were balled into tight fists at her side.

"I promise you, Fletch. I never would have chosen that path if I knew. I would let this entire realm burn to ash before I'd let you become a martyr."

She nodded slowly, belief dousing her eyes. "I know, Math."

Mathieson swore his shattered heart broke all over again as relief swam through his body. The weight he had carried for so many dark months lessened, and gratitude spurred through his bones.

"Tell me when you're ready," she murmured.

As Mathieson stared into her bottomless eyes, he could see the brilliant mind of the warrior racing. His brow crinkled.

"I know you," she continued. "And you don't have to tell me now, but I know there was a reason for it. For all of it. So, tell me when you're ready. When you can."

A weight he had held for too long finally lifted from Mathieson's shoulders. "Thank you," he breathed, pulling her against his chest in an earnest embrace.

There was something so pure about unconditional love. Something so raw and rare and beautiful about the concept.

And, for the rest of his days, no matter how the events ahead would unfold, Mathieson knew he would forever thank the Dominions for giving him a family—a sister—so extraordinary, it allowed him to experience the notion of unreserved love.

A loud screech echoed in the distance, and the pair broke their embrace, turning their gazes upward.

A flash of deep blue and violet plumes swept across the morning sky, gracefully landing in the open sand beside the other firebirds. Mathieson's heart swelled.

Bashiri.

A genial, beaming smile broke across his face.

"How did she know?" Asha marveled; her eyes focused on Mathieson's phoenix.

"As soon as we took off the iron shackles, I called for her down the Bond."

A bright smile, the kind that met his eyes, rested on his face as he looked over at his firebird for the first time in years. "She never left. She had been waiting close by the whole time for me."

Asha let out a soft laugh. "I always liked Bashiri. Never understood how she put up with your stubbornness, but I always admired her for it."

Mathieson chuckled and gave his sister a playful shove.

A heavy squall of frost-bit wind thrashed across the ice-lined shore. A strand of hair was pulled loose from Asha's braid by the gust, and she reached up to tuck it behind her ear. As her hand moved up to the side of her face, a long line of Marked ink peeked out from beneath her jacket.

Mathieson stared absorbedly at the misty line; his heart twisted inside his chest. "I'm so sorry, Ash," he whispered.

She turned to face him, her eyes burning brightly; the same eyes that matched his own—their mother's eyes. She saw his gaze was locked on the ribbons of ink etched on her arm.

"Ever since we were kids," he confessed, "all I ever wanted was to protect you."

"I know, Math," she replied softly, with kindness and conviction in her voice. Her voice was filled with the strength of a hundred warriors as she continued, "But for too long, so many people dared to tell me all the things I could not be. They told me of the protection that I needed to wait for from others. Of the goals I would never accomplish. Until one day, I decided to stand up and remind them that I have been forced to learn how to protect myself. I am both war and woman, and they cannot stop me."

Heavy was the crown she wore, yet it sat upon her head as if it were a feather. There was strength in her heart, determination in her eyes, and the will to survive resided within her soul.

She was a warrior, a champion, a fighter—a queen.

Her voice tempered as she added, "So, I don't need you to protect me anymore. I need you to stand beside me. I need you to walk with me through the Darkness ahead, so that neither of us must endure it alone. Because until last week, I never thought we would have that chance again."

He swallowed the rising lump in his throat, and with kind eyes, Mathieson looked at his sister and nodded. "No matter where, I promise I will be by your side. Until the day I am called home. And even after, when you look towards the sunlit ground by your feet, my shadow will forever be standing tall next to yours. No matter what."

Asha smiled, a flame of hope sparking in her heart. "No matter what," she promised him back, and Mathieson knew his sister would burn the world to ash to keep the promise she made—to always stand by his side.

That was the moment he realized she had changed.

Mathieson could see it in her eyes, hear it in her tone. She was not the same as she had been before, and he understood that the girl he'd once known was never coming back.

And in that moment of awareness, Mathieson smiled. Pride for his sister swelled in his heart, for he was convinced she had never been born to be soft and quiet.

Asha Akselsen Raynor had been born to make the world shake at her fingertips.

PART
TWO

SEAL-BREAKER

CHAPTER THIRTY-ONE

Jeremiah paced back and forth along the shoreline, his mind unsettled and frenzied.

It was nearly midday, the blazing sun having already climbed to its highest peak in the open sky, and the warrior group was still stuck waiting on the coastline of Gull's Landing.

"Your pacing is making me anxious, Jer. Come sit down." Asha motioned to a spot in the sand beside her, patting the ground with her scarred hand.

Jeremiah shook his head and continued his restless walk.

He couldn't be seated. Not now. Not while his mind raced, and an inexplicable feeling of worry pressed in on him from every direction. He kept glancing down at his wrist, at the open gash scraped across his Brand as it burned in the salted air.

He hadn't been able to rid himself of the angst for hours. It had come upon him like a tidal wave, and nothing he did seemed to ease the fear—so he paced.

But, even with the attempt of quieting his anxiety

through endless steps across the sand, Jeremiah couldn't shake the ominous feeling that had settled in his bones. He couldn't shake the persistent, undimming feeling that he needed to return home.

✤ ✤ ✤

"What is up with him?" Asha asked, staring at Jeremiah from across the sand.

Kaira lifted her head and glanced over at the Soturi. She let out a long breath. "Maybe he is struggling?" she offered, her voice quiet.

Asha pulled her eyes over to the Amarok. "With what?"

Kaira lifted her gaze. The golden pools poured out an unsettling amount of bafflement. "Not everyone is built like you, Ash."

Asha did not reply and silently waited for her friend to continue.

Kaira sighed. "Not all of us can handle Darkness like you. Not everyone was destined to encounter so much brokenness and continue to forge forward." Kaira glanced over to Jeremiah as she continued, "Some of us experience Darkness, and it remains etched onto our souls, and we never find the entire way back to the Light."

"What happened?" Asha questioned, fearful of the answer she would receive.

Kaira was quiet for a long moment before she replied. "On our way out, after Jeremiah had grabbed the staff," she began, her voice low and focused.

Asha's brows bunched together as the Amarok spoke, confused about the staff she had referenced.

Kaira did not see the look of confusion sweep across Asha's face, and she continued without pause. "A group of guards came into the chamber. There was only a handful of them, and the entire brawl was over before it even began, but—" Kaira's voice broke. She swallowed a lump in her throat and composed her unsteady voice. She looked down at her hands, as if she could still see the blood that stained them.

Asha took her friend's hands in her own and said softly, "It does not make you weak to feel, Kai."

Kaira's golden eyes, lined with tears, looked up and met Asha's. The Thurisaz offered her a soft smile. The words the shadow-wielding warrior had whispered atop the Grounds of Sephone flooded her mind, and she added, "Do not let it harden you. Hold on to the parts of you that make you human. The parts that make you kind."

Kaira smiled and gently nodded.

Asha looked across the sand to the pacing Soturi, and worry filled her heart. Fear for the Darkness swirling in Jeremiah's veins seeped into her thoughts, and concern for the day his powers manifested sat at the forefront.

But Asha knew her Tribe. Knew her chosen brother far better than most. He was a warrior. A fighter. And she knew he would have no issue fighting for those he loved. Fighting to survive.

Asha said nothing, but deep down, an uneasiness began to fester within her chest, because Asha assuredly recognized there must have been another awful reason for his angst.

Before he cracked open his eyes, Iskander sensed the nipping breeze brushing against his face, took in the smell of the salt-filled air, felt the grainy sand beneath his hands.

He heard the muffled whispers of feminine voices close by, and as he opened his moondust eyes, excruciating pain tore up his leg.

The General shot upright, sipping in ragged breaths as the wave of pain washed over him.

The two warriors sitting nearby were swiftly at his side, but in the midst of the pain, his swirling shadows obscured the women's faces.

His shadows violently churned as he raged against the wrenching pangs. He could hear the scuffling sand as the rest of the group ran across the shore. Shouts and questions of concern filled the air.

"I don't know," Asha replied. "He just woke up and..."

"How long?" Anselem asked, his voice calm and composed—the ever-collected tone of the Commander.

"It just started," Kaira answered, her voice low but strong. Even amid the swirling darkness, Iskander could envision the piercing gold eyes that accompanied the voice.

"Did he say anything beforehand?"

As soon as the final voice spoke, Iskander's shadows ceased.

Light replaced the swirling tendrils, and Iskander forced his piercing pain down as he crawled to his feet. He looked at no one else as he rose, his moondust eyes fixed on the Prophet.

The General forced himself to cross the small stretch of sand, a heavy limp in his stride. Each step sent shattering shocks of pain up his leg, like a blade was slicing through the flesh.

"Iskander..." Mathieson started, his voice unsteady.

But before the Soturi had the chance to offer another word, Iskander closed the gap between them and sent his curled fist straight through Mathieson's face.

A loud crunch sounded as Iskander's knuckles crashed into Mathieson's nose, knocking the warrior off his feet. Blood instantly began to pour from the Prophet's face.

The warriors began shouting. Asha and Kaira bent

down, helping Mathieson back to his feet. Anselem stepped between the two Septant warriors, pushing Iskander back a step.

The General let him, but he kept his death-filled stare locked on Raynor.

Mathieson rose, shaking off the two warriors attempting to help. He pinched the bridge of his nose, but the bleeding did not slow.

Iskander shook off Anselem. "Unbind it," he growled, staring at the Prophet.

Mathieson said nothing, just continued to burn his sapphire gaze into Iskander.

"Iskander, let's just take a minute to talk this out..." Anselem broke in, attempting to ease the tension.

Iskander ripped his sleeve up and screamed, "Unbloody-bind it!"

Mathieson's jaw clenched. He dropped his hand, the bleeding in his nose having begun to clot. A line of crimson trailed down the front of his face, and the blood slowly dripped off his chin, falling onto the sand below in sporadically splattered droplets.

He remained silent as he stuck out his hand. Iskander forcefully reached for it, wrapping it in his own.

The brothers looked at each other for a long moment, tension and animosity filling the air between them.

"Hagalaz," Mathieson breathed.

Destruction.

A cold, ice-filled breeze swept across the shore, and nothing but grating screams filled the surrounding air as the Binding Mark was violently burned away from each of the warriors' skin.

CHAPTER THIRTY-TWO

Jarring silence saturated the air after the final cries rang out.

"Tell them," Iskander commanded, his voice cold and iced over.

It was not Mathieson who responded, still attempting to catch his breath, but Anselem. "Blaidd, you need to take a walk."

"No," he snapped, cutting his eyes to the Commander. Iskander drew in ragged breaths. "Not until he tells you everything."

Anselem stepped forward, his face a mask of steel, and growled, "I'm not going to tell you again."

Iskander, with his chest still unevenly rising, held the Commander's gaze for too long a moment, defiance dancing in his moondust eyes.

His jaw feathered. He blew out a huff and turned around, heatedly limping away from the group.

Mathieson released a thankful breath.

Anselem snapped his eyes over to the Prophet. "I wouldn't look so relieved if I were you," he snarled.

Mathieson's eyes narrowed and his lips pursed, but he did not chance a response.

"You better start talking," Anselem bit. "Now."

Mathieson took a deep breath, his eyes scanning each of the onlooking faces. He held the Commander's gaze for a long moment before finally resting his eyes on the pair of sapphire blue that matched his own.

Then, Mathieson proceeded to tell the warriors everything he knew about the Six Princes of Shadows.

He told them about the staffs, and the Crowns harbored within; about the Ossuary, and the vault resting deep inside the core of the Iron Mountains. He explained how the tales of old were anything but fables, and how the Princes had been born from the depths of Darkness itself, long before the First War. Then, with an expression of guilt covering his face, Mathieson admitted how he Bound Iskander to silence.

From across the sand, close enough to hear the rumblings of the Prophet, Iskander sat brooding, a mask of loathing and ire covering his face.

As Mathieson spoke, the rage resting inside of Anselem grew.

Kaira and Jeremiah sat still, with fear-filled expressions as they realized the meaning behind the mission Iskander had sent them on.

Asha went rigid.

Tension filled the air once Mathieson finished speaking.

"So, these staffs have just been hiding in Darnella for millennia, and they just happen to resurface *now*?" Kaira questioned, her brilliant mind racing.

Iskander ambled back over to the group; his interest piqued.

Mathieson nodded. "I don't have all the answers," he replied. "There are still a lot of blanks missing."

"Of course there are," Iskander muttered.

"I had a vision before we went to Montu," Mathieson explained, his use of the word vision eliciting a scowl from Iskander. "It was about a man—a warrior," Mathieson continued, adding to the already lengthy explanation he had given. "He was stumbling up a hill, climbing towards a colossal rock perched above a battlefield. There were mangled bodies littered all over the ground below, wrapped in armor with breastplates carrying the crests of kingdoms that have not graced this world for many millennia. Not since the First War."

Mathieson paused, gathering his thoughts as he relived the vision once again. "The warrior scaled the hillside until he reached a large stone, with seven erected staffs plunged into its core. Each scepter possessed its own unique features, but all of them were covered in dark, looping shadows. A crown was etched into their hilts." He took a deep, tired breath. "After the vision, I did as much research as I could on the First War. It was difficult, as many of the tombs of that time have been burned or destroyed, but eventually I was able to get my hands on a few ancient texts.

"That was when I read about the Warriors of Old, and their leader, the Warrior of Praenuntius. It took several more months to track down any lingering information about him. It wasn't until I visited a library in Peitho that I learned about his crypt. The Ossuary. I was only able to track down one of the staffs before we were captured in Montu."

A long-standing silence covered the shore.

"That all makes sense…" Kaira began, her voice hesitant as she worked through everything Mathieson had revealed. "But I think the big question that remains is why? Why did the Dominions—or whichever subset of the Authorities sent you those visions—want you to collect the staffs? What is the purpose?"

Mathieson's expression turned grave. "Because war is

coming to our lands. Darkness is coming."

"What do you mean war? War with the *Hells*?" Anselem questioned, his voice sharp.

Mathieson cut his gaze over to the Commander but did not answer. His silence was confirmation enough.

"I think the better question is *why now*?" The words came out softly, but there was a sense of dread in Asha's voice.

Mathieson turned his gaze to the Thurisaz. "I don't know that either, but my best guess is that the Dark King has been waiting for the right time. The right person."

Asha's eyes narrowed and her brow crinkled.

"The right person for what?" Jeremiah muttered, voicing the question running through every warrior's mind.

Mathieson did not turn his eyes from his sister as he replied, "The person powerful enough to wield his final Crown."

CHAPTER
THIRTY-THREE

Asha's head spun, and from across the shore, Uriel let out
an angst-filled screech.

Blaidd's voice broke through the air. "What in the Sev-
en Hells does that mean, Raynor?"

Asha did not turn her eyes to the General; she kept her
gaze locked on her brother.

Mathieson drew in a deep breath and ran his scarred
hand through his matted hair. That was when Asha saw it.
The fatigue in his eyes. The utter exhaustion that had seeped
inside his bones over the last two and a half years.

"I don't know," Mathieson replied, his voice weary.
Drained. He glanced from Asha to her snow-white firebird
nestled across the shore. "That's the thing I've been trying to
work out for years," he continued. "But why else would I be
sent those visions other than to uncover the answers? Other
than to know that this war the Hells plan to wage is going
to be more closely aligned with the First War than we may
realize."

Asha could see that her brother was holding back, that

he was refraining from sharing everything he had theorized over the years. She didn't press.

"Well, how are we supposed to figure it out?" Jeremiah asked softly. "Just wait around and pray the Authorities send you more visions?"

Mathieson turned towards him, and before he was able to answer, Asha chimed in, "The Empress knows, doesn't she? The Empress of the Forgotten City."

Mathieson shrugged. "It's the only being on the Continents that might be able to provide some insight."

Asha's mouth was drier than the sand beneath her feet. She tried to swallow the lump in her throat but could not force it down.

"Why don't you just tell us where this *Adversary* is, and we can go take care of him now?" Iskander rumbled, as though he wasn't speaking about fighting the Dark King of the Hells. He shifted back and forth on his feet, like there was an obscene amount of pent-up frustration rushing through his bones and he was itching to take it out on someone — anyone. "Or, better yet," he continued, "just tell us where the bloody *Crown* of the godswaning King of the Abyss is located, and we can go destroy it and be done with this nonsense." Iskander didn't add *and be done with you* to the end of his statement, but his irate tone conveyed the sentiment.

Mathieson rolled his eyes. "That's not how it works, Blaidd. I don't possess the gift of omnipotence." Ire filled the Prophet's tone.

"Oh, well, excuse me, *Mr. All-Seeing*," Iskander mocked. His perfect jaw clenched tightly, and he added through gritted teeth, "Is there anything you *can* tell us, or are we just supposed to take your word for it?"

"Iskander..." Anselem warned.

The General did not listen as he concluded, "Because your *Word* doesn't stand for shit, Raynor."

Booming thunder shattered overhead.

"That's enough!" Anselem barked.

But Iskander paid him no mind, continuing to throw insult after insult towards Mathieson. The Prophet deflected and returned the spitting slights with his own.

A crack of lightning flashed across the clear sky, and an earth-rumbling voice echoed through the space, "I said *that's enough!*"

Iskander shut his mouth, and Mathieson did not breathe another unrequested word. The two Septant warriors bowed their heads.

The remaining warriors turned their heads, and all three of their bodies went rigid.

Risen before them, with towering, gold-plated wings splayed out behind him, stood the unwavering Commander of the Septant.

Asha's eyes went wide, her mouth agape.

Anselem's breathing was deep, ragged, like he was straining to maintain the last semblance of control he had over his being. After a long minute, he calmed his breath and moved his worried eyes over to her. Rage eddied in the emerald seas, but it was quickly replaced with something else. Something darker. Something deeper.

Fear.

And as he gazed into her eyes, Asha realized it was not fear of himself, or fear of losing control, for she was certain he had learned long ago how to harmoniously dance with the raging power inside him. It was fear for her. Fear *of* her— and whether she could love him in all his forms.

She forced her feet to move. Forced her boots to drag her across the packed sand.

And with each step, staring into his deep green eyes, the world around them melted away.

As she approached him, she dragged her eyes down his

wings.

The feathers were pure, unblemished gold, tipped with electric flecks of silvery blue. They shimmered in the sunlight, like a collection of dazzling gems. A hum of charged light buzzed beneath the surface, and she watched as flickers of lightning flashed across the top, wrapping around the outer edges.

They were beautiful. Otherworldly.

Infinite.

She could feel his eyes as they bore into her, and she dragged her flaming sapphire to meet them.

Worry and Darkness danced across his iris.

She pulled her hand up and caressed his face. He closed his eyes and leaned into her touch, as if it were the only comfort he had ever needed, as if it were the first and only touch that had ever made him feel whole. Feel accepted.

She brushed his cheek, and his emerald seas slowly opened.

She smiled softly and said, *I told you before, no matter the horrible things you have done, no matter what form your being takes or the vows to which your life is tied, I will love you just the same. Always. Into every lifetime.*

The Commander released a sigh, pressing his forehead to hers. And for the first time in his life, Anselem Eros did not hate who he was or the Vows he felt cursed to uphold for the remainder of his days—because it had all brought him to her. She was the first thing in his cracked and broken world that ever made him feel whole. The first thing that had ever made him feel like he was enough—pieces and all.

Sand shuffled beneath several of the warriors' feet as they uneasily shifted their weight, unsure of what was unfolding in the silent conversation between the two warriors.

Anselem pulled his brow away from Asha.

I love you, he murmured.

He pulled his focus back to the group before him. Jeremiah and Kaira's eyes were still wide as he glanced sideways at the pair. He trailed his gaze over to Mathieson and Iskander, and vexation crept back into his bones.

Anselem took a deep breath, tucking his wings in close behind him. He rubbed the bridge of his nose as he spoke. "Is there anything useful that you *do* know, Raynor? Or is all of this simply just speculation and visions?"

His breathing had calmed as Asha helped ground him once again, but an edge of frustration still eddied in his voice.

A flash of pain flickered through Mathieson's eyes, but he shoved it down as he met Anselem's stare. He nodded. "I know how to find Thotha. The Empress of the Forgotten City is in—"

"We already know," Anselem cut in, an edge of impatience seeping into his curt tone. "We spoke to Raziel weeks ago. It was one of the few things I had been able to understand in those godsflaming journals of yours. The Secret-Seeker told us how to enter the city when Asha and I visited his Manor over a month ago. It was the next place we had planned to go before we discovered you were still alive."

Memories of the plan Anselem and Asha had made flashed through her mind. They had planned to go to the Midnight Castle, destroy the city and its queen, and then continue on the path they had been slowly uncovering through Mathieson's journals. It was why Anselem had put in a request for her transfer to the Elysian Fort—so they could travel to the Forgotten City and discover why her brother had wanted to go without raising too many questions with Leadership.

"What I don't understand," Anselem continued, "is *why*." He stepped towards Mathieson. "Why in the Seven Hells did you need to go there? Why did you have the Empress's name scribbled in your notes? Why do all of these troubles keep pointing back to *you*?" Anselem growled the last of the words.

Mathieson did not balk as the fury-filled snarl ripped from the Commander's throat, but his voice still trembled as he stumbled over his response. "I—I don't..."

"Don't you dare tell me you don't know, Raynor," Anselem spat.

Asha saw a small smirk slide onto Iskander's face. She narrowed her eyes at the General. He only raised his brows, daring her to say something.

Mathieson took a deep breath. "Commander," he started, his voice made of steely professionalism. "I do not have a definitive answer for you."

Anselem opened his mouth, readying to unleash whatever fury he had stored for the last two years inside his chest.

"But," Mathieson proceeded, keeping the Commander's storm at bay. "I *do* know that there are answers for us there. Knowledge that lies beyond the visions the Dominions have sent to me. Beyond the things I was able to understand inside the Chamber..." His voice trailed off, as if his mind had been clouded by unhappy memories.

The smirk on Iskander's face vanished.

"But I have tried," Mathieson continued. "Over and over, I have tried to make sense of them. To piece it together." His words sounded desperate—broken. "But all I have managed to understand is that war is coming to Darnella. The Hells want to return. And the only being who has lived long enough to grant insight on the Princes of the Hells and the King of the Abyss is Thotha."

A great silence stretched. Anselem's breathing returned to normal, but his hands remained firmly clenched at his sides. "Fine," he said, voice tight. "We will go to Verloren, and we will see what insight the Empress may have." The

Commander shook his head and twisted towards the fire-birds across the sand.

He had not made it more than a step before Mathieson's voice broke through the air. "Do you have the amulet already?"

Anselem turned back, his head tilting to the side. His eyes narrowed. "The what?" he asked, the question coming out more like a command than an inquiry.

"The amulet," Mathieson repeated. "The Empress will require it before she will speak with outsiders."

A storm-ridden wave of fury threatened to crack across Anselem's face. "There was nothing in your notes about an amulet," he seethed. He slid his gaze to Kaira. "Did you read anything about an amulet?" he asked.

Kaira did not answer, not daring to correct the Commander. Her silence was answer enough.

Anselem let out a long exhale and rubbed the bridge of his nose. "Where is it?" he asked, turning his attention back to Mathieson.

"I don't know," Mathieson replied. "We went to the Midnight Castle before I had the time to find it."

Anselem gritted his teeth. "Samson?"

Kaira shook her head.

He turned to Asha. "Looks like we will be paying your twisted friend a visit sooner than expected."

"Raziel?" she asked, surprise flooding her tone.

"I don't see another option," he huffed.

Asha could see a million options racing behind his emerald eyes. *Any* other option.

"Does the amulet have a name?" Anselem asked, shifting his gaze back to Mathieson. "I don't want that spineless sneak to squirm his way around giving us the answer."

"The Amulet of Tisiphone," Mathieson answered.

Anselem nodded, his only sign of acknowledgment.

Silence spread over the shore once again.

"While you all go back east, I'm going to take this," Iskander interjected, bending down to pick up the iron-wrapped staff, "and head up to Lorca."

"I'll come with you," Mathieson boldly offered.

The look Iskander cut at the Prophet was filled with so much aversion, Asha wondered how it did not maim the warrior on the spot. "You will *not* be joining me," he growled. "She will," he added, gesturing to Kaira.

The Amarok's golden eyes flared wide. "Excuse me?" she snapped.

He turned his alluring, stardust eyes onto Kaira and, with a wolfish smirk, he replied, "You can read the Language of the Founders, after all."

Kaira's face dropped, and her striking eyes narrowed. "No," she barked.

Anselem nodded, taking in all the information. "Yes. Samson will go with Iskander. Mathieson." He turned to the Prophet. "You will not be joining them. I can't trust the two of you to behave. We will all reconvene at the Mount."

The Commander shook his head, annoyance swimming through his veins as he realized he was having to make strategic war decisions based on two quarrelling children.

"I'm not going with him," Kaira opposed, her voice lacking its normal softness.

Anselem's endless patience snapped. He turned to the Amarok, no placidity left in his body, his golden wings splaying wide. "If you want to be part of this warrior group, then you'd better get in line. There is structure for a reason, Samson, and I know you, of all people, are bright enough to understand that. I may not be in your direct command, but he sure as Hells is," he explained, motioning to the General of the Vanguard. "And he answers to me. Which means you do too. So, I don't care how you have to reason it out in your mind, but you'd better figure it out—fast."

He turned and began walking towards his midnight fire-bird. "Asha, Greystone, let's go. We will have to stop in Elysia to prepare before we visit the Secret-Seeker."

The two Valorous warriors silently followed him.

Before the trio had walked too far down the sand, the last remaining Septant warrior chimed in, "And where would you like me to go, Commander?"

Anselem, the ever-composed leader, halted; his hands curled slowly into fists at his side. He spun on his heels, and his harsh glare landed on Mathieson. "Right now, I don't give a damn where you go, Raynor," he spat. "And unlike him," he continued, pointing to Iskander, "I don't have the luxury of openly detesting you. But don't be naïve enough to think my command over you holds anything more than the Oath I took."

The Commander twisted back around without waiting for an answer.

He did not see the wave of pain wash over his brother. The crushing weight of the guilt he had carried for years. The brokenness etched in his heart.

Jeremiah swiftly trailed the Commander, and Anselem's wings abruptly tucked in, disappearing from behind him.

Before heading to Uriel, Asha walked over to her brother, squeezed his hand once, and then jogged across the sand to catch up to the two Soturi.

The three warriors wasted no time fastening the saddles onto their phoenixes. Pale green orbs were promptly secured around their heads, and soon after, their firebirds launched into the clear, open sky.

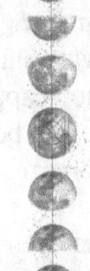

CHAPTER
THIRTY-FOUR

The first half day of flight was bursting with fury-loaded silence and nervous angst. Asha wasn't sure which temperament was worse.

Jeremiah and Khalfani flanked her on the right. She hadn't missed the strained expression perched upon his face since they left the shores of Gull's Landing, nor how he persistently grasped at his scarred wrist.

Behind her, Mathieson sat atop the violet plumes of Bashiri, keeping a far distance from Anselem at the front. He had trailed silently behind them as the trio took to the skies after Anselem's dismissal. The Commander had been less than pleased to see he had followed.

As the group glided through the biting air, she guided Uriel over beside Kapheria. His snowy wing brushed against her midnight feathers, and the firebird turned a piercing glare towards him, but she did not snap her beak in his direction.

Anselem shook his head.

Asha smiled. "Shameless flirts."

A small grin tugged at the corner of his lips, and he

glanced over at her.

Truth for a truth? she asked.

He turned his eyes away, staring directly ahead at the mist-covered forest and snowcapped mountains in the distance. The wind picked up his bound hair, and it fluttered fiercely behind him in the breeze. He nodded and pulled his emerald eyes back to hers.

Talk to me, she said, her eyes full of concern.

Anselem forced a grin to his mouth as he replied, *That isn't a question, Seven.*

She rolled her eyes. *What are you thinking?*

He raised a brow, and a snarky smirk curled on his lips.

Asha pulled the reins on Uriel and balanced his flight path. She huffed out a breath of annoyance, remembering Anselem's advice to be specific in her questions.

She glared at the Commander and asked, *How do you feel about everything with Math?*

Anselem's playful grin soured as he glanced backward, his flawless jawline feathering.

Even across the winds, Asha could see the tenseness entering his shoulders.

I'm angry, he admitted, and even through the silence of the words between them, Asha sensed the fury in his tone.

I've been racking my brain all day. Trying to see what I missed, where it all went wrong. But it just doesn't make sense. I can't find any valid reason why he kept it from us, Anselem added bitterly.

Asha gave him a sorrowful smile and shrugged. *I don't know, Ans. But I know he had a good reason.*

The Commander huffed and rolled his eyes, *You can't know that, Seven.*

I can.

How?

Asha turned her gaze to the whipping winds before her,

to the passing mountains and the far-off coast. She closed her eyes and felt the chilled breeze brushing across her burned cheeks, felt the whisps of her hair as the wind tossed them violently behind her.

She took a deep breath and looked back at him. His emerald eyes were dark and filled with swimming resentment.

Because, she replied, *I trust him. I believe in him. I know him. And even when it does not make sense, even when I don't understand the why or the how, and even when all the odds are stacked against him, I will always stand by his side. Even when everyone else has abandoned him. No matter what.*

Anselem's jaw clenched, but he did not counter her claims. He did not reply with the unkind comments primed on his tongue.

Because one of the things he loved most about Asha was her unwavering loyalty to those she loved most. And he knew that love forever extended to her brother. Even when he had felt his own adoration for the Prophet vaporize as soon as Mathieson spoke.

His friend's deceit had sliced straight through his flesh and buried itself like a sharp knife in his back.

The warriors finally landed outside the tall, glass walls of the Elysian Fort, and the overwhelming angst in Jeremiah's chest had grown so great that he could hardly breathe. The burning in his wrist had shot up his arm and was now coiling in his skull.

He sipped in short breaths as they dismounted their firebirds and walked down the alabaster stone path towards the Fort's main doors.

They had not made it more than halfway down the trail when the dragon glass gates opened and an older, white-haired warrior with deeply tanned skin came out to meet them.

With each step, Jeremiah's spirit slowly descended further and further, and his knees began to tremble.

The man was silent as he approached, with a sorrowful look set on his wrinkled face.

"Cathan," Anselem greeted the man.

He nodded at the Commander, but his wise gaze turned directly to Jeremiah. An unusual sadness crowded his grey eyes.

Jeremiah swallowed a lump in his throat, and his stomach twisted.

Cathan's wrinkled hand slowly reached inside the pocket of his dark, weathered jacket.

Time slowed, and Jeremiah felt the thump of every anxious heartbeat thundering against his chest.

The Overseer pulled a rounded piece of silver from his pocket.

Jeremiah's heart sank.

In Cathan's hand rested a delicate, silver chain with a brilliant topaz gem fixed on the end. A necklace that perfectly matched the ring sitting in Jeremiah's jacket pocket. The same one he had taken to the merchant down the street only weeks before, when he asked the jewelsmith to craft a marital band that would match the necklace his future wife wore every day of her life. The one her grandmother had gifted her as a child.

Jeremiah tore off in a sprint, heading straight to Tahira's house.

"WOLVES AND WARRIORS BOND FOR LIFE. ONE CANNOT SURVIVE WITHOUT THE OTHER."
— THE AMAROK: A DETAILED UNDERSTANDING OF THE CANINE BOND

CHAPTER THIRTY-FIVE

Iskander had always found the sentiment of unconditional love to be strange. Foreign.

Like the idea could not exist easily inside his bones. As though it wanted to claw its way out as soon as it entered the empty space that was his soul.

El was the only time in his life he had felt it, understood it. But even that glimmer of light was short-lived in his endless dark.

And some days, his darkness was harder to navigate. It was hard to stay afloat in the shadows swimming beneath his skin when he looked out and saw how others were loved, of the unconditional love they experienced.

And what made the struggle even more difficult was that those loving souls reminded him of everything that had been taken from him.

Of everything he had lost.

Of the family he knew he was too broken to ever have.

And it would always bring his mind back to El.

Missing her came in waves.

And for the last few days? Iskander had been drowning.

Kaira's chest was on fire by the time the warriors reached the base of the Iron Mountains. The cold air burned her lungs, and her chattering teeth refused to rest for the last several hours of the trek.

As they scaled the side of the mountain, the remaining feeling in her feet went numb against the snow, and the sweat on her brow quickly froze over.

Iskander, keeping a fair distance ahead, kept glancing backwards at her. She wasn't sure if it was from disgust for her slow speed or concern.

After a grueling ascent, the side of the mountain broke open, and Kaira followed Iskander inside the break, thankful for the reprieve from the bitter winter winds.

The General, iron-wrapped scepter in hand, continued without word, descending into the dimly luminos-lit cave.

As the pair plunged deeper inside the core of the Iron Mountains, Kaira swore she heard dulled whispers and muffled cries between the scuffing of their boots against the iron floors.

After roughly an hour, the pair turned the final corner, and a large, gold-plated door greeted them. A seven-headed dragon was carved in the center of the rounded metal, and a deep-black keyhole was fixed in the center.

The Wraiths of War and Ruin was carved into the top of the door.

As the General dug through his jacket pockets, Kaira ran her gaze over the ancient words etched below the door.

"Can you read it?" the General asked, breaking his long-standing silence. He was holding an onyx key in his hand, made of the same stone resting in the center of the door.

She nodded and glanced over the words once more. She took a deep breath and replied, "The Light shines in the Darkness, and the Darkness has not overcome it."

Iskander stared at her blankly, and without a response, he shoved the metal piece into the lock, twisted the key, and the warriors slipped inside the Ossuary.

Curved walls greeted them, and a towering, domed ceiling stretched far above, adorned with gold and onyx shingles. On the floor rested an intricately painted mural, seemingly untouched by marks or wear.

On the far side, opposite the round entry door, lay an archway covered in gold bars. An onyx chest rested inside the cage.

Additional arches wrapped around the side walls, with obsidian platforms placed inside each opening. Two of the stands held erected staffs, and, even from the entrance, Kaira could see small swirls of clouded Darkness wisping around the hilts.

She did not move as Iskander marched around the room, seemingly finding the proper home for the staff. She could feel a shift in the air as he approached the archway directly beside the caged box. He paused in front of it, and a soft glow radiated from the opening. The gilded letters at the base of the platform began to glimmer.

He carefully placed the rod into the post and pulled the iron-laced blanket off the staff.

Kaira slowly made her way across the space, and as she approached the scepter, tendrils of smoky Darkness began to pour out from the newly seated Crown.

Kaira dragged her golden gaze down the obsidian metal. Burnished cracks of molten magma stared back, and she swore she could hear the Dark, hushed murmurs of whatever ancient power was locked inside.

She dropped her stare to the ancient, glimmering letters at the base, and her eyes paused on the large, rounded gap with overlapping triangles carved into the center that was placed below the script.

Kaira said nothing as she ran her eyes across the old symbols. The carved triangles looked familiar, and she tried to recall where she had seen the marks before.

She was fairly certain she knew what foreboding word was etched beneath the staff, but she held her tongue, apprehensive to voice her theory without first confirming her suspicions.

Kaira ambled around the room silently, stopping in front of each archway to take in every detail of the sanctuary.

Once she had made a few rounds, she glanced over at Iskander, silently brooding in the corner.

"Mathieson doesn't know anything else about this place aside from what he told us?"

Iskander shook his head. "He claims he doesn't," he answered bitterly.

Kaira raised her brows at his implication. "Isn't truthfulness a requirement for your position?"

"Apparently not," Iskander snipped.

Kaira waited for the General to expand upon his reply, but she was left with resounding silence. She wandered over to the barred opening. "And you haven't found out anything about this chest?"

Iskander shook his head.

Kaira pursed her lips. "Or the keys that presumably unlock it?" she asked, pointing to the six small holes on the front of the box.

Another dismissal.

"Or the symbol inside these openings?" she asked, pointing to the carved gap beneath the staffs.

"No," Iskander curtly replied, his voice filled with an

edge of annoyance.

Kaira was not sure if his frustration stemmed from her ceaseless questions or if the General did not enjoy his new-found feelings of ignorance.

She moved her attention to the mural painted on the floor. The design dipped slightly in the center, as if the stone itself had once been lowered, its weight not entirely resting on the earth beneath. Her gaze moved slowly over the detailed brushstrokes. The painting depicted a great battle, with thousands of slain warriors and beasts sprawled across a shoreline. Dozens of winged creatures rampaged overhead, bursts of light and shadow ripping from their hands and colliding with one another in the sky. In the background, a warrior climbed a narrow path towards the top of a hillside. At the top, a large boulder rested on the edge of the rim, and a bundle of lines jutted out from the large rock.

"Do you think..." Kaira began, staring down at the picture. "Do you think this was what Mathieson was talking about? About his vision of the First War? About the Warrior of Praenuntius?"

Iskander flinched at the word vision, but ambled over to Kaira's side and looked down at the mural. "Yeah, well, this is his crypt, isn't it? It would make sense if he devoted some portion of this bloody sanctuary to himself." He shrugged and sauntered back towards the door, leaning against the wall with his arms crossed.

Kaira posed no more questions as she walked around the small room once more. She paused in front of the curved staff hewn from pale blue rock, examining it with meticulous scrutiny. After memorizing the image of the scepter, she crossed the room and fell into place in front of the staff made of burned copper.

She clicked her tongue.

"What is it?" Iskander asked tersely.

Kaira rolled her eyes at his impatience, as if the General and his lack of transparency about the staff she was sent to retrieve had not been the cause of her suppressed voice in the first place.

"I'm wondering..." she dwelled, running her eyes over the two staffs mounted in the Ossuary. "I'm wondering," she repeated, "if Mathieson was right. If the staffs all look different because they are hewn from the power of the Princes. And perhaps their Dark Power reflects their Province within the Hells. Like the staff holds a likeness to the Province they govern."

Iskander ran his inked hand through his hair and sighed. "Why would the Princes' powers look different from the Lord of Darkness's? Or from each other, for that matter? Wouldn't Darkness just be... Darkness?"

Kaira shrugged. "I'm not sure," she admitted, "but I remember reading something long ago about the various Provinces of the Hells... maybe that book could give us some insight."

Iskander raised a brow. "Where is the book?"

Kaira clenched her jaw. "We have to go back to the Ageless Library in Velsen."

CHAPTER THIRTY-SIX

Jeremiah's lungs burned, and his legs were shaky as he broke through the front gate of Tahira's yard.

The pale blue cottage looked the same as it always did, with a rainbow of dainty flowers lining the front edge and two wooden rockers resting on the front porch. He remembered helping her build those chairs, and as he raced up the walkway, he thought about the soft laughter that had escaped her lips on so many nights when she sat in one of the chairs, hand-in-hand with him, and they watched the sun set beyond the city.

It was his favorite sound—her laugh. He could listen to it for the rest of his life and never tire of it. Never desire to hear another noise besides her happiness in all his days.

His shaking hand reached for the brass knob, and he tore open the light-grey door. The warrior nearly fell over himself as he rushed inside.

Warm air smacked into him, and the familiar smell of lilac greeted Jeremiah as he flung himself around the corner and into the front room.

It was the smell of her. The smell of home.

But as Jeremiah barreled into the small room, his feet tripping over themselves, his heart plummeted. His entire body went rigid, and the color drained from his sun-kissed skin.

An unending moment passed. Then another.

The world seemed to stop spinning, frozen in time. Hung in place like an unbending statue.

And then, all at once, it came crashing back down, ripping the very breath from his lungs, the light from his heart.

He felt like he was in free-fall, and his knees cracked against the blood-stained floor.

The world went silent. Numb.

He could hear far-off murmurs, voices that were once familiar but now sounded foreign and detached.

A relentless ringing hummed in his head, and his mouth turned to ash. The burning in his wrist and arm winked out.

A vague stinging sensation ripped across his skin, racing up his arm and neck until it curled around the left side of his face.

He did not move. Did not breathe.

He was not sure he ever would again.

And as the last part of the Mark was etched onto his pale skin, Jeremiah heard his once whole heart splinter; and he knew it would never heal again as he stared down at the mangled form of Tahira's body.

Asha stood unmoving as dark, black Marks carved themselves up the side of Jeremiah's body. Lines and curls of geometric shapes formed together to make dreamlike arrangements. A mixture of words from the *Language of the Founders* was strewn throughout the dotted swirls, stretching all the way up the side of his distraught face. Tears slid down her cheeks.

"Go find Ronin and Varrick. Get them here," Asha choked out in a hushed whisper. "Now."

Anselem disappeared without a word.

She slowly moved towards Jeremiah. He was sunk on the floor, his knees soaked with pooled blood.

The marred body wrapped in his arms looked nothing like the kind, quiet friend she had come to know. To love. The small, missing piece that had completed their Valorous Court of Misfits.

Jeremiah's body shook with silent sobs, and Asha kneeled beside him and wrapped her arms around her chosen brother, praying to the gods of old that she could hold him tightly enough to forge his broken pieces back together.

And as Asha gently folded her arms around Jeremiah, blinking away the blurry tears that had collected in her eyes, that was when she saw it.

Her breath caught and her throat tightened as she read the jagged, bloodied letters carved onto the pale skin of Tahira's stomach, right beside the small, silver pin of the Vices:

THERE IS A PRICE FOR EVERY CHOICE.
NOW YOU KNOW NOT ALL THE VALOROUS
COURT WILL LIVE ON AND BURN WELL.
BUT LONG LIVE ITS QUEEN.

CHAPTER THIRTY-SEVEN

"Where are we going?" Kaira questioned, breathlessly trying to keep pace with Iskander's brisk steps.

"I have something I need to take care of," he replied
sharply.

Kaira huffed.

That was how the last few hours had been since they
left the Ossuary, snaking their way down the mountainside
and into Lorca—snippy comments, followed by deafening
silence.

"What is your problem?" Kaira challenged, tired of the
bitterness he had been directing her way.

Iskander halted his hurried walk, and Kaira barely
avoided running into the back of him as he whipped around.

"Excuse me?" he barked.

Lorcan citizens passing by glanced in the direction of
his raised voice with wide eyes.

Kaira clenched her jaw but did not bite back.

He stared at her intently, waiting for an answer.

She took a deep breath, remembering Anselem's words

from hours earlier. Kaira changed her tone, selecting one with more sincerity and respect, and said, "Is there something I have done wrong to make you so... angry at me?"

She pursed her lips, anticipating another heated reaction.

A flash of surprise crossed his eyes, as if he had not expected her to swallow her prideful, spitting remarks. His moondust eyes burned into her. She did not move.

"No," he replied briskly, and turned back to begin walking down the path once again.

"Are you sure? Because—" Kaira started, but Iskander's impatient tone quickly cut her off.

"Samson, I appreciate the attempt, but following orders also includes taking the answer you are given and then shutting up afterward."

Kaira blinked.

Iskander let out an exasperated sigh. "I need to stop by an old friend's place to get a message to Anselem and Asha to let Conri and Tala out of the kennels in Elysia so we can get to Velsen. Unless you would prefer to walk halfway across the kingdom." She stayed silent as he added, "And I also need to inform them to meet us there."

Kaira noticed his apparent avoidance of her second question, but she did not press the matter.

He stared at her intently, as if he expected her to come up with a list of additional questions. She only nodded.

The warriors said nothing more as they continued their walk into the heart of the city.

They wound through the endless streets, filled with broken buildings and rundown homes, and similar whispers to the ones Kaira had heard in the iron tunnels resurfaced.

Her head began to pound as the warriors plunged deeper into the Slums, and Kaira swore she heard petrified screams and gasping breaths ripping through her mind.

She tried to concentrate on the path before her, placing one foot in front of the next, never once taking her eyes off the General guiding the way.

The stirring whispers receded as she made her way out of the Slums, and she forcefully pushed the remaining murmurs from her mind as she neared the Citadel.

As they passed the towering blue-grey walls, Kaira wondered how it was possible she had never seen the renowned General in all her years of training.

"I'm surprised I never saw you," she mused, breaking the standing silence.

"What?" Iskander asked, confusion in his tone.

"At the Citadel. I'm surprised I never saw you when I was there for Fenri training."

Iskander shrugged. "I haven't spent a lot of time at the Citadel in the last few years. I was always either out on a mission with the Septant or up at Iron Rock with the Vanguard."

Kaira nodded, knowing she had never ventured up to the Vanguard Training Quarters on the high side of Lorca. Iron Rock sat at the northernmost base of the Iron Mountains, just off the edge of the Hoarfrost Sea.

His eyes slid over to her as they continued walking. "Do you think you will ever try out?" he asked, his voice softer than it had been for days.

Kaira's eyes went wide, and she huffed out a laugh. "I'm not so sure about that."

"How come?" he asked, genuine intrigue in his tone.

Kaira looked at him with astonishment.

"What?" he asked.

"You know I am from Atropos Den, right?"

Atropos—the notorious Den of the Amarok.

When Kaira had first learned about the Soturi and how their Divisions were based upon the warrior's own volition,

Kaira couldn't help but feel a tinge of envy.

She had never once felt jealousy towards the other branches, always thankful for the Bond she had forged long ago with Tala; but sitting inside the second story Base classroom in the east wing, and learning from the Soturi warriors about how their Division assignments had been selected, Kaira had not been able to shake the covetous feeling that washed over her—a wishful desire that her own branch would have practiced a similar custom.

But the Fenri soldiers, the Amarok warriors, and the entirety of the branch's Leadership had decided long before Kaira's time to pay homage to the three-phased Moon Goddess.

In an effort to thank her for the magic she bestowed upon them with her Wolves of the Night, each Fenri cadet received their Den assignment on the night of their Bonding.

From the final light on the Autumnal Equinox until the last of the midnight darkness on the Winter Solstice, the Moon Goddess's wolves were released to roam the kingdom, searching for a child they deemed worthy of their magic-releasing power.

Throughout her Fenri training, Kaira had always been taught that the wolves were guided by Selene's supreme power, a force that was strongest when the moon was wholly full.

And, to honor that tenuously instilled belief, the Den assignments of the soldiers became forcefully predicated upon which phase of the lunar cycle was present at the time the child bonded with their wolf.

The choice few who were selected by their wolves on the night of the full moon were considered valued and powerful, and it was rumored that Selene had generously gifted some of her own power to those chosen children—the Fenri soldiers of Lachesis Den.

A majority of the children bonded when a variety of crescent-shaped phases were draped across the sky. These children were assigned to Klotho Den—the largest faction of the three units—and were known for their deference and resolve.

The final Den—Atropos—was comprised of the smallest number of soldiers and was often referred to as the *Dark Den*, for the soldiers who were assigned to the unit were marked as defective and tainted. The Leaders claimed Selene did not find favor with the choice of her wolves on the night of the Dark Moon, as her power was not present without her shining light. So, in supposed honor of the Moon Goddess, the Amarok Leaders formed a Den to house the rejected.

On the night Kaira bonded with Tala, the Dark Moon hung high in the midnight sky.

As a young child, before their death, Kaira's parents had told her countless times to never wander outside on the evening of the Winter Solstice, but sitting in her Uncle's cold house, watching drink after drink flow down his throat, Kaira knew she would not escape his sickening, salacious gaze for long.

She pulled on her boots, wrapped a thick coat around her chest, and silently slipped out the back door and into the Mist.

Kaira had found the Olden Oak a couple of years before, when she first chanced spending a night in the Redwoods over a harrowing evening in her Uncle's home.

Wandering through the vaporous winter haze, her small legs had violently shivered inside her thick, wool-lined pants. She forced them to continue forward, unknowing where they would lead until she stumbled upon an ancient tree, with a deep-green door carved into the base.

She never truly knew how she found the Olden Oak. It was as though it had capriciously appeared in the middle of the Mist, specially for her.

A small haven in the midst of her endless Dark.

After the first night the Mist had gifted her a place of safety, she had spent nearly every evening curled up inside the protection of the Olden Oak.

As she ducked out of her Uncle's home and made her way through the eternal haze covering Velsen, Kaira glanced up to the winter skies and found no trace of light from the moon to help guide her.

She forged forward nonetheless, sending a prayer to Selene for a safe passage.

But the Goddess of the Moon was not near on that night, and Kaira's pleas went unheard, for Selene's power was scarcely present during the Dark Moon.

Weaving her way through the towering, reddish-brown trees, Kaira's gaze whipped towards the sound of every cracking tree limb and every rustling of leaves, until the forest-green door came into view and her shoulders finally untensed.

As she crossed the last bit of space separating her from the shelter of the Oak, a massive, snow-white wolf stepped out from the cover of the Mist and paused in front of the door.

Kaira froze, her entire body unmoving. She did not breathe as the wolf turned its all-knowing, ice-blue eyes onto her. And when their gazes met, the Bond snapped into place.

From that night on, Kaira had been publicly marked as one of the children bonded without Selene's blessing.

"I did not," Iskander replied simply, bringing her drifting mind back to the present.

There was no judgment in his tone, but Kaira stayed quiet as insecurities pilfered their way into her mind.

"Some of my best guardians are from Atropos," he stated, his tone even and unemotional. "Fellowes, my Second, she came from Atropos Den." The faintest smile turned up on the corners of his mouth as he mentioned the honorable Second of the Vanguard.

Kaira noticed that, unlike most other Amarok warriors, the General had not once referred to it as *Dark Den.* She slowed her steps.

"Imara Fellowes came from Atropos?" she whispered, disbelief flooding her words.

Iskander let a full, pride-filled grin cover his face as he nodded. "She certainly did."

His feet started back up, and Kaira fell in stride beside him.

"Are you in Lachesis?" she asked, presuming the General's strength and power were likely formed with great influence from the Moon Goddess.

Iskander shook his head but offered no further explanation.

"So... what Den are you in?" she tried, unsure if he would answer any more of her questions.

Iskander continued his steps, and without a falter in his stride, he answered, "I have no Den assignment."

Kaira slowed her pace, and to her surprise, the General shortened his steps to match hers.

Her brow furrowed. "What do you mean you have no Den assignment?" she whispered.

The General cleared his throat. "I mean that I do not belong to Lachesis, Klotho, or Atropos."

"How?" she asked, her voice hardly carrying across the short distance between them.

Iskander let out a long sigh. "When I bonded with Conri, it did not fit into the typical... phases," he answered, his voice trailing off.

Kaira looked the General over once as the gears in her mind began racing. "How old were you when you bonded?" she questioned, her voice beginning to fill with disbelief.

336

Iskander glanced sideways at the Amarok, attempting to assess her expression before he answered. Her face was unreadable.

"Ten."

Kaira sucked in a sharp breath. Her boots halted in place, and her golden eyes splayed wide as the revelation clicked.

The only reason Iskander Blaidd could have been unassigned to one of the three chosen Dens was that he had Bonded to his wolf on a night when neither full, crescent, nor dark moon hung in the sky. On a night when the rarest of lunar phases occurred.

She looked the warrior over once more, knowing that a little over a decade and a half ago, a Perseisian child was rumored to have bonded with a wolf on the sacred night of the total lunar eclipse, when a super blue moon hung high in the midnight sky.

The event was so extraordinary, the scholars and academic Instructors at the Citadel claimed the moon phase would only occur in the lands of Perseis once in a lifetime.

"It was you?" she breathed, all semblance of composure having left her body.

Iskander's jaw feathered, and he gave her a nearly imperceptible nod before turning and continuing through the Lorcan streets.

The General had only made it a few steps before Kaira collected herself and followed swiftly behind. "You're Selene's Favored One."

"Don't call me that," Iskander grunted.

Surprise washed over Kaira. She had never known an Amarok warrior to blaspheme the Moon Goddess. And she certainly never would have expected it from the Favored One.

A sharp tenseness fell over the General's shoulders.

Kaira sensibly dropped the subject, gleaning there was a

deep-seated bitterness attached to the story that Iskander was decidedly unwilling to share.

After another half hour of walking, they arrived on an ordinary street in the middle of the Merchant's Guild.

Iskander knocked heavily on a maroon door, exchanged quick pleasantries with an aged man hiding beyond the cracked doorframe, and swiftly slipped inside. He returned to the empty street moments later.

Kaira fought the urge to ask him any questions about what had transpired behind the closed door, and instead she silently paced beside him as the pair leisurely meandered back down the street.

They rounded a corner, heading southward, and the setting sun slowly dipped behind the buildings overhead. A blanket of deep orange covered the sky, painting the city below in a dusky, burning hue that was delicately softened by the powdered white snow resting atop the sloped roofs.

"Hungry?" he asked, turning onto a street lined with taverns and shops.

Kaira's stomach rumbled as the mixed aromas of smoked meats and spices flooded the air.

She nodded, and the General slid inside a small, nearby eatery packed full of hungry patrons.

Sitting at a small table along the back wall, Iskander stifled a laugh.

He had not realized the guilelessness of the woman before him.

When they had entered the tavern, nearly every head in the room had turned. At first, Iskander believed it was thanks to the persistent recognition he received whenever he frequented the public streets of Lorca. But the longer he sat, watching the crowd and observing the clientele, he quick-ly gathered that the longing gazes and wish-filled eyes that were ordinarily fixated on him were instead focused on the striking woman seated opposite him.

Feelings he could not place stirred inside of him as he noticed a group of men passing by with lustful gazes locked on the Amarok.

Kaira paid them no mind, her glorious, golden eyes fo-cused on the food before her.

Iskander laughed.

Kaira glanced up from her stew with raised brows. "What?"

He shook his head. She was so distinctly different than him in every way imaginable.

Her beauty, like his, was unmatched in any room she en-tered, but unlike the General, she did not wield it to her ad-vantage, nor did she use it as a honed weapon. It was almost as if she deemed the entire notion of exterior beauty to be unimportant—trivial. Like she did not give her otherworldly looks a second thought, believing she had more important—stronger—assets to wield.

Kaira narrowed her eyes.

She looked like waves on a sunset, the kind he'd let crash into him time and time again. A devastating temptress, harboring the force of a raging tempest.

But it was not her looks that had captivated the attention of the cold, heartless General of the Vanguard. It was her mind.

Bold. Resilient. With an edge of viciousness that re-minded him so intently of the resolute spirit of a fighter—a survivor.

The same spirit that had been etched into the very depths of his bones.

After Kaira had scarfed down a second helping of stew and Iskander finished another mug of ale, the pair made their way back onto the hectic streets of Lorca.

Kaira followed silently behind the General as he led the way through the city.

They wound back through the different districts, passing by the towering walls of the Citadel, and as they reentered the devious streets of the Slums, the harrowing screams and chilling whispers crawled back into Kaira's mind with newfound force.

She kept her eyes forward, locked on Iskander, and she forced herself to take one step after another.

The cries continued to grow louder and louder, thundering inside her head with the forceful violence of a vicious storm. Her vision began to blur, and she reached out to steady herself against the brick wall beside her.

The General, focused on the dimly lit streets ahead, continued along the path, unaware of the internal war waging behind him.

Kaira shut her eyes and focused on her breathing. The screams persisted, and the heaviness inside her head grew so loud it became unbearable.

She pressed her hands against her temples, sucking in a sharp breath. A low whimper escaped her lips as she fought to stay upright. It felt like sharp, lifeless nails were being dragged down the insides of her mind.

A tormented scream escaped her lips as she struggled to remain present. Not a moment later, the world began to shake, and she felt strong hands gripping her shoulders.

The grating scrapes of the lifeless nails slowly receded from her mind, and a calm, steadfast presence replaced the harrowing screams within her mind.

She did not move as the last of the Darkness withdrew from her mind, filled in by a soft, moondust Light.

Kaira slowly opened her eyes, and as they readjusted, she was met with a warrior's gaze.

Iskander stared down at Kaira, his face painted with concern.

"Don't look at me like that," she snipped, rubbing her temples to soothe the passing pain. "It's unbecoming."

Iskander morphed his face back into the unemotional mask he always wore, but a trace of worry lingered in his eyes. "How long?" he questioned, his tone holding nothing but command and poise.

"A few days," she replied facilely.

"It's still too early to know…"

"I know the odds, Iskander."

Kaira had run through the probabilities for days. Ever since the first bone-chilling scream rang through her head when she entered the misty forest just beyond the streets of Velsen.

She ignored it at first, when the cries and whispers were so low she'd been able to convince herself she had imagined them.

But as the hours and days passed, and the death-filled shrieks grew louder and more pronounced, she knew. Deep in her scarred and mist-filled soul, Kaira knew what she was.

A Revenant.

Maybe it was from too many nights spent inside the Mist as a child, or perhaps the Dominions had always known that her broken soul was more closely aligned with the dead than the living, but no matter the reason, Kaira Samson had been cursed with the power of necromancy.

The number of wielders granted the gift of death-magic was rare, and Kaira believed the paucity to be a blessing, as she knew far too well the tales of old.

She had memorized the ancient stories as a child, the ones depicting the waning mental status of every Revenant, and, as the storytellers never failed to mention, how a Dark Mist would creep into the wielder's minds and eventually drive them mad.

As a child, she had found the gift of speaking with the dead mesmerizing. She had longed for the chance to talk with those who had lived long before her, those who held wisdom and insight into the limitless questions that rolled through her mind.

But what she did not realize as one so young was that a great price came with fracturing the established balance between worlds. Because whenever the ones before her had attempted to toe the line between the realm of the dead and the living, convincing themselves that they could maintain the balance between the spirits, they found themselves wobbling across a blurred track. And, inevitably, every Revenant had crossed into an eternal place from which there was no return.

Iskander looked down into her devastating, golden eyes and muttered, "Don't."

Kaira's brows bunched.

"Fear is often the worst form of torture. Never let those who came before you tell you who you will be. Never let them tell you your destiny." He held her gaze for a long moment, like he was looking past her bright smiles and quiet disposition and deeply gazing into the scarred parts of her soul, and added, "And do not fear Death. Instead, make yourself into something Death begs to never meet."

Kaira nodded, unsure what to say to the General's words.

She glanced down the quieting streets of Lorca, and just before she stepped away from the brick wall to resume their journey, Kaira looked up at the General, and a sudden, newfound reverence filled her heart.

And as she gazed into his moondust eyes, she realized

Iskander Blaidd could very well be the perfect person to teach her how to become something Death feared.

CHAPTER

THIRTY-EIGHT

Asha was sitting in the corner of the room, staring out the window blankly, when the front door to Tahira's cottage swung open.

She palmed a dagger but quickly loosened her grip when three warriors entered the home.

Anselem's emerald eyes looked tired, and his hair was wind-blown and knotted.

Ronin and Varrick did not look any more rested than the Commander.

The two Valorous Soturi warriors silently crossed the small space and grabbed Asha in a quick embrace.

They unwrapped their arms from around the Thurisaz and their gazes twisted to the opposite corner, landing on Jeremiah.

He was sitting on the floor, cross-legged, staring into the fireplace. Asha had ensured a constant fire remained burning within the wooden planks, occasionally reigniting the firewood with her flames.

He had not moved from his spot on the hardwood floor

344

for hours. He had not even reacted when the door opened, and Asha had jumped to her feet.

All he did was stare, motionlessly, into the flickering flames.

In the aftermath of the massacre, Asha had peeled Jeremiah's numb body from Tahira's and dragged him to the washroom. Silent tears streamed down her cheeks as she gently washed the blood from his hands and arms. She rummaged, blurry-eyed, through several dressers in the bedroom until she found a drawer containing his clothes. Carefully, she helped him out of the blood-soaked leathers crusted onto his skin and into a clean pair of trousers and a top.

Asha sat beside Jeremiah on the bed for a long while as he rocked back and forth. After several hours had passed, she brought a vile from her leather bag in the front room and coaxed him into drinking the draught. She waited beside him silently until the warrior gave in to the sleeping powder and was carried off into a deep slumber.

No more tears left his amber eyes.

She unfeelingly managed through the rest of the day and the ones that followed, disposing of the bloodstained carpet and scrubbing the stained floors. She requested a local Rapha to stop by and tend to Tahira before making arrangements with Cathan to ensure her body would be properly kept at the fort until her water burial could take place.

Standing beside Ronin and Varrick, Asha could still see a faint shadow of where the blood had seeped too deeply into the floorboards to be washed clean.

Anselem's towering form appeared in front of her, pulling her eyes away from the stained wood.

He caressed her face, brushing his thumb across her cheek. She offered him a soft, tired smile.

I received a note from Iskander, he explained, digging in his jacket.

345

Asha tilted her head to the side and dropped her gaze to the note he pulled from his pocket.

She could see the broken Septant seal on the front as he handed her the parchment.

Asha silently unfolded the letter and read the scribbled writing:

RELEASE CONRI AND TALA AND MEET
US AT THE AGELESS LIBRARY.

I'll head over to the Kennels now, and I will be back shortly, Anselem stated.

Asha nodded.

The Commander turned to head out the front door, and she grabbed his hand.

Wait, she requested.

She walked over to the small desk tucked away in the corner. She pulled an ink bottle and quill from the drawer and placed the parchment onto the mahogany surface. She flipped the paper over and scrawled a few short sentences on the back.

She walked back over and placed the note in Anselem's hands.

Attach this to Conri.

Anselem stared down at the inked letters instructing the two Amarok warriors to meet them at the Mount before heading to Velsen.

He nodded, folding up the letter and tucking it away in the front pocket of his flying jacket.

I'll be back as quickly as I can, he promised. He leaned down and pressed a soft kiss against her lips.

The Commander said nothing else as he left the cottage, swiftly disappearing into the City of Glass.

For the next hour, Asha caught Ronin and Varrick up on

everything that had transpired. During her explanation, she heard the front door softly open and close, but the Septant warrior that had returned did not join them in the front room.

"You think it was Leadership?" Ronin questioned, his body tense with rage as he glanced over at Jeremiah.

Asha nodded. "It's the only explanation."

"Why?" Varrick asked, attempting to understand how she had arrived at the conclusion.

"No one else knew about our Court. Our family. No one but us and Anselem. But the Council had eyes on us—on me—the entire time I was there," she explained.

The warriors nodded, recalling the sight of their friend in the East Wing hospital bed after the Tartarus and hearing her explanation of why everything had happened.

Asha dropped her voice low and added, "And just beneath the words they had carved into Tahira's stomach, there was an eye etched into her skin."

Ronin and Varrick's jaws clenched at the mention of the symbol of the Vices.

"Do you think it was the Snake?" Ronin's eyes were dark when she met them, but she shook her head.

"Bardick disappeared after the Nameless Place, and Anselem has kept tabs on any rumors circulating about his whereabouts ever since, but nothing has surfaced among any of his informants. Especially not in Elysia," she replied.

"I'm fairly certain it was one of the other Vices on Base after our final Benchmark. I don't know which one, and I have no proof, but those are the only ones who had close enough access to us to learn about our Court. To learn about Tahira."

Varrick pursed his lips. "And now you have to go to Reyka to meet...?"

"Raziel," Asha finished, filling in the forgotten name for Varrick.

"The Secret-Seeker," he resolved.

Asha nodded.

"That's the next step in all of this?" Ronin asked, attempting to clarify the load of information that had been dumped onto the warriors.

"Yes," she confirmed. "At least that's what Math seems to think. I'm hopeful he will have some answers for us about the Amulet of Tisiphone whenever Anselem and I go to the Manor."

"What do you mean *whenever you go*? How long are you planning to wait?" Ronin asked. His voice was strained, as though he recognized time was not on her side.

Asha agreed. Time was certainly not a luxury she could afford to waste. She sighed and glanced over to Jeremiah, who remained unmoved on the floor.

Asha turned her eyes back to Ronin and Varrick. "I just don't think right now is the best time for me to be leaving..." she whispered, her voice trailing off.

Her heart was heavy with grief. With guilt.

She couldn't bring herself to look again at Jeremiah.

She had no idea if he blamed her for it; he hadn't muttered a single word in the days since he had awoken. But if he did, Asha didn't fault him for it. Gods knew she blamed herself.

Varrick and Ronin glanced at each other, then over to their brother. They brought their gazes back to Asha and nodded in understanding.

"Maybe after some time—" she started, but was interrupted by an unrecognizable, lifeless voice.

"Go," the voice stated flatly from the corner.

The three Valorous warriors whipped their eyes to Jeremiah.

"Jer?" Asha questioned softly.

He twisted his neck and looked back at her with depthless eyes. Eyes that held a thousand oceans of Darkness. "Go," he ground out, his voice firmer than the first command. "It's what she would have wanted."

Asha swallowed and nodded resolutely.

She pulled her eyes to Varrick and Ronin. They held her stare, and Ronin offered, "We will be here with him. Go."

She squeezed each of their hands and spun towards the door.

As she turned the corner and exited the front room, the heaviness of the past few days rammed into her like a tidal wave, thrusting her out into a tempest of Darkness. But when she looked up and met the soft, quiet eyes of the Commander, her shoulders untensed, and her heart calmed, as though his very presence had lightened the Darkness she was swimming inside.

"NUMBER 14 - REVENANT (NEKROS): POSSESSES THE CAPABILITIES OF NECROMANCY AND SPIRIT MANIPULATION."

— THE KNOWN POWERS AND KRATOS OF MAGIC WIELDERS (ABRIDGED VERSION) BY INSTRUCTOR C. BARDICK

CHAPTER THIRTY-NINE

After the voices inside her head had fully quieted, Kaira and Iskander made their way through the snowy streets of Lorca and into the eastern outskirts of the city.

Staring out the large, glass window of Iskander's cottage, Kaira observed the pattering of snow as it trickled from the sky, lining the trees and mountaintops.

For a moment, in the silence of her mind, watching the pure, untouched flakes fall from the clouds above, she felt at peace.

"Want some?" Iskander asked, pulling a glass from the nearby cabinet. He had a large craft of black-crescent whiskey curled in his hand.

Kaira glanced over from her place on the couch and shook her head. "No, thank you."

Iskander raised a brow as he poured the blackened liquor into a mug.

"Do you ever partake?" he questioned, lifting the canister. There was no judgment in his tone, simply a quiet curiosity.

She placed her gaze back on the endless fire before her. "No," she answered softly.

"How come?" he tried.

She shrugged. She did not mention that every horrible memory she had experienced as a child had been accompanied by drunken debauchery.

"You know the bedroom is a much more comfortable place to fall asleep..." he began, stopping short as Kaira's gaze whipped to face him.

Her eyes were wide, and he smirked. "The *guest* bedroom, Samson," he clarified.

Redness spread across her cheeks at her wrongful assumption.

"I mean, unless..."

Kaira narrowed her eyes, but the General had already released a huffing laugh.

"Oh, loosen up, I'm only kidding," he teased. "Not even in your nightmares, I know, I know."

Kaira caught the faintest hint of pain in his words. "Iskander..." she began, not wholly sure what to say. But her words stopped short as Iskander held up his hands.

"No need," he said. "I deserved it." A long moment of silence passed between them before Iskander interrupted the quiet and said, "I'm going to bed. Just knock if you need anything."

Kaira nodded and watched as the General headed out of the main room and down the hallway, canister and mug in hand.

The Amarok pulled a book from the satchel at her feet. She flipped through the pages, occasionally pausing to watch the snow outside fall from the heavens. As the night went on, the steady crackling of the fire softly lulled her to sleep.

She awoke a few hours later, and it took her a moment to gather her wits and realize where she was. The room was still dark, and the sun had not yet risen.

Kaira peeled herself off the cognac couch and placed her feet on the warm wood floor.

She decided to make her way towards the guest bedroom, but as she stood, her novel fell from her lap and clattered to the ground. As she grabbed for it, she clumsily knocked into the small table set in the center of the chairs, and the wooden feet scraped against the floorboards.

"Bloody moonlight," she cursed, grabbing the book and placing it on top of the table.

As she spun around, aiming for the guest room, her heart leapt into her throat. A towering figure stood inside the archway that led down the hall.

Iskander took a step forward, the fire illuminating his face, and Kaira released a deep breath as her heart calmed.

"Sorry," she murmured, making her way across the room.

Iskander did not move from where he was leaning against the wall.

As she neared, an enveloping smell of cedarwood and snow wrapped around her.

He gazed down at her with glassy, red-lined eyes. Even in their glazed state, the moondust color was entrancing.

"Sorry," she murmured.

"You said that already," he replied, glancing over to the floor beside the couch.

He lifted his hand, and soft spirals of shadows poured from his fingers. A moment later, the book she had left inside her bag was in his hands. Iskander glanced at the scripted title printed on the front and raised his brows.

Kaira's heart dropped as he began to flip aimlessly through the pages.

The General's hazy eyes went wide, and a dark libidinous twinkle sparked through them. "Grab onto the bed posts?" he taunted, reading one of the salacious lines from her endless collection of romance novels.

His eyes trailed down the rest of the page, and Kaira tried to snatch the book from the General's hand, a deep crimson painted on her cheeks.

He teasingly raised the novel higher, just above her reach, as he let out a dark, sensual laugh that trickled down her spine. "I've been wondering what that vicious mind of yours indulges in when it's not uncovering the hidden secrets of the world."

She rolled her eyes and huffed at the warrior. "You know it's rude to rifle through other people's belongings."

Kaira knew the General likely thought the book was one of the journals from the Ageless Library, but she was still vexed, nonetheless.

"You know, the most breathtaking words are not the ones printed into novels," he told her, "but those drawn on soft skin and breathed through hushed moans." His voice was full of dark promises and fantasy-filled wishes.

Kaira's breath hitched, but before she could reply with a snippy remark, he placed the novel back in her hands. She glanced up, into his stunning stardust eyes, and she swore she could see the glassiness dissolve, as if staring into her gaze had brought him more clarity than a thousand days of sobriety.

Her gaze dropped as she realized the closeness between them, and as her eyes trailed down his body, she noticed the lack of clothing he wore.

Aside from a pair of midnight-black shorts, every inch of his skin was exposed. Hundreds of Marks were inked upon his flesh. It looked like violent whispers of Darkness had carved themselves onto every surface.

Her breathing deepened as she pulled her eyes back up to his silver stare.

He looked down at her with intrigue and wonder, as if he wished to know her thoughts on the many Marks scarring his body.

Kaira caught a flicker of fear as it flashed through his starry eyes, but before she could say anything, the General murmured, "Goodnight, Samson."

Kaira took her cue and quickly turned away, shuffling down the hall. She closed the door to the guest room without a word.

Iskander smirked as he shut the door to his bedchamber and crawled into bed.

Even in the dim light, the General had not missed the deep red brushed across Kaira's cheeks as she dragged her gaze down his half-dressed body.

As she lay in bed, staring at the ceiling, an overwhelming sense of self-loathing settled into Kaira's bones.

She hated herself for staring. She hated herself even more for blushing.

She was just as bad as the rest of them, all the women who undressed him with their eyes. She would've had to be blind not to notice the women nearly tripping over themselves when the General walked past.

She shook her head.

Kaira didn't blame them. He was objectively the most beautiful man she had ever seen in her life.

But what caused the warmth that washed over her cheeks was not from Iskander's undeniable beauty or his sculpted physique. No, the redness painted across her face was from the burning shame she felt stirring deep inside her bones as her eyes dragged themselves across the darkly etched thorns splintered across his skin.

Shame for judging the warrior without realizing there was much more to Iskander Blaidd than dreamy eyes and flirtatious smiles.

Because the heavy Marks covering his torso told Kaira there was a brokenness swimming inside of him that reminded her so patently of her own fractured pieces.

"THE DEAD DO NOT WHISPER TO THE SANE. IT IS ONLY WHEN THE MIND BEGINS TO
UNRAVEL THAT THE VEIL BETWEEN LIFE AND DEATH BEGINS TO SPEAK. ONE MUST
ALWAYS REMEMBER THERE IS A PRICE TO HOLD AUTHORITY OVER DEATH. IT IS NOT
PAID IN BLOOD, BUT IN MEMORY."
– QUOTE FROM K. MORTIVOX, THE LAST KNOWN REVENANT OF THE
SEVENTH GATE; EXTRACTED FROM WHISPERS OF THE VEIL: THE DIRGE OF
BONE AND SOUL

CHAPTER FORTY

Asha and Anselem entered the Mount in silence. Kage and
Mathieson were already in attendance, positioned at opposite ends of the room. A thick tension clung to the air between them, sharp and unspoken. Asha wondered if their
reunion had been as strained as Mathieson's and the other
Septant warriors at Gull's Landing. From the lack of blood
and scuffed knuckles, Asha assumed it had gone at least
slightly better than his and Iskander's.

Mathieson stood against the far wall, arms folded across
his chest. Kage lounged in a chair at the table's edge, his
posture deceptively relaxed.

"Sacha's on his way from the fort," Kage said, leaning
back as the two warriors took places at the table. "He was
speaking with the Overseer. Said he wouldn't be long."

Anselem nodded. "Then we will wait before diving in."

There was a brief pause, then Kage asked, quieter this
time, "How is Greystone?"

Before Anselem had departed to retrieve Varrick and
Ronin, he had stopped by the Elysian Fort to inform Cathan.
The Overseer had passed along the news of Tahira's death to

356

the others.

Asha's chest twisted. She opened her mouth to answer, but words did not form. Her throat tightened.

"He's managing," Anselem answered for her, reaching across the table and clasping her hand. "As well as anyone could."

Kage gave a solemn nod.

From his place against the wall, Mathieson asked, "Has his Kratos manifested yet?"

Asha understood the implication of his question immediately. The threat of being Marked before one's powers came. The swallowing Darkness that preyed on those when their magic was finally released. She had dealt with the struggle only a few short months ago, and from what Anselem had told her atop the clocktower roof at Sveaborg, both he and Mathieson had experienced the same fate.

Asha shook her head. "I don't think so," she answered, voice low. "Not that I've seen."

Mathieson nodded once, grim and tight. Anselem's grip on her hand tightened.

Tense silence filled the room, and just as Asha's thoughts of Jeremiah began to spiral, the door to the Mount swung open, and in strode Sacha.

He gave a brief nod to each of them seated at the table before his gaze landed on Mathieson, still standing in the corner. Sacha's tanned face drew tight.

The two men stared at each other, still and unblinking.

Asha held her breath in the silence.

"Oh, good," Sacha said at last, voice cracking somewhere between a laugh and a snarl. "You're alive. That means I can punch you."

Asha's eyes widened. She braced herself, expecting a remake of Mathieson's encounter with Iskander. But neither Anselem nor Kage moved. They didn't even tense.

The Pontos took a step forward, fists clenched, eyes wild. "You have *no* idea how much grief-rage I've been bottling. Two godsdrowning years, you beautiful, undead idiot," he called, voice made of loving mockery rather than rage. "I thought you were gone. I buried your favorite boots, you ungrateful bastard." He glanced at Mathieson for a long moment, and with a shaky breath, he added, "You owe me boots."

Mathieson's mouth twitched into a faint smirk.

Then, in a quieter voice, he added, "I cried, by the way. Actual tears. Full snot situation. I looked like a drowned, feral cat. Which is *not* the image a soldier of the sea wants etched into legend." He paused, the bravado fading. His crass voice dropped low. "I mourned you. And now you're just... standing here." His tone was laced with disbelief and bewilderment. A grin tugged at the corner of his mouth—sharp, unhinged, and laced with something dangerously close to joy. He snorted. "I should've known Death wouldn't take you. Too stubborn. Too loud. And probably too irritating for the Afterlife to deal with."

Silence stretched for a beat. Then the warrior moved in with a choked laugh and arms flung wide. "Don't just stand there, you walking miracle—get over here before I start leaking from the face again."

Mathieson let out a quiet laugh, the sound light and genuine, and crossed the space in three strides. He pulled Sacha into a rough, grateful embrace. For a moment, the sharp edges between them dulled.

Anselem cleared his throat, the sound slicing through the heartfelt silence. "Now that we're all here," he said, voice steady. "We have a few things to discuss."

The subtle warmth of the reunion evaporated. Mathieson and Sacha found seats at the table.

Anselem leaned forward, bracing his lightning-streaked

forearms against the table. "Mathieson believes we need to obtain an artifact—the Amulet of Tisiphone—before we can request a meeting with the Empress in Verloren. We don't know what it is or where it is hidden, which is why we will be going to the Boeotian Manor. I believe Raziel may know."

Kage's brow lifted, skeptical. "The Secret-Seeker?" he asked. "You really think he will know where to find a buried relic that's been hidden for gods know how long?"

"I think he is our best option," Anselem answered. "He knew the location of the Forgotten City. If there's anyone who knows where to find the payment for convening with the Empress, it's him."

Sacha tilted his head, frowning. "And where exactly did this amulet come from? Why are we chasing something none of us has ever heard of?" His face was twisted with confusion as he attempted to catch up in the conversation.

"The same way I know there will be answers waiting for us in Verloren," Mathieson said quietly, his voice cool and distant. "It came to me in a vision. Long before Montu."

A weight fell over the room. Kage's jaw clenched. Sacha's expression darkened. Even Anselem, ever composed, went utterly still at the mention of the city.

Anselem was the first to speak. "We move tomorrow night. My sources inform me that Raziel is hosting another one of his insufferably grand parties. With enough noise and masks, we'll slip in unnoticed."

Mathieson exhaled through his nose. "There's something else," he added, almost as an afterthought.

Asha turned to him, brows drawn.

"What do you mean?" Anselem pressed, voice tight.

"During one of my visits to the Chamber of Reflection, I saw images of the Boeotian Manor. The Room of Secrets."

Anselem's gaze narrowed. "How did you know what the Room of Secrets looked like?"

"Because I've been there," he replied simply.

Asha's chest tightened.

"In the vision," Mathieson continued, ignoring the shift in the room, "I saw a box tucked inside an onyx desk drawer. It was wrapped in crimson thread."

"What was in the box?" Kage asked.

Mathieson shrugged. "I don't know," he replied. "The visions from the early days are... hazy. Fragmented." He shook his head. "But it felt important. Important enough to find."

Anselem stared at him for a long, unreadable moment.

"Who's going?" Sacha asked, breaking the growing tension.

Anselem turned his attention to the Pontos. "Asha and I." He slowly shifted his gaze to Mathieson. "And I suppose Raynor will be joining us, seeing as though we have another item to retrieve." Anselem's words were clipped, and he did not hide the edge in his tone.

He turned to Kage. "You will remain at the fort to run interference. Sacha, you go with him and start preparing the supplies for travel. Depending on what Raziel gives us, we may be covering more ground than we think, so be sure to request an aerial orb from Cathan for the flight."

Sacha nodded once and grunted in affirmation.

"Anything else?" Anselem asked, scanning the table.

The warriors shook their heads, all except Asha, who turned to face her brother. A sobering graveness rested inside her sapphire eyes.

Her voice was lower than before as she finally voiced the question that had been racing through her mind since the moment she had laid her eyes on her brother on the western shores of Gull's Landing. "What was the price?"

Mathieson cocked his head to the side.

"For your deal with Raziel. What was the price?" Her

voice was not cold, nor harsh, but instead held a deep-seated concern for the dark deal her brother had made with a scheming devil.

Confusion spread over the Prophet's face. "I never made a deal with him. He invited me to play, but I lost."

"Then why was your name on one of the journals in the Faustia Room?"

Mathieson's brows knotted together. "What are you talking about?"

Kage and Anselem inched closer. Asha could feel a strumming of power vibrating off the warriors.

She ignored the men and replied, "When I was walking out of the Room of Secrets, there was an onyx book beside the door with the initials *M. Raynor* on it."

Mathieson's face turned pale, and Kage, seated beside him, went rigid. The Transferent's eyes flickered rapidly back and forth between the siblings.

"What?" she choked out, her mouth drier than the desert sands of Peitho.

Mathieson's voice was grim and hollow as he answered, "Micaiah Raynor."

Asha's stomach dropped, and her throat tightened.

"Dad?"

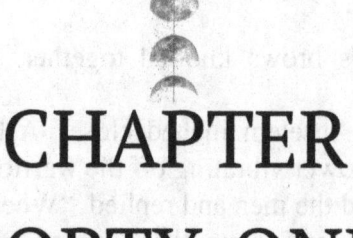

CHAPTER
FORTY-ONE

Salt stung Asha's nose as she neared the iron archway, its frame carved with the jagged letters *Boeotian Manor.*

Her lavish dress trailed behind her as she approached the gate. The gown was covered in an assortment of Septant-black gemstones and hugged snugly against the top of her body before falling in loose layers down to her feet.

After the meeting at the Mount, she and Anselem had scoured the Luminos District, visiting three separate seamstresses in search of a gown before leaving empty-handed. With much reluctance, she begrudgingly surrendered to Anselem's suggestion to visit the one person he knew would have a lavish, hand-sewn gown waiting in reserve.

As she strolled towards the Manor, Asha was mindful to avoid tripping over the extra length bundled at her feet. Even with the heeled shoes she wore, Asha still did not reach the height of the Spinner.

Anselem, calm and steadfast by her side, offered an arm to steady her. She looped her hand around his honed muscles and peered up at him with an appreciative glance.

He donned an off-white jacket with matching trousers that were perfectly tailored to fit his brawny form. Intricately stamped etchings were impressed into the thick material, and down the backside of the coat, just beneath the collar, fell a crafted piece of fabric structurally shaped into the form of alabaster wings.

The Commander trailed his emerald eyes down her tightly fitted gown, and a libidinous twinkle sparked through the green.

Asha's red-painted lips tipped into a teasing smile, and as they continued their walk, Anselem leaned over and whispered in her ear, "You are killing me in that dress, Seven."

He pulled himself back upright, never once faltering in his steps.

Asha peeked back at the warrior trailing closely behind them.

Mathieson was outfitted in a simple ensemble of deep, forest green and gold—the traditional colors of Valhol.

She pulled her charcoal-lined eyes back to Anselem's, and with a devious smirk on her lips, she replied, *Maybe if you're lucky, you'll see it on your floor later.*

Flashes of desire and hunger rushed through Anselem's gaze. He matched her taunting grin with his own. She could hear his sensual, breathy laugh as it reverberated through her mind, and he looked at her with passion-filled eyes as he replied, *You better make sure a great deal of time accompanies that promise, Seven. Because I plan to take a long while with all the things I want to do with you.*

A tempting smile was still set upon her mouth as she stepped through the archway and onto the iron-laced grounds of the Manor.

She waited for the shift to happen. For the dulling feeling to wash over her well of power.

She noticed the dampening of Anselem's thrumming

electricity beside her, a clouding of the sensation she experienced whenever he was near—the feeling of her own magic's desire to devour and consume.

From the stiffness that came over the Septant warrior behind her, she assumed Mathieson had experienced the same quieting of his magic within the iron-fortified border.

But as she continued up the stone path, nearing the sinister walls of the Manor, the dampening of her obsidian-lit Chaos never came. She could feel no change in the magic running through her veins, nor any hindrance to accessing the limitless well of power inside her glittering onyx.

She slowed her pace before they ascended the stone staircase, allowing the warrior behind her to draw closer. "I'm confused. Why would Dad have made a deal with Raziel? How did he even know who he was?" Asha whispered.

Mathieson shrugged. "I don't know, Fletch."

Asha contemplated bringing up the inquiries made about their mother during her time in the Nameless Place, but the unsettling feeling that poured through her veins as the haunted thoughts entered her mind kept her lips sealed.

As the warriors climbed the entrance steps, overcast by the crimson hue of the overhead luminos, they fastened their respective masks into place and warily entered the Boeotian Manor.

The Manor looked the same as it had every other time Anselem had apprehensively entered its walls.

Dozens of partygoers ambled around the room, all donning ornate masks and lavish ensembles as they mingled with one another.

Servers floated around the room with bottles of fine wines, refilling the unsteady glasses of the half-drunk guests.

An opium-mixed haze filtered out of a corner room, with tendrils of smoke rolling into the main ballroom.

The warriors waded through the boisterous crowd, with Asha purposefully and gracefully leading the group directly to the far corner.

She tossed the onyx curtains open with daunting resolve, unveiling the red doors of the Faustia Room.

Without hesitation, she marched to the doors, ripped open the hinges, and ducked inside. The Septant warriors followed silently behind her.

The Secret-Seeker was hunched over the onyx desk in the corner. His eyes splayed wide as the warriors poured into the room, but he quickly composed himself, carefully placing the quill in his hand upon the table.

Opposite him stood a lean young man, no older than eighteen. His posture was poised, but the tension in his limbs betrayed his cool exterior. His jet-black hair was cropped short, and on his pale neck, just above his collar, rested a tattoo inked in deep carmine red. It was the outline of a single droplet of blood falling from a hollow circle. The Mark of Death Without Trace.

Anselem stiffened. He knew that Mark; he'd seen it once before during a Septant mission on the Southern Continent. It belonged to the Nightshade Assassins, a network of elusive spies, poison masters, thieves, and murderers, all of whom answered to the Queen of the Assassins. Anselem's eyes narrowed as the men shook hands, and he watched with heightened suspicion as the boy silently departed from the room. He knew the underqueen had spies in every corner of Darnella, but the idea of her dealing with the Secret-Seeker made his skin crawl.

The Muses began to swirl in the center of the room, pulling his attention from the assassin.

Asha raised a hand, and the waters ceased, as though her

own will commanded the eddying pool.

Raziel's eyes darkened, and a sly grin curled onto his lips. "Hello, Asha darling."

The warriors wrapped around the room, lining the edge of the boundless pool resting in the center. Asha ambled to the far side, and Raziel walked over to meet her, his usual sultry look displayed smugly on his face.

"To what do I owe the pleasure?"

He dragged his red-flecked eyes down Asha's body, and it took every ounce of self-control Anselem held inside to keep from crossing the short space and grabbing the Secret-Seeker by his throat.

"You owe me an answer," she demanded.

A spidery smile crawled onto Raziel's mouth. "Is that so?" he taunted.

Asha did not reply but instead held his gaze with eyes that looked as though they could cut through dragon glass.

A sensual laugh escaped his lips, and he murmured, "So tense, Asha." He glanced at Anselem and added, "Are you sure your needs are being met?"

Buzzing waves of electricity thrust themselves to the surface of his skin, but before Anselem could release any rage-filled bolts, Asha let out a mocking laugh and replied, "I'm more than satisfied, Raziel. But if you would like me to indulge your curiosities, I have no problem enlightening you of just how well the Commander lives up to his reputation." She paused as the Secret-Seeker dragged his gaze back to her sapphire eyes. "*All* of his reputations," she added, a sultry smirk set upon her face. "Just let me know how detailed you'd like me to be."

Raziel offered her a false smile. "Glad to hear," he replied through gritted teeth.

Mathieson uncomfortably shifted his weight from one foot to the other, but the Secret-Seeker did not notice.

"My answer," she demanded, bringing the conversation's focus back to its intended purpose.

Raziel narrowed his eyes, clearly displeased with offering answers without the recompence attached to his games. He nodded stiffly.

"Tell me where to find the Amulet of Tisiphone," she said cooly.

A spidery smile crawled onto Raziel's face. "The amulet is hidden in a forgotten sanctuary on Skull's Rock, buried deep within the center of the isle. Follow the Spine of Sorrows and you shall find your prize."

Asha's face remained made of stone as the weight of Raziel's answer settled over the room. But, with her answer in hand, Asha did not make for the exit; she instead took a step towards the Secret-Seeker, eyes filled with fire. "What did my father want to know when he made a bargain with you?"

Anselem and Mathieson kept their faces fixed in unreadable expressions.

Raziel pursed his lips and tilted his head to the side. Darkness danced inside his gaze. "Now, now, dear Asha, you know that I require compensation for my answers." His lips turned upward. "But," he proceeded, his voice filled with amusement. "Because you have been such a... delectable guest," he crooned, flashing a smug look towards Anselem. "I'm willing to offer you one more." A devious twinkle sparked in his red and black eyes, as if offering her a free answer was just another move in his twisted games.

"He wanted to know about the Warrior of Praenuntius," Raziel said, picking at his nails. "Your father was clever, I'll give him that. He wagered for an interwoven question. I think he may have come out ahead in the end. He had so many of his questions answered for one simple price." His lips curled up as the last words escaped.

"What did he want to know about the Warrior?" Asha questioned, voice calm and emotionless.

Raziel pressed his lips into a thin line. "He wanted to know of the Warrior's power."

Asha remained silent as the Secret-Seeker continued, a dismayed look perched upon his face. "It was the only time my Muses have ever gone wholly silent. I had no answer for your father's inquiry." The unease vanished from Raziel's face, and a sinister grin replaced the worry. "But I did offer him something extra for his participation, a small token for his troubles."

Asha did not move. Anselem was not sure she was even breathing.

"I allowed him one more question," Raziel stated, perfectly placing the tempting bait.

"And what did he ask?" she enquired evenly.

A sly spider's smile twisted onto Raziel's face. The smile of a monster born in the depths of the Seven Hells. "Oh, sweet Asha, as I already said, you only get one answer from me. That was your prize, after all. And I'd like to believe I've been quite generous already, wouldn't you agree?" He took a step towards her and raised his hand to her face. As he trailed his thumb across her cheek, he added, "Unless you would like to play a game?"

The hunger in his eyes pulled Anselem's roaring power back to the surface. A small crack of lightning snapped in the room before it was quickly stifled by the iron-laced air.

Raziel smirked, and with his hand still caressing Asha's face, he twisted his gaze to Anselem. "Careful, Commander, you wouldn't want to tarnish that spotless reputation."

"I'm not the one you should be worried about, Raziel," Anselem replied, disgust wrapped around his words.

Asha shook his hand from her face and glared up at the Secret-Seeker.

"Sweet Asha would never hurt me. Would you, darling?"

Asha's painted lips turned upward as she sneered, "Answer my question and you won't have to find out."

Raziel took a step backward, and with his pale hand, he gestured to the pool centered amongst the warriors. "You know the way to have your questions answered." A dark twinkle sparked through his eyes as he added with excitement. "Unless you would rather make a deal, Asha? Perhaps just like daddy dearest?"

Asha's patience splintered.

In a rushing burst, fire ripped itself from Asha's hands. Flames stretched up to the ceiling, encircling every onyx book inside the round room. The blazes encompassed the leather-bound manuscripts but did not touch them as she held her fire just above the surface of the parchment.

Suffocating warmth flooded the room, and an engulfing heat radiated from the towering flames.

A devious grimace crawled onto Asha's face as she stared at Raziel.

The Secret-Seeker went pale as he watched his Room of Secrets erupt in flames.

"I told you before that you would watch your precious Room of Secrets go up in smoke," Asha hissed. "And if you would like for it to survive another day before it is turned to ash, you'd better start answering my questions."

Raziel swallowed.

Asha held his petrified stare, and she did not falter. Her flames, raging through the iron-laced air, did not flicker.

His fear turned to fury, and his eyes went dark. "He asked how to find a cure for Chaos. How to stop the Burning from taking place. He asked, with desperate pleas, for me to tell him how to stop a Thurisaz from combusting," he spat.

Asha's fire continued to swallow the room as she looked

into his onyx eyes, internally debating whether she would trust his answer. The Mueses behind her did not move.

Darkness danced in Raziel's eyes as he added, "And I will tell you what I told him. There is no cure. There is no way to stop the Chaos from consuming you. One day, that fire raging through your veins will burn you from the inside out."

Asha gave no indication that the answer had shaken her. She remained firm, like a statue molded from the Iron Mountains. From the corner of his eye, Anselem watched Mathieson stiffen.

Raziel glanced down at the Muses, as if he expected the waters to save him from the Thurisaz's wrath. The pool remained still. Not a single ripple waded through the abyssal well.

"Anselem," Asha called, never taking her eyes off the Secret-Seeker.

Anselem silently strolled to her side.

"Check the drawers."

Raziel's face drained of all color.

A wall of fire stretched before Anselem, separating him from the onyx desk in the corner. He took a deep breath and, trusting Asha with his entire soul, he stepped forward into the flames.

As he entered the fire, the flames morphed around him, and not one roaring ember touched him.

He rifled through the desk drawers, opening them from the top down.

In the very bottom cabinet, tucked far in the back, lay a small box wrapped in crimson thread. He pulled it from the drawer.

"Don't you dare touch it, *Lightless*," Raziel snarled. His red-flecked eyes were wild, and he spat the slur at the Commander as though there was no greater insult.

Anselem ignored his cries and lifted the lid. Resting inside the deep red container was a brushed bronze key. Five curved loops were centered around an off-white rose. The rings bowed around the edge of the flower in twisted metal curls with intricate details. Underneath the elaborate hilt, stretched a polished shaft lined with dozens of deep engravings in the metal.

Anselem placed the lid back on the box, tucked it into his coat pocket, and wordlessly nodded to Asha.

"I'll tell you whatever you want, just please don't take it," Raziel begged, his voice strained and fretful; a tone vastly different than the confident, tempting lilt he normally wielded.

The Secret-Seeker was abruptly flung across the room, his body thrust against the round wall by an unseen force. Asha had not moved from her place beside the Muses, but a stretching band of fire sprang from her hands, reaching across the space and wrapping around Raziel's exposed neck.

"Unless you would like a permanent ring of scorch marks to match the purple collar Anselem gifted you the last time we were here, I suggest you stay put as we leave."

Anselem waded back through the flames, and as he approached Asha's side, the roaring flames encircling the onyx books dwindled, but the fire-coated rope around Raziel's throat remained in place.

"This does not end how you think it will. We will rise again. The Darkness will conquer once more," he spat, his onyx eyes blazing a bright red.

The warriors made their way to the exit. Mathieson opened the wooden door and slipped back into the ballroom. Anselem lingered in the threshold, waiting for Asha.

She glanced back at Raziel. The rope of flames dwindled, and a small flicker of embers was left in her hands.

The Secret-Seeker did not move as he took in deep

breaths from across the room.

Asha placed a swaggering smirk upon her face as she replied, "That's where you're wrong, Raziel. Light will always find a way to shine in the Darkness. And the Darkness will not overcome it."

She twisted around and made her way towards Anselem, patiently waiting at the door.

Before she joined him, she stopped at a nearby shelf, running her fingertips across a stack of onyx books. She grabbed one from the end of the line and sauntered over to the exit.

She paused on the threshold and looked back at the Secret-Seeker, still attempting to catch his breath.

"And Raziel?" she chimed.

His red-flecked eyes narrowed from across the room.

"You should know a warrior never breaks her promises."

His brows bunched, and he tilted his head.

Asha raised her empty hand, and flames erupted from her palm, enveloping every onyx-bound book inside the curved shelves.

She met Raziel's frightened eyes as she concluded, "You and your games can burn to ash in the darkest parts of the Seven Hells where you belong."

She twisted around, and the two warriors exited the Faustia Room, leaving the Secret-Seeker behind without a second glance.

As they departed the Manor, Anselem could hear the guttural screams crawling from Raziel's throat as he watched his Room of Secrets go up in smoke.

CHAPTER
FORTY-TWO

Two days passed as the Amarok warriors awaited the arrival of their wolves.

The pair lounged in the warm embrace of Iskander's living room. The General was perched on one of the onyx armchairs, a glass of crescent whiskey in hand, and Kaira sat sprawled out on the cognac couch, a worn book resting on her lap. An endless fire crackled in the corner.

"I'd like to teach you a few things," Iskander said, breaking the comfortable silence in the room. He glanced over at her and added, "If you'd let me."

Kaira met his moondust gaze. "You mean magic?"

Iskander smirked, and his voice and eyes grew dark as he replied, "Whatever else, witchling?"

Kaira tried to hide the red that blushed across her cheeks as she narrowed her gaze. "I'm not a witch," she sneered.

Iskander let out a playful laugh, and Kaira hated how it twisted that stupid little thing fluttering inside her chest. "Would you prefer Deathweaver?" he teased. "Or perhaps Gravewalker?"

373

She rolled her eyes and picked her book back up. "How about neither?" she snipped.

"Oh, you're definitely getting a nickname," he replied, eyes gleaming. "Maybe Little Reaper," he mused, resting his head back against the chair. "No, that one's too much of a mouthful. How about—"

His words were abruptly cut off by a loud thud that sounded on the ground beside him. He lifted his head towards the noise and then glanced over to Kaira. "Did you just chuck a book at me?" he asked, astonished.

"Yes," she answered curtly.

He chuckled. "Well, your aim is terrible," he replied, handing the book back to her.

She rolled her eyes once more and buried her head inside the pages.

"So, what do you say?" he asked.

Kaira lifted her eyes towards him and raised a brow.

"To me helping you," he clarified, his voice taking on a more serious undertone.

Kaira pressed her lips together in a thin line. She could feel the unremitting chill awaken in her veins. Could feel the misty, bone-white haze of her power wrap around her mind.

"How does it present itself?" Iskander asked, voice low but firm.

"I just hear screams," she answered, her voice distant. "It's mostly when I'm in a place where death has recently occurred. Or a great deal of it."

Iskander nodded, as though he had come to that conclusion in the Slums. "What would you say to trying to see the Veil?" he asked delicately.

The Veil was a liminal plane between worlds, a realm made of eternal dusk where the unclaimed wandered, lost between death and whatever came next for their lost souls. A place where time itself stood still—a haunted void between worlds where the dead lingered, but never truly rested. A realm made of gray skies and shifting mist, where echoes of the dead were left to wander without memory.

It was the place In-Between. A place visited before the Afterlife or the Underworld.

Most passed through the Veil quickly, their souls eager to move on towards awaiting judgment. But others lingered. Others remained lost. Keen to remain wraiths of their former selves rather than face the Final Judgement of Anubis.

Those who lingered too long in the Veil became cold, lifeless, as their emotions slowly vanished. They became symbols of unfeeling cruelty as their spirits were sucked out. And they continued to wander in the plane of the In-Between until there was nothing left but a hollow husk of the hearts they used to own.

The worlds referred to them as Reapers.

"I'll be here with you, if you would like to try," Iskander added, his voice genuine and abnormally soft.

There was a kindness wading within the silver of his eyes. Something that told Kaira he had likely navigated something similar when trying to make sense of his own magic long ago. It made the tightness in Kaira's chest loosen. Made her feel as though she might have a chance at surviving. Might.

"Alright," Kaira whispered, nodding to Iskander.

He held out his palms, and she placed her own atop them. His skin was warm, his touch gentle as he wrapped his fingers around her hands. He explained the concept of mental grounding and a few points on how to control her Kratos.

Kaira nodded, having read up on the concept many times before, and after a few attempts, she quickly established a solid groundwork to build up her mental walls.

"Ready?" he asked, his warm hands still wrapped around her icy fingers.

Kaira paused for a heartbeat, her pulse hammering in her ears. Fear coiled tight in her chest, whispering that a single misstep inside the In-Between could leave her hollow, a wandering shade among the Reapers. Yet beneath the fear, a quieter, stubborn thread drew taut. A yearning to see what lay beyond her self-imposed limits, an ache to understand the depths of her magic. She lifted her gaze to his moondust eyes. A shiver rippled down her spine, but her shoulders squared, steadied by resolve. With a deep, bracing breath, Kaira closed her eyes, summoned the icy, bone-white mist stirring inside her veins, and stepped into the Veil.

A cold, vaporous haze eddied around her, clouding the undimming dusk sky painted overhead. A blanket of silence covered the misted space, and the winds stood unnervingly still.

The world here was not made of earth or air, but of memory and eternity. A place where time bowed its head and did not dare to speak.

Dark shadows churned beside Kaira, and a great hall appeared beyond the mist. A white-stone building with large obsidian doors rose before her. Painted on the doors sat a detailed drawing of a golden scale.

Kaira's breath hitched.

She knew that Hall. Had read about it many times before as a child in Velsen. The Hall of Two Truths. The sacred place of Anubis's Final Judgement.

Beside her, from the mist, a man emerged. His dark, oily hair was slicked back from his pale, gaunt face, and a large, bleeding scar was cut across his cheek. The pallid man stared up at the onyx doors before him for a long moment, studying them with intense focus. Then he climbed the dozen stone steps and entered the Hall of Two Truths.

Kaira followed him, her boots near-silent against the stone steps. She pulled open the heavy, two-story doors and entered the building. An endless chamber of black stone and golden light stretched before her.

Lined along the walls sat a large assembly of Reapers.

Gaunt, skeletal-shaped figures wrapped in long, tattered robes made from shrouded dusk. Their cloaks were crafted from the mist of the Veil, with unraveling tail ends swathed in smoke. Their lifeless bodies were ashen and gray, caught between the borders of decay and permanence.

Beneath the creatures' hoods peered two void-touched eyes, lifelessly hollow and glowing.

Floating above their veiled hoods hovered faint, broken halos of haunted mist. They were jagged and splintered and crackled like a fractured star. In their skeletal hands, the half-lifes carried rune-encrypted scythes made of shadows and twisted chains. Flecks of ash and pallid dust fell from the tip of the curved blades, and a cloud of spectral mist curled around the foot of their robes.

Not one of the hooded Reapers glanced in her direction.

At the far end of the hall, a golden scale hung suspended in the stillness. On one side, a pan gleamed with the soft shimmer of a single, impossibly white phoenix feather. The other pan remained empty.

A pair of gold and silver doors stationed behind the massive scale burst open, and a towering figure drifted into the room.

He was tall, silent, and draped in midnight linen. His head was crowned with the mask of an obsidian jackal, and his pale eyes burned through the blackness with an ancient mist. When he moved, he did not step; he merely floated across the floor as it shifted beneath his body. There was no malice nor mercy in his gaze. Only the clarity of Final Judgement—as eternal and unyielding as the cages of the Underworld itself.

Anubis, the God of Death.

The sallow man was led forward by two Reapers, shuffling slowly across the stone floor until he stood before Anubis, the golden scale towering beside him.

With a slow, deliberate extension of his hand, the God of Death reached out, and his fingers twisted in the air. The man's heart floated towards him like a petal on water. It beat slow and uncertain in his spectral hands, pulsing with memory. With regret. With love and cruelty and doubt. It pulsed with *truth*.

Then Anubis placed it in the pan opposite the glowing feather. The scales trembled. Kaira tried to draw in a sharp breath, but she found that there was no air to fill her lungs in the liminal place.

From the shadows near the dais, a dark-skinned woman with ancient eyes stepped forward. Ink-stained and ageless, the scribe unfurled a scroll, and her ibis-sharp eyes glinted as she watched the scale sway.

The feather did not move, but the heart quivered. Sagged. As though it remembered every breath the man had stolen. Every truth he had spoken. Every name he had betrayed. Every kindness he had left unsaid.

And as the scales teetered back and forth, Kaira understood. It was the weight of a life.

A low growl curled from a corner of the hall where darkness pooled deeper than elsewhere. There, waiting, was an onyx-scaled beast made of nightmares. Crocodilian jaw, leonine claws, eyes like suns swallowed in pitch. The creature paced as the scale balanced and trembled, its razor-sharp teeth gleaming with anticipation.

For a moment, the scarred man's heart seemed to move higher. Lighter. Then, the scale tipped with a violent crack.

A soundless cry echoed through the Hall of Truths as the pale man fell to his knees.

Anubis did not speak. He simply turned, nodded to the

corner, and smiled as the scaled beast leapt from the shadows.

Kaira flinched. Not for the soul the creature devoured, nor the cries that rang from the man's throat as the beast tore him limb from limb, but for what came after.

Nothing.

No scream. No light. No fall. Just absence—a hole where a life had once been.

And then the Hall of Truths was empty again. The feather untouched. The scale waiting. Anubis, still.

Then the mist-shrouded Veil faded, and the fire-warmed space of Iskander's living room wrapped around her once again, and Kaira wept without tears.

"Though the initial maneuver was executed under favorable conditions for conquest and pillage, the retreat from Skull's Rock marks one of the deadliest collapses in recorded Perseisian military history. Over three thousand soldiers from the Takaman Fort perished, not in battle, but in the chaos that followed. Swallowed by swamp, starvation, and silence, their bodies remain claimed by the isle to this day."
— The Marshland Campaigns: An Analytical History of the Collapse at Skull's Rock

CHAPTER

FORTY-THREE

"So let me get this straight," Kage said, rubbing his temples. "The amulet is out on Skull's Rock, and you're planning to grab it before traveling all the way to Verloren?"

Anselem gave a nod.

Kage and Sacha had arrived at the Mount shortly after the warriors returned from Boeotian Manor. Anselem had spent the better part of half an hour briefing them on the meeting and everything that followed.

"And you think I'm going to be able to keep Vice Rook from noticing *another* prolonged absence of yours?" Kage asked incredulously. "You do realize I'm running out of plausible lies, don't you?"

"At least you're not the one who has to go to that cursed rock," Sacha muttered, arms folded tightly across his chest as he leaned back in his chair.

"What's wrong with Skull's Rock?" Mathieson asked.

"It's haunted," Sacha grumbled. "And I'm tired of missions with godsdrowning haunted ghouls and ghosts."

Asha arched a brow and glanced at Anselem, who gave

her a subtle *another time* glance before turning to Sacha. "It's not haunted," the Commander replied calmly.

Sacha scoffed. "Tell that to the entire army that was slaughtered there. Left to rot in the swamps. Damn saltwench queen didn't even have the decency to bury their bodies…"

"The Emir was fair when I met her," Asha said, voice clipped. She remembered the woman's sharp eyes and un- wavering face from her Soturi benchmark. She still had the belt that the resilient woman had gifted her before she left the island.

Sacha slid his eyes to Asha. "Yeah, well, your people weren't the ones piled into mass graves," he said bitterly. "You know, they say that sometimes, after heavy rain, their skeletal remains still surface in the marshes. It's a disgrace."

Asha didn't respond, but she wondered if the reason for the men's slaughter had been the true disgrace.

"You'll need to set your feelings aside, Kaz," Anselem said, voice firm. "As fast as Iskander can ride, there's no way he's making it here in the next few hours, so you're going to have to come with us."

Sacha clenched his jaw but nodded.

"Do you know anything about the Spine of Sorrows?" Anselem asked.

"Only from the legends," Sacha replied. "It's a ridge that snakes through the island from south to north. I believe at its highest peak it bends above the inky marshes."

"Maybe you can ask the Emir to confirm when we ar- rive," Anselem suggested, turning to Asha.

She nodded.

Anselem reached into his pocket and pulled out the key taken from Raziel's manor, handing it to Kage. "Take this to the Undercroft. We will figure out what it's for when we get back."

Kage tucked the key in his jacket and offered a vague

grunt in response.

Anselem pivoted toward the door. "Alright then," he said, a flicker of anticipation in his tone. "Let's go find ourselves an amulet."

❖ ❖ ❖

Two days later, the warriors landed with practiced grace on a stretch of the southern coast of Skull's Rock, grains of pink and white sand flying into the air beneath the phoenixes' impacts. Asha and Anselem slid from Uriel and Kapheria, their boots sinking into the warm, powdery beach. A beat later, Bashiri descended, violet wings splayed wide, and Mathieson and Sacha promptly dismounted.

Sacha grumbled something beneath his breath as he wiped sand from his leathers.

The shore lapped lazily at low tide, revealing a bone-white reef that curled like snapping vertebrae. Further down the shore, jagged rocks jutted from the sea. They were weather-worn and hollowed into the likeness of skulls. Waves crashed through their gaping mouths, filling them with foam and an eerie howl that sounded like the dying gasps of the drowned.

Asha turned from the grim sea to the dense thicket of palms rising beyond the hills. From within the trees, a tribe of women began to emerge. They moved in silent formation down the rocky hillside, clad in golden armor, and at the front, standing tall and regal, marched the Isle Emir.

She looked every bit the warrior queen Asha remembered. Forged from sun and steel, muscles corded beneath skin the color of burnished copper. Her golden-brown hair was twisted into intricate braids that crowned her head, and the sweeping paint of the isle tribes covered her skin in curved lines. The gold of her armor caught the light in sharp flashes, and her amber gaze scanned the newcomers with the weight of one who had seen war and won.

The Emir's eyes swept across the group, pausing briefly on Sacha. A glimmer of something unreadable crossed her face, and then her attention shifted to Asha. When she spoke, her voice rang with authority, low and unyielding.

"I see your men come with tension in their eyes," she said coolly, gaze never leaving Asha's.

Sacha stiffened but held his tongue.

Asha stepped forward, bowing her head respectfully. "Emir. There's an amulet hidden on your isle we wish to retrieve. We believe it to be hidden in a sanctuary atop the Spine of Sorrows."

The Emir's expression remained unreadable. She folded her arms across her chest, glancing toward the sea for a long moment before returning her gaze to Asha. "And what claim do you have to it?"

"We don't seek to claim it. Only to retrieve it—to bring with us for payment to another," Asha said openly.

A pause stretched between them, and then the Emir nodded once. "The Spine is not easily crossed. It winds like a serpent through the center of the isle, cutting through marsh and stone and ruin. Most who try to reach it sink or turn back. And it punishes those who walk it with arrogance." The Emir flashed a glance towards Sacha.

Asha's jaw tightened. "We shall walk it with care."

The Emir stepped closer, eyes narrowing. "You may all walk the Spine, but only you may enter the sanctuary."

Asha blinked. "Only me?"

The Emir's voice was quiet but firm. "The sanctuary was sealed by rites your companions cannot pass. The wards will not open for them."

Sacha scoffed, the sound sharp. "Of course. Let me guess—some mystical womanhood bloodline test?"

The Emir's eyes cut to him, cold and sharp. "You should choose your company more wisely," she said to Asha, her tone like honed steel. "Your dog would not bark so freely if he knew what happened on these shores. What was buried in our marshes. What his kind did to mine."

Sacha opened his mouth, but Anselem stepped forward, voice laced with authority. "Enough," he barked at the Pontos.

The sharpness of the command made Sacha clamp his mouth shut, but his jaw worked behind clenched teeth.

The Emir gave a small, unimpressed glance toward Anselem, then looked back to Asha. "I see he only listens when a man bares his teeth. That may prove troublesome for you later." The Emir offered a wry smile. "Still. Every queen needs a mangy dog to do her bidding... no matter how unsavory he may be." She let her gaze linger on Sacha one final time. "Just don't let him drag fleas into your tent."

Despite the tension coiling in her chest, Asha couldn't stop the corner of her mouth from twitching. She bowed her head. "Thank you for granting us passage," she said evenly.

The Emir nodded. "Head inland. When the stone turns black and the air begins to hum, you'll know you've reached the Spine." She paused, eyes narrowing slightly. "And be wary of the mire," she added, voice low and clipped. "There are things that fester in the waters around the sanctuary. Wretched creatures born of bloodshed and bone rot. They were drawn here after the massacre and have not left since. Some sleep. Others... hunger."

Without another word, the Emir turned. Her gold-plated warriors fell into formation behind her, vanishing into the palms as swiftly as they had come. And as the jungle closed behind them, the island began to whisper.

"WHEN THE SEVENTH SHADOW SPILLS AND THE FINAL DUSK IS DRAWN, ONE SHALL RISE, NOT CROWNED BUT CHOSEN—MARKED BY THE AUTHORITIES, AND CARVED TO CARRY CHAOS IN THEIR BLOOD. THEY SHALL NOT BE BORN OF PEACE, BUT OF FIRE AND SILENCE, AN ECHO OF THE FIRST WARRIOR OF PRAENUNTIUS, WHO BORE THE ETERNAL FLAME WHEN LIGHT AND DARKNESS FIRST BLED INTO WAR. BUT KNOW, IT IS NOT THE GODS ALONE WHO WATCH. BENEATH THE HOLLOW GATE, THE DARK KING WAITS—SEALED NOT BY STRENGTH, BUT BY ABSENCE, AND YEARNING NOT FOR AN ENEMY BUT FOR A VESSEL. FOR THE FINAL SEAL SHALL NOT BREAK BY SWORD NOR SPELL, BUT BY THE BLOOD OF THE ONE BORN TO BEAR IT. ONLY CHAOS MADE FLESH CAN UNLOCK THE LAST GATE, AND ONLY THE CHOSEN CAN DECIDE WHETHER THE KING RETURNS. THE WARRIOR WILL NOT COME TO SAVE THE WORLD, BUT TO UNMAKE WHAT MUST FALL AND TO CHOOSE, IN THE END, WHAT BURNS AND WHAT ENDURES."
— LAST LIVING TESTAMENT OF THE FIRST ORACLE
(TRANSCRIBED IN THE CODEX OF PRAENUNTIUS AND ENTOMBED WITHIN THE SILENT VAULT OF IANODA)

CHAPTER

FORTY-FOUR

The journey inland began beneath a canopy of dense palms and twisted mangroves, their roots clawing through mud the color of old blood. The air turned thick with brine and rot, heavy with moisture that clung to the skin. Swarms of glass-winged insects skimmed over dark, stagnant pools, their wings catching flecks of light that filtered weakly through the tangled branches above.

Jagged stone formations jutted from the ground like shattered ribs, slick with moss and veined with black minerals that glimmered faintly beneath the mist.

Over time, the green began to fade. The jungle thinned. Vines withdrew. Shadows grew longer, cooler. And then, in a blighted clearing, the wind went still and the soil turned black.

The Spine of Sorrows rose from the earth like the bones

of a long-dead god. Jagged, volcanic stone was twisted into cruel, unnatural angles. Ancient carvings marked its surface, pulsing softly with the residue of forgotten magic. Bones lay scattered at its base. Pale, feral trees grew in crooked clusters along its flanks, their bark bleached white, their branches stripped bare.

The warriors began their ascent in silence, carefully picking their way across the jagged ridge as mist curled low around their boots. The stone beneath their feet was slick and uneven, forcing them to move in single file, balancing between clusters of bone-littered ground and twisted roots that jutted like grasping fingers. At times, the trail narrowed to nothing more than a knife's edge, and they had to brace themselves against the rock wall to continue. Hours passed like that—an endless rhythm of climbing, slipping, adjusting. Shadows moved where they shouldn't. No birds called.

Time bled away in a slow, grueling rhythm as they moved in single file, navigating the sharp incline and narrow ridges.

Around midday, the ascent began to ease. The stone underfoot grew broader, more stable, the incline softening into a long plateau of black rock.

Asha slowed her pace, pulling beside Mathieson as the tension in her limbs began to ease.

"What else do you know about the Warrior of Praenuntius?" Asha asked, voice low.

Anselem, still leading the way, glanced backward at her, and she knew he could hear her hushed words.

Mathieson cut his eyes over to her, knowing full well the question had been brewing in her mind since Raziel had revealed their father's question. "Not much more than I already told you. That he was the leader of the Warriors of Old, and he crafted the Ossuary shortly after the First War."

Asha nodded. "There's nothing about his power in any

of the old texts?"

"Not anything I could find," he replied, but Asha caught the tension in his voice.

"Liar," she snipped.

He took a deep breath. He didn't turn to look at Asha as he spoke. "I saw something. Last year, inside the Chamber of Reflection." His voice was steady, but his jaw had a tightness in it that Asha recognized. The weight of knowing too much. "It was something ancient. Carved. A stone wall covered in writing I didn't recognize, but I understood it all the same. It was a message—a prophecy." He glanced at her before he continued. "It spoke of someone rising. Not born for peace, but for fire and silence. Chosen—not by mortals, but by the Authorities of Ianoda. Someone marked by Chaos in their blood."

She felt the shift in his tone, and the air around him thickened.

"Someone called to be an echo," he added, "of the first Warrior of Praenuntius. The one who carried Chaos into the First War, when Light and Darkness first clashed. The first to bear it fully—and survive." His jaw clenched. "Warrior of Praenuntius was a Thurisaz."

Asha whipped her head towards her brother and stared. She forced her feet to continue moving.

Mathieson huffed out another long breath. "I don't know for certain. Much of the vision and the prophecy carved into the wall was difficult to recall after I was out of the Chamber, but from what I gathered, the Warrior possessed power so great, it only makes sense for it to have been Chaos. That's literally what Chaos is—the raw, unpredictable, and fundamental primordial energy that is interwoven into the fabric of existence itself. It is the most powerful magic the worlds have ever known."

She slowed her steps, voice dropping to a whisper, "You

said you believe the Dark King has been waiting for the person powerful enough to wield his final Crown..."

Mathieson said nothing.

"Tell me what you know," she demanded.

Mathieson cut his eyes at her. "I don't *know* anything," he replied, voice hushed but sharp.

Asha narrowed her eyes. "But you have a theory," she countered. "I saw it written all over your face when we were standing on the shores of Gull's Landing."

Mathieson gave her a weary look. "I have my beliefs, but there is nothing written in any of the ancient scrolls. At least none of the ones I was able to find. All I have is that half-formed vision from the Chamber."

"What do you believe?" Asha asked.

Mathieson took a deep breath. He opened his mouth, then closed it, as though unsure if he wanted to voice his thoughts. After a long moment, he said, "I think history is repeating itself once again. I think..." He hesitated, taking another long moment before he continued. "I think another Warrior of Praenuntius has been chosen," he said carefully, avoiding Asha's gaze. "I believe the Authorities have selected another to entrust with the power to combat Darkness."

"You think there is going to be another Warrior of Praenuntius?" she asked incredulously.

Mathieson nodded, keeping his eyes pinned on the path ahead.

"Who?" she questioned.

Mathison said nothing, but his sapphire eyes turned towards her intently.

Disbelief flashed across Asha's face. "Me?" she said, a wave of shock swelling over the word.

Anselem looked back, his face unreadable.

Mathieson shrugged. "It fits."

Asha scoffed. "Just because Dad was looking into the

Warrior doesn't mean it fits, Math."

Mathieson shrugged again.

Asha let out a huff of frustration but dropped the subject.

They walked in taut silence for a long while before Asha broke the quiet once more. "You said war is coming," she murmured, glancing at her brother.

"Yes," Mathieson replied. His footsteps were even, as if this topic of conversation was easier for him to swallow.

"What did you mean exactly?" Asha pressed.

Mathieson pursed his lips and took a deep breath. "When I was in the Chamber of Reflection," he began, his voice wavering across the words. "It made my visions stronger. Clearer." He rolled out the growing tightness in his shoulders. "My visions... They were of dark places. Of places so sinister, I knew they could not have existed in a realm such as our own."

Anselem's footsteps slowed ahead as he allowed time for the warriors to amble closer.

"I was sent visions of the Hells. Of the Seven Provinces, and snippets of their meetings."

Asha stopped abruptly beside him, her hand softly grasping his arm. She heard the crunching of boots against the rocks cease ahead. "You..." Asha began, struggling to find the words. "You went to the Seven Hells?"

Mathieson shook his head. "I did not go, Fletch. But I saw them. And the face of one of the Princes."

"What were they like?" Sacha asked.

Asha cut her eyes at him, her fist curling at her side as if readying to strike him for asking her brother to relive such horrors.

Mathieson put a hand on her shoulder, and she turned back to face him. "Gruesome," he answered. "Horrid. And..." He paused, sorting through the best way to describe the unspeakable. "Ordered."

Asha's brows bunched together. Everything she had ever been told, everything she had ever *believed*, about the Seven Hells was that it was a world of turmoil and chaos. A realm of endless dread.

"Each of the Provinces was filled with wretched things," Mathieson proceeded without pause. "A whole collection of gruesome creatures that varied across the regions. But the Hells themselves… they were structured. Ruled by lasting and established hierarchies." Mathieson glanced around, scanning the trees and shadows before he continued. "It took months—years—of visions to even understand the most basic of their systems. I'd catch fragments of conversations, clips of secret meetings held between the Princes of Shadows." His voice dropped lower. "I never saw the King of the Abyss. I only heard his voice. Once. From behind a closed door, as he spoke to all six of his sons." Mathieson took a deep breath. "That was when I heard it. The smallest segment of a plan. To return. Here. And wage a war for the realm."

Suffocating silence pierced the air.

Anselem was the first to speak, his voice holding nothing but unwavering leadership and strength. "Did he say how he would wage this war?"

Mathieson turned his gaze to the Commander and shook his head. "No," he answered. "I think," he started, his eyes going dark with memory. "I think he knew I was there. Behind the door. Listening."

"What do you mean?" Asha's voice was strained and sounded far away as the question fell from her lips.

"As I stood there, surrounded by an endless pit of darkness, I heard the king's words fall silent, and he laughed." Mathieson's face went pale, all color draining from his cheeks. "I'd never heard anything so dark. So alluring. So beautiful. So… wicked." He swallowed audibly. "And then he said from the other side of the door, *Mathieson Raynor, Prophet of the Light, come inside. We are not mere thieves who come only to steal and kill and destroy. Join us, and you shall see your true potential for greatness. Join us and claim your destiny.*"

Asha's chest tightened. Her heart slammed against her ribs.

"And then the vision ended," Mathieson concluded, his voice tight and haunted. "As if I'd been hastily pulled back from the Dark."

Silence stretched for a long while, and the warriors' steps began once more.

As they walked, Sacha asked, "So that's all there was in the Hells? Endless Dark?" His voice was full of grave intrigue.

Mathieson shook his head. "No, that's just the Abyss. The deepest and final region that the king presides over. The Seventh Province is a void of absolute oblivion. The other regions are different."

Sacha looked at him with interested eyes, but he did not press the warrior to elaborate.

"I didn't visit all of them," Mathieson proceeded, quenching Sacha's thirst for more details. "Even spending more than two years in the Chamber, my visions did not become clear enough to understand all of the Provinces." The warrior stepped around a large boulder in the path. "The First Province was a frozen waste, littered with callous, soulless Reapers that travel from the Veil. The cold there was bitter and angry, deep enough to chill through bone." Mathieson clenched his jaw, a phantom shiver running down his spine. "The Second and Third were equally wretched places. One made of violent, wind-ruled storms and seas, the other of dry, barren sands and sun.

"The Fourth Province was the only one whose Prince

I had been able to glimpse. His fire-red hair matched the bloody grounds of his lands. And his eyes had been half-filled with matching crimson.

"I do not know of the other two Provinces. I never visited them. But I'll never forget how pitiless the reigning Prince of the Sixth Hell had sounded as he spoke to the others behind closed doors. As though he had earned every bit of power that came from governing the second deepest level of the pits."

Silence fell heavily over the group. The forest path swallowed their footsteps, and no one dared to speak for a long while.

Asha's chest felt tight, Mathieson's words coiling tight against her ribs like a constricting snake.

A world of ordered Hells. Princes who plotted in secret. A king who knew her brother's name. She lifted her gaze towards the thin sliver of moon cutting through the warped trees as night pressed in. Above the treetops, clouds slid across the sky, smothering the pale light of the stars.

For a moment, it felt as if the Darkness had noticed them, had turned its face toward the mortal realm, and was leaning in close, listening.

And somewhere, deep in the unseen Hells, Asha could almost imagine the sound of laughter.

CHAPTER FORTY-FIVE

The warriors traveled until dusk, pushing through dense overgrowth and winding mountain paths until the terrain finally opened into a wide, shadow-rimmed meadow.

Lush tropical ferns unfurled from dark, damp soil, and heavy floral scents hung thickly in the air. A littering of jagged rocks jutted from the earth in irregular patterns, curving around the edges of the open meadow. A canopy of tall trees loomed at the field's edge, the humid ocean breeze whispering through their palms in steady breaths. Shadows stretched long and deep along the trunks, and a scattering of glowing eyes blinked intermittently throughout the surrounding dark.

Mathieson had collapsed on the far side of the field almost instantly, his weapons half-unbuckled from his waistbelt. Sacha sat a few feet away, back pressed against the thick trunk of a hooked tree. He kept one hand on the hilt of his sword, eyes sharp and alert as he took first watch.

Anselem and Asha lay curled beside one another on the opposite side, tucked between two broad slabs of stone where the wind could not reach them. Asha rested her head against his chest as Anselem's arms wrapped tightly around her.

Silent tears fell from her eyes, soaking the thick shirt clinging to his chest. "It's all my fault," she whispered. "What they did to Tahira." Her voice broke on the name.

Anselem gently rubbed her back as more tears slid down her cheeks.

"I was the one who went to get Jeremiah. I was the one who asked him to come."

Anselem remained silent, listening as the warrior finally allowed herself to feel.

A soft sob escaped from Asha's mouth. "She was so kind. Innocent. She was good." Asha sucked in a deep breath, trying to calm her shaking voice. "It was Leadership. The Council. I know it."

Anselem softly nodded.

"I don't know how they knew about our Court. Or about Tahira. But it was them, I know it deep in my soul."

"It was Leadership," he acquiesced, no uncertainty in his words. "I assume his absence was noticed by the Elysian Vice, and he was commanded back to the fort. And when Jeremiah did not respond to the Brand's summons..." He let his words trail off.

She sniffed. "Why?"

Anselem shifted onto his side and gazed down at Asha. He wiped the tears from her cheeks as he replied, "Because when snakes feel threatened, they unhinge their jaw and go straight for the throat."

He was right. She knew he was right. That the Vice was sending a clear message: defy the Council's authority and reap the consequences.

But knowing it did not stop the weariness from washing over her, shoving her beneath the waves of an infinite ocean. And it didn't stop the rage that was roaring inside of her, burning her to ash from the inside out.

The Darkness crawled into her mind, settling into the newly formed cracks. She shoved at it, knowing the effort was futile. She rested her head against Anselem's chest as the war raged inside her soul. As she fought to forge the broken splinters back together. She was so weary. So tired of fighting.

"Ans?" Asha whispered.

"Yes, Seven?"

She exhaled, hesitating. Wind whistled through distant canyons. "I think..." she began, pausing as though she did not want to speak her thoughts into existence. "I think I might be a terrible person."

Anselem swallowed a laugh as he looked down into her eyes and realized she had voiced the words with genuine sincerity.

In that moment, Anselem understood with unrestrained clarity that at some point or another, those who are truly good all believe they are terrible people; they simply wait to voice it aloud until they are asking someone to love their darkest parts.

But Anselem already knew all of Asha's darkest parts, and he did not shy away from her shadows.

"You are not a terrible person, Seven. Sometimes, good people must do terrible things in order to survive. Sometimes we have to don a mask that we wish we never had to wear." Anselem spoke with gravity and transparency, knowing deep inside his heart he had worn many guises he never wished to display. "But know this," he continued, "no matter your darkest moments, or the terrible roles you have to play, it will never stop me from loving you. You can show me every splintered thorn inside your heart, and I will meet you there with hands ready to bleed."

She melded into him, as though his words were all she

needed to hear for her body to release the tension. That she only needed to know he would love her through the dark.

Stars flashed overhead, and the wind began to quiet its shrills.

She traced a delicate finger down his neck, wrapping around the coiled muscles in his shoulder until her gentle touch trailed down his back. She paused as her hands hovered close to the center, just over his shoulder blades.

A smirk twitched on his mouth.

"Are you going to tell me about them?" she asked, her voice quiet and inquisitive.

He pulled himself upright, and she adjusted beside him.

"What would you like to know?" he replied, his voice low and even as he stared into her intense flames.

She was quiet—contemplative—as if she was unsure of what to ask.

Another grin crept onto his face, and he leaned forward, his wings unfurling with a rush of air.

Asha's eyes widened, a glimmer of astonishment sparking through them. She trailed her gaze up and down the gilded feathers, watching as flickers of electric light flowed through the plumes. They were made of pure, unblemished gold, with a metallic sheen that covered the surface while still holding the inherent softness of feathers.

"How?" she whispered, wholly mesmerized.

Anselem smiled and closed his eyes, recalling a distant memory. "I was assigned to the Elysian Fort when I was approached."

"It sounds creepy," he continued, "like something out of one of the dark tales of old that your parents would read you when you were little. But I was walking back to the fort from my post near the Grounds one night, when a hooded figure, cloaked in all black, appeared on the path. I remember staring ahead at the empty trail, and then, in the split second it took me to blink, suddenly a shadowed figure was no more than ten yards before me, like he had formed from the misty night's cover."

Anselem paused for a moment, attempting to find the best words to recount the memory. "Truthfully, I'm not sure why I followed him. The figure didn't even say anything. He just held out his hand, gesturing away from the fort, and I knew he was asking me to follow him towards the seaside."

Anselem took a deep breath, and Asha's stare shifted to his eyes. "Deep down," he continued, "I think I knew—in my soul, or my heart, or some preordained part of my mind—I think I knew I had to go. To follow. Wherever the shadow was going to take me."

Asha held his gaze assiduously, her attention focused solely on the warrior before her.

"The hooded figure brought me to some half-ruined tower on the outskirts of the city. Turns out it was part of an old temple dedicated to the Virtues."

Anselem remembered every intimate detail of the sanctuary. He had spent such an uncountable number of days training with the Septant on the outside grounds that he knew he would never forget the temple.

Wind slipped through the stone corridor as Anselem and the shadow entered the sacred space. Broken stones, scattered across the uneven ground, crunched beneath his boots. Sweat clung to every surface of his skin as he walked across the wide, open room. The warm summer heat had remained settled inside the temple; the vast, open archways surprisingly provided no flow from the nearby sea breeze.

The ceiling overhead stretched three stories high, providing ample space for the seven crumbling statues at the front of the sanctuary. The gods and goddesses, seated shoulder to shoulder in detailed stone thrones, towered nearly two stories tall, their ruined presences still governing the space.

Weather-worn stone pillars lined both sides of the sanctuary, creating a wide, guided path up to the sculptures.

Inscriptions and carvings were etched into the bases of the thrones, and the entirety of the stone wall erected behind the seated gods was covered in words from the *Language of the Founders*.

The curved ceilings overhead, made up of pristine dragon glass, seemed to be the only portion untouched by decay in the years of abandonment.

Moonlight crept in through the glass windows above, illuminating a stained, sculpted archway in the far corner, lined on either side by towering spires. Inside the archway rested a spiraled staircase, half covered in hidden cobwebs, that led up to the high tower.

The shadow silently guided Anselem towards the spire, the only proof of his silenced existence being the soft clap of footsteps against the cobbled floor.

"The others were already there when I arrived—all dressed in Septant black," he recounted. "They didn't have to say anything. I had heard enough tales in my few years as a Soturi to know what the meeting demanded."

As he continued speaking, Anselem described the five-sided room at the top of the temple's tower. "I remember thinking it looked rather plain to belong to a building dedicated to the third entity of the Authorities. But as I turned my attention to the focal point in the center of the floor, I realized the reasoning for the blankness of the walls and ceiling overhead."

An enormous, silver-plated crest was set in the center of the floor. Two onyx wings were carved into the triangular metal, and the crest looked as if it were glowing. A transparent, dragon glass window overhead let in the light from the moon, illuminating the insignia.

"Cathan was the only one to speak as he walked me

through the process—the choice to join." Anselem huffed out a laugh and shook his head. "I suppose if he possessed a portion of Mathieson's power, he had already known I would say yes."

Anselem glanced down at the nearly imperceptible scar on his palm and smiled. "After I expressed my agreement, he explained that I would have to complete the Passage before proceeding. Mathieson was my Guide, and after I survived the flooding of power, Cathan handed me a long, obsidian-tipped blade. I ran the knife across my palm, and we all watched as my blood dripped onto the silver crest beneath my feet."

Asha glanced down at the silver line on his palm.

"It was my Vow—my promise to serve the brotherhood with both blood and breath. To serve the Septant with my life."

Asha ran a gentle finger across his scar, and he curled his hand around hers.

"The Septant Mark was inked onto my back as soon as my blood hit the onyx wings." Anselem's eyes were bright and clear as he concluded, "And as soon as the wing was Marked on my back, I felt it."

He pulled up his sleeve and unclasped the onyx bracelet on his wrist—the one he never removed—and unveiled the clean Unbranded skin beneath.

Asha's body went stiff, and her eyes were wide.

"My Passage erased the Brand. I was no longer bound to serve a wicked crown; no longer a slave to a cruel king; no longer forced to answer to the Council." He took a deep, thankful breath. "It was the first time in my life that I felt free."

"You made the Passage?" she whispered, still caught on the first revelation he had divulged.

The Passage was the voyage of a warrior's descent into

the deepest reaches of their power—a sacred rite that awakened the full extent of the magic that stirred within their veins. It was discovered during the era of the Warriors of Old, born from a profound desperation to unlock the true limits of their power.

But the journey inward was dangerous, and it became clear that no warrior could endure it alone. To survive the depths of one's magic, a warrior needed to be tethered to a Guide—another who was strong enough to anchor them to the Light.

Most of the warriors chose not to make the Passage, content to live with their partially unlocked power. But those who trusted their Guides stepped willingly into the unknown.

Over time, the journey came to be known as the Passage. A name born from the transformation it required, as well as the sacred stages that defined it: the Dive, the Void, and the Rising. Each phase echoed the legacy of the three branches and reflected the trials one endured to awaken true power.

The Council had forbidden it long ago. And now, staring at the unmarked skin of Anselem's wrist, Asha finally understood why.

Anselem nodded. "It's part of joining. The Septant Mark cannot be imprinted without it." He was quiet for a long moment before adding, "They don't know. No one knows we've made the Passage—survived it. That's why we wear the cuffs. That's why we still have to play the Council's games and feign following their rules."

Asha ran her thumb across the pristine, unblemished skin on his wrist.

He could see the longing in her eyes—the desire for freedom. The desire he had always seen in her for a different life. A better world.

"And the wings?" she asked, her eyes drifting to the

gilded feathers. "You only received them after the Septant Mark was imprinted?"

Anselem nodded. "They demand immense strength to summon. That's why we had to make the Passage first. We wouldn't be able to access the wings without the entirety of our power."

Asha's brows raised. "They drain your magic?"

"Yes." His voice was steady, but heavy with weight. "Everything comes at a cost. That was why we couldn't use them when we escaped Montu. The iron shackles prevented us from accessing them. And even if we had managed to remove the shackles, our magic had been drained for so long that our reserves were empty. There wouldn't have been enough depth to summon the wings."

"So—" Asha began, pausing as waves of surprise and confusion draped across her face. "So, you don't need Kapheria?"

Anselem smiled softly, unsurprised that her thoughts would drift to the bonded beast they had left back on the shore. "I will always need Kapheria. And our Bond will live on until Death comes to claim me. But no, I do not require the Bond to wield the magic that runs through my veins. The Passage, as well as the Purelight, allows me to access my fully unlocked power." Anselem paused, glancing around the meadow and the stretching darkness beyond, weary of the shadowed corners where he did not want his words to carry. He lowered his voice and continued, "The Bond can only unlock a fraction of people's power. I think it was Ianoda's way of ensuring there was a check—a system of balances, if you will—on the powers of chosen wielders. As if the God of Light had always known our propensity to twist his gifts into something dark."

Anselem's jaw clenched as the image of his fallen brother flashed through his mind. Betrayal, as fresh as if Balam's disloyalty had happened mere moments ago, sliced through his mind. He cleared his throat. "The Bond releases a large portion of one's magic, but never its entirety. The Passage— it unleashed the rest."

Asha was quiet for a long time, letting Anselem's words settle in her mind. With a wrinkled brow, she asked, "If you were the last of them to join, why were you named Commander?"

Anselem smirked. "You mean aside from the gold wings?"

"You don't all have gold wings?" she asked, her interest piqued.

He laughed softly. "No, Ash, just me. I'm the only one."

"So that's it?" she asked, a hint of disbelief in her voice. She arched a brow. "They made you leader because your wings are flashy?"

He huffed a laugh. "No, Seven. It wasn't just for the color of my wings, dashing as they are."

She rolled her eyes at his smugness. "Then what was the reason?" she asked more quietly.

He took her hand in his and looked deeply into her fire-filled eyes—the same eyes that had captivated him from the moment the stunning sapphire pierced his soul. "The Septant Mark does more than unlock our power. It grants... other abilities." He paused, glancing at the trees. His voice dropped to a hush. "But that is a tale for another time," he whispered. "When we are not surrounded by shadows and unseen creatures lurking in the dark."

Asha nodded, sensing the weight behind his words, and said no more, understanding Anselem would tell her when the time was right.

CHAPTER
FORTY-SIX

Anselem stared out at the murky-black water stretched before them, still and silent beneath the weight of dusk. A veil of mist clung low to the surface, threading between moss-laced reeds. Across the far side of the mire, nestled against the marsh's dark edge, stood a small sanctuary crafted from deep green granite. Its domed roof curved inward, topped with a thick coat of moss and lichen, and a narrow, unlit opening rested at the front.

The warriors had set out at first light and spent the day tackling the final stretch of the Spine. The distance had been shorter, but the climb had taken them nearly as long as the first day. A steep, winding path had greeted them once again, and the obscenely narrow ledges had required extremely measured assessments. They had made it to the summit just as the sun reached the horizon.

Beside Anselem, Asha stood stiffly, her face fixed in an unpleasant expression as she stared down at the inky water.

"Don't worry," Anselem murmured, glancing at her with a crooked smile. "Wings, remember?"

Before she could reply, a rush of wind broke the stillness as the three Septant warriors unfurled their wings.

Asha's eyes flared wide as she took them in.

Anselem's wings, vast and gleaming, stretched outward in a sweep of brilliant gold, each plume catching in the fading light like strands of liquid sun. On his right, Mathieson's wings shimmered in a glowing shade of silver, with streaks of gold strewn throughout the feathers. To his left, Sacha's wings splayed out in a breathtaking display of pale, oceanic blue, with gilded tips that glinted like the edges of sunlight against a breaking wave.

Anselem rolled his shoulders, settling the familiar weight of his wings with practiced ease.

Asha's gaze moved between them, but her expression was unreadable as she met Anselem's eyes.

"Ready?" he asked, stepping towards her.

She arched a brow. "You're seriously going to carry me?"

He extended an arm around her waist. "I certainly don't mind having a reason to wrap my arms around you." He gave her a wink.

"I feel like I'm setting warrior women back at least three centuries," she muttered, but stepped closer, reluctantly sliding her arms around his neck.

He chuckled, the sound warm against her ear. "You're the last warrior I would accuse of setting anyone back, Seven."

Asha rolled her eyes, but as her cheek brushed against the curve of his wing, her gaze lingered. Sparks of electric light danced across the gold feathers.

"I'll tell you everything you wish to know about them later," he whispered, his voice so low only Asha could hear.

She met his deep emerald gaze and nodded.

But before their feet left the muddied earth, movement

on the far side of the marsh caught the warriors' eyes. Beneath the sanctuary's edge, the water rippled unnaturally, and slowly a figure began to rise from the swamp.

Its body emerged half-drowned, slick with pondweed and silt. It was small, no taller than a young child, but there was nothing innocent about its shape. Its body was hunched, its limbs stiff with unnatural tension.

The creature's skin was a mottled green, slick with a mossy sheen that shimmered in the dimming sun. Scales clung tightly to its limbs, some overlapping like armor, others peeling at the edges as though they'd rotted underwater. Its arms hung low, and its fingers were long and reed-thin, ending in webbed claws that carved slow rivulets through the mud as it stepped forward. Water oozed from its joints, and the stink of stagnant rot followed in its wake.

Its back arched beneath the weight of a dark, rounded shell, and jagged grooves cracked along the ridges like a weatherworn stone. It looked like an overgrown tortoise shell, but the splitting exterior made it seem as if the shell had grown there in defiance of the body beneath it. Algae clung to the rim, and fat black leeches pulsed along the spine, twitching with every movement. Its movements were jerky, frog-like, but there was purpose in every step.

Its face was humanoid in structure, but it twisted and stretched into a grotesque mask. Its eyes were bulbous, yellow, and glassy like a dead fish, and its mouth curved into a hooked beak lined with needle-sharp teeth. When it blinked, its lids slid in from the sides.

But the most disturbing part of the creature was its head.

Bald, save for a few patches of greasy, matted hair, its skull sloped inward in a shallow dish-like bowl carved into bone. Inside it sat a thick, motionless puddle of dark water. As the creature crept forward, the water did not slosh or spill. It simply clung there, unnaturally still, as if it were part

405

of the creature's blood. When the creature tilted its head, the surface rippled, like something living moved beneath it.

It smelled like wet earth and old bones, and nothing kind lived inside its lifeless eyes.

"What in the Seven Hells is that?" Anselem breathed, his gaze locked on the rising amphibian.

"By the Deep," Sacha swore, his hands dropping to the blades at his side. "It's a godsdrowning kawataro."

"A what?" Mathieson breathed, reaching for his weapon. He raised a double-edged axe above his shoulder and widened his stance.

As the warriors palmed their weapons, the murky surface behind the creature began to break once again. One after another, a small army emerged, rising like water-logged Reapers from the mire. Over a dozen creatures eddied in the black bog.

"A kawataro," Sacha repeated grimly. "I faced a nest of them once in Delphagia. Rot-born fifth. Scaled like reptiles, move like frogs, but smarter—and meaner—than either. They drown their prey and drain the blood before dragging the bones back down into the muck. That bowl of water on their skull? It holds their strength. Spill it, and they're nothing but husks."

Anselem's gaze skimmed the marsh. More shapes were breaching the surface, rising in twisting, hunched silhouettes. "How many?" he asked.

"A few dozen, maybe more. Too many to fight on the ground," Sacha replied.

Mathieson's grip tightened around his axe.

"Then we take the sky," Anselem decided. "And hold them off long enough for Asha to get inside." His calculating gaze swept across the sanctuary. "I'll drop you on top of the dome," he said, turning to Asha. "Find a way to slip in from there."

Asha nodded.

A low, guttural rasp echoed across the mire. The lead kawataro, now fully risen, lifted its grotesque head, its dead-yellow eyes gleaming beneath the dusk sky. "Your trespass ends here, children of sky," it hissed, voice like rot and gravel.

Anselem didn't hesitate. He grabbed Asha firmly around the waist and launched skyward, his wings ripping through the heavy dusk.

Mathieson and Sacha were on his heels, wings rusting sharply as they soared into the fight.

As they neared the far side, Anselem veered off toward the sanctuary's roof, throwing Asha atop the dome. She landed with feline grace atop the curving stone, feeling for a break in the moss-covered dome as Anselem dove back towards the swamp's edge.

Anselem's gold feathers cracked with power as he slammed into the front line, electricity surging through his arms. He sent an arc of lightning through the first kawataro's skull, aiming for the indented pool of water resting in the center. The creature shrieked as electricity met standing water, and it crumpled into a lifeless pile of scales and slippery skin beneath Anselem's feet.

Sacha arrived a moment later, his blades a flashing blur as he spun through the air, slicing through shell and scale. One collapsed instantly, the other hissed before its throat split open beneath Sacha's second strike. Mathieson descended like a falling star, axe cleaving clean through two kawataro, their wet shrieks echoing over the mire.

From the corner of his eyes, Anselem caught a glimpse of Asha slipping inside a shadowed crevice atop the dome and disappearing inside. Below him, a kawataro crept out from the water, skulking towards the small opening at the front of the sanctuary.

Anselem tucked in his wings, barreling toward the ground. As he landed, mere inches in front of the scaled creature, he sent a raging blast of lightning straight through the kawataro's chest. The creature spasmed violently before it collapsed in a hiss of steam.

Mathieson and Sacha touched down beside him, boots sinking into the muddy ground, wings folding in tight.

"Don't let them breach the front," Anselem barked, flinging another bolt through a kawataro's chest. "Asha made it inside."

The warriors grunted in agreement and fanned out, trying to cover as much space around the marshy entrance as possible.

The battle blurred. Steel clashed against claw and shell, lightning hissed, feathers and mud streaked the air. Anselem's sword, *Soulmaker*, moved like a living current, his lightning wrapping around the serrated blade. He carved through creature after creature, cracking power bursting through each strike. Mathieson rose and fell in wide, brutal arcs, his axe ringing with each skull it shattered.

Then, from the right, a scream tore through the mire.

Anselem whipped his head towards Sacha, watching as a hooked claw raked across the Pontos's ribs, drawing a deep, red line. He staggered, blood slicking his fingers, but didn't fall. With a savage roar, he drove his blade through the kawataro's throat, pushing upward until it pierced through the water-filled bowl atop its skull. The creature let out a wet gurgle and dropped.

Wave after wave of kawataro emerged from the inky waters, but the warriors did not falter. Shells cracked beneath steel. Light flashed through the mist. Screams echoed through the air. One after another advanced, until the number of emerging creatures began to dwindle, and only the leader remained.

It skulked toward them slowly, black claws dragging through the mud. Its lips peeled back into an ominous grin.

"You do not know what you reach for," it hissed. "That relic belongs to a monster cloaked in a maiden's form. A creature of hunger and ruin. She bled half a continent dry to bury it from the world. But she is not gone. One day, she will return for what is hers. And when she does, night will swallow the sky."

"Let her come," Mathieson snarled. "I'll still have enough steel left for her throat."

The Septant lunged as one, Mathieson striking high, his axe slamming into the creature's left arm. Sacha darted low, slicing its knee. As the kawataro screamed, Anselem flew above it and crashed down, lightning surging through *Soulmaker* as he drove it straight through the bowl on its skull.

The kawataro convulsed, water spilling out in one final splash. It collapsed, hanging lifelessly in the mud.

Silence fell across the swamp. The air hung heavy, thick with steam and blood.

A moment later, the sanctuary door burst open. Asha stepped out, a silver amulet clenched tightly in her fist. "Sorry," she panted. "There were an obscene number of locks. I had to burn through half of them."

Mathieson, breathless but grinning, leaned on his axe. "No worries, Fletch. It was easy work."

Anselem, grinning, huffed a breathless laugh. "Yeah, Sacha, those weren't as bad as you made them out to be."

Sacha did not respond.

Anselem turned towards him, and he saw the warrior's normally sun-kissed skin drain of color.

"You okay, Kaz?" Anselem asked, stepping closer to the Pontos.

Sacha stumbled, his body swaying at the mire's edge. He pressed a hand to his side, wincing as his fingers curled.

Then, slowly, as if his thoughts lagged behind his body, he pulled his hand away, and his fingertips were slick with dark-red blood.

Their eyes met.

"Sach—" Anselem started, stepping towards him. But the warning came too late.

Sacha crumbled, his body folding as he toppled forward, his body crashing into the murky water.

The water rippled around him, and then the blackness slowly began to bloom with haunting crimson.

CHAPTER FORTY-SEVEN

Iskander stood in the kitchen, swirling a glass of black-crescent whiskey, his gaze drifting to the Amarok warrior curled up on the couch. Kaira sat motionless, staring out the wall of windows that overlooked the Iron Mountains. Outside, under the pale cast of moonlight, two wolves lay nestled in the snow. One was midnight black, the other soft snow-white with ice-blue eyes.

Conri and Tala had made it to Lorca a few hours before, just after sunset, and Iskander had decided to delay their departure until morning. He knew the wolves needed a great deal of overdue rest.

He slid his eyes back to Kaira, who sat quietly on the corner of the cognac couch. A worn book rested in her lap, but she had not turned a page in several minutes.

It had been two days since she had gone to the Veil. When she returned, something in her looked... haunted. Iskander hadn't asked what she saw. And in the days that followed, Kaira hadn't offered.

Iskander took a sip from his glass and ambled over to

one of the onyx armchairs flanking the couch, watching her in silence. She did not look up from her book.

"Someone ought to teach you manners," she said, flipping a page. "It's impolite to stare."

A smile tugged at the corner of Iskander's mouth. "Oh, but life is so much more fun without them," he replied.

Kaira cut her eyes at him but returned to the book.

"You want to talk about it?" he asked. He could hear the clumsiness in his voice as the words spilled out. Comforting others was *not* a skillset Iskander had mastered.

She kept her gold eyes locked on the page before her. They remained unmoving. "Not particularly," she replied tightly.

A loud pause stretched between them, thick and lingering.

"The journey will take us an extra day now that we have to go back to Elysia," Iskander said, ungracefully attempting to shift the subject. He'd been redrawing their route ever since pulling Asha's note from Conri that instructed them to return to the Mount.

Kaira nodded faintly, her eyes once again moving over the words scribbled on the page.

Iskander turned his attention to the fire, welcoming the return to usual silence.

"Have any of you ever thought to use a more... accessible means of communication?" Kaira asked, pulling Iskander's gaze from the fire.

He met her glinting gold with a furrowed brow. "Meaning?"

She looked over to the wolves outside the window. "Notes tied to fur? Not exactly confidential."

"We have the Deliverer," he countered. "He handles our more sensitive messages." Iskander had told Kaira about Al once they had returned to his cottage on the first day.

"But he's only in Lorca," she said. "What about when you need to get a message to the others when you are in another city, or another kingdom?".

Iskander blinked. "We usually just use Al."

Kaira pursed her lips. He caught her stare dip down to the obsidian band on his wrist, and her eyes narrowed. "You all wear those," she said, no hint of a question in her tone.

Iskander involuntarily stiffened, but he forced his voice to remain neutral as he replied, "We do."

Kaira nodded again, slow and thoughtful.

Iskander could see her mind working behind the golden gaze. "What is it?" he asked.

A beat passed, and then she shook her head. "Nothing." She returned her focus to the book in her lap, and Iskander didn't press.

Silence lingered, thick and unmoving. The hearth crackled softly, and firelight cast dancing shadows across the warm room. Outside, the wolves lay still beneath the waning moon. Inside, Iskander leaned back in his chair, liquor glass resting idly against his thigh. His gaze was half-lidded with sleep. Kaira did not stir; she sat motionless, face fixed on the rune-locked hearth. The fire painted flickers across her face, mirroring the shadows that had come back with her from the Veil. There was something hollow in her posture, and her face was drawn and thoughtful, but lacking in presence.

When she finally spoke, her voice was quiet and brittle, like something inside her was straining itself so it would not splinter. "Is that all there is to my magic?" she asked, her voice so low that Iskander almost didn't catch it. "Seeing the Veil…is that all I can do?"

He studied her for a long moment, waiting to answer until she brought her eyes up to meet his. "Your power is what you make of it, Samson." He took a deep inhale and ran a thorn-inked hand through his dark hair. "When my powers first manifested, the instructors at the Citadel told me I was meant to be a counter against things that shine. That crafting darkness was all I would ever be. Just a void meant to swallow light. But I didn't accept that." He paused, the corners of his mouth curling slightly. "And thankfully, neither did the Grandmaster who trained me." He extended his hand. Coils of shadows rippled in his palm. "This was all I could do at first," he said, letting the smoky tendrils writhe and flicker. "A wisp. A cloudy thread. Nothing more. For months. Years. That was all there was, until I learned to shape it. Form it." The shadows in his palm shifted, elongating and morphing into a long, cracking whip. "I began to forge weapons. To fight with something other than wisps of darkness. To create forms with purpose." He twisted his hand, and the whip dissolved, reforming into the image of a broad, snarling wolf. A creature made of living shadow. "And then," he said, rising to his feet, "I eventually learned to Shadowstep." He took a step forward, and his form vanished.

A small gasp escaped from Kaira's mouth as he appeared on the far side of the room, tucked in a corner of shadow and darkness. Kaira's eyes flared wide. "You can flicker?"

Iskander shook his head. "It's not flickering. It's different. Shadowstepping only works when there's shadow to move through. But it's useful. Especially in combat." He smirked. "Anselem still hasn't figured out how to counter it. I usually knock his sword from his hand before he knows I'm behind him."

Kaira didn't respond; she just stared at him blankly, her face unreadable.

He let the silence breathe again, then said, "So, no, I don't think crossing into the Veil is all you're capable of. You've barely begun to understand your Kratos. There's more in you if you choose to find it."

Kaira swallowed hard. "Unless I lose my mind," she

murmured.

Iskander took a long, thoughtful moment before answering, "Only you can decide what breaks you." His voice was steady and certain.

Kaira stared into the fire. Then softly, almost absently, she said, "I saw him."

Iskander shifted in his chair, leaning forward, his elbows propped on his knees in anticipation.

"I thought I would have been terrified to meet the God of Death," she said, eyes fixed on the fire. "I would have thought I'd be consumed with fear, that the Reapers and the dark creatures in the Veil would have torn me apart." She shifted her eyes from the fire to Iskander, meeting his awaiting moondust silver. "But I wasn't afraid. I was… hollow. Unfeeling. Like everything had been emptied out." Her voice was steady but distant as she spoke.

Iskander nodded. "The Veil does not allow emotion. Not in the way we understand it. It is judgment without warmth. Memory without feeling."

"You speak of it as though you have been there," Kaira replied, tilting her head.

Iskander shook his head. "No, I have not. But my shadows… they speak a similar language. They were born from the darkness that resides there. The silence."

"I want you to teach me," she said, voice soft but firm and unflinching.

Iskander held her gaze, and after a quiet pause, he leaned back and lifted the glass to his lips. "What is it you would like to learn?"

Kaira stared at him with focused intent. "I want you to make me someone the God of Death will fear."

Iskander smirked and raised his glass in a silent toast, nodding once to the warrior he knew would one day become a reckoning.

CHAPTER
FORTY-EIGHT

Asha stared down at the glinting metal amulet in her hand.
It was hewn from brushed silver, with onyx dragon scales
lining the outer edge and a detailed carving resting in the
center.

Made of a tinted crimson, the engraving was an outline of three interweaving serpents. The center snake's neck
crawled upward, and its tail turned to the right before curling
back in towards its body. The two other serpents were perfect
duplicates of the first, with the curled tails all intertwining
in the middle to form touching circles. The three serpentine
necks stretched outward, looping in opposing directions.

Asha ran her thumb across the smooth surface, and an
ominous, humming power stirred from within.

"Do you know what the Empress wants with it?" she
asked, glancing over at Anselem.

He was securing the final straps on Kapheria's harness
and shook his head.

"No clue. Raynor said he didn't know anything about
it." The Commander attempted to hide the bitterness in his

416

tone when her brother's name crossed his lips, but the hostility buried within was not lost on Asha.

Asha glanced back down at the rounded metal in her hand. "And he is not going to meet us there after he drops off Sacha?" she inquired, her voice trembling more than she intended.

The question was heavy, weighed down by the uneasy feeling that accompanied the uncertainty of whether Sacha would survive the journey.

Mathieson had departed just after dawn, with Sacha strapped on the back of Bashiri. He had not wanted to waste any time getting the Pontos back to Elysia. Sacha's skin had been pale and clammy, his breathing so shallow it had made Asha's stomach knot.

The Isle women, after several flame-filled threats from Asha, had reluctantly agreed to tend to Sacha's injuries after Anselem had carried his limp body down the mountain. But the healing magic of the Isle women was inadequate, and the warrior of the sea still needed a great deal more to mend the gaping hole in his side.

Every moment that had passed felt like sand draining from an hourglass that the Soturi warriors could fill. Once the Isle Healers had slowed the bleeding enough for Sacha to be moved, Anselem helped secure his sagging body in Bashiri's harness, and the warriors watched with worried expressions as Mathieson took to the sky. A shadow of red still stained Anselem's hands from where he had hoisted Sacha onto the firebird.

Anselem's jaw clenched, and his hands stopped moving on the harness's straps. "No," he replied simply.

The singular word landed like a weight against Asha's chest, and she looked to the east, out past the choppy waters of the Straight. She tried not to picture Bashiri's wings beating furiously against the wind as Sacha bled out on her back.

Beneath her breath, she whispered a plea that Sacha would hold on long enough for her brother to find help.

Asha released a weary sigh and pulled her gaze northward, in the direction of the mountains lying far beyond what her eyes could see. She looked back down at the amulet once more before tucking it inside her shirt and climbing atop Uriel. She brushed a gentle hand over his feathers. He let out a soft sigh and stretched out his wings.

Anselem hoisted himself onto the back of Kapheria and leaned forward to whisper something inaudible to his firebird. When he returned upright, he fixed an arial orb around his head, and Asha followed suit.

She seized one last glimpse of the stony shores of Skull Rock, and then the pair of warriors took to the skies, heading straight for the Kunlun Mountains.

It had been many years since Anselem had wandered into the Alps of Perseis's southern mountain range, but he had never forgotten their mystical allure. After an arduous day of flying, they crossed over the small village of Silversage, and the snow-dusted peaks finally came into view.

The Kunlun Mountains were so vastly different from the neighboring iron-filled range of the North.

With sharp, imposing peaks made up from jagged ridges of light-colored rock, the mountain range was unlike any other on the Northern Continent. The distant sunset hues painted the white rocks an array of warm colors, and the Mist from the Redwoods seemed to rest at its foothills, never climbing higher than the gravelly base.

The warriors landed in an open space at the southern edge of the mountains, just west of Silversage.

Once Kapheria's claws hit the pebbled ground, Anselem

released the orb around his head and gracefully slid off her back. Asha slipped out of her saddle and landed softly beside Uriel.

"We will have to go on foot from here," he explained, pulling off a large pack that was strapped to Kapheria's harness. "There is nowhere for them to safely land inside the mountains," he clarified, glancing up at the towering rock forms. He fastened his twin blades against his back and slung a leather pack over his shoulder.

An eerie feeling washed over him as he stared up at the peaks. Kapheria released a loud huff of air beside him, and he brushed his hands over her feathers.

The dense clouds overhead blocked out the highest peaks of the ridgeline, but a gusting wind ripped across the skies, and the thick fog high above swirled. Anselem kept his eyes locked due North, at the mountain peak resting in the heart of the Kunluns. The misty billows began to pull away from the eight prominent peaks lining the ridge, and as the clouds disappeared, the crown summit of the Kunluns came into view.

The Horn.

The domineering peak dwelled in the centermost portion of the mountain range, and the towering crest could be seen from any angle on the ground below. The Horn's jagged, pyramidal shape was realm-renowned, and citizens traveled from as far as the Southern Continent to view the band of sides that faced each compass direction.

The sun continued its descent on the far side of the towering mountains, dipping below the silhouetted peaks, and as night began to emerge, the stars hanging high above littered the darkening sky.

Anselem let out a relieved sigh as a brilliant star emerged above the western ridgeline. His gaze circled the sky, finding the three additional vivid lights hanging overhead.

He had learned of the stars long ago, on a dark night spent on the outskirts of a foreign city south of the Straight.

Anselem had been on an assignment with the Septant, and the night before they planned to execute the mission, the warriors set up camp and lay beneath the stars for their rest.

As they stared up at the evening sky, waiting for sleep to claim them, Iskander told the Commander all about Selene and the goddess's *all-seeing eyes of the night*.

The General had explained her relationship with the moon and stars, and how her power was linked with the Amarok Wolves of the Night.

The goddess was recognized for her strength and influence amongst the gods of old, but everyone who worshipped her was also aware of her fury; because, just as the moon had forever possessed a dark side that stifled out life, so too did the Moon Goddess, and her wrath was more devastating than a thousand wrecking armies.

Iskander had spoken so highly of the goddess on that night, going into vivid detail about the power the deity possessed. But as he sat there, staring up at the stars hung in the night sky, Anselem realized his brother had not mentioned the goddess once since their reunion, and he prayed that his brother's bitterness towards the Moon Goddess would not impact their journey.

The four primary stars overhead slowly brightened as the sky faded into twilight.

Selene's favored companions.

Directly North rested the most brilliant of her treasures, with a smoky black ring surrounding the collection of vivid lights.

The Eastern sky held the second constellation, with a faint cobalt hue encompassing the stars.

Anselem twisted around to see the scarlet tinge filling the darkening sky to the South, and a scattering of bright lights was littered throughout the haze.

At last, he turned his gaze to the West. A pure-white vapor engulfed the single, brilliant star floating in the twilight air.

Selene's White Tiger of the West.

Anselem let out a long, deep breath and pointed towards the star. "We will head that way until we lose the last of the daylight."

Asha flung her pack onto her back and walked over to Anselem's side.

He stared down into her sapphire eyes for a long moment before pressing a soft kiss against her lips.

Ready? he asked.

She nodded and offered him a soft smile, and the pair began their ascent with the White Tiger guiding the way.

❖ ❖ ❖

The warriors walked for hours, well past the closing light of the sunset, when they finally found a cutout in the rock wall wide enough to set up camp.

Asha had guided the way for a while, using an orb of moonfire she had summoned in her hand, but the further they ascended into the mystical mountains, the stranger the air felt, so when the first opportunity for shelter presented itself inside a cavernous hollow, the warriors seized it with comforted relief.

Asha, lying beside Anselem, stared at the stars hanging outside the cave's cover. The night sky was clear, and the only light filling the space came from the bright moon hanging high overhead. Her head was resting against his chest, and she could feel the rhythmic rise and fall of his breath.

The warrior closed his eyes, content to fall asleep beneath the stars, wrapped up beside the woman he loved.

"You were right, you know," Anselem said quietly.

She twisted her neck and looked up at the warrior. He let out a soft laugh at the twinkle shining in her eyes—a twinkle he knew emanated from hearing those three words uttered from his lips.

"About what?"

He smiled. "When you told me you would ruin me."

A glimmer flickered in her eyes.

He brushed a piece of hair from her face and traced his thumb across her damp cheek. "You have ruined me, Asha. Completely. In the most beautiful way I never could have imagined. You have been my undoing. And sometimes I think that maybe the greatest thing I have ever done in this life was wait. It was like my soul knew you were there, somewhere in the world, I needed only to find you. And as I waited for you to come into my life, into the perfect place and time, I made an art form out of the endurance." He let out a breath. "I think deep down I always knew the wait would be worth it. That *you* would be worth it. And gods, you were worth every single moment."

She pressed her lips to his, deep and sure. Anselem wrapped his arms tightly around her shoulders, and the warriors silently drew their gazes to the stars above.

Several minutes passed, and just as sleep was beckoning to claim him, Asha's soft voice broke through the air.

"Ans?" she asked again, her tone grave and distant.

"Yes, Seven?" He opened his eyes.

"Why did my power manifest itself as fire? Iskander wields Chaos too, and his revealed itself as shadows…" Her words trailed off, as though she had wondered the thoughts for quite some time but was unsure why she had chosen to voice them out loud that night.

Anselem's voice was low and steady as he answered, "I think darkness and hollowness are things Iskander has always known. And when his magic was released, those sentiments were something he was comfortable with—something familiar. So, that was how it manifested for him. I think the same goes for you. Fire was something familiar. I think there has been something burning deep inside of you for a long time, and it needed to finally be set free."

He paused for a moment before adding, "I think if you trained and focused on it, there's a possibility you could form your magic into whatever you want. You have before."

Asha glanced at him with confused eyes.

"At your final benchmark," he continued, "you told me you froze one of the Eligos with ice before you burned it."

Asha could barely remember what had happened over the last several days, much less every detail from her concluding benchmark weeks before.

"I don't even know how I did it," she admitted, reflecting on the shards of frost that had spewed from her fingertips.

"Perhaps it was what you needed at that moment."

Asha tilted her head.

"Time," he supplied, answering her unspoken question. "Time to get to Jeremiah—to save him. Maybe your power recognized that plea and manifested itself into something that could satisfy your greatest need."

She loosened a sigh and did not speak for a long while, lost in thought.

He was quiet as he held her, letting the warrior battle through the war in her mind, steadfast by her side. "Talk to me," he murmured against her hair.

She stayed silent for a long moment, staring out at the White Tiger. "What if the Chaos consumes me?" she whispered.

"It won't," he replied, his voice full of belief.

She shifted her body, twisting around to look up at his eyes. "But what if it does?" she breathed.

He tucked a piece of hair behind her ear. "Then we will deal with it."

"What if I'm too far gone? What if… what if I'm not *me* anymore?" Her voice was shaky, filled with a fear he had never heard fall from her lips.

He smiled softly, and his words were wound with earnest candor as he replied, "Seven, I would know you even if I found you in the midst of ambient shadows, in the middle of devouring Darkness, or in the depths of all-consuming Chaos. I would recognize the feeling of your soul in another life altogether. In a different vessel, a different form, a different world. And I would love you in each. You have me. Always. Until every last light in the star-strewn sky fades into midnight obscurity, I am yours. And even after, I promise to find you, even without the light."

And with those professing words, he felt Asha's heartbeat calm. He pulled her in close and pressed a gentle kiss to her forehead. Staring down into her radiant eyes, his soul felt full — complete.

And in that perfect moment, he knew if Death ever tried to steal her from him again, he'd rip the worlds apart with his bare hands.

CHAPTER
FORTY-NINE

When morning light broke in the sky, Asha and Anselem continued through the rest of the trek, creeping further and deeper into the heart of the Kunluns.

As they rambled through the mountains, Asha's mind mirrored her feet—precariously wandering through the unknown.

She thought a lot about where they were headed, and the mysterious Empress they were fated to meet, but Asha's mind also drifted to the night before, and the steadfast warrior before her, guiding the way.

She stared at his back, wingless and clothed in a Septant black jacket. If she hadn't seen the golden wings with her own eyes, hadn't studied every ornate detail of the gilded plumes, hadn't felt the constant thrum of electricity that buzzed off the surface—she never would have believed it to be true.

Asha had heard the tales as a child and learned the history during her training in Valhol about the higher and lesser winged peoples of Darnella, but never in her life did she

425

think she would see one with her own eyes.

As far as she had been told, no more even existed. They had all been wiped out during the First War or in the days soon after.

The most notorious group of the higher wings—the select few groups of winged peoples who wielded powerful, devastating magic—was the Daire.

The Daire were formed long ago in a time before the First War, as the offspring of an unnatural joining between the Princes of Shadows and the Elven peoples.

Known for their otherworldly beauty, the Elves had been forced to breed with the Dark Princes; ultimately creating a collection of descendants—all females—that earned their name of the Goddesses of Vengeance.

The black-winged warriors possessed all the beauty of their Elven mothers, along with every ounce of bitter Darkness granted by the creatures who sired them.

But much the same as the other immortal creatures that had been eradicated in the First War, the Daire were wiped from the realm, with no repudiable trace or mention of their vengeful sisterhood in the Desert Isles, or their originally inhabited lands of Erebus.

Legend claimed that the handful of Daire children who survived the eradication of their kin were beholden to pay for the sins of their mothers. The Leaders, employed in the beginning times after the First War, forcefully tied down the young girls and brutally clipped the remaining black wings from the backs of the Daire children.

The vengeful goddesses had not been seen since.

As for the lesser winged peoples of Darnella—the immortal creatures of the Continents who possessed smaller, more finite magic—they had all gone into hiding to preserve their limited magic.

And the select groups that had refused to conceal their

gifts were forcefully exiled—permanently banished to the remote areas of the Southern Continent for their unnatural ability to wield unbonded magic.

But in all her studies throughout Kappi training, Asha had never once heard of higher winged people belonging to the Septant.

A harrowing, mist-filled wind whipped across the mountainside, and Asha tucked her absorbed thoughts about the warrior before her into a dark corner of her mind, for she did not want to know if the strange winds of the Kunluns—or the questionable creatures that called it home—had some ethereal ability to burrow through her mental shields.

After miles of mounting slopes and scrambling across uneven rock faces, the warriors rounded the final corner of a jagged, rising rock wall, and a plunging canyon greeted them.

Two colossal sculptures of stone hands were carved into the far mountainside, reaching outward and across the chasm to form a bridge with their upturned palms.

The Hands of the Wise One.

Asha glanced up to see a large, four-faced pyramidal peak towering above them.

Just beyond the bridge, at the crook of where the statue's supposed elbows would meet, was a small entrance that led into the heart of the Horn.

Asha swallowed and took a deep breath. Neither of the warriors knew what they would encounter inside the mountain, but if her past experiences served her right, she knew that no virtuous creatures ever willingly dwelled inside the darkest corners of the world.

Asha and Anselem crossed the bridge overhanging the canyon. The whipping winds thrashed her knotted hair in all directions, and the warriors fought to keep upright against the forceful gusts.

After making their way across the stone passage, the pair quickly ducked inside the small archway leading into the heart of the Kunluns, and the ripping winds instantly ceased inside the cave's walls.

The air was damp, and a narrow passageway was carved into the rock. Asha conjured an orb of moonfire in her palm, and Anselem unsheathed *Soulmaker* from his back.

The warriors slowly entered the tunnel, curving downward until a faint light came into view from below.

Anselem took Asha's hand and led them the rest of the way through the lightless tunnel, until they broke through the passageway and entered the luminos lit space.

Asha sucked in a breath as she took in the scene. The tunnel opened several hundred feet above the rocky floor, and from their elevation, she was able to see every portion of the Forgotten City.

Shrouded underground within the core of the Horn, rested a fully formed settlement, with hundreds of homes ingeniously carved into the cave's walls. Far below, covering nearly the entirety of the rocky ground, sat a transparent lake filled with ice-blue water. Dozens of small boats, occupied with Verloren citizens, were scattered through the serene centerpiece, floating from one side to the other.

Isolated from the outside world, untouched by the Darkness of the past, the Forgotten City was a refuge. An unscathed symbol of promise for the future. For a better world.

Across the cavern, hanging high above the tranquil lake below, rested a second, larger archway, manned by two men outfitted in golden armor.

As Asha traced her gaze along the wall, searching for a route that would connect their path to the other side, a small, delicate-looking woman ambled up the exterior trail. She slowly ascended the stone path until she stood before the

Soturi warriors.

"We've been expecting you," the girl murmured. Her voice was soft and gentle, effortlessly matching the welcoming smile stretched across her face.

Anselem shifted his weight, and his grip tightened around *Soulmaker*.

The girl looked young, but a great sense of wisdom rested in the depths of her doe-shaped eyes. Her jet-black hair was cropped short, exposing the pointed tips of her ears, and a littering of freckles was sprayed across her pale cheeks. Her high-cut, deep-blue dress matched the navy hue of her eyes, and the golden accents of the gown's embroidery accentuated the metallic veins dispersed throughout the wings protruding from her back.

"I'm Evie," the fairy introduced, tilting her neck back to look up at the warriors. The top of her head struggled to reach Asha's chin.

Neither of the Soturi replied.

Her inky blue eyes shifted between the two warriors before landing on the tightly gripped blade in Anselem's hand.

The innocent smile remained on her face as she stated, "You won't be needing that, Commander. If the Empress did not want you here, you would have been dead as soon as you crossed the Hands."

Anselem set a menacing smirk upon his face as he replied, "Well, you can tell the Empress her wisdom seems to falter in areas of war if she thinks the only weapon I brought was a blade."

The sweetness in Evie's voice turned sour as she replied, "Tell her yourself, Lightbearer."

She quickly spun around and curled her way down the path lining the exterior wall.

Asha and Anselem exchanged a look before silently falling into step behind her, and the trio made their way around the outer edge of the city.

As they walked, Asha scanned the walls and floors far below, straining her eyes for any sign of another archway or opening.

Her hand instinctively felt for the hidden dagger in her waistband when she realized there were no other visible passageways. Only one way in and one way out.

Asha was staring at the glinting veins scattered throughout Evie's wings when Anselem slowed his pace and fell in line beside her. She glanced up at his waiting gaze.

There is one other, he claimed.

Asha's brows bunched, and he smirked.

You're looking for additional exits, I assume.

Asha sighed. *Was I that obvious?*

He grinned and shook his head. *No, I just know you.*

A genuine smile curled at the corners of her mouth. She loved the truthfulness in such a simple statement. That he sincerely and earnestly knew her. To the depths of her soul.

At the bottom, in the far corner just past the row boats, he added.

She glanced down at the lake, straining her eyes to the far corner of the city. She could not make out any hidden exits, and just as she was about to tear her eyes from the docked boats below, she saw a small wooden watercraft float out from a dark cutout in the stone wall, leading out of the city and back into the underground mountains.

She looked back over to Anselem and nodded once, quick and concise.

As they walked, Asha continued to rake her gaze across the hundreds of vibrant citizens hastily moving through the underground city.

Verloren was beautiful—so vastly contrary to the obsidian tunnels and dark corridors of her home in Valhol.

But what fascinated Asha more than the stunning homes

and the crystalline lake perched in the center was the assortment of people strewn throughout the city, all tranquilly moving about the cavernous space.

Like Evie, there were dozens of lesser winged peoples, the ones Asha had learned about from the tales of childhood. The stories about ethereal fairies with wings spun of gold and temperaments crafted from endless serenity. The same legends that had claimed the fairies had been eradicated by Darkness in the First War.

Her gaze shifted to an arboreal woman walking by on the path, and Asha's heart skipped a step.

Her ears, similar to Evie's, were pointed, and the light brown skin on her face was freckled. Her dark hair was twisted into dozens of braids, and a crown of forest-green leaves wrapped around her head. The leaves stretched out from small wooden branches that connected to a central point that plunged into the crest of her forehead. A single, deep-green gem hung from the bottom of the branches and matched seamlessly with her stunning jade eyes.

The earth-blessed woman smiled as she passed, and Asha nodded.

The People of the Woods.

There were dozens of other beings scattered throughout the cave, each more unique than the last. Various aquatic creatures lined the lake below, and aerial beings buzzed overhead, transporting goods from one side of the cavern to the other. There were multitudes of beings that had not been seen or spoken of for centuries.

Asha realized that even with their apparent visual differences, all the citizens inside the city shared one singular commonality: they were the forgotten peoples of the Continents.

And as she drew her gaze back to the majestic wings of the woman guiding their path, Asha understood one thing with unequivocal certainty: the Forgotten City was not an abhorrent place tucked inside the darkest corners of the Horn.

It was a haven. A place full of tolerance and acceptance. A place for the lost.

The Forgotten City was a glimpse into a better world.

CHAPTER FIFTY

Mathieson had flown nonstop to Elysia, Sacha's unconscious body strapped behind him on the back of Bashiri.

Before he took to the skies, Asha had pressed a half-full vial into his palm. A pale green liquid swirled inside the bottle. It was all she had left of the restoration elixir.

It had been better than nothing. It slowed the hemorrhaging just enough to keep Sacha from bleeding out, but it hadn't been enough to close the gaping wounds kawataro's claws had ripped in his side.

Dawn had not yet touched the horizon when Mathieson landed outside the City of Glass. He hadn't waited for the Kappi warrior on gate duty to come out and greet him. He couldn't risk being recognized.

He'd moved swiftly through the alabaster stone streets, Sacha's limp form draped across his back. Not a soul stirred in the alleys as he made turn after turn, memory guiding his way.

His body ached, and his legs began to cramp beneath the weight as he darted towards the center of the city. He rounded another corner, and then he saw it.

Bathed in the soft glow of the luminos strung along the buildings, it stood tall and commanding, its stained-glass windows reflecting a rainbow of fractured light across the square.

The Lighthouse.

Mathieson didn't hesitate. He crossed the cobbled square, twisted the golden knob of the pristine white door, and pushed into Elysia's main center for the Rapha.

He knew exactly which turns to take, exactly which door to find as he clamored through the halls. His Septant black hood was drawn low over his face, and he ensured he kept Sacha's fastened as well as he dragged his bleeding brother through the hall.

And just before he entered the onyx door that would lead him into the reserved room for the Septant, Mathieson glanced back and saw a cluster of pale-blue-robed healers whispering urgently to one another.

"Get Panacea!" he roared, his voice sharp and unrecognizable in his own throat.

The healers' eyes went wide, and as if shaken from a trance, the Rapha scattered into motion.

Mathieson turned and shoved open the door, hauling Sacha in with him.

The chamber was wide and rectangular, walled in pale ivory stone veined with silver. A large glass dome arched overhead, catching the dawning light in fractured beams across the marble floor. At the center stood a single stone bed. It was smooth and sterile, and draped with clean linens. Shelves lined the walls, filled with polished vials, bundles of dried herbs, and scrolls marked in dark ink. Everything smelled faintly of lavender, ash, and something unplaceable and ancient.

Mathieson moved toward the center, each step echoing

against the marble. Carefully, he lifted Sacha from his back, muscles trembling from the strain of the journey. Blood had soaked through the wrappings around his brother's side, warm and sluggish now.

He laid the Pontos warrior down gently on the table. Sacha didn't stir. His skin was pale, his breathing shallow and uneven.

Mathieson stepped back.

The room was still. Silent. Cold.

Mathieson's chest rose and fell with quiet urgency. The adrenaline was fading, leaving behind only the ache in his limbs and the weight in his stomach. He didn't pace. Didn't speak. The chamber demanded stillness. Demanded reverence.

So, he waited. And he prayed to whatever gods would still listen that he hadn't brought Sacha here too late.

Only a quarter of an hour had passed before an ancient woman, clothed in pale-blue robes, entered the room.

Her white hair was twisted into a neat bun at the base of her neck, and her bright gold eyes beamed with power and wisdom. Deep-set wrinkles were etched into her dark-brown skin, and she moved with slow, methodical grace across the room. Her aged hands were folded delicately in front of her, and she wore an unyielding mask of inexpression. Neither smile nor grimace adorned her face. Only the boundless knowledge of healing sparked within her eyes.

The High Regent of the Rapha.

"Regent Panacea," he greeted, dipping his head to the Supreme Healer of the Rapha.

Much the same as the warriors of Perseis, the healers of the Rapha adhered to a strict hierarchy of their own, each rank a reflection of mastery of their healing Light.

At the foundation were the Rapha Acolytes, newly inducted healers who had recently completed their initial training. These initiates spent their days learning to brew potions, tend wounds, and control the glowing Light that flowed within their veins.

Above them stood the Rapha Ascendants, the largest tier of the healers. Comprised of practitioners who had honed their connection to the Light and could wield it with skill, clarity, and precision. Whether stationed at forts or active field postings across the kingdom, the Rapha Ascendants were the steady lifeblood of the healing arts across Perseis.

Presiding over them were the Rapha Exalted, a rare and revered few whose power surpassed the rest. They were master healers who served as heads at each of the forts and oversaw complex rites of restoration.

At the pinnacle stood Panacea, the High Regent of the Rapha, whose word was law among the healers. She alone answered to no one but the Light itself.

Panacea nodded in acknowledgment of Mathieson and silently made her way towards the corner where Sacha lay slumped atop the table.

A second woman Mathieson had never seen before strolled in silently behind her.

She was small and softly built, with a dusting of freckles that spanned across her fair skin. Her amber eyes held an easy warmth, like a hearth's fire on a cold morning. Vivid red hair was braided neatly away from her face, and she carried a kindness in her smile that seemed crafted for healing. Every motion she made was deliberate, gentle, as though the world around her deserved a softer touch.

"Tell me what did this," Panacea ordered, her golden eyes drifting across Sacha's wounds.

Mathieson pulled his gaze from the red-haired Rapha

and strode over to the examination table. "A kawataro," Mathieson answered, eyeing the young Rapha as she quietly ambled to Panacea's side.

Panacea hissed, "You lot always know how to get in the worst of trouble."

"It was a necessary mission," Mathieson said, earning a sharp look from the High Regent.

"Of course it was," Panacea muttered, exhaling through her nose, slow and annoyed. "You should stop letting your Commander lead your little death-squad into the homes of creatures that eat bone."

"You should know by now he doesn't like to listen," Mathieson snorted. "But I'll be sure to pass along your concerns."

Panacea raised a brow but said nothing more. She approached the table and studied Sacha with narrowed eyes. "He's lucky to be breathing," she murmured. "Claws tore deep... right between the ribs. Any closer and his lung would've collapsed."

"We got to him quickly," Mathieson replied.

"Clearly not quickly enough," Panacea said dryly. She let out a soft click of her tongue, then reached out. Her voice dropped, almost tender. "Hold him steady."

Mathieson and the red-haired Rapha placed their hands on opposite sides of the warrior's unconscious body.

Panacea pressed her hands gently to Sacha's ribs, fingertips splayed over torn flesh. A soft radiance bloomed beneath her palms—light not blinding, but warm, like sunlight caught beneath water. It pulsed in time with his breath, threads of gold and white seeping through muscle and bone, stitching what had been broken.

Sacha's body jerked faintly beneath her touch. His limbs twitched, jaw tightening as the Light surged through damaged nerves. A fine sheen of sweat broke across his brow, and for a moment, his shallow breathing hitched. The body remembered pain, even when the mind did not.

Panacea's expression did not waver. She held her hands steady, letting the Light guide the reweaving of flesh, the mending of vessels too small to see. Magic threaded through muscle, coaxed bone into alignment, and soothed the broken architecture of his chest.

The glow dimmed gradually, ebbing like a receding tide, as the skin beneath her hands began to smooth and seal.

The High Regent looked over to the young Rapha and wordlessly nodded to a cabinet across the room.

The Acolyte silently glided across the floor and returned a moment later with a small vial in hand. A pale light-yellow liquid sloshed inside. She uncorked the bottle and tipped the contents gently into Sacha's mouth.

"It will be a few days before he is fully recovered," Panacea explained, stepping back from the table. "There will be some swelling where the muscles have been forged back together. He's been given a sleeping draught to ensure he sleeps through the worst of the pain."

Mathieson cleared his throat. "Thank you."

Panacea nodded and began to make her way towards the door. She paused, her wrinkled hand clutching the brass knob, and glanced back at him. "Glad to see you have returned," she said sincerely, and before Mathieson could reply, the High Regent slipped back into the stained-glass halls of the Lightpost.

Mathieson glanced over at Sacha and watched the slow rise and fall of his chest. Then he took a deep breath and made his way to the leave, knowing the best thing for the Pontos warrior was uninterrupted rest.

"I didn't catch your name," the red-haired Rapha said softly as she gathered a bundle of clean cloths from a nearby cabinet.

"Amos," he lied, not wishing for the unfamiliar girl to know his name. There were not many people he trusted to know he was still alive. And a healer he just met—student of the High Regent or not—wasn't one of them.

The Rapha smiled politely and replied, "I'm Brighid."

Mathieson offered a nod and turned without another word, striding out of the room and back into the quiet streets of Elysia.

439

CHAPTER

FIFTY-ONE

The trio finally made it to the other side of the cavern, and the large, guarded archway they had seen from the opposite wall greeted them.

The two soldiers, outfitted in solid gold, rotated to the side as they approached. Evie entered the corridor first, and Asha and Anselem followed closely behind.

The walls in the passage were damp, and a collection of warm-hued luminos lined both sides of the tunnel.

It was eerily quiet as they made their way through the short channel; the soft trickle of water was the only sound present in the narrow space.

Evie exited the passageway first, entering the brightly lit space beyond.

Asha ducked through the opening next, followed by Anselem closely at her heels.

A second, smaller room had been carved out within the mountain. Hundreds of feet above, a large hole was cut out in the ceiling, allowing a portion of the breaking sunlight overhead to enter from outside.

The room was much smaller than the one from which they had come, but even in its comparative smallness, the chamber remained abundantly spacious.

Dozens of columns had been carved directly into the stone lining both sides of the curving walls. Towering sculptures of illustrious figures were etched between the pillars, with great hearths of fire resting beneath each of the statues' feet.

A large, round table, lined with great, stone chairs, sat in the center of the room, with an array of candles scattered across the cream-colored top.

On the far side of the cave, erected atop a platform of matching cream stairs, sat an occupied throne.

As Evie led the warriors over to the throne, passing by an assortment of guests gathered at the table, Asha noticed the abyssal, onyx stone resting at the base of the throne's steps.

The flattened rock was perfectly circular, with a glittering hue that glinted when the overhead sunlight shifted. Small, nearly imperceptible tendrils of smoky shadows coiled around its edge.

Evie stopped just before she neared the obsidian rock, and Asha and Anselem took their presumed place beside it.

As she looked up to meet the sagacious eyes peering down at her, Asha could feel the humming buzz emanating from the blackened circle.

The Empress had deep-lined, tawny skin with curly grey-white hair that fell halfway down her back. She wore dozens of gold-plated bangles around her wrists with flowing cobalt robes scattered with flecks of silver.

She possessed an eternal beauty, with wise eyes that looked as though they held the answers to every question under the sun.

"Are you the Empress?" Asha asked.

Thotha offered Asha a kind smile and replied, "I am many things."

Asha held her intense gaze.

"I am of Mist," she continued, "I am the keeper of the veil that separates the worlds of the gods from the mortal realm. I exist to ensure good triumphs evil and to manage the cosmic order of our dimension. I am a guardian of knowledge and prophecy."

Asha's breathing became jagged, and Anselem brushed the back of his hand against hers. Her eyes flickered to the staff resting beside the throne.

Asha could see no inky tendrils billowing from the hilt, nor did she see a seven-pointed crown etched into the handle.

The scepter was pure-white, matching the snow scattered across the mountaintops above. The shaft was smooth and straight, stretching up to a linear crystal fixed at the pommel. The translucent gemstone twinkled in the overhead sunlight, and the reflecting beams created a myriad of colors painted across the stone walls.

Asha stepped forward, careful not to cross the deep line carved into the onyx ring before her, and placed the silver amulet on the ground before the Empress.

Thotha stared down at Asha from her throne and ran her hand down the side of the staff resting in the post beside her.

It was simple and pure, with a faint hint of blue spiraling around the snow-white shaft. At the top rested a glass orb, with a transparent flame flickering in the center—an everflame.

The Empress dragged her gaze over Asha, and a light filled her eyes, as if she was seeing something familiar once again after a long time. "What guidance of mine do you seek?"

Asha drew in a deep, bracing breath. "I wish to know of

the war with the Hells."

The Empress studied her for a long, silent moment before inclining her head. "Very well," she replied. "But to understand the present, one must first glimpse the past."

Asha held the Empress's stare with steely determination.

"Millennia ago," the Empress began, "in a world long since destroyed, wars raged, and the realms fell into chaos. A great battle took place, the one your people refer to as the First War, that was fought between the Gods of Light and Darkness. And as the battle raged across time and space, the gods ripped through dimensions, and many realms were destroyed. The war was fought for a long time, each side enlisting its own soldiers and armies. But in the end, the God of Life triumphed, and Darkness was defeated. Afterward, the God of Light created a new world, born not from the chaos and voids of battle, but from peace and order. He cast out the Lord of Darkness, imprisoning him in the Underworld, and the Founders forged the seven kingdoms from the ashes of a broken world.

Asha's hands clammed with sweat. Words could not form on her lips. Her head spun—throbbed. "And Anubis, he is the Lord of Darkness?" The questioning voice sounded far from Asha, and the words barely registered over the ringing in her ears.

The Empress of the Forgotten City laughed softly. "No, Anubis is merely the Guidon of Death, directing mortal souls into the Afterlife or the Underworld. Guiding them across the Veil that separates words. He bows to powers higher than his own."

Asha swallowed. "How will the Lord of Darkness return?" Asha asked, voice thick.

"You already know," the Empress stated coolly. "Your brother has already told you."

Asha shifted her weight, her only sign of distress. A rim of sweat beaded on Asha's brow. "My brother was right, wasn't he? History is once again repeating itself. The gods have chosen another Warrior of Praenuntius."

Thotha tilted her head. "It is not solely the gods who wait for the one who will fulfill the prophecy, child," she murmured. "The King of the Abyss waits as well."

Asha pursed her lips. A trickle of sweat trailed down her back.

"He waits not for battle," Thotha said softly. "He waits for release. For the one whose blood burns with chaos, whose power can open his gate in its entirety, whose soul was chosen by the Authorities themselves. When that vessel rises... the age of ruin begins. And only through ruin can a new world be born."

Asha's voice was calm. "And this vessel—what are they meant to do?"

Thotha looked back at her. "They are not meant to save the world," he said. "They're meant to *unmake* what needs to fall. To decide what burns and what endures. To harbor an end to the Darkness of our world so something new can rise from its ashes. Whether the world ends or survives will depend not on power, but on who commands it. The vessel is the Champion meant to carry this age to the edge of ruin... And through ruin, to a new world—a *better* world. Made of Light."

Asha forced herself to clear her mind. Her voice strained as she spoke. "How do we send them back?" Her voice was barely above a whisper, as if the question alone would summon the Adversary's wrath to the very spot. "How do we win a war against the Hells?"

The Empress's face was schooled into an expression of poised neutrality. "The path will be long, Seal-Breaker."

That name again.

"And even I do not hold all the answers you seek," Thotha added. "But you must first decide if this journey is one you wish to embark upon, because once the choice is made, there will be no turning back. You must decide to accept your fate or turn from it."

Asha's lips pressed into a thin line, and she nodded once.

"Knowledge demands knowledge," the Empress added, motioning to the dark circle on the floor.

Asha glanced down at the onyx stone before her. She could feel it calling—beckoning—for her to enter, and deep inside her Chaos-etched soul, she knew she must cross into the ring to accept the path lying before her.

Before she could take a step forward, Anselem's hand grabbed her wrist. "What is the price?" he asked, his voice was heavier than the entire weight of Iron Rock.

The Empress offered a soft, sorrowful smile as she glanced down at the onyx stone. "The only price required is a simple test," she answered, her ancient hand gesturing to the obsidian stone before her. "To know if you are worthy of the knowledge, or if the Darkness will swallow you."

Anselem glared at the Empress. "And what is the cost if the Darkness wins?"

She stared a long while at Asha before she replied, "Your mortal soul."

The color drained from Anselem's face. "No," he muttered to the Empress. The word was filled with unreserved disbelief as the whisper left his lips. He grabbed Asha's wrist tighter as he repeated, "*No*."

Asha placed a hand on top of his and turned her eyes up to his face. His expression was stone, carved in an unrelenting mask of pain and horror. Silver lined his eyes.

No, he pleaded, turning to face the woman at his side. We will find another way. His voice cracked across the words inside her head. His eyes scoured Asha's face, looking for an answer, a reply.

"I will do it in her place," he begged Thotha, turning back to the Empress in a desperate plea.

The ruler's voice was gentle, kind. "Only the Chosen One may break the Seals. Only Chaos has the power to destroy what Chaos has forged."

Asha grabbed his hand in hers and squeezed once. He broke his stare from the Empress's to meet hers.

This is it, she said into his mind. This is when I need you to trust me. Believe in me.

He looked down at her. Into the flame-filled eyes of the warrior who had faced Darkness before and won. Into the chaos-forged heart of the woman he loved, who had emerged on the other side. Into the gaze of one who had been built for triumph. Who had been made, not for cowering in the face of evil, but with power that could conquer the Dark.

She gave him a warm smile as tears slid down her cheeks. "Until we are ash and embers," she breathed.

Tears began to fall from Anselem's eyes as he wrapped his hand around hers. He took Soulmaker from his side and pressed the hilt of the blade into her hand. Then he looked deep into the burning sapphire, into her very soul, and nodded. "Into every lifetime," he promised.

Then Asha released his hand and stepped forward into the ring of Darkness.

446

CHAPTER
FIFTY-TWO

Asha stood in the center of stretching blackness. Bitter silence filled the air. A deep, sickening chill shuttered around her, and she could feel the wave of frost lick across her skin. A cold so bitter, it cut through bone.

She tried to squint past the blackness, tried to see something illumed in the lightless place. Another gust of icy wind brushed over her, tugging at the loose strands of hair that had fallen from her braid. It smelled of ice-covered rot and death.

She did not know where she had been transported. Did not know where the obsidian stone inside the Empress's throne room had flickered her. All she could see was a stretching expanse of midnight black as she waited for her eyes to slowly adjust to the dark.

In the distance, a frost-blue light began to pulse, webbing across the icy floor like spidery veins. Asha pulled her jacket tighter to her chest and began to walk towards the glow, her boots crunching on shattered ice.

Each step echoed across the barren expanse, swallowed quickly by the frigid wind. The ground beneath her looked like a fractured mirror, black and glassy, webbed with veins of frost that glowed beneath the icy surface.

Above, the sky was a desolate void. No stars sparked inside the blackness, no moonlight pierced through the misty clouds. There was only a pressing darkness that permeated every corner of the lands. The silence was boundless, save for the distant cracks of shifting ice, and the angry howl of wind that curled like a living thing through jagged ridges of stone.

Frost began to feather across Asha's sleeves, creeping toward her skin. Her jacket stiffened around her, and her breath came out in pale, shallow bursts.

As she walked, her eyes slowly adjusted to the dark, and before her, the land gave way to a frozen lake covered in a thick mist. Its surface gleamed like obsidian glass, undisturbed and deathly smooth, reflecting her form in warped fragments. The ice was too perfect. Too still.

Asha hesitated, taking a long pause before stepping onto the surface. A hollow groan echoed beneath her boots as her feet brushed the glass-covered lake. Spiderweb cracks bloomed outward across the surface, and Asha's heart stuttered.

She waited for the surface to crack open. For her body to slip into the black waters below. But the glass exterior did not break, and the ice held.

Asha moved slowly, each step placed with delicate intention. Below, shapes drifted through the murky blackness. They were too large to be human, too slow to be alive. As she crossed, faces rose beneath the ice and faded again, eyes open. One floated just beneath her step, mouth open in a silent scream, hands pressed to the underside of the ice as if trying to claw upward from some deeper chasm.

Asha did not stop to look again.

Halfway across, the wind shifted. The wild gusts twisted into purposeful squalls, and the cold deepened, curling through her bones, as if calling her to the opposite side.

On the far edge, the lake cracked sharply beneath her last step, a jagged sound like tearing glass, and she stumbled onto solid ice-crusted earth once more.

She passed through a curved entrance, made from the ribcage of some forgotten creature. Bones the size of towers jutted up from the ground; their gleaming-white shells were half-buried in snowdrift and shadow. As she stepped through the gate, the mist thinned, and shapes began to rise around her. A vacant village, half-buried in ice and snow, stretched in broken outlines ahead. Shattered windows and caved-in roofs littered the square. Everything was coated in a thick sheen of ice and shadow, like the entire place had been flash-frozen by an ancient god.

It didn't feel abandoned. It felt paused. As if it were holding its breath, waiting for permission to move once again.

She made her way to the end of the village, and the wind shifted once more, making a space for her through the misty cold. She stepped out from the cover of the frozen buildings, and through the drifting curtain of frost and shadow, a large, distant structure peeked through the mist.

She trekked through the vaporous fog until she reached the base of a palace made of black ice and frozen stone. The glass walls were streaked with veins of trapped ghost-light, like lightning captured beneath a glacier. Jagged spires lanced the sunless sky, rimed with hoarfrost so thick, they cast a glowing blue haze onto the surrounding black stones. Icicles, thick as oak trunks, hung from the arched parapets like spears. There were faces frozen inside the crystals, mouths open in a scream that had no heart left to carry it across the bitter winds.

The front doors were tucked back behind monolithic

pillars, covered by a shroud of impenetrable shadows. Asha heard the creaking of hinges as she approached the bottom of the grand, black-marble staircase.

"Don't be afraid," a voice beckoned from the shadows. The tone was soulless, made of depthless ice. A collection of faded, glacier-blue luminos ignited overhead. From the doorway, a man with long onyx hair and snow-white skin stepped onto the portico. He was draped in robes of snow-laced shadow. A crown of shattered ice and splintered bones wrapped around his head like a fractured halo. His face was callous, and his dark eyes burned with glacial malice. As Asha drew closer, she could see the irises were nearly filled with flecks of bright crimson.

The man looked like a harsher, more devious version of Raziel, the resemblance between the two a near duplicate.

Asha's heart sank.

A wicked smile, one that could easily rival that of the Secret-Seeker's, crawled upon the man's face. His voice was filled with ice and malice as he crooned, "Welcome to my home. The Province of Anarchy is delighted to have such a delicious guest."

And as his chilling voice cut through the dark, Asha knew she was no longer inside the Forgotten City. No longer inside the Horn, or the southern mountain range of her home kingdom. No longer Perseis, or even her realm of Darnella.

Asha Akselson Raynor was standing in the First Province of the Seven Hells, staring up at a Prince of Shadows.

CHAPTER FIFTY-THREE

Asha stepped over the threshold and into a grand, glacial hall. The air was sharp with frost, biting at her lungs as her boots clicked against ice-slicked stone.

The foyer was vast and echoing. Its walls were carved from dark basalt veined with silver and looked like frozen rivers locked in stone. Towering pillars flanked either side, sculpted into the likeness of robed figures with veiled faces and outstretched arms, a motionless throng of chiseled Reapers reaching out towards the long hall ahead.

Overhead, the vaulted ceiling arched high above, draped in webs of frozen mist and crowned by a massive chandelier of jagged crystal. Each shard was illumed with pale-blue light, and the spikes were frosted over to look like skin-piercing icicles.

The walls shimmered with a layer of half-melted frost, and the sconces lining the passage flickered with cold light.

The prince moved ahead, his footsteps as silent as snowfall. "Come along," he beckoned cooly. "Let's get this little trial of yours over with. I have more pressing matters

451

to attend to."

Asha narrowed her eyes but said nothing, matching his pace as they moved deeper into the hall.

Silence stretched as they wound their way through a series of twisting corridors.

"What sort of trial is this?" Asha finally asked, her breath misting the air.

The prince gave a dry chuckle. "The kind without mercy." He glanced at her sideways, eyes glinting. "If you're lucky, there will still be something left of your soul to weigh when it is done."

"And if I'm not lucky?" she snipped, eyes narrowing.

The prince smiled thinly as they turned another corner. "Then you will die twice—once in body, and again when your memory is wiped from the worlds and thrust into oblivion."

A knot in Asha's stomach twisted.

They entered a long corridor that ended in a pair of wide, onyx doors. Frost coated the glittering stone, and beneath the thin glaze of ice rested a silver-plated carving of an unbalanced scale. On the right, hanging ever so slightly beneath the center, lay a single phoenix feather. In the other, the tray held a half-devoured heart.

A chill snaked down Asha's spine.

The prince stepped forward and pushed the doors open, slithering through them with perfected grace. The chamber beyond was square and stark. Its walls were made of black stone, its floor bare, save for a thick iron chain bolted to the far wall. It snaked into a shadowy corner, disappearing into darkness. Dim luminos glowed faintly above the twin doors that led in and out of the chamber, casting long shadows across the room. The warmth that had greeted Asha as she entered the fortress had not followed her here, and it made the room feel like a cold, barren dungeon.

A cage of stone, Asha thought. And she noted the room to be an odd corridor to pass through on their way through the bastion.

Asha cleared her throat as they crossed the cage. "And if I fail, will you be the one to take my soul?" she asked, voice even as the frosty air bit at her skin.

The prince laughed coldly, the sound sounding unnatural and forced. "No, no. I have no use for such things. There is another who is tasked to deal with such tedious affairs." He glanced to the shadowed corner. "But I'm sure he will be grateful. His pet does enjoy a warm meal from time to time," he said, his slender hand motioning to the gathered darkness.

The darkness stirred, and there, waiting in the shadows, lay an onyx-scaled beast so sinister, it could only have been crafted in the darkest corners of the Abyss. It had a wide, reptilian mouth, with mincing claws, and eyes like molten tar. The creature lifted its head and bared its sharp fangs towards Asha, watching her with deliberate hunger.

A Soul-Eater.

The prince frowned. "Poor thing. I imagine Ammit grows rather tired of frozen fare when he visits."

Asha's eyes widened. *The wretched beast has a name?* She glanced over once more at the creature. "Pet sitting? Seems like a lowly task for a prince."

The prince glanced back at Asha as he continued to lead her across the room. "Please. Call me Ipos," he said, his voice a blend between sensual intrigue and amiable charm. "And it is only for a temporary stint. His owner had... obligations."

Asha made a mental note of how the prince referred to the beast's possessor as its *owner* and did not call the keeper his *brother*.

They exited the Soul-Eater's quarters and filtered into a second, larger chamber.

The circular room was lined with towering shelves of onyx-bound books. A thick, crimson and cream carpet bled across the stone floor, echoing the hues of suspended luminos hanging overhead. On the far side, a silver-dusted window stretched from floor to ceiling, illuminating the icy darkness outside. An ebony desk was positioned before the window, overlooking the midnight frost. Atop it sat a black leather-bound book and a red quill.

Asha couldn't help but notice the similar taste in record-keeping and ornamentation that the prince shared with Raziel. Same taste in drama, same flair for intimidation. Clearly, showmanship ran in the family.

"Just a few formalities before we begin," he said, strolling toward the desk. He picked up the quill and dipped it in the blood-red ink. "I'll need your name and signature. Standard procedure."

Asha paused and looked up at him, fighting to keep her face neutral. "You don't know my name," she said, more statement than question.

He gave a mock gasp. "Oh, don't look so insulted. I can't be expected to keep up with every one of your unremarkable ilk. Thotha sends candidates down to me weekly, sometimes twice. You all start to blend together after a while. Eventually, I stopped asking."

Asha's fingers twitched at her side with annoyance. Another spoiled immortal playing games with mortals like they were cards in a deck.

"Aella," Asha lied smoothly. "Aella Vendaval."

It was the first name that sprang into her mind. One of the women she had met at Raziel's Manor the first time she had visited. The one who had cut a deal with one of Hells' devils.

The prince smiled and scribbled the name onto the book's spine in a clean, looping script. "Lovely."

He set the quill down and gestured towards the contract. "Very simple terms," he murmured. "Once your trial begins, all you need is to pass through the golden door."

"That's it?" Asha asked skeptically.

"That's it," he echoed. "Nothing extravagant. No riddles or sacrifices. No blood or bones. Just a door." His smile widened. "And a few... friends, perhaps. To keep you company, of course."

Asha didn't flinch, but her stomach curled.

He slid the contract towards her. "Now, before you sign, you should know: the only rule is truth."

She blinked. "Truth?"

"Yes. Clean, simple, absolute," Ipos said, frosty eyes gleaming. "No lies, no fabrications, no omissions. Knowledge demands knowledge."

Knowledge demands knowledge.

"What do you mean by—"

"Ah, ah," Ipos reprimanded, waving a finger. "No need to spoil the surprise. Besides, surprises are half the fun." His smile lingered, but it did not meet his eyes.

His warped version of fun made Asha's skin crawl. He was exactly like Raziel. The mirrored pair wore their twisted masks the same way. Like boys playing kings.

But Asha had outplayed one Secret-Seeker before. She could do it again. She picked up the quill and signed *Aella Vendaval* in deep-crimson ink.

Ipos grinned and gently closed the book. "Good girl," he purred and stepped back. "Then by all means," he said, gesturing to the far wall. "Let your trial begin."

Without another word, the wall on the far side groaned, stone shifting as a slit of shadow opened into a narrow hallway.

Asha exhaled once, straightened her shoulders, and stepped into the dark passage.

CHAPTER FIFTY-FOUR

Asha stepped into a shrunken amphitheater, its tall domed ceiling arcing overhead with layered veins of frost. Curving stone walls enclosed the space, and the sides were lined with rows of benches carved from slate. Each tier overlooked the central depression in the floor: a sunken pit framed like an elongated stage, purposefully built for spectacle.

The benches wrapped around the arena in a half-circle, granting every onlooker a perfect, unobstructed view of the entertainment that would unfold beneath.

Lining the upper tiers were dozens of figures cloaked in silence. Reapers made of blackened bone, their faces lost beneath deep, hooded robes, sat in perfected stillness. Statues of mourning. Asha could feel the cold precision of their gazes pressing down on her like a noose cinching tighter with every breath. Among the Reapers sat an array of obscured silhouettes, half-devoured by darkness. Most were swallowed by shifting shadows, their features blurred as though the frigid air refused to hold their shapes. But among the throng, a handful remained visible. Creatures formed of nightmares. Twisted beasts born of the Hells.

One loomed with obsidian scales that covered its skin like plated armor, a covering made of dark volcanic glass. Another was thin and long-limbed, but its head was a smooth stretch of flesh where no features rested. Several others bore clawed limbs and fanged grins of deep malice.

A band of Shadowblades.

A heaviness coiled in Asha's stomach, loosening only when she realized there were no Eligos among the crowd.

The pit itself stretched long and rectangular, hewn from pale frost-colored granite. Its walls rose more than fifteen feet in height, seamless, smooth, and utterly unclimbable. Asha's stomach twisted. The walls reminded her of the inescapable confines that had formed the Minos Maze during her Rite at Sveaborg. Walls built to hold screams.

Set against the far end of the chamber, a throne of frosted glass sat raised atop a platform. It overlooked the pit with unfeeling judgment. At the base, mist hugged against the corners of the stone floor like churning clouds. Translucent threads formed a tangled web across the pit, vibrating faintly against the mist.

On the far side lay a single golden door, brandished with a gleaming silver knob.

"Your absolution," the prince said, nodding towards the door. "Reach it and you may leave, soul in hand."

Asha's eyes swept the arena floor, scouring the mist-draped ground for threats. Small shadows twitched erratically in the center of the stone. A cluster of massive, fanged spiders crept silently along the floor. Several hung from the silver threads, swaying gently on the woven web as their hundreds of black eyes trailed up to where Asha stood. She took a closer look and realized they were Widow Weavers. Nasty creatures, bred within the middle Hells. They had segmented black-and-purple carapaces that shimmered like oil.

457

Their legs were barbed, thorned like thistles, and their swollen abdomens bore jagged crimson markings that seemed to pulse in time with their breaths. From their open mandibles dripped a thick, glistening venom, and the green-hued poison hissed when it touched stone. Some of the Weavers were the size of wolves. Others were larger.

Asha's heart raced as one of the Weavers turned its body towards her, its two dozen eyes narrowing into small slits as its fang-lined mouth clicked open.

And then the mist stirred.

Slowly, from the corner, a towering beast crept out from the fog. Asha's breath caught in her throat.

A gaunt, skeletal humanoid with deer-like features floated from the mist. Its ashen-grey skin was stretched tautly over protruding bones, and deep, hollowed eyes burned with a malevolent glow. Jagged fangs filled its lipless mouth, and claws like sharpened bone extended from its long fingers and toes. The air around the creature hung heavy and foul, carrying the stench of decay and decomposition through its half-open ribcage. Clumps of flesh still clung limply to the rotted bones.

A Wendigo.

And then, as quickly as it appeared, the beast vanished.

Prince Ipos stepped to the side and smiled, slow and wicked, as his gaze swept the pit below. "Good luck, Miss Vendaval," he said, voice laced with ominous excitement.

Before Asha could respond, the floor beneath her feet gave way. She dropped with a jolt, crashing hard into the arena below. She heard a loud crack of bone as her body slammed against the frost-slick stone. A loud cry snapped from her mouth, and she tried to regain the air that had been knocked from her lungs. For a moment, all she could hear was the echo of her fall ricocheting off the granite walls.

At the sound, a flicker of movement bloomed within the

mist. From the edge of the pit, a pair of glowing red eyes flared to life, hollow and feral.

Asha froze, heart pounding in her throat. She didn't move. Didn't breathe. And then the crimson glow blinked out. She reached down and unsheathed *Soulmaker*, her shoulder howling in protest.

Above, the crowd erupted in a sudden roar. Cheers rang and chants echoed, all the howls begging for her death. Yet their voices sounded distant, muffled, as if buried beneath layers of snow. Asha looked up to see them pressed against the edges of the tiered balconies, their expressions warped by shadow. Some wore masks, others painted smiles of cruelty across their faces, but all were jeering. All were watching.

She rose slowly to her feet as the mist began to thicken, roiling in steady, unnatural waves that poured more heavily into the arena from unseen vents along the stone floor. The air turned damp and cold against her skin, clinging like breath. The silver threads shimmered faintly, catching the low torchlight in flashes of glass-like glint. She watched as a handful of Widow Weavers scampered across the threads until slowly, one by one, the silver disappeared into the darkness, swallowed by the crawling fog.

Asha stepped back instinctively, her pulse thudding beneath her collarbone. She took a deep, steadying breath.

I am a master of my fear. I have power beyond measure. I am unbreakable.

And as the comforting words rang through her head, over and over, Asha forced her legs forward and stepped into the mist.

The crunch of frost beneath her boots echoed loudly in the silence. The mist stirred at the sound, curling higher in fitful ripples.

She scanned the space before her, careful not to brush against any silver threads. The Weavers' claw-tipped legs chittered against the surrounding stone, growing louder as she ducked beneath their spindled threads. Somewhere above the darkened fog, the crowd continued to shout, but their noise dimmed to a distant hum like a heartbeat heard through water.

The mist stirred, breaking overhead, and Asha could see the frosted throne at the far end. Prince Ipos now lounged on the chair, one leg draped casually over the other, his chin resting on his pale hand. His crimson eyes gleamed, sharp and eager, as he drank in every breath Asha took. He wore an unsettling smile, as though he and his guests could see through the mist from overhead, and he was gleefully awaiting her screams.

Asha forced her eyes back to the path before her. The golden door was scarcely visible through the thickening haze, and mist licked across her hands and face as she crept forward, the frost burrowing into her very bones.

A few more measured steps, and a pinching snap cracked to her left. Asha pivoted sharply, watching with wide eyes as three Widow Weavers skittered low across the arena floor, their glossy black legs moving in a stuttering rhythm. She raised *Soulmaker* higher, ignoring the sharp pain the splintered through her arm, and stepped backward as the spiders herded her towards a narrow channel of space between two glinting threads.

Another Weaver dropped from above, landing with a sick, wet crunch beside her. Asha's heart leapt into her throat. The Weaver's venomous jaws clicked loudly as it reared, fangs glistening with thick, hissing spit.

Asha struck with one swift swing, *Soulmaker* singing through the mist. The dragon-glass blade sliced towards the spider's bulging abdomen and, with a loud clang, ricocheted off, flinging back towards Asha with a useless clamor.

Her stomach dropped. Panic flared. But without a second of hesitation, Asha summoned the flames inside her and thrust her magic into the blade. A faint, muted glow rippled through the glass as heat surged along the edge. She swung again, and *Soulmaker* sliced straight through the armored underbelly of the Weaver, serrating clean through the spider's swollen abdomen. The creature shrieked as it splintered in two, legs twitching violently as black blood poured onto the stone.

She finished off the other three with swift, calculated strikes, their cries piercing through the air as the beasts curled inward. Puddles of dark blood painted the frosted stone, and mist began to twist around their limp bodies until it swallowed the carcasses whole.

Asha stepped back, breath uneven, heart hammering in her chest. She quickly reclaimed the flames crawling up the blade, swallowing the heat before it could illuminate through the mist.

No flare. No light. No fire.

Not in the Hells. Not before a Prince of Shadows. She would wait to reveal that secret.

The sound of the Weaver's scream had shattered the stillness, and from the far end of the arena, footsteps began.

Soft. Bare. Wet.

A slow, deliberate pace echoed through the fog. Asha turned, every hair on her neck rising as she was met with two glowing-red eyes, burning through the mist like coals caught in the wind.

The Wendigo.

She paused, holding her breath as her eyes tracked its gradual, methodical movements.

The eyes paused. And then, they vanished, swallowed whole by renewed silence.

Asha's lungs ached as she released her breath. Her heart slammed more rapidly as the realization settled cold and sharp in her stomach.

Sound was the Wendigo's invitation, and silence, the only protector.

Asha edged forward, weaving between the threads as the mist thickened to a near-solid veil. Every step was made with precise calculation. Every scuff of boots against cracking ice had her tightening her grip on her blade.

As she made it halfway through the arena, a faint scuttle echoed from the side. A Widow Weaver darted out from the haze, its legs slamming into the ground as it lunged. Asha twisted, leaping backward as *Soulmaker* sang through the air, fire forged through its edges.

The spider crumpled beneath her, but its shredding cries were drowned out by a loud shredding snap.

Asha felt the cord fray before she saw it, and as she turned, she watched the silver thread break beneath her impact, snapping as her boot broke through the webbing.

For a moment, the worlds seemed to move in slow motion. The air stilled. The silence that followed the break stretched. Even the spectators above grew quiet.

But as the moment broke, pain exploded in her throat like a coiling flame. The silver thread wrapped around her neck like a noose, tightening on impact. Asha clawed at the cord, gasping frantically, but no air came to greet her.

Then she felt it—something sharp and alive piercing beneath her collarbone. Needle-thin stings sank into her skin, and her body turned icy.

Asha staggered, vision dimming. Her hands went slack. And then she heard it. A voice. Dry, whispering, and ancient. And it echoed palely through her mind:

Breath is a gift, and gifts are earned.
Bestowed by the shadows, who hunger to learn.
Love will cost and love will save.
Say a name or meet your grave.

To escape oblivion's eternal churn,
Tell me the one for whom you burn.
The voice edged through her skull, cruel and hungry. The thread pulsed tighter. Asha's knees buckled. Stars burst in her vision, and her lungs began to scream. The mist rippled.
Breath is a gift... gifts are earned.
It wanted a name—a name she burned for. That was the cost. Breath for truth. Life for love. Her mind clawed for clarity through the suffocating dark.

The cord pulsed tighter, her chest rattling with each stolen gasp. It didn't want her dead—not yet. It wanted her answer. A bargain. She would give it truth, and it would give her air. *Knowledge for knowledge.*

Her vision swam as the stings beneath her collarbone throbbed with icy pain. *But which truth? Which name will it take?*

The realization struck like a blade: not family, not a friend. It wanted the name of the one she loved. The one she would burn for.

The noose seared hotter, and her lips trembled as she understood the only way to earn her breath was to bare her heart. Asha's lips parted, the name tearing through her throat ragged and raw. "Anselem."

The thread loosened instantly, slithering off her neck and disappearing into the dark fog.

Asha collapsed to her knees, coughing loudly. She pressed her hand to the collar of small stings below her neck. They throbbed with an icy cold hollowness.

In the distance, faint footsteps began once more. She looked up to see the glowing-red eyes of the Wendigo, closer and brighter than before.

She swallowed her ragged breaths, watching as the wet footsteps stilled, and the crimson eyes vanished once more.

Above the beast, the mist split in a curling draft of frost. The stands overhead erupted in a collection of cheers and snarls. Some of the Shadowblades shouted her name—*Aella's name*—their voices raised in cruel delight. Others leaned forward, clapping fervently, as if the show had finally begun. One of them hurled a curse from above, another demanded blood. Near the highest tiers, a handful remained utterly silent.

The Reapers.

The dense mist swallowed the overhead space once more, and silence fell like a whetted blade.

In the stillness, the words rang through her mind again, carved into the hollow space between her breaths.

Knowledge demands knowledge.

Asha's pulse continued to rattle, but her thoughts burned sharp and certain. The name had been the key. But what did the trial gain from forcing her to speak it?

Her eyes lifted toward the throne above. Through the haze, she could make out the faint outline of Prince Ipos. Perched atop his throne, the Prince of the First Hells shifted, leaning forward, hands curled tightly around the arms of his frosted chair. His eyes narrowed in focused curiosity. And then he slowly sank back, a wicked smile curled on his lips as he resumed his picturesque posture of pleasure. His crimson-flecked eyes glinted with hunger.

A collector. Just the same as his twin. But this devil did not deal in the currency of secrets. The Prince of the First Hells traded in names. Names weighed with love, torn from the chest while the heart still beat.

Asha's fingers curled around the hilt of *Soulmaker*. Flames ignited in her veins.

The mist shifted around her like breath pouring into a giant's lungs. The pit was watching. Waiting. She knew every name she offered would carve something loose from

464

her soul. And somewhere in the stillness, clawed hands were waiting to catch it.

Asha rose slowly, the clarity biting harder than the sinking frost. And with profound understanding, Asha realized her trial was not a test of survival. It was not a test of resilience or endurance. It was an extraction. And the First Prince of Shadows was not present to judge her strength. He had come to listen. To feed. To harvest what she held sacred— one name at a time.

He was a Reaper of cherished things.

CHAPTER

FIFTY-FIVE

Asha pressed onward, threading her way through the veil of mist.

The golden door loomed ahead, close enough she could see the silver knob gleaming through the shifting fog. Her breath steadied. Her pulse eased. A flicker of hope sparked in her chest.

No more than fifteen yards from the door, the mist skittered.

The sharp click of bones sounded from the left. Then another high-pitched scrape echoed from the right. Above, one by one, half a dozen Widow Weavers dropped onto the stone floor. Foot-long fangs gleamed in the dim light. Glass-black bodies bristled with armored hide, and putrid venom leaked from their serrated mandibles in long, hissing strings.

The first Weaver lunged, forcing Asha to duck just in time before its stygian claws struck the space where her throat had just been.

Another pounced, and she rolled beneath it, slashing up-ward as she forced a burst of flames back into the blade of

466

Soulmaker. The edge severed clean through the creature's abdomen, pouring a pool of dark black blood onto Asha's body.

Snarling, she sprang to her feet and swept her eyes across the throng of Widow Weavers encircling her. One by one, they converged, and Asha fell into the dance of battle. The song of war.

Shrieks filled the silence, and one after another the Weavers fell, collapsing on the ground in twitching heaps. She spun and twisted, the fire-forged edge of *Soulmaker* slicing through abyssal black hides. She met the next with a wide arc, her sword cutting through legs and fangs. One leapt onto her back, its limbs clawing at her ribs. She slammed into the arena's wall, crushing it against the stone before turning to sever its head clean from the body. Another webbed her prominent arm with a shot of silver silk, dragging her towards an open maw. She summoned flames and shadow-fire into her unbound hand and jammed the magic into the threads. The Weaver screeched as Asha's flames met the silk strands, and she tore free, leaping forward and splitting the beast in two.

Arm burning, breath ragged, the final Weaver sprang, and Asha turned swift and wide, the arc of her blade looping upward and through the clamping jaws of the spider.

A loud crack snapped overhead as she pulled *Soulmaker* back from the open jaw of the Weaver, and Asha's eyes splayed wide as she saw the thrust of her blade sever clean through a silver thread.

Pain exploded in her throat. Her sword dropped to the stone with a loud clank. The hiss of the slain Weaver died off, and silence swallowed the air. A collar of frozen stings wrapped around her throat, just beneath her collarbone, and she felt the cold, merciless venom seep slowly into her veins.

She staggered back, clutching at her throat. Her lungs

locked, and the thread tightened as she grasped at the silver string. Her vision tilted. The world around her narrowed, and the roar of blood rang in her ears.

Then, the cold, shrill voice returned.

Blood remembers the bonds of kin,
Speak their name or burn within.
When silence drops and kingdoms fall,
Who would you shield through fire and thrall?

Asha's knees hit the stone again. Her chest heaved, her heart thundered.

Her mind clawed for meaning through the haze. Another riddle. Another cost. It wanted a name. Blood of her blood. Heart of her heart. Her family. Her kin. The venom froze her veins as she struggled to grasp the thread of the trial's cruel logic. It would not release her until she gave it the one she would die to protect.

Panic sharpened her thoughts. It wasn't testing her strength. It was prying her soul open, demanding the name of the one she would shield—no matter what.

The name pressed like fire behind her teeth. Her lungs began to break open. A tear slipped from her eye. She gasped, her choked voice barely a whisper. "Mathieson."

The thread hissed loose, falling away with the mist. Asha collapsed forward, coughing hard. Her breath burned through her throat like rusted steel.

For a long moment, only silence fell.

Asha stayed crouched, one hand pressed to the stone, the other reaching for *Soulmaker*. She curled her fingers firmly around the hilt. Her breath rattled in her chest as she attempted to calm her uneven breaths.

And she waited, eyes scouring the dark fog. But the mist held still, and the Wendigo did not come. No glowing-red eyes pierced through the haze. No wet footsteps echoed across the granite. Just still, merciful silence.

She pushed to her feet, blood pounding in her ears. She took a deep inhale, settled her trembling hands, and stepped forward.

As her foot struck the icy stone, the mist twisted, and her heart sank into the pit of her stomach.

Two glowing-red eyes emerged from the frosted haze, inches from Asha's face. Towering above her, its skeletal frame veiled in icy fog, the Wendigo peered down at her with hollow eyes. The scent of rot seeped from its open ribs, and before Asha could even lift her blade, the beast struck.

Jagged, stygian claws ripped through her side. A horrid scream tore from her throat as flesh and sinew were shredded open. Blood poured freely from her ribs, hot and wet, pooling at her hip and dripping in heavy splatters onto the cold stone below.

Her vision blurred. A guttural groan rang from her mouth, and a wave of sharp needles prickled over her body. Her slick fingers clutched *Soulmaker* more tightly as she steadied herself. She raised her sword, and shattering pain ripped up her side as she activated the flayed muscles. Flames guttered weakly along the blade as the Wendigo loomed over her. Its red eyes burned into the sputtering fire, and something like a sneer curled on its gaunt face.

Asha plunged deeper into her magic, pulling fire and ice and shadow deep from the marrow. It bloomed in her chest, surged through her arms, and poured into *Soulmaker*. The fire licked along the blade, the shadows veiling the roaring flames.

The Wendigo's gaze narrowed, its crimson eyes contracting into thin slits. A wicked snarl tore from its throat, and then the creature lunged, claws slicing towards Asha's face. This time, she met it. Dragon-glass clashed against obsidian nails, cracking with blunt impact. Asha rolled left, crying out as pain tore through her ribs. More crimson blood seeped from the wound. The Wendigo struck again, its claws rattling against the granite as she leapt sideways. The talons impacted brutally against the spot where she'd stood a heartbeat before. She swung upward, steel clashing against raw bone. Sparks flew and the Wendigo shrieked, the sound warping the mist into violent spirals. It darted with unnatural speed, moving like a shadow made flesh.

Asha roared, driving her flames down into the blade until it glowed white-hot. The Wendigo charged, arms wide, claws ready to rend her into pieces. She crashed into the beast head-on, her blade carving upward in a vicious arc. The singeing edge sliced through the Wendigo's extended arm, and the severed limb fell to the ground with a loud thud. Black ichor spurted from the gaping wound, and the beast howled. Its wicked shriek drummed through the mist, and the Wendigo reared back, readying to counter, but Asha was already moving.

She feinted right, ducking under another forceful swing, and with a second upward slash, she drove *Soulmaker* deep into its chest. The dragon-glass blade hacked directly between two jutting ribs and straight through the ruined mass of what should've been the Wendigo's heart.

The blade pulsed. Flames surged. The Wendigo shrieked.

Its body convulsed violently as fire raced through it, devouring rot and shadow as it spread through its skeletal frame. Its antlers cracked. Its skin split down the center, peeling like scorched paper. A choked hiss escaped its open maw, and with a deafening smash, the Wendigo collapsed, its lifeless form smacking against the frosted stone.

Asha stood over the body, shaking, blood still dripping from her side. Her grip on *Soulmaker* faltered. Her knees buckled. Her head felt light. Her vision came in spots.

Asha staggered forward, each step sending splintering shards up her side. Blood soaked through her leathers, trailing crimson across the stone behind her. She pressed a trembling hand to her ribs as she limped forward, but the pressure did nothing to stop the pooling blood. Her fingers came away slick with red.

The golden door shimmered ahead, tall and gleaming, untouched by the filth and horror she'd crawled through.

The world reeled with each step, every movement pulling at the torn flesh. Her breath came in shallow gasps. She reached the door with a strangled cry, crashing into the cool metal. A blood-slicked hand fumbled for the silver knob, slipping over the cool handle and painting it with a long streak of red. She reached for the knob again, gripping it tightly on the second try, and wrenched the door open.

Blinding light spilled through, and Asha stumbled inside, flinging the door shut behind her with a loud, echoing *boom*. The sound rumbled like thunder, and then silence fell.

She stared out at a small, circular chamber, crafted from pale stone veined with obsidian. The mist here was thinner, the air colder, sharpened like a honed blade. No torches lined the walls, but an eerie glow emanated from cracks in the floor like moonlight bleeding through broken glass.

There were no threads. No Widow Weavers. No Wendigo.

But the silence was heavier. Expectant.

A slow, deliberate clap broke the stillness. Asha's gaze snapped upward. Prince Ipos sat reclined upon his elevated throne at the far curve of the chamber. His smile cut like glass.

"Well done," he said, voice soaked in mockery

Asha did not respond.

"Oh, come now," he drawled. "You survive my arena, you best my creature, and still, nothing to say?"

Asha stared, silent and shaking, her blood pattering softly onto the stone floor.

Above, the Shadowblades remained motionless, silent silhouettes perched in the upper seats. Watching. Waiting.

Ipos leaned forward, resting his chin against his knuckles. His smile widened. "I have one final test for you," he said, eyes glinting.

Flames ripped through Asha. Burning, fury-filled flames.

"A simple walk is all I desire." He rose slightly, just enough to point across the chamber to an onyx circle. "Just cross the room and reach the obsidian stone," he said. "It will flicker you back to the place from which you came." He paused, as if expecting thanks.

Across the room sat a flat, stone circle, crafted from a glossy, glittering onyx.

Asha did not move. She did not blink.

The smile on Ipos's face sharpened. "Or is that too much for you?" He tilted his head with mock pity. "Poor little thing, you look like you're bleeding out."

Asha could feel her limbs beginning to shake. She knew she did not have much time before her blood loss would be too great. She looked across the space once more, towards the onyx circle no more than twenty yards away. From the mist coiled in the corners, two Eligos stepped forward, their long limbs twitching erratically.

Asha narrowed her eyes. "No," she said sternly, voice wrapped in defiance.

Prince Ipos blinked. "No?" he questioned.

"I said no," Asha bit, her voice steady despite the fury ripping through her. "You gave me terms. I fulfilled them. I crossed the pit. I faced your creature. I survived."

Ipos raised a brow, amused. "Oh, but I'm afraid you have no choice."

"You're just as deviant as your brother," she barked, the fire erupting inside her. "Always twisting everything into a game. Always changing the rules. Never holding up your end of the bargain. Well, I'm done. I'm done playing your stupid little game, just like I was done playing his."

Prince Ipos's eyes narrowed into thin slits, and Asha knew she had made a mistake, knew she had shown her hand too early.

The prince and Asha locked eyes for a long moment, and before he was able to raise his hand, she tore off in a sprint, aiming straight for the obsidian circle.

Shadow-coiled ice surged forth like a tidal wave. Shards, needles, a full curtain of jagged frost poured toward her, snow-white and blinding cold.

Asha threw both arms up, fire bursting from her palms in twin plumes. She threw short, compact orbs of flame to meet his frost, melting the sprays of frozen magic as fire met ice. A snapping hiss cracked overhead, and a shower of shattered icicles rained down onto the chamber. She darted through the torrent of ice, cloaked in smoke and embers. The first Eligos lunged, and she ducked beneath its long stygian nails, her side screaming in protest. She met its second strike with *Soulmaker*, the flame-wrapped blade meeting the claws with a ringing clash. She thrust her hand towards its chest, and a blast of fire poured out, singing through skin. The beast fell with a wet thud, black blood pooling beneath it on the pale stone.

She did not hesitate as she spun, flame trailing from her palm to the floor, and met the second Shadowblade with a wave of fire and light. It let out a hissing screech as it erupted in flames, jerking erratically before falling into a clump of charred bones.

Overhead, Ipos snarled, and she looked up to see the prince summoning another wave of shadowed ice.

She thrust her hands up, blood seeping from her side at the movement, and flames met the ice midair again, this

473

time louder, hotter. Fire wrapped in gold light. The sound cracked like flame-wrapped thunder as the magics collided. Steam and vapor churned outward in all directions. The impact threw her back several feet.

She hit the ground hard, rolled, and came up with fire still sparking in her veins. She swept her hand in a wide arc, flame spilling from her fingers in a circle. It raced across the floor—then up—curling into a towering wall of fire that shot toward the ceiling like a reborn sun. Heat swept the room in a furious gust, melting the coating of frost that clung to the corner of every surface.

She threw a wall of fire towards the ceiling, a dense curtain of flames separating her from Ipos. Sweat poured from her face. Blood began to trickle from her nose as she held the wall of fire.

The First Prince of the Seven Hells froze, his body unmoving. A dark sneer crept over his face. "You—" he snarled. His form flickered beyond the flames, his crimson-flecked eyes went wide, and his body froze as disbelief rooted him to the seat.

Fear.

Asha turned, bloodied, burning, but unbroken. A triumphant smile curled on her lips. A living fire danced inside her eyes. "Tell your father I do not kneel to his sentence of oblivion," she snarled. "Let him hear that the Warrior has risen—" She stepped onto the obsidian stone, flames searing in her wake. "—and she comes bearing war."

"YOU WILL HEAR OF WARS AND RUMORS OF WARS. NATION WILL RISE AGAINST
NATION, AND KINGDOM AGAINST KINGDOM. BUT THE END IS STILL TO COME."
— PROPHESY 12 OF THE RECORDED VISIONS OF THE FIRST ORACLE
(UNSANCTIONED EDITION)

CHAPTER
FIFTY-SIX

Sweat beaded on Anselem's brow as he watched the Darkness eddy around her. But just as quickly as the violent shadows had begun to swirl, the tendrils ceased. The entire cy-
clone of Darkness shuttered out in less time than it took for
him to inhale.

The soft whispers in the back of the room quieted, and
the Empress, unmoving from her throne, raised a brow.

Asha, still standing within the onyx stone, clutched
her side. Then, straightening to her full height, she glanced
down at her hand. A fleeting look of confusion drew across
her face before her eyes narrowed and she settled her gaze
back on the Empress. She stepped forward, face twisted in a
snarl. "You'd better have a damn good explanation of what
is about to unfold after sending me into the godsflaming First
Province of the Hells," she spat.

There was a tangible shift in the air as the warrior commanded the Empress. The whispers from the men and wom-
en gathered at the round table were revived, and the golden
guards lining either side of Thotha's throne wheeled towards

475

the Thurisaz.

The Empress held up a hand, calling off her sentinels, and as she gracefully placed her wrinkled hand back onto her lap, a twinkle of reverence flickered in her sagacious eyes.

Anselem stiffened behind her, eyes jutting to the black circle she stood inside. He palmed the blade at his side, as if thinking the Hells themselves would materialize from the stone.

"It is a one-way portal," Thotha said, glancing at Anselem as though she could see the thoughts swimming in his head. "As for you," Thotha said, turning her gaze to Asha, "knowledge commands knowledge."

"Oh, spare me the self-righteous *worldly balance* nonsense," Asha snarled.

"You would be wise to hold your tongue on things you do not understand, girl," Thotha replied coolly.

"Why? Afraid your little city will find out exactly who you work so closely with?" Asha snapped, gesturing to the corridor leading back into the main cave.

A long silence stretched as the women stared at one another.

The Empress glowered, her eyes burning into Asha's very soul.

"Speak," Asha demanded.

A sneer curled on Thotha's mouth at the command. Her ancient eyes narrowed. "To end this war, you must first understand how it began—long before the First War scorched the world." The Empress's tawny eyes glowed like coals as she leaned forward on her stone throne. "When Light still reigned sovereign, and the three factions of the Authorities governed the celestial order," Thotha began, "the Lord of Light called upon each to choose a Champion. Not soldiers, not armies, but living extensions of the High Gods' will."

"Soldiers chosen by the gods?" Asha asked.

"Not gods—Authorities. Older. Stricter," the Empresses corrected, voice firm with ancient reverence. "The Dominions, stewards of law and might, chose the Warrior of Praenuntius—a blade made flesh, strength without cruelty, the first shield against annihilation. The Virtues, keepers of vision and judgment, chose the Lightbearer—a soul of wisdom and living fire. And the Thrones, guardians of protection and strength, chose the Herald of Promise. A ruler without a crown or throne, with only the raw truth of command. One who could bend the wills of kings and shape nations with a word."

Asha's pulse thundered. "And together they defeated the Lord of Darkness?"

"They unmade him. There is a difference," Thotha said, eyes glinting with ancient memory. "The Three bore a harmony the Dark King could not break. The Champions cast him down in the final battle—but he was cunning, even in defeat. Rather than perish, he shattered himself. He forged Seven Anchors—living prisons of agony and will, brimming with the thousands of souls he had devoured. The Anchors were formed by shards of his Dark Power, and they served as his tethers to this world. As long as the Anchors endured, so too did his shadow."

Asha's mouth went dry. "So, they failed."

"No. They chose restraint," the Empress replied. "To destroy the Anchors would have doomed every soul locked within them into oblivion. So, the Champions forged the Seven Seals, wards crafted from their own essence and power, to bind the Anchors. They did not destroy them, they simply made them inactive... frozen."

Asha's whisper trembled. "Why do the Seals no longer hold him?"

Thotha's voice hardened. "Because one of the Champions broke the oath. The Herald. Closest in mind to what the

Dark King had once been: a soul made for conquest. When he beheld the Anchors' power, something in him shifted. Perhaps he turned. Or perhaps he only revealed what was always there. The Seals weakened—not from frailty, but because corruption bled into them. And slowly, subtly, over time, they have begun to weaken. Just enough for the Dark King to slip through, for moments at a time."

The cavern seemed to breathe with her words.

"After the Herald's betrayal, the surviving Champions—the Warrior and Lightbearer—crafted a crypt deep within the core of the Northern Continent to contain what fragments of Darkness could still be bound."

"The Ossuary," Anselem reasoned.

"Yes," Thotha confirmed, nodding to the Commander. "Six vessels were carved deep within, each designed to house a Seal. Wards woven from the Authorities' magic ensure that the Anchors bound within can never be reforged. Above the vessels, the Champions built alters for the scepters, podiums filled with the magic of the High Gods to hold the Darkness of the Crowns of Shadows and remove them from the presence of mortal hands."

Asha's voice tightened. "Why must they be hidden?"

"As I said before, the Crowns act as gateways to the Hells. When touched by mortal hands, the Dark Power inside the scepter is awakened. A Prince of the Hells becomes bound to the wielder's flesh. Their heart becomes the door to that level of the Hells, and in return, they claim a fragment of the Prince's power."

Asha's stomach sank. "And the rulers of Darnella—the Kings and Queens of the Six Kingdoms—are the ones who have opened the gateways?" Asha questioned, her voice solemn.

Thotha nodded.

"Why?" Asha asked, voicing the very same question

running through Anselem's mind.

Thotha's faint smile turned into a grimace as she answered, "The same reason any ruler chains themselves to Darkness. Power."

Asha and Anselem sucked in sharp breaths.

Thotha was quiet for a long moment before she added, "Why worship the gods when you can become one?"

Anselem's stomach knotted, and his breath became shallow.

Asha's chest constricted. "So, if the monarch dies, the gateway will close?"

Thotha inclined her head. "Yes, but not forever. Strike down a monarch, and the Prince of Shadows will lose his grip, but only for a time," she clarified. "The shard of his Darkness will seek another willing hand. The Princes are patient. The Hells play politics as sharply as our own realm."

Asha and Anselem exchanged a grim look, fully understanding the Empress was alluding to killing the six rulers of the kingdoms of Darnella—the people with the greediest hearts, unquenchable thirsts for power, and entire armies at their disposal.

Anselem's stomach crawled into his throat. A Prince of the Hells was willing to give his power to another monarch of these lands if his gateway closed. Anselem's mind flooded with images of Kalevala, the Queen of the Obsidian Throne.

"What if we secure the scepters before any more of them are wielded and the Princes enter Darnella?" Anselem asked, his voice thick with desperation.

Thotha's ancient face turned grave, and the warriors braced themselves for the words that came next. "All of the gateways have been opened, and the Dark Power of the Six Princes of the Hells is here," she said, confirming his worst suspicions.

Asha's body went cold, but she forced her voice to remain steady as she asked, "And what about the Dark King? You said his power is splintered into seven Anchors. Who wields the power of the King of the Abyss?"

Thotha's gaze sharpened as she dragged her eyes over the warrior still standing inside the circle of obsidian stone. "Each Anchor is a relic containing a fragment of his Dark Power, objects he forged when he splintered himself. They are not gateways, but tethers, bound to this world by magic older than time itself. They were never meant to be wielded, only to bind the Dark King's essence." She leaned forward, voice dropping. "But the Dark King was cunning. He forged a seventh, living Anchor. The Soulvion Scepter. It holds the largest shard of his power, the very heart of his will. Only this Anchor can be wielded. Only this Anchor may serve as a gateway, and through it, the Lord of Darkness can return in full."

Thotha's ancient eyes bore into Asha. "The Princes of Shadows," she continued, "mimicked their king when they forged the Crowns of Shadows. The scepters house shards of their own Dark magic, just as the Soulvion Scepter harbors the Lord of Darkness's. The Hells learned well from their king."

"So, who has wielded the Soulvion Scepter?"

Thotha's gaze deepened to something almost reverent. "No mortal can bear that weight alone. Most who try will perish. The Soulvion Scepter is the Dark King's soul-key. To be wielded, it needs a host whose blood burns with the same likeness of its kind. A being made of immeasurable power and strength. A warrior who burns with Chaos."

"The Warrior of Praenuntius," Asha whispered.

Anselem's jaw tightened. "Then the only true way to win the war against the Hells is to destroy the Anchors and the Crowns."

Thotha did not remove her eyes from the Chaos-wielding warrior before her. The resilient women stared at each other with resolute gazes until the Empress broke the silence and answered, "Yes. Destroy the Seven Anchors, and the Dark King's lingering essence will be forced to return to the Abyss. Secure all six Crowns in the Ossuary and remove the living piece of Dark Power from the monarch who wielded it, and the Princes will lose their mortal gateways. But if even a single fragment remains unclaimed or unbroken, the Lord of Darkness will claw his way back, as he has now."

Asha's eyes flickered back and forth as she absorbed the enlightening words of the Empress. After a moment, her jaw tensed, and she pulled her sapphire eyes up to meet the intense gaze of the woman atop the Throne of Stone.

"You were not chosen by chance," Thotha said, voice quiet but immense. "The Warrior's echo calls to you. Soon, you must do what even your predecessor could not: confront the Anchors, unmake them, and end this cycle. If you fail… the Lord of Darkness will rise again. Not splintered. Not shackled. But whole. And this world will not survive the destruction."

Asha did not reply. Her head spun. Her throat bobbed. "Where are the Anchors and the Soulvion Scepter?" she ground out. The words sounded thick.

Thotha looked into Asha's fire-filled eyes for a long time. "As I said before, even I do not hold all of the answers you seek." The Empress ran a hand down the staff resting beside her stone throne. Her gaze seemed to drift beyond the cave. "But the Volvana holds the answers you desire," she said, her voice dipping to a hush that carried weight beyond the stone chamber.

Asha's brow furrowed. "Who is the Volvana?"

"She is the last who walks between Light and Shadow," the Empress replied, her gaze distant. "The witness to the Seals' fall, and the keeper of the path you must walk to find them."

"That's not an answer," Anselem snapped, his mind spinning at the unknown title.

The sentinels crowded around the Empress shifted. "It is the only one I can offer," Thotha replied. "When she wishes to be found, she will find you. Until then, Seal-Breaker, tread carefully. There are some paths where even the gods dare not follow."

Anselem's honey-brown skin reddened with rage, and his eyes narrowed.

Thotha stared down at him unflinchingly. "In the future, you would be wise to remind yourself that not all stories are as they seem, Commander."

Asha, still standing within the heart of the obsidian stone, remained steadfast.

The Empress quieted her voice as she repeated, "The path will be long, Seal-Breaker." Thotha ran her hand down the ivory scepter beside her again, and with predictive wisdom, she concluded, "You will encounter many barriers along the way. But remember—though obstacles can hinder progress, nothing can stop the will of the gods."

Asha stared up into the wise eyes of the Empress, and with a wolfish sneer set upon her lips, she replied, "The Darkness has winked out too many Lights in my life, and I have no intention of allowing the Shadows to dwell in this realm any longer." She took a deep breath as she concluded, "May Ianoda save those who stand in my way; for I will spare them no mercy, and I shall show them no kindness, and I am not afraid to make all of them wish that I would."

CHAPTER FIFTY-SEVEN

The warriors did not utter a word to one another as they trekked back out of the Forgotten City and crossed over the Hands of the Wise One. The only sounds that filled the air were the crunch of the newly packed snow beneath their boots and the occasional howl of the wind.

The path looked exactly the same as when they traveled it mere hours beforehand, but Asha knew something had changed. Something was different in how she saw the world. How she felt it.

Deep inside her bones, she felt the shift the moment she stepped inside the obsidian circle.

The moment she accepted her fate.

That same ache kept pulling her hand to her side, braced for the sticky warmth of blood, certain she would find her palm painted in crimson. Yet each time, her fingers found only clean, unbroken skin. The strangeness of it unsettled her, and a thought lodged itself into her mind, sharp and bold: she would have to ask Kaira if she had ever come across records of someone crossing realms. Did wounds persist through such passages? Or did time and distance strip them away, reshaping the body as it slipped between worlds?

The question lingered in Asha's mind, but another truth pressed free from her lips. "Math was right," she murmured, breaking the silence. Her voice was low, barely carried by the wind.

Anselem's brows knitted together as the pair began their descent of the southern mountain pass.

"He knew it was me," Asha continued, stepping around a large boulder blocking half of the path. "I think deep down, he always knew it had to be me. Even before the Chamber of Reflection. Even before he saw that prophecy carved into the wall of some ancient vault. He knew I was the one the Lord of Darkness waited for. The one who can break the Seals and unlock the Anchors. The only one able to wield the Soulvion Scepter and release him in our world." Her throat tightened as the words fell from her lips. A shiver ran down her spine. "But he also knew I was the one destined to destroy them. The only one who can cast him back into the Abyss."

They continued to walk in silence for a short while, their boots crunching against the newly fallen snow, until Anselem broke the renewed quiet.

"I still don't get it," he pondered, a sentiment of displeasure in his tone. "Why did he not tell us before Montu?"

Asha sighed. "He had a reason."

"How do you know that?"

"He told me," she answered, stepping up onto a jagged rock covering the path.

"He told you why he did it? Why he lied to us? Why he let us mourn him?" Bitterness marked every word that fell from the Commander's lips.

"No," she replied, hopping down onto the gravel trail. "He didn't tell me the reason. But he told me there is one, and that's enough."

Anselem let out a loud huff, and Asha was unsure if his frustration was directed towards her or her brother.

"I think it was one of two things," she added, attempting to ease his vexation. "It was either something to do with Leadership—with the Skia or the Arch, or whatever title the Council calls the Lord of Darkness and his Princes."

"Or?" he prompted, continuing in his unwavering steps.

"Or it had to do with the Chamber of Reflection."

Anselem raised a brow.

Asha's boots kicked up a collection of loose pebbles, and the small rocks toppled over the edge of the descending ridge that lined the outer portion of their path.

"I don't know how to explain it," she expressed, carefully assessing her footsteps as they neared a steep decline. "Something just felt… different in there. Other. Like it was enhancing my power, and I'm not sure what type of Dark Magic was stirring inside the walls, creating that atmosphere, but it was inviting and comfortable—and it worked. I could feel my power as it was strengthened by the mirrors, just as I could feel the glass reflect and reinforce the iron in the air."

Asha took a deep breath. "And ever since we landed on the shores of Gull's Landing, I have wondered if Math needed that enhancement for his power—his visions. Maybe there is a piece of the puzzle—a part of the prophecy—that he is still trying to figure out; and it's possible he believed going to the Chamber was the only way to force the visions to be revealed."

"But why wouldn't he just tell us that?"

Asha shrugged. "Maybe he couldn't. Maybe there was a reason he didn't want us to know he is an Oracle."

Anselem was quiet as he took in everything Asha had attempted to work through in her head over the last several days. Every explanation she had conjured in her mind to justify the choices of her brother. For the pain he had caused.

485

"But the visions are supposedly designed prophesies sent by the Seven High Gods, are they not?" he questioned, bringing the focus of the conversation back to the Chamber.

Asha nodded, her pace slowing as she looked over to the Commander.

"And he thinks he can force the will of the Dominions?" Anselem disparaged.

Asha shrugged again, "I don't know, Ans. But clearly something positive seemed to come from it. We seem to be headed in the correct direction. And at least *some* of our endless questions are starting to be answered. So, I suppose he didn't piss off the Dominions too much."

Anselem was quiet for a long moment, and then the Commander glanced over to her with weary eyes and said, "That's the problem with the gods. Their wrath and their pleasure often look the same."

CHAPTER FIFTY-EIGHT

Two days passed before Asha and Anselem made their way down the Kunluns and onto the backs of their awaiting firebirds.

Soaring high above the rolling grounds of Perseis, Asha pulled back on Uriel's reins as the Seidon coastline came into view.

He slowed his flight to a leisurely glide as they neared Elysia's eastern shore. The firebird's talons gracefully landed in the white sand, and Anselem and Kapheria joined them a moment later.

After she had unhooked the saddle and placed it on the ground beside her, Asha reached up to brush a hand over Uriel's feathers. The phoenix nuzzled into her touch and looked down at her with his gold, otherworldly eyes. He stared at her for a long moment, as though he knew more than even she had learned inside the Forgotten City.

The wind stirred, and the sea's breeze carried the sharp scent of salt and brine. The familiar cry of gulls echoed across the sand, and the calming rays of the evening sun danced across her skin, but Asha felt removed from the world around her. The Empress's words pressed like cold iron against her ribs. Every Anchor, every splintered shard of Darkness, every looming revelation weighed on her like stones in a drowning tide. She lifted her gaze to the horizon where the sky bled into the sea, and for the first time since leaving the heart of the Kunluns, she noticed that the world felt fragile. Delicate. As if something ancient stirred beneath the rolling waves and endless blue.

Uriel ruffled his wings, the heat of his feathers warming her hand. For a heartbeat, she drew strength from the firebird's steady heat. Yet even as his warmth steadied her, a chill lingered. A whisper in her bones that the path ahead would burn, and there would be no turning back from its awakening.

The Mount had never felt so crowded.

Iskander sat in the corner of the room, leaning back in a small wooden chair with his boots kicked up on the nearby table.

The group of warriors had gathered each day at sunrise, patiently waiting for Anselem and Asha to return, and each day at sunset, they had left without any appearance of the two Soturi.

Kaira sat across the room with the three Valorous warriors, piles of ancient journals stacked around her.

The crown prince of the bunch looked numb, lifeless— like every morsel of Light had been drained from his heart.

The two others—Ronin and Varrick—had introduced themselves on the first morning they arrived at the Mount. They unfailingly remained beside Jeremiah, with little words exchanged between the trio.

Kage and Sacha, now fully recovered, sat silently at the table with Iskander, uninterestedly flipping pairs of playing cards back and forth.

Mathieson remained by himself against the far, center wall, seemingly isolated from the group.

When the Prophet arrived, it had been a tense reunion between the Septant warriors.

Iskander supposed it was likely attributed to his adverse recounting of the events in Montu, but he didn't care. He figured Raynor should just be thankful he hadn't shoved his fist through his duplicitous face for a second time.

Iskander had just begun contemplating how much longer he was willing to wait before he headed into the other room and downed several mugs of ale when the handle on the Mount's door unlatched and two Soturi strolled in.

The warriors looked tired and worn, and there was a change in Asha that he could not place.

✤ ✤ ✤

"Thank you all for meeting us here," the Commander began, his voice heavy. He exhaled deeply before continuing. "I suppose we might as well get right into it."

The warriors in the room shifted their weight. Ronin and Varrick stood from their relaxed places on the floor.

Asha moved to the corner of the room, near the Septant warriors that were gathered around the table.

Kage and Sacha placed their playing cards down, giving their full attention to the Commander.

Iskander was stagnant, the only one to remain unmoving. Anselem figured his Second had already prepared himself for the worst.

He glanced over to Asha, and she nodded. He took a steadying breath, dragged his gaze around the room once

more, and proceeded to tell the group everything they had
learned from their journey to the Forgotten City.

He outlined every detail of the trip. Everything from
their voyage to Skull's Rock and acquiring the Amulet of
Tisiphone, to their journey to the Forgotten City and their
meeting with the Empress. Asha followed him, recounting
her visit to the First Province of the Hells, the Prince of
Shadows, and slaying the Wendigo.

A stretching silence filled the room once the warriors
had finished.

Iskander gracefully placed his feet onto the floor and
leaned forward. "So you're telling me there are six Anchors,
each bound by a Seal, and a seventh—the Soulvion Scepter—that holds the largest fragment of the Lord of Darkness's power and can be wielded to open a gateway to the
Abyss?"

Anselem nodded.

"And," the General continued, "the six Crowns of Shadows have all been wielded by the monarchs of the most powerful kingdoms of Darnella, and they are currently serving as
gateways to the various levels of the Hells?"

Asha murmured her affirmation.

Iskander ran a hand through his hair. "*And*," he continued, "the Warrior of Praenuntius, and the two other Champions of the Authorities—titles none of us have heard before—led the first war against the Lord of Darkness and the
Princes, but conveniently forgot to destroy the Anchors and
instead created the Ossuary and the Seals to bind him to our
world."

Anselem nodded.

"... Did I get all of that, or am I missing something?"
Iskander scoffed.

"Yeah, you forgot the part where the Herald of Promise betrayed them and now the Seals are weakened," Asha

replied cynically. "So, the Lord of Darkness can enter our realm for fleeting moments because of the connection he has to the shards inside the Anchors."

"Perfect," Iskander grumbled, his annoyance on full display as he perched his feet onto the table once more and leaned back in his chair.

"And no one knows who the Volvana is?" Kage questioned.

Asha and Anselem shook their heads in unison.

Asha turned to face Kaira. "Have you ever read about anyone with that title? Or of the Champions?"

Kaira shook her head. "The only one I have ever heard of is the Warrior of Praenuntius," she clarified.

The same as the rest of those in the room. Even if the tales had been stripped from the kingdoms, almost every soldier across the Continents had heard of the Dominion's Favored Warrior.

"I can look through some of the journals in the Ageless Library and see if either of the names comes up," Kaira offered.

Asha nodded.

Anselem released a long breath and rubbed the bridge of his nose between his fingers.

"And the Empress didn't say anything about where the Anchors or the Soulvion Scepter might be?" Mathieson asked.

Anselem shook his head. "She only said the Volvana holds the answers, and when she wishes to be found, she will find us."

"Did the Empress mention anything about the chest?" Kaira asked, her voice soft and low.

Anselem shifted his gaze to the Amarok. "What chest?"

Kaira cut her eyes over to Iskander.

The General remained fully relaxed, with his feet still

resting upon the top of the table. He picked at his nails as he indifferently replied, "There is a chest locked behind several gold bars inside the Ossuary."

"And you didn't think that was an important thing to mention?" Asha questioned, impatience entering her tone.

The General glanced up and snidely replied, "I would have figured Raynor might have thought to inform you of the details, being as he is the one who has known about the crypt for a lot longer than I have."

Asha pursed her lips.

Anselem turned his eyes back to Kaira. "What about the chest?"

Kaira, feeling the growing tension in the room, hesitated before answering. "The seventh opening in the Ossuary is barred. And instead of a platform crafted to hold a scepter, an obsidian chest sits inside of it."

"Does it have a lock on it?" Asha probed.

Iskander scoffed beside her. "You could say that."

The warriors shifted their gazes to the General.

"Are you going to elaborate or simply throw out useless comments with no explanation?" Asha snipped.

Iskander rolled his moondust eyes. "It has six locks."

"Six?" Kage interjected.

Iskander nodded.

"We think, but we are not certain," Kaira added, her voice unconvinced. "There are six small holes on the front of the chest, possibly keyholes."

"Keyholes?" Sacha chimed in, his first comment of the afternoon. "For what keys?" he asked.

Kaira shrugged.

Anselem glanced over at Asha, whose jaw had clenched tightly.

"I'm not sure," Kaira answered, "that's why I was hoping the Empress had explained it."

Anselem composed himself and replied, "No, she did not mention the chest or any keys that would open it."

"Convenient," Iskander grumbled.

"Is there anything else from the Ossuary we should know?" Asha inquired.

"It would make a lot more sense for you to just go and see it for yourself..." Iskander muttered.

"Yes," Kaira interrupted, cutting off the complaints of the General, "beneath each of the scepters, there is an empty space with a symbol carved into it. It looks like three overlapping triangles with an eye in the center. Do you think that those spaces are the vessels for the Seals?"

Asha was quiet for a long moment before she replied, "Yes. And I think I know where one is."

Iskander stopped fidgeting with his nails, and the other warriors in the room went still.

"I have an amulet with the same symbol you described etched into it. It was connected to the collar on the Hound from our final benchmark," she explained, turning to the Valorous warriors as she concluded.

Jeremiah, for the first time since Asha and Anselem had entered the room, turned his attention to his friend.

"Where is it now?" Kage pressed.

"It's locked inside the Undercroft," Anselem answered.

The Transferent nodded.

Asha looked over to Anselem, and with her mental shields in place, she murmured, *Should I tell them about the key you locked inside the Undercroft with it?*

Anselem nodded. *At this point, I don't see why we would need to keep it from them.*

Sacha cleared his throat.

"Also, without seeing the chest," Asha continued, ignoring Sacha's impatience, "I can't know for certain what kind of keys will open the locks, but I asked Anselem to put

493

one that I found inside the Undercroft as well. Seeing where it came from, there's a possibility it could be connected."

"What do you mean where it came from?" Mathieson questioned.

His eyes had returned to their normal clarity, but a graveness remained in his expression.

"It was given to me when I was at Sveaborg."

"By whom?" Iskander asked, an edge of intrigue in his tone.

Asha sighed, knowing the response she was bound to receive once she explained the key's source.

"An Adaro gifted it to me."

Silence filled the Mount. Wide eyes stretched across the faces of her Tribe, and narrowed gazes appeared on the Septant warriors.

Asha glanced over to Valorous, "It was their king, actually. I encountered a group of them when I fell into the Lake during the fifth Wargame."

Jeremiah glanced up from his place on the floor, the first reaction he'd shown since the warriors had returned.

But it was Sacha who chimed in, the sole warrior belonging to the sea, and stated, "The Adaro have been extinct for centuries."

Asha focused on letting the smallest, most specific gap open within her mental walls, careful not to let Kage see any other memories stirring within her mind.

The Transferent captured her stored memory of the encounter with the Adaro King and proceeded to share it with the other warriors gathered in the room.

"I'm not sure if the key he gave me is anything we are searching for, but I think it would be worth looking into," she concluded.

"You almost drowned," Jeremiah murmured, his voice solemn and detached.

494

Surprise washed over Asha as she twisted to face her friend. She nodded slowly.

Jeremiah made no other comment and instead moved his eyes back onto the floor beside him, as though he had lost all interest in the conversation taking place around him.

"Should we stop by on our way to Velsen?" Asha asked the Commander.

Without giving her a response, Anselem turned to Iskander and questioned, "What is so important that we need to go back to the Ageless Library anyway?"

"Samson seems to think there might be some journals that contain answers about the Ossuary. Or at least expand upon what we already know," the General replied.

Anselem glanced over at Kaira, and she nodded.

"Alright," he concluded. "I agree, we need to stop at the Undercroft first and then—"

"We have a problem," Mathieson cut in.

Iskander huffed out an irritated breath. "Would killing you solve this problem?"

Asha shoved his boots off the table and glared at the General.

"What?" Iskander grunted, but the Thurisaz caught the mischievous spark that flickered through his starry eyes.

Mathieson continued, ignoring Iskander's sardonic comment, "What are we going to do about the First Prince of the Hells?" he asked, glancing at Asha.

"What do you mean?" Anselem questioned.

"Well, Thotha said all the staffs have been wielded. All of the gateways have been opened. To include the gateway for the Prince of the First Province. I'm sure he has a score he wants to settle with you," Mathieson said, looking over to Asha. "A rather vehement one."

"What makes you think you're such an expert on the resentment of a Prince of Shadows?" Iskander snarled.

A healthy amount of skeptical disdain filled the General's voice as he looked towards Mathieson.

Mathieson snapped back, "Because I've had regrettably close views of the Hells, *General*."

Iskander narrowed his eyes and stood, taking a step towards Mathieson. Thick tension filled the air between the warriors. "And how would you have had those, *Prophet*?"

Iskander spat the title out as though it were a slur—like a name that held disgrace and shame rather than a label of extraordinary, prestigious honor.

The group fell silent. No one had dared voice it. They knew—they had all known since Mathieson first mentioned his visions on the shores of Gull's Landing. But there was something surreal about the truth being spoken out loud, as though the audibility gave the notion a more concrete basis in reality.

As the word hit the air, there was a shift inside the Mount. A palpable change in energy.

Mathieson pursed his lips. "Because I may not have gone, but I have seen visions of the Hells," he replied tensely.

Iskander scoffed. "How convenient. You've *seen* them."

Anselem cut a glare at the General but did not reprimand him.

Asha's strong voice cut through the rigidity in the room. "I don't think we have to worry about Prince Ipos, Math."

Iskander snorted. "On a first-name basis with a Prince of the Hells, Kappi?"

Asha ignored him. "Truly. I have a feeling he's going to be getting reamed out for not knowing who I was for quite some time."

"Yeah, well," Mathieson said, "I'm more concerned about after the Dark King is done punishing him. Princes in any realm tend to hold grudges."

"I think I'd be more concerned about the fact that he

looks like an identical replica of Raziel," Kage chimed.

Anselem shook his head and scoffed. "Add that to the endless list of things we still need to sort out."

"On it," Iskander jeered, and made a mocking gesture of dabbing an invisible quill and scribbling on his hand.

Anselem rolled his eyes. "Alright. Then it's settled," he said. "We will all head for the Ageless Library and see what we can find about the First War, the gateways, and any other information the Empress told us." He glanced around the Mount as he sorted through his strategy. "The five of us will go to the Elysian Fort first," the Commander directed, nodding at Asha and the three Valorous Soturi warriors. "I'll figure out something with Cathan for a temporary assignment to keep Vice Rook from making any more inquiries until we can work out the details for a larger plan."

Anselem cut his eyes across the room. "The two of you," he continued, pointing to Kaira and Iskander, "will head to the Ageless Library and begin looking through the documents there." He shifted his eyes to Iskander. "Make sure you submit a change of station for her to keep Leadership from asking questions."

Iskander nodded.

"And you two," he added, turning towards Kage and Mathieson. "Go to the Undercroft and grab the Adaro Key, the Hound's Amulet, and the key from the Manor. Then meet us in Velsen."

The warriors all nodded.

"Good. Then it is settled. Does anyone have anything else to add?" Anselem questioned, addressing the group.

The warriors all shook their heads.

The room fell silent, the faint hum of the Mount's wards thrumming in the background. Asha's gaze drifted to the door, to the night sky she knew waited just beyond the tavern walls. Vast, cold, and black.

Images of the First Province of the Hells rose in her mind like a phantom. The frozen mist curling around her feet, the silver collar of fangs biting into her flesh, the venomous voice that had coiled like smoke inside her skill.

And in the heavy silence, Asha knew with bone-deep certainty that the Darkness awaiting them in this war would be worse than anything she had faced.

The First War had left the world in ruin. But the next would leave nothing but Abyssal oblivion.

"The Dominions: the seven high deities purposefully and exceptionally selected by Ianoda to enforce and carry out his divine will. They protect the moral order and intervene amongst the human realm to uphold justice, righteousness, and harmony; executing judgment on behalf of the Lord of Light."
– A Partial Excerpt from the Incipiency & Formation: A Succinct Overview of the Establishment of the Seven High Gods

CHAPTER FIFTY-NINE

Standing in the heart of the Redwoods, with a dense mist dancing around them, the warriors cracked open the forest-green door set inside the Olden Oak.

Jeremiah, Ronin, and Varrick stepped around the massive, ruddy base of the tree and swiftly ducked inside the curved door, pleased to be removed from the unnerving reach of the Mist.

Before Asha could follow behind the Septant warriors, Anselem grabbed her hand, stopping her from descending the staircase into the Ageless Library.

She turned to face him, her eyes hazy in the vaporous forest.

"Are you okay?" he asked, voice low.

It was the first time either of them had mentioned it. The first time they had taken a long enough pause to acknowledge what she had endured. Where she had gone. A moment to acknowledge the immense weight pressing in on her shoulders. A second to recognize the war that loomed before them.

Her jaw flexed, and she nodded slowly.

Anselem pulled her against him, wrapping her up in his arms. "We will figure it out," he promised.

She nodded silently against his chest.

He did not know the how or the when; all he knew was that now that he had found her, he would not lose her.

Even if that meant defying Death.

Even if it meant defying the gods.

Kaira was sitting against the far wall when Asha entered the open room, striding past the hall of bookshelves. The Amarok had a pile of aged journals strewn across the stone floor beside her, and several of the worn tomes were opened to pages covered in the *Language of the Founders*.

"Find anything useful?" Asha called, ambling over to her golden-eyed friend.

Kaira shrugged. "Possibly."

She pointed at a navy-bound book with scripted letters drawn onto the spine. "This one talks about the Princes of Shadows," she explained.

Asha glanced down at the parchment, but all the lines were written in a script she could not comprehend, with letters and symbols that had not been used for many centuries.

"What does it say?"

Kaira pulled the book closer to her, and as she began to read, the warriors in the room fell silent, and the incessant flipping of pages ceased.

"Each of the Wraiths," she began, reading the ancient name the Founders had given the Princes of Shadows, "was given charge over a Province in the Hells, allowed to govern and rule as they saw fit. The Princes transformed their bestowed territories into inconceivably sinister places. Some ruled with wrath and greed, others with covetousness and voracity. But the deepest, darkest pit of the Hells dwelled within the Seventh and final province, where the Lord of Darkness reigned over them all as the supreme King of the Abyss."

Asha's mouth was dry, and she could feel a stirring inside her soul, as though the Chaos that flowed through her veins had awakened from the mere mention of the Adversary.

"Anything else?" she choked out, forcing her voice to appear calm.

Kaira glanced over the collection of books at her feet. She picked up a thick journal made of onyx leather, with golden symbols scattered across the front. It was opened to a page containing a sketched photo of an unassuming key.

"I still need to translate more from this one. There are a lot of words I have never encountered before, but I believe it says something about a power that is connected to the keys. I think this word here," she stated, pointing to a script Asha could not comprehend, "means imbued. So, perhaps the keys are imbued with magic or power of some kind."

Asha nodded and offered her friend a soft smile. "Great work, Kai," she praised.

A couple of hours passed as the warriors flipped through the delicate pages of dozens of journals. The stretching silence was interrupted by a dull voice across the room.

"Is this what it looks like?" Jeremiah called, his voice impassive and numb.

"What, what looks like?" Asha prompted.

"One of the keys."

Every warrior in the room ceased and turned to Jeremiah. There was an open book in his hands with a large rectangular hole cut out in the center of the thick pages; the object stored within the secret hollow was grasped between his fingers.

In his hand, he held a vibrant, gold key with a pearlescent gemstone set in the middle. Diamonds, fixed against looping adornments, wrapped around the bow, and a small, detailed sword was carved into the shank.

Jeremiah gently placed the key onto a nearby table, and one by one, the warriors strolled over to examine the metal.

Anselem picked it up first, flipping it over several times in his hands. He handed it to Kaira, who focused greatly on the carved sword etched onto the body. After a short glimpse, she handed it to Iskander and returned to the other side of the room, and began rifling through the pages of one of the journals.

The other warriors each took turns studying the key.

Asha was the last to approach the table, and as she glanced down at the metal, dragging her gaze over the vibrant gold, she noticed the key appeared to have a soft glow. It looked as though it had not been touched for millennia.

After a long moment, Asha reached down and picked up the glinting metal.

Suddenly, as soon as her hands touched the key, it transported her into another world—a time and place far from where she existed.

A group of otherworldly men and women, perched atop thrones covered in gold adornments, gathered around a large, stone table. The scene was subdued and hazy, as if Asha was viewing it from underwater.

Puffs of clouds floated under her feet, and she felt weightless, as though she was suspended in the boundless air beside the kings and queens.

Splinters of sunlight battled to break through the haze, and a thrumming buzz of familiar energy filled the space around her, as though uncontainable power was emanating directly from the gathered monarchs.

Asha glanced around the table, and as she studied the royals, she realized she was not able to be sensed by those gathered, as if she had been transported into a locked memory of a different time.

No words were exchanged amongst the kings and queens. Instead, they sat silently staring at an infinite flame flickering in the center of the marble table.

A regal-looking man with snow-white hair strummed his fingers on the stone top. Stress filled his jade-green eyes, and there was a noticeable tenseness in his shoulders.

Beside him sat a pair of poised, raven-haired twins. Their violet eyes looked like they held the knowledge of a thousand reigns, and their delicate, fair features looked as though they could decimate kingdoms with their beauty.

A golden-blonde woman with kind, sapphire eyes and a soft smile resided beside the twins. Her hair fell down her back in loose curls that reminded Asha of Tahira, and a great tightness twisted in her chest as the woman hummed softly to herself.

Beside her sat an auburn-haired queen with lively, tawny eyes, tanned skin, and a bright smile that looked as if it held the kindest of spirits.

The last occupied throne was filled by a gentleman with fierce, piercing gold eyes highlighted by his deep-brown skin and warm disposition.

Asha glanced from monarch to monarch, and everything felt motionless—frozen—as though time did not exist in the space where she found herself.

She studied the details of the occupied throne beside her, and as the woman seated in the chair readjusted her weight, Asha gasped.

Peeking out from behind the queen, etched deeply into the center of the throne, was the carving of a seven-pointed star. The sacred symbol of the Dominions.

A whipping wind whisked across the hazy space, and Asha felt the breeze gently caress her face as it moved across the skies.

"My apologies for the delay," a voice uttered from across the room. Asha spun her gaze to the seventh chair, now occupied by a silver-eyed man with close-cut hair and tawny skin.

A god, she corrected herself. Not a man.

The gathered beings in her presence were powerful, immortal High Gods.

"Is it done?" the white-haired deity tensely asked. His inquiry led Asha to believe he was likely the leader of their group.

The god beside him nodded and pulled out a small, weathered key, covered in burnished gold. It held a pure white gem in the center, with ornate diamonds wound around it.

"It has been a long time," the golden-eyed divinity murmured.

The leader reached across the table and took the key from the recently arrived deity.

"Not long enough."

A stillness fell over the group as the leader ran his hand across the jagged surface of the metal key.

"The last was Mikkal, was it not?" The golden-haired goddess asked softly.

The leader nodded once more. "The last Warrior of Praenuntius."

One of the twins sighed deeply and chimed, "I had always hoped we would never need another."

The others harmoniously agreed—all except the white-haired leader, who remained silent at his throne.

As the group fell silent, he slowly peered up from the

key in his hand and avowed, "The worlds will always need a Warrior."

The gathered gods said nothing, and the leader looked over the key once more before placing it onto the table before him.

When he removed his hands, the brushed gold was no longer withered or worn, but instead looked renewed and vibrant, as if life and Light had been poured into the vessel once again.

"I'm not sure how long it will be," he commented, turning his eyes towards the others. "It could be many millennia before the next is chosen."

Several heads nodded in agreement, but their lips remained sealed.

"But we can all agree that Uriel will choose wisely."

Asha's mouth went dry. Her lungs twisted, and breath could not enter.

The leader of the High Gods rose, and the others followed suit. In harmony, the Dominions pulled their polished Swords from beside their thrones.

The leader placed the whetted blade against his palm and pressed. Blood began to pool in his immortal hand. Silently, the six other deities mirrored his movements.

He raised his bloodstained hand and affirmed, "I willfully pledge my power to the next. May the Chosen One deliver the lost into a better life and a better world."

One by one, the Seven High Gods and Goddesses repeated the idiom, vowing their power to the Warrior of Praenuntius.

And once the final deity had declared his oath, the Dominions all leaned forward and held their dripping hands above the everflame.

Asha ripped herself from the memory locked within the

Recollection Key, forcing herself back into her own world—her own vestige of time and space.

And in that moment, between ragged gasps of breath and worried whispers, Asha realized she had been wrong.

They had all been so very, very wrong.

The permanent darkness residing deep inside her soul—the same blackness that had entered her heart the day Uriel chose her, and her powers manifested—was not Darkness at all, but rather an infinite flame forever intertwined with her own devastating Chaos.

An everflame gifted to her by the Seven High Gods, intended to enhance her own well of endless power.

And, as she glanced around the room at the awaiting eyes of the ones she loved most, Asha understood the crucial, fate-altering implication of the memory gifted to her by the Authorities.

She did not just hold the power of unremitting Chaos in her blood.

No, she wielded something much greater. Much stronger.

The only magic more powerful than Chaos. The same limitless magic that had been gifted to the Warrior of Praenuntius three thousand years ago.

Asha Akselsen Raynor possessed the entire, unrivaled power of the Dominions.

Acknowledgments

My Lord and Savior, Jesus Christ: You know every word, every expression of thanks, every acclamation of gratitude written in my heart before I ever pour them on the page. But I will still continue to shout your praises to the world. Not one word on in this story would be possible without you. Thank you for so many blessings. Thank you for being the Light of my life, for giving all of us a Way through the Darkness, and for your endless and infinite love.

My husband & the love of my life: I've said it many times, but this entire journey would not be possible without you. Your endless support and love have given me the courage to continue pursuing my dreams, even when they seem unattainable. You inspire me in more ways than I could ever express, and I hope you know, when death takes my hand, I will grab onto you with the other and follow you into every lifetime. Always.

My sister, Maddie: Never has there been a truer, more loyal friend to exist. I thank God every day that He allowed you to be the first born, so there's never a day I have had to live without my best friend. It's you and me always, moo. No matter where. No matter what.

My Mom: I have no words to express my love for you, for your encouragement, and your support in everything I set my sights on. Thank you for always cheering me on so loudly, I never think twice about the ones who stay silent. Thank you for helping me navigate the world of writing and publishing without a clue, but always a heart of gold and an attitude that we will figure it out together. I love you bunches.

My Dad: Thank you for supporting me so fully in every endeavor I pursue. From following so closely in your footsteps, and sharing every bit of knowledge I could need, to diving headfirst into the realm of fantasy and cheering for me every step. I love you.

Jamie, my greatest friend: I thank Jesus every day for you and this friendship of ours. And I hope you forever know, that old note your friend wrote in your yearbook was right— you truly are an incredible person that inspires the fiercest and most loyal of storybook characters. But I'm especially thankful I get to have the real version of you for myself.

Clayton: Thank you for saving our family from my endless book ramblings, and for losing yourself in wild stories with me!

Gabriel: I know you're still too young to read this but thank you for making me Aunt Cam Cam. There is not another title I have ever held so close to my heart. I promise as you grow, I will read all the stories to you, and selfishly make you as obsessed with reading as your dad and me. (Clayton, don't worry, I promise to let you read him the Red Rising Saga first).

Malcolm: Thank you for nearly two decades of friendship, and for being one of my oldest and truest friends. Thank you for your love of audiobooks and giving me the confidence to pursue a medium of publishing I never could have imagined

I would find myself in the midst of. Thank you for supporting me and this journey in every way you have, and for dealing with my social media mayhem. You're a true warrior for that alone.

Elena Anderson: Thank you for bringing Asha & The Dominions to life in a way that is more incredible than I could have ever imagined!

To my family: The true heroes. I thank God every day for each of you, and for blessing me with people who will support me and love me in every facet of my life. If there was ever a true version of a Tribe, it would be ours. I love you all.

To my closest friends: I wish there was an endless number of pages to name every one of you, but I hope you each of you know exactly how important you are to me. There is no one I would wish to have in my circle more than all of you.

Finally, to you, readers: This dream would never have come to life and flourished without you. I truly mean that from the bottom of my heart. This world, these characters—your love for them brings it all to life. And there is no better group I would want to share them with than you. And, as always, may you live on and burn well.

Until the flames claim us,
  Cam